FOREVER AND ONE DAY

A love story

Jacqueline Simon Gunn

This book is a work of fiction. All names, characters and events are from the author's imagination. Locations are used fictitiously. Any similarity to actual persons, living or dead, is purely coincidental and not intended by the author.

ISBN: 1979983860
ISBN 13: 9781979983860

In loving memory of my mom.

Between the empty spaces is a place called forever.

"Your task is not to seek for love, but merely to seek and find all the barriers within yourself that you have built against it."

— *Jalaluddin Rumi*

1

"I'm having an existential crisis." Olivia folded her arms across her chest.

"I love when you try to avoid the specifics of your distress by hiding under the blanket: existential crisis, my ass. Your contemplation is specific, Liv: Do you want to go to your twenty-year high school reunion or not?" Sebastian shot her a pointed look.

"I hate when you simplify. Come on, you're a philosophy professor. It's a bigger question for me: Do I want to go back and revisit that part of my life?"

Sebastian raised a dark, thick eyebrow. "It's been twenty years. Everyone has something from that time in their life that they wish they would have done differently. What happened in high school? It can't be that bad."

"I'm thirty-eight and single. Everyone is married, most of them have kids."

"So, your life is different than theirs. You've never been one to buy into convention. You have a big career. You're a doctor, Liv. A professor of psychology."

"Yeah, so. That area of my life has never been a problem. It's the romance that's always gone awry. I've never even lived with a man. Since college, I've never even made it past the one-year mark."

"So I've noticed." Sebastian smirked. "However, my dear, I've never seen you so bothered by this. I know you want children. Is that what this is about?"

"No. I dunno. It's the reunion. These sort of life events make you reevaluate, I guess." Olivia looked up at the ceiling of the subway station as they exited the car, contemplating.

Swarms of people hurried down the stairs, yelping and screaming for the car to wait. Like life and time, subway cars didn't wait because people screamed at them. Olivia observed the phenomenon: pointless calls at a car that was pulling away, the rushing, the energy of the city. It distracted her from her private reverie and the truth she didn't want to say aloud. In fact, New York City was full of distractions. Millions of untold pasts were hidden in the concrete, which was convenient for Olivia.

Olivia pulled her hair off the back of her neck and fanned herself with her other hand. "Boy, I overdressed. It's warm."

"Mercurial May in the city." Sebastian shrugged his shoulders. "Take your sweater off."

"You know I like my layers."

"Then hide behind your sweater and sweat."

Olivia rolled her eyes at him. "I'm not hiding." She removed her cardigan as they walked up the subway stairs at Union Square, navigating the crowd of people. Daylight dwindled, leaving only a muted light as the sun settled.

"We have time for a cocktail." Sebastian looked at his watch.

"I don't even feel like going to the signing."

"What? You've been carrying that book around, waiting for the Adam Summers' signing all week. What has gotten into you?" They crossed the street. Standing along the square, Sebastian tapped an impatient foot. "Spill it. I know you. Something's cooking in that complicated head of yours. I'm not moving until you tell."

She looked at his piercing expression. He wasn't going to budge, and she knew it. *Justin,* she thought, but she didn't even want to say his name aloud. It made it more real if she did.

Justin, one word, six letters, and no matter how hard she tried to deny it, she had been thinking about him since she got that invitation for her twenty-year reunion. And that damn Facebook page where she could see who was going. Justin and Petal would both be there.

Olivia took a heavy breath. "There was a guy in high school. Justin Steeler. He was my first love. My first everything. And he'll be there."

"First of all, how can you not have mentioned him in the ten years we've been friends? And two, it's been twenty years. You are a beautiful, strong, successful woman."

"You're right. I'm being silly. I guess it feels strange to go back when I've spent every day since we broke up going forward."

"Isn't that what a breakup is? An ending and then movement forward to new beginnings." Sebastian pushed his glasses up the bridge of his nose with his pointer finger.

For a smart person, Sebastian could be obtuse, Olivia thought. His highly intellectual thinking didn't leave a lot of space for emotional speculations, like her past still having a hold on her.

"See? It is an existential crisis. This milestone is causing a deep contemplation of my life. That's not necessarily a bad thing. Reveries about life are important. I'm just looking back and mulling over decisions I've made, good and bad, and thinking about my life going forward."

He wrapped his arm around her narrow back. "Listen. I didn't go to my twenty-year reunion. No big loss."

"My high school was different than most. So many of my friends are still friends. I skipped the ten-year. I was busy with my dissertation." *And I didn't want to see Justin and Petal,* she thought. "I'd really like to see some of my old friends. It's stupid. It would just be nice if I actually, at thirty-eight, had a date."

"You want me to go with you? I can be handsome and charming and straight for a night." He gave her a warm smile.

"Thanks, Bash. That's OK. It's only gonna feel right if it's an actual date. You are awesome for offering, especially to fake being straight when I know you hate that." She smiled and they both laughed.

He grabbed her hand, "Come on. Let's go get Adam Summers to sign your book."

"Let's."

2

2000

"**S**he caught my eye, didn't try / her playful hair / cascading red, like a dare." Justin strummed his acoustic, making up lyrics as he sang and played along. Justin always acted cool, but when they were alone he was romantic.

"Liv, I've been thinking."

"You're always thinking." She batted her eyelashes and smiled.

"I don't think we should wait. What do you think about us getting married when you finish college?"

She looked at him through wide eyes.

"*Liv, with your long red hair, will you marry me on the day after your college graduation?*" Justin sang, a playful lilt in his tone.

Justin had dark brown eyes, almost black. They were intense, always filled with emotion. Olivia could see how much he loved her by looking at him look at her. It made her tingle all over.

"Are you serious, Jus? Don't tease me like that." She gave him a coy smile.

"I *am* serious."

"What about graduate school?"

"Married people go to graduate school."

"No. I mean, I'm going to be even busier when I'm in graduate school. Maybe we should wait until I'm finished."

"I don't want to wait that long. We can get married in the summer after your college graduation, and then I can support you while you're in graduate school." He gave her those intense eyes.

"Yes. I want to. But– "

"But what?"

"What if you're not done with college? How will you support me? It's less than a year before I graduate."

His eyes looked heavy. "Don't worry. I'll figure it out. Don't I always?"

"You do." She said, but she worried that he wouldn't figure this out fast enough. They were young, sure, but discussing marriage meant they were stepping into a mature life, one that had a different level of responsibility.

Justin had his band, Furious Whiskers, and he wrote music. He studied music and education at New Jersey City University. Justin was talented too; friends, family and teachers all believed that he had potential to take his music to the next level. But Justin seemed satisfied playing with his band, which was mostly cover music.

The lyrics he wrote piled up in notebooks, maybe to be used one day, maybe not. Olivia loved his artistic, creative, dreamy side. But now, if they were to be engaged, to be married — which, of course, she wanted more than anything; Justin was her love — she needed him to focus more on the long-term.

"Jus, don't you ever worry about the future."

"I don't worry about the future because I know things are going to work out. Life is good. I think about the future, though. I think about *our* future." He pulled her close. There was nothing like feeling Justin's arms around her, warm, strong, secure. She settled into his embrace. "Don't worry, sweets. You put so much pressure on yourself. Sometimes, I worry that you don't enjoy your life because you're so concerned about the future."

"But what do you want to do with your life? At some point you've got to figure that out."

"You know what I'm going to do."

"Become a teacher, play with your band?"

"Right."

"But you have to finish college to be a teacher. Your natural brilliance will only take you so far."

"And I will be done by the end of next year. Look at me."

She looked into his eyes.

"I promise I will take care of you."

"I know you will. I just– I get scared sometimes. I wish I could be as easy-going about life as you are. I wish I believed that things worked out without putting so much pressure on myself."

He held her in his arms. "You have to relax. It's going to be OK. You will get into graduate school." He stroked her hair. "If you don't get into Rutgers, which I doubt will happen, but if you don't, you will get in somewhere else and we'll make it work. Right?"

How did Justin do that? He always seemed to know exactly how to comfort her. "Right." She rested her head on his shoulder. "You know, Jus, you should do more with your music."

"I like where it's at right now, playing with Furious Whiskers. We're getting more and more bookings. This is what I had always hoped."

"And it's awesome. But maybe it could be even bigger. Your songwriting and singing could be a career."

"Yeah, maybe. Let's figure out our life first, then I can figure that out. Liv, with your long red hair, please don't worry so much." He twirled a lock of her hair.

"OK, Justin, with the striking dark brown eyes, I promise I will try to stop worrying."

3

Adam Summers.

Romance novelist Adam Summers wrote captivating stories about love and lust, weaving existential themes through the narrative. Turns out, Adam Summers was also impossibly handsome, thick dark hair, broad shoulders and facial scruff. Boy, did Olivia enjoy a man with some scruff. He wore a light-blue collared shirt, which accented the little bit of gray hair along his temples.

Wow.

Olivia fanned herself with her hand as Sebastian and she sat.

This stunning man, Adam Summers, sat in front of an audience of people, mostly women, and read an excerpt from his newest release, *An Inconvenient Coincidence.* A story filled with romance and intrigue. It followed protagonist, Penelope Tam Fellows, as she fell into an affair with a handsome stranger with a dark past and many secrets. Meanwhile, Penelope struggles with her identity as she now is on the other side of an indiscretion and feels she doesn't know the woman she has become.

Any woman who enjoyed a romance story with strong and profound themes couldn't read Adam Summers and not have an imaginary love affair with him. He seemed to know what women found romantic and sexy, and how they wanted to be touched.

She hadn't realized from his headshot how handsome he was. *Jesus Christ.* She caressed her hardcover copy of *An Inconvenient Coincidence* as if she were running her fingers through his actual hair.

"My, he's quite the looker," Sebastian said.

"Yeah." Olivia smiled.

A heavy-set blonde woman beside Olivia turned, giving them a hearty nod of agreement.

When Adam Summers finished his reading, he answered a few questions. Olivia needed to ask this man something. *Are you single?* She thought, smiling to herself.

Her hand went up before she even knew what she wanted to say.

"I see. All we needed was a handsome man to relieve your existential crisis." Sebastian said under his breath.

"Existential crisis? That man could cure cancer." The blonde woman said, holding the book against her chest.

"Yes?" Adam Summers motioned for Olivia to ask her question, the question she didn't even know she had.

She twirled a thick lock of her hair through her fingers. "Will there be a sequel? I'm wondering if we will find out if her friend dies or not."

Adam Summers smiled. *He smiled at me!* Well, maybe he smiled at everyone. No, no, he smiled at *her.* He looked her right in the eye and smiled.

She gave him her most unabashed look, even though her heart raced. Adam Summers was the kind of guy whose smile made a woman feel twelve and awkward, like she was a girl and he was her first crush.

That smile morphed into a mischievous grin, when he said, "No. This is not part of a series. However, you may find some of these characters in my next book. I do like to leave my readers with something to think about. For example, how would the experience of Penelope differ based on if Tamara died or not? I have some of those questions on my blog for consideration."

He smiled again, right at her.

It definitely wasn't generic. This was a smile for *her.*

"Thank you." She smiled through quivering lips, and she wondered what her non-generic smile for *him* actually looked like.

"He smiled at me, didn't he?"

"Liv. I love you, you delusional romantic. He smiled at you, just like he's smiled at every woman who asked a question. The man is a charmer. You always go for the charmers. He's just your type."

"He's everyone's type."

"Not everyone's. I, for one, wouldn't go out with him. When I say he's just your type, I mean he is dangerously charming and emotionally unavailable. Oh, and too into himself. A man like that is never good in bed."

"He's not too into himself. Where are you getting that from?"

"There's no way that man is bad in bed. What I wouldn't do to see him naked." The blonde woman said, her face flushed.

"I hear that." Olivia said to the blonde woman, then she elbowed Sebastian. "See."

When Adam Summers finished, Olivia got in line to have her book signed by him. Sebastian waited off in the philosophy section of the store.

She wished she had put more effort into what she wore when she left the house for this event. She looked down at her red sundress, pressed away a wrinkle at the bottom part with her hand. Well, she didn't look that bad. She put her cardigan sweater back on. Inconspicuously, she took a barrette out of her handbag, pulled the front of her hair back off her face. The line inched up. She took her sweater off again.

Adam Summers now sported wire-rimmed glasses, which hung from the tip of his nose as he looked up at the woman whose book he was signing and asked, "Your name?"

And he smiled at the woman.

Sebastian was right. He smiled at everyone.

Her turn. He gave that crooked smile.

"Olivia. I mean, Liv, make it out to Liv. Thanks."

"I liked your question."

"Oh. Ha, thanks," she blushed.

He tapped the top of his pen on the inside cover of her book, looking over the rim of his glasses into her eyes.

Tap, tap, tap. She watched his pen going up and down. It matched the *boom, boom* of her heart beating against her chest. What on earth was he doing? His stare made her nervous.

She looked at him, a curious consternation.

"Perhaps you would like to discuss your question over coffee?" He rubbed the scruff along his face.

She swallowed. "Um... yeah, yeah, sure. I'd like that."

"Great. Here's my number." He slipped a small piece of paper into the book. "I look forward to your call."

He smiled. This time it was an intentional and inviting smile.

"Thanks." She tried to sound casual.

As soon as she was out of his sight, she opened the book and his folded note. He had written his phone number and: *I look forward to sharing wisdoms. X*

Sebastian had his head buried in a commentary on Heidegger when Olivia finally found him. She dangled the note at him. "He *was* smiling at me."

Sebastian read the note. "Liv does it again. Beguiles another handsome stranger. This time a best-selling author. Not bad, sweetie."

"He's very handsome."

"You'll get bored of him if he's available. And if I'm right, and he's not, he'll provide some sex, string you along, and then you'll have to toss him into your collection with all of the other emotionally unavailable men of Manhattan you've accumulated over the years." He winked at her.

Olivia gave him a severe look. "It'll be different this time."

"Uh huh."

4

Facebook should come with provisions against scrolling through pages filled with pictures of ex-fiancés and their wives. She almost never looked at Justin and Petal's pages. She couldn't see much of their pages, anyway; they weren't *her* Facebook friends. But her perusal of their lives was fairly successful, since all three of them had gone to North Bergen High School together and had nearly 100 mutual friends. She had visited their pages before, but not like this. The reunion had her trying to piece together a past that remained untold, as well as figure out what their current lives were like. All of which was unreasonable to expect from a social media page she didn't have full access to.

Justin looked as attractive as he always had, which was unfortunate. She wished he had gained weight like so many of the other guys. A double chin would have made it easier to pretend that she didn't still find him handsome.

The distance of observing a photograph when they had been so close felt strange. She didn't even know that person anymore and yet, she had never been closer with anyone. His thick, dark hair was short now. He used to wear it hanging to his shoulders. Those penetrating dark eyes always looked intense, even when he smiled wide. She could remember exactly how his eyes looked when he would gaze at her, filled with so much love.

The memory of the first night they had made love entered her mind. She would never forget how filled with emotion Justin's eyes were that night. It had all seemed so magical back then, so perfect, just the way every budding young woman imagines. It was 1997 and the summer after their senior year of high school, right before Olivia left for college. They discussed it beforehand; they were both ready. Justin's parents were away for the weekend. Olivia went over with a bottle of wine. Trying to act like it was an ordinary night, they sipped wine and talked and listened to music. But intense and unbearable desire hung between them, making her breath catch every time he looked at her. She remembered thinking that it would be one of the most important days of her life: the day she would lose her virginity and to the only boy she had ever loved.

Things would be different from then on. There would be the Olivia *before* she lost her virginity and the Olivia *after* she lost her virginity.

She still remembered quivering at his touch that night. She had always liked when Justin caressed her, but that night was different. She was giving him something she would never give anyone else.

"You're shaking." She remembered him whispering in her ear.

"I'm OK. Are you?"

He touched her face, "Never better. You sure you're ready."

"Yes. I love you." She kissed him — his lips, his cheeks, his neck — with everything she had.

He took her clothes off, slowly. He must have been as nervous as she felt because he kept checking in on her. "Are you OK?" "Everything alright?" "Is this OK?" And when he removed her bra: "I love you, Liv." The first moment she saw his eyes wandering along her naked body, she felt like she wanted to cover herself. It was an intense feeling, to be uncovered before him; his eyes scanning her. But at the same time, she wanted him to see her. She lay naked next to him as he caressed her so tenderly, kissing her face, rubbing her hair. Then, they removed his clothes together. The flutter of her heart tickled inside her chest and stomach. His body felt warm and smooth against hers.

They went slowly, each massaging the other to arousal, and then he entered her. While he was inside of her, she thought that she would never feel as close to anyone as she did to Justin. Those dark eyes looked moist as he moved slowly back and forth on top of her. It was then that she believed for certain that they would spend the rest of their lives together. No one could feel the way they felt about each other and not have it last forever. Afterward, they lay together, no words, arms around each other, eyes glued to one another's. She loved Justin more than ever. As it turned out, the Olivia *after* she had given her virginity to Justin felt that he was now a part of her. They were each one piece of a whole. This is what forever felt like, to have an eternal connection.

"I love you more than ever," he said, as if he read her mind.

"Me too."

He pulled shorts on and grabbed his acoustic guitar. Olivia loved when Justin sang to her impromptu, making the words up as he went along. She knew when he sang to her privately, he was giving her the most private part of himself. The part of him that was so deep he could only express it through his art.

God, had she loved Justin. Justin Steeler, the boy who she had believed would one day be her husband. She had given her whole self to him and him to her. Turns out, along with her virginity, Justin had also taken that feeling of total idealization, the pure unadulterated love that she had for him, when he betrayed her.

She shook the memory off by switching to a photo of Petal Taylor, her once best friend, now Justin's wife, Petal Steeler. She looked blonde and curvy and perfect in every picture, which was sort of sickening, as much as Olivia hated to admit it. They had no kids. Interesting, because Petal used to go on and on when they were in college about how she couldn't wait to be a mother. Anyway, what did she care? They were both part of her history. She wasted enough time and tears on those two.

Maybe Adam Summers would go with her to the reunion.

She did have to have an actual date with him first. It had been three days since he passed her his phone number at his book signing. What was she waiting for? She unwrapped the white paper where he wrote his number. She wished she had given him her phone number instead.

Her nose practically touched the computer screen, as she switched her screen to Adam Summers' Facebook author page and then to his Twitter account. Her elbows rested on her desk, her chin in her palms. What would she say when he answered?

Dangerously charming. Sebastian wasn't always right. Besides, she enjoyed dangerously charming.

She pressed his number into the phone. *Briiiing.* She tapped her toes on the floor under her desk, looking at his picture, waiting for him to pick up.

"Hello, Adam Summers, here."

"Hello. Hi. It's Olivia. Liv. From your signing." She tried to sound confident.

She was confident.

"Liv. Hi. I was hoping you would call."

"I was hoping I would, too. I mean. I don't know what I mean."

20

"Usually you're the one answering the calls, not making them. I'm guessing."

She blushed at his accuracy. "Something like that."

"So, I appreciated your curiosity about the ending of the book."

"I still want to know if Tamara dies or not."

"That's open to your interpretation."

"What was your intention when writing it?"

"Ah, writer's secrets. Have dinner with me and we can talk about it."

"I'd like that. Although, I do get the feeling you're not going to tell me."

"You are a smart woman, Liv." He laughed. "Are you free tomorrow night?"

"Yes." She smiled into the phone.

"Where do you live?"

"The Upper Eastside. And you?" She asked.

"Upper West. There's a great Italian place on 86th and Lex. Would you like to go there?"

"Sure." She said.

"Would you like me to pick you up?" He asked.

The man picking the woman up for a date was not always a given in Manhattan because most people walked everywhere. Adam was chivalrous, she decided, but declined with, "that's sweet, but it's alright. I'll meet you at the restaurant."

"8:00?"

"Sounds perfect."

A wide smile crossed Olivia's face.

That was easy enough.

Although, the first date, the first few months even, were never the problem. The problem: finding a man she wanted to spend most of her time with who wanted to spend most of his time with her. This was the basic impasse of every Manhattan woman who was over thirty-five and single.

She switched her screen back to her high school reunion Facebook event page, clicked "**Going.**" Now her picture with her name "Olivia Watson" sat next to Petal and Justin's pictures, all marked going. She had put the past behind her seventeen years ago. It would be awkward seeing them at first, but she wanted to see her other friends.

She enlarged Justin's picture again. This man was a stranger, not the boy she had once known. But the old sadness coursed through her nonetheless. Pain kept him close in a way she didn't even realize.

5

2000

Christmas break. Justin's band, Furious Whiskers, was playing in Hoboken. Petal and Becka picked Olivia up at her parents' house where she was staying while home for the school break. Light snow had accumulated the night before. Olivia wore corduroys and a thick sweater. Her red hair spilled out of the bottom of her favorite black knit hat.

She hopped in the car with Petal and Becka, both clad in short skirts and high boots. Olivia immediately felt underdressed. "You went for comfort not fashion," Becka giggled.

"Walking across campus has taught me that I freaking hate being cold. Besides, Justin loves the grunge look." With her fingers, she touched the little bit of extra body fat she now had around her waist. She sucked her stomach in.

Petal and Becka were always thin and curvy and perfect. Never an ounce of extra flab, stomachs taut. She had always been the one with just a little extra. Never overweight, just not *skinny* skinny. Justin always said that he loved her body and that she never obsessed over what she ate. "Being comfortable in your skin is sexy as hell," he always said. "No man wants a woman who's afraid to eat. I don't think I've ever seen Petal bite into something and look like she enjoyed it. You should talk to her about that. Food is to be fucking enjoyed."

She pinched the skin that hung over her pants, again, reminding herself that she liked the way she looked. College had added a few pounds, no biggy. She had more important things to concern herself with, like getting into a doctoral program.

Hall and Oates' "Kiss on My List" reverberated from the stereo. Petal and Becka sang along.

"Is C.J going?" Olivia asked.

"Yep. He'll be there and Travis, Cory, and maybe a few of the other guys. I'm not sure who though."

"So, it's going well?"

Petal sang, drowning out Olivia's question.

"Petal? It's going well between you and C.J.?"

"We sort of broke up. But we're still hanging out. If you weren't always with Justin when you came home, you'd know what was going on."

"We talk on the phone."

"It's not the same. You never make time for us. And we miss you." Petal said to Olivia, then turned to Becka, "Right, Bex?"

Becka nodded in agreement.

"I miss you gals, too. It's just so busy at school. Especially now that I'm applying to doctoral programs."

"Knowing you, you'll get in wherever you apply. You're good at everything you do." Petal said.

Becka turned. "She's right. Hopefully, you'll pick somewhere close."

"Hopefully." Olivia didn't share her anxiety that she wouldn't be accepted into Rutgers, her first choice. Only Justin knew that.

They had to walk four blocks to the bar. Petal and Becka huddled together, both wearing thin leather jackets. "It's freezing," Petal squealed through chattering teeth; her breath became a cloud of gray in the frigid air. "C'mere, Liv. Body heat." She squeezed Olivia close. The three walked briskly toward the bar.

Justin noticed as soon as they walked in and strode toward them. He had a cool, edgy manner, especially when he played with his band. His dark hair hung carelessly, hovering just above his shoulders. He wore a flannel shirt and jeans with a tear in one knee.

"Hey, Jus," Petal and Becka said in a sing-song harmony.

"Hey," he nodded to Petal and Becka as he scooped Olivia under his shoulder. "Hey, Sweets." He kissed her lips while they walked.

Parker, Scully and Raul were setting up. Justin walked her over so she could say hi to his bandmates. "How was your Christmas?" Scully, a tall dude with bulging arm muscles and a magnanimous smile, asked her.

"Excellent. And yours?"

"Can't complain. Good to see you." He smiled again, went back to his set up.

Petal and Becka sat at a wood table with C.J., Cory and Travis. Two pitchers of beer and a row of cups sat in the middle of the table.

"Liv, hey. How's it going?" C.J. threw her a nod.

"Everything's going well."

Petal leaned in to C.J. One leg crossed over the other, her long, lean thigh muscles exposed and obvious, as she swung her leg.

C.J. seemed oblivious, but that's how he was all the time: polite, even nice, but too cool to care.

What Petal saw in him, Olivia couldn't be sure. The guy was alright, nothing special. He was tall and athletic with a big personality and too much confidence. In high school, C.J. had been popular, the leader of their friend group. High school had been over for three years and C.J. still acted like a cocky teenager who thought he knew everything. Petal was drawn to it. "He's strong. A leader type. It's sexy." She would say.

"He's a player, P. Be careful with him. C.J. loves C.J. I'm not sure there's room to love anyone else."

"Not everyone is as perfect as *Justin*." Petal would respond through pursed lips.

Petal turned her chair toward C.J. He sat straight forward, elbows on the table, talking with Cory about a business they were trying to start together. Olivia felt far away from all of them. She wanted to regain that sense of belonging to a group that she used to feel with them, but she felt distant.

She watched them interacting, drank her beer, said nothing. "Let's get some shots," she finally suggested. She wanted something stronger to dull the discomfort she felt. She was there to see her love play with his band. She wanted to enjoy every minute.

Justin sang most of the lead vocals, Parker and Scully, backup. Although Furious Whiskers had some of their own songs, for this event they played only cover.

Justin looked straight into her eyes as he sang "Wonderwall" by Oasis, a favorite song of theirs. Sometimes when they were alone, she would sing "Wonderwall" with him. She loved singing with Justin — in private. She loved singing in general, although she could barely carry a tune. From as early as she could remember, her mother played the piano and sang while Olivia and her older sister, Abbee, would sing along. When Justin started coming around, he would sing with her mom while her mom played the piano. "That's hot," Petal yelled to Olivia over the music. "He's singing right to you in a crowd of people.

That is fucking hot as hell. I hope you know how lucky you are."

"It is, and I do." She smiled at him through the crowd.

"Let's dance," Petal pulled on C.J.'s hands.

"Nah. You go." He said without budging.

"C'mon. One dance." She shot him flirty eyes.

"Maybe later, P. Liv'll go with you. Right, Liv?"

Petal's eyes looked disappointed.

"Yeah. Come on." Olivia got up.

The two hit the dance floor smack in front of the band. Holding hands, Petal and she swung around in a circle. Soon Becka joined them and the three of them danced together. The whole time, Olivia kept her eyes glued on Justin. His fingers glided across his guitar while he sang. His expression intense, his voice affecting. Whenever he looked at her, he'd smile.

Now he sang "I Wanna Be Sedated" by the Ramones. The crowd bopped to the rhythm of the music as the dance floor quickly became packed with swinging arms and jumping feet of people singing loudly. Justin was captivating when he sang. He amazed Olivia. For someone reserved, even shy in crowds of people, when he got a guitar in his hands and a mic in front of him, he transformed into someone powerful, confident and magnetic.

The night went on, more drinks, more chatter, more dancing. Petal now had an exposed leg across C.J.'s legs; his hand rested on her knee. Still, he talked more to the guys than to Petal, but she seemed content that he at least paid her some attention. Travis ordered another round of shots, another pitcher of beer, then another.

At the end of the band's third set, Justin spoke into the microphone to the audience. His eyes zoomed toward Olivia's, gripping hers like a magnet. His smile faded, replaced by a serious expression.

Petal swung her gaze between Olivia and Justin. "What's he doing?"

The bar fell silent. "I don't know," she answered, not peeling her eyes away from Justin's.

Justin looked vulnerable.

Her stomach fluttered.

"Tonight's a very special night. I have been lucky. Luckier than most."

Cheers and screeches from the crowd.

C.J. whistled.

Olivia's heart raced.

"Oh. My. God. Is he gonna propose?" Becka hollered.

"Liv, with your long red hair." He got down on one knee on the stage. "You are the most beautiful woman I have ever known and *I love you*. Will you marry me?"

Olivia couldn't move.

"Liv." She heard Petal say. "Go to him."

Justin looked at her from across the crowd and through all the noise; it was the two of them alone in that moment. This was one of the most important moments of her life: the night the only man she had ever loved asked to spend his life with her. The two of them. Together. Forever.

Blood rushed to her face.

"Yes." She went toward him.

The cheering in the bar sounded like faraway noise. "Yes."

Justin, still on one knee, took her ring finger and slipped a diamond perched atop a white gold band onto it. "I love you, Liv. Forever and one day." He said into the microphone, then put it down. He stood up and pulled her tight.

The crowd applauded. She felt something moist against her neck. "Are you crying?" she whispered in his ear.

"No." He said, but he looked her in the eyes through a tearful smile, so she could see how emotional he was.

Tears welled in her eyes. "I love you so much. I can't wait to be forever and one day."

"We already are."

6

Olivia left Hunter College, where she was a full-time professor, and walked north on Third Avenue. Date one with Adam Summers. She wished she had had time to go home to shower and change. Her wavy hair had lost some of its bounce throughout the day. Sebastian, who had stopped by for a pre-date assessment, had twirled strands of her hair around a pen, making a few corkscrew-shaped curls that framed her face.

"Much better." He had said when he stood back to give her a once over. "Lose the sweater."

"It makes the outfit."

"Um, no. Take it off. You look like a college professor."

"I *am*."

"By day, yes, but not by night. By night, my dear, you are a goddess. I don't know why you insist on covering that body of yours."

"Fine." She had huffed and took it off.

Taxis zoomed past. She stood on the curb at 65th Street and hailed a cab. Better than walking all the way up to 86th Street. Sebastian had been right about the cardigan. The May air was smooth, but it was warm enough that walking 20 blocks would leave her sweaty.

First dates used to make her nervous, but not anymore. After being on-and-off single for so many years, she had become accustomed to the awkward chitchat and the inconspicuous assessment of intention and desire.

It often felt like a charade: the guy acting a certain way to get whatever it was he wanted. She always kept one eye open to the possibility that whatever it was that a man said he wanted, there was a chance he could change his mind. Desire came and went. It was the commitment that made things last. Even then, it wasn't a sure thing.

She knew that, unfortunately, from firsthand experience.

The pressure of her age sat in the back of her mind too. She had always imagined having at least two children, but time was tick-tick-ticking away her dwindling opportunities. It irritated her that outside forces, such as time and age, had some sort of control over her life.

On the bright side, because everything should have a bright side, she was about to have dinner with Adam Summers. If things went well, she might ask him to her high school reunion, which wasn't until September.

She still had four months to find a date, but like her child-bearing chances, the days to the reunion were tick-tick-ticking away. *One date at a time*, she admonished herself.

When she stepped out of the taxi, the heel of her shoe got caught in a crack on the street. She yanked her foot, trying to dislodge it, and the heel broke off. *Crap*, she picked up the broken heel, and hobbled onto the curb.

She knew the stilettos were a bad idea. Those thin little heels were precarious. She liked a sturdy shoe, but Sebastian had convinced her that her shoes were too safe and that she needed to take more risks in fashion. She looked at her watch, thinking she might have time to get a new pair of shoes before she met Adam.

Then she heard, "Olivia," and turned to see Adam standing beside her, an amused expression across his face.

Just perfect. Naturally, she wouldn't escape the quiet mortification of Adam Summers, her attractive dinner companion, witnessing her flair for calamity. Without intention, she revealed her occasional lack of grace before they even sat down to dinner.

She batted her eyelashes. "Hi, Adam. As you can see, my heel decided it no longer wanted to be attached to my shoe." She waved the heel and chuckled.

He smiled at her, a devilish glint in his eyes.

"You look entertained." She said.

"It's cute."

They looked at each other and laughed.

"There's a shoe store on the next block. Would you like to start our date there?"

"Yes." She smiled.

As it turned out, Olivia's mild disaster eliminated any awkwardness. By the time they walked to the restaurant from the shoe store, their rapport felt easy.

"So, you know what I do. Tell me what you do. What does Liv like to do when she's not getting her heel stuck in cracks on the street?" He peered over his wire-rimmed glasses; his eyes glimmered, almost teasingly, but she noticed the concentration in his gaze. He seemed like someone whose feelings ran deep.

"I'm a professor. I teach psychology."

"That's interesting. A psychology professor. I could see that. Do you have your doctorate?"

"Yes. From Duquesne University."

"In Pittsburgh, right?"

She nodded. "I was torn during my senior year at Rutgers. I had applied to both psychology and philosophy programs, in New Jersey and New York, as well as other areas of the country. Originally, I thought I'd stay at Rutgers, if I was accepted, and study clinical psychology, but," she sipped her wine. "Some things I thought were in place, weren't."

"How so?"

"In addition to my affinity for breaking heels off shoes, I have a knack for saying more than I want to. Please excuse my awkwardness."

He looked at her inquisitively, while rubbing the scruff along his face. "Excused."

"There were many reasons I chose Duquesne, but the main reason really is that it has a unique program. Existential Phenomenological Psychology, a psychology that takes the diagnostics out of clinical psychology and focuses more on the experience of the whole person. Existentialism has always been a passion of mine. I can remember reading existentialism as early as seventh and eighth grade.'

"No kidding. That young?"

"Some things that feel like decisions aren't really choices. When I stumbled upon existentialism as a young girl, I felt like I had found a part of myself. It drew me in. No volition. Like it was already inside."

"Interesting," he contemplated. "So, you believe that existentialism was your calling and no matter what it would manifest itself somehow?"

"I do." She nodded. "I think what we want is within us from the beginning. I think fear can distract us from knowing the truth of who we are and what we want. Just my opinion, of course. But I love thinking about these things. It's one of the reasons I love your writing. It's rife with existential themes."

Adam took a long sip from his glass. "I have always been fascinated with the big questions. Existentialism seemed to answer some things for me. Or rather, it gave me a way to ask the questions. The writing gives me an outlet to explore it."

"I can see that. I write too."

"Oh, anything I might have heard of."

"No. I don't think so. My publications are all academic."

"Perhaps, you'll share them with me one day." Their eyes met.

He had a quiet intensity, which she felt as his eyes wandered across her face and along her shoulders. There was something about sitting with a man who didn't say too much, but, she could tell, had a lot to say that was terribly alluring. She wanted to know what he thought about things. "Maybe we could make a deal: You tell me if in your mind Tamara dies, and I'll let you read one of articles."

"You drive a hard bargain, Liv. I do enjoy your tenacity over the fate of Tamara."

"You are one attractive man, Adam Summers." *Shit. Shit.* That flew out of her mouth before she could stop herself. She needed to switch to water. Wine made her words too untidy.

He rested his hand over hers. "You are a very attractive woman, Olivia...?"

"Watson."

"Olivia Watson. You are also a very interesting woman. Would you like to go for a walk? Or another drink somewhere?"

The intensity in his eyes disarmed her, making her stomach flutter. "Another drink sounds nice." she said, trying to hide the anticipation she felt in her throat.

As they stepped outside, Adam weaved his fingers through hers. "Any preference on where you want to go?"

She felt a tingle up her spine. "How about your place?"

He smiled. "Let me get a taxi." He squeezed Olivia's hand, as he used the other one to wave down a cab.

She looked at their fingers woven together. She felt secure holding his hand, and although she knew it could be a mistake to go back to a man's place on the first date, in the moment it felt right.

Adam escorted her out of the taxi in front of his apartment building. He hadn't mentioned at dinner that he lived in a duplex on Central Park West, rubbing shoulders with celebrities in the elevator, or that he was wealthy.

They walked through a narrow hallway into a huge living room with high ceilings. There was a large black leather sofa and three matching love seats; large canvases with colorful, amorphous designs hung on three of the walls. Next to the living room, there was a dining room; a long thin black table with three chairs on each side, spotlights along the ceiling, more modern artwork along the walls.

When she saw the staircase to the second floor, she asked what was up there.

"My bedroom and writing room," he responded, not seeming too interested in showing her around the inside of his apartment.

Before she could even take in the surroundings, he said, "I think you'll like this." He walked her outside to his balcony, which overlooked a magnificent view of Central Park. The city buzz was muted from above, replaced by the quietness of the expansive greenery and rolling hills. She saw the runners, cyclists, walkers, roller bladders, tourists and city dwellers enjoying the warm evening. A spring breeze blew across the balcony, carrying the sweet aroma of flowers.

"Wow. This view is amazing."

"I love it out here. Especially this time of year. So, what can I get you to drink?"

She sat down on a cushioned lounge chair. "You have red wine?"

"Coming right up. Make yourself at home. I'll be right back."

Adam came back out with a bottle of red wine and two glasses. They sipped wine and talked. Adam touched her hand gently, on and off, as they spoke, desire filling the spaces between them. She learned that he was nearly ten years older than she, just three years shy of fifty. He looked young; his skin was smooth and tight. His manner suggested that of an older person, though, like he held a wisdom that only came from life experience.

He rubbed his hand along his five o'clock shadow as he reflected on what she said before he answered. She enjoyed watching the concentrated gaze he had when she spoke. And she enjoyed how expressive his eyes were. A few times she noticed laughter in them before the laugh came out of his mouth.

A scratching sound came from the screen door; Olivia turned to see a beautiful black cat with a white neck, white paws, white whiskers, big yellow eyes.

"Hey Tucker. You hungry, boy?" Adam asked the cat.

Tucker lifted a paw up, almost as if he said yes. Adam opened the screen door and picked him up. "This little guy is Tucker." He rubbed under the cat's neck. A small meow released from Tucker.

"Come in for a minute. Let me give him a little food."

"You didn't mention that you had a cat."

"Oh." He chuckled. "I guess I had my mind on other things." He gave a devilish smirk.

Olivia blushed.

Now they were in the kitchen, which had all black appliances. There was a high bar table with four stools, two on each side, more expensive artwork. "This place is huge." She exclaimed. "You gonna show me around?"

She wondered where he made his money. She knew a few writers and though some did reasonably well — well enough to live comfortably from writing — she had been in the city long enough to know that this apartment probably wasn't in a writer's price range, even a best-selling author. Unless of course, he was as famous as Stephen King or James Patterson, which he wasn't. At least not yet. Old money, she wondered. He had a dignity about him, almost like he had gone to finishing school.

"And this," he opened a door adjacent to the living room, "is my sanctuary."

The oak door swung open to reveal a huge room filled with books. Awe-stricken, she looked around. Shelves covered every wall. The shelves displayed row after row of books. Countless volumes stuffed every nook and cranny. In the middle sat four sturdy black leather chairs, two on each side and facing each other with two square tables in the middle. It had a late nineteenth-century New England feel to it; like Olivia had stepped through a time warp and had entered the library of a classic literary figure, maybe Emerson or Thoreau.

Olivia took a sharp breath. "Wow. I've never seen anything like this before. It's magnificent." She spun around, taking in the splendor of being surrounded by ages of literary brilliance. She walked over to one shelf and scanned the books. Old books, used books, some first editions from classic writers. Impressive, perhaps one of the most impressive rooms she had ever been in. She turned to go toward another shelf and noticed a half-smoked cigar in an ashtray. "You smoke?"

"Occasionally. You?"

"I quit ten years ago."

Strange, as she looked around, she realized that there were no photographs, not one. Nothing in the apartment on that first floor, besides the books, that told her anything about him except that he lived in opulence.

"Can I see your writing space?" She covered her mouth gently. "I'm sorry. As we get to know each other better, you'll see that I often don't have a filter. Words just sort of fly out, surprising even me."

"I like that." He moved closer toward her. "You can always trust someone who says what's on their mind."

"How about you?" She blinked at him through wide eyes.

"What?" He took her hands in his.

She looked up at him. "Can I trust you?"

"You can." He kissed her.

"About your writing space?" She searched his face. "Can I see it?"

Their faces were close. "It's a mess. Next time. I promise."

"I'm gonna hold you to that."

"I know you will." Adam wrapped his arms around her, kissing her face and then her lips, desire swelling. "Do you want to go into the other room? The couch is comfortable." He whispered in her ear.

She nodded. Soon they were naked on the couch. Her hands wandered across his back and along his ass. Adam was fit, fitter than her. The lights were dim, but she could feel his wide shoulders and trim waist and strong butt. She enjoyed feeling him on top of her, as his fingers explored her body. "You are beautiful," he said, caressing the side of her face.

He felt good slipping inside of her.

7

Adam slept on the couch. The warmth of his breath skimmed the top of Olivia's hair as she lay nestled against him. It was nearly one in the morning. She disentangled herself and quietly got dressed.

"Where are you going?" He said in a groggy voice.

"Sorry. I tried to be quiet. I didn't want to wake you."

"I'm glad you did." He sat up. "You don't want to stay? We could go into the next room and sleep on the bed. The guest room." He smiled, boyishly.

Olivia found him gentle; not pushy, but inviting. Other guys always seemed to come on too strong, nearly overwhelming her with their desire or to be too aloof, which quickly got boring. Adam seemed to have a balance to him, like he knew what he wanted, but wouldn't push. "I have to get up early for work," she said, but it was more than that. She needed to be alone, or at least

42

not with him. Sleepovers on the first night usually were no big deal, but she had the unsettling sense that if she stayed with Adam she'd never want to leave. Worse, maybe he wouldn't want her to leave, either. And it was too soon to have those feelings.

He stood, the blanket loosely covering his lower body. His chest was wide and sturdy. He had the smallest layer of body fat around his waist, which made him feel warm and soft, natural. She gave him a strong hug, then said, "I had a wonderful time."

"Me too, Olivia Watson." He held eye contact. For a second, his gaze reminded her of Justin. Maybe Adam was the first guy to look at her as intensely and completely as Justin had. Or maybe it was the way *she* felt that reminded her of Justin. Exposed. Like he saw inside of her.

"Next time I want to see upstairs. You promised."

"I did. And I will keep that promise. I'll call you tomorrow. Actually, it's already tomorrow. I'll call you later today."

"Good." She kissed him at the door, turned and left.

Outside, the streets had an eerie quiet. A few people strolled along the park. Doormen stood outside buildings, acknowledging her as she walked passed. A peaceful feeling flowed through the darkness, and it felt like the city that never slept was taking a respite from the usual buzz. She decided to walk a few blocks before she hailed a taxi to go across town.

What had Sebastian said? Dangerously charming? That's right. Dangerously charming.

He was charming. It was more than that, though. Adam had depth, a reflective, thoughtful side. He also had a story, something he kept tight, something dark and painful. Something that he covered, but added dimension to his personality.

Then her mind diverted down a path she didn't like. She wanted to bring him to the reunion. That was a fine, respectable thought. However, the next thought made her cringe. She wanted the whole gang to see that she was now with best-selling author Adam Summers who owned a magnificent duplex on Central Park West. Her handsome, charming and intellectual new beau.

She especially wanted Justin to see.

Yikes.

She was over him and what he did. What *they* did. Why on earth would she want to rub Adam in Justin's face? She didn't care what Justin thought, right?

Closure: one word, seven letters. A word Olivia felt should be eliminated from every dictionary. It was a superfluous word, and she wanted it expunged from her vocabulary and everyone else's on the planet.

Smith had said it. Smith Rose, her college roommate, whose last name was a first name and first name was a last name. Smith was tall and lanky with stringy blond hair. A natural athlete, she played basketball and ran track, running circles around most of the guys. Smith had said it: *closure.*

Olivia totally disagreed.

"You need closure," Smith had said one night, a few months after the breakup, when Olivia was still crying on a regular basis. "You should return his calls. Hear him out."

"I heard him out right after it happened. There's nothing more to say. I have my closure."

"Bullshit. Here." She had handed Olivia a jar of peanut butter and a spoon. They ate that whole jar until there was nothing left. "It helps, right?"

"The peanut butter?"

"Yeah."

"For now."

Smith had hugged her. "Until the door is closed, it's real hard to totally move on."

"Believe me. The door *is* closed. It's not just losing him. It's the betrayal. I trusted him and I trusted Petal. I feel spun around. I need time, not closure."

"Maybe you should take up a new hobby. You could start running with me." Smith gave a hopeful smile.

"I dunno. Maybe. I was thinking more along the lines of a dance class. I used to dance as a kid. I was pretty good at it."

"Dancing is good. Just do something. This moping around isn't good."

"I know. I'll try."

She didn't need closure. She hadn't needed it back then, and she certainly didn't need it now. Justin and Petal were married. Married! *Things don't get more closed than that.* She had picked up her pace and hadn't even realized it.

She turned and hailed a taxi. All she had to know was that she enjoyed her evening with Adam. The best way to keep her heart safe and her mind sane was to take things one step at a time. If things progressed with Adam, she'd take him to the stupid reunion. If they didn't, she would go alone. She had nothing to prove to anyone. A proud, successful, strong woman didn't need to prove anything to anyone other than herself.

The next day when she spilled the Adam story to Sebastian, he said, "Your face is flushed."

"It's hot out."

"It's air conditioned in here." They sat in her office. "You like him."

"I do."

"A. Lot." He gave her a shrewd look.

"I dunno about a lot. I just met him. I had a nice time and would like to get to know him a little better." She felt her face burning up.

"Just as I suspected. You like him tons. I don't think I have ever seen you blush while talking about a guy before."

"Shut up." She threw a pen at him.

8

After Justin's band finished their last set, they started packing up. Petal and C.J. stood next to Olivia, kissing like two animals. Becka laughed drunkenly with Cory and Travis. "Should we go to the diner or back to our place for another round?" Becka asked between giggles.

Becka and Petal shared an apartment off Bergenline Avenue.

When Petal finally unglued her lips from C.J.'s, she shouted out to the gang. "We should go back to our place and pop some bubbly to celebrate Liv and Justin's engagement." She turned toward Justin and batted her eyelashes. "You're such a romantic."

"Nah. I'm just lucky." He smiled at Olivia and squeezed her hand.

Her face beamed with an exuberant smile.

"I've gotta finish up here with the guys. Wait for me." He said to Olivia.

She nodded to Justin, then turned to Petal. "You girls go. He's got to finish up and I'm tired. We'll celebrate another night."

In a pointed tone, Petal responded, "Another night? What other night? You're going back to school in a few days. I wish you wouldn't have taken that job at the bookstore."

"I'm still home for three days."

"You're not even celebrating New Year's with us. I can't believe you and Justin are going out with Smith and her boyfriend instead of us." She eyed Justin who was busy packing up with his band. "Did you ask Justin what he wanted to do on New Year's? I bet he'd say he wanted to be with us."

"I don't know what to say. I love you guys. My life is just different now. And I'm balancing a lot of things. We'll go out tomorrow. OK?"

"Sure." Petal softened her tone. "Sounds like a plan."

"And just for the record," Olivia placed her hands on her hips, "Justin and I make all of our decisions together. New Year's plans included."

"Of course." Petal smiled, then turned and rolled her eyes.

The next evening, Olivia's parents took her and Justin out to celebrate. When Olivia learned that Justin had asked her father for her hand in marriage before he proposed, she hugged and kissed him. "Petal's right. You really are a romantic."

"Nah. Just the luckiest dude alive."

Petal and Becka were having everyone over to their place. When Olivia and Justin arrived after dinner with her parents, they found only Petal and Becka with a case of beer, two bottles of vodka and a pack of Marlboro lights.

Petal cried, wheezing out words between sobs as she explained to Olivia and Justin that C.J. had cheated on her with Ashlee Lynn Burgos.

"I'm confused. I thought you guys broke up. Then you were kissing him last night?" Olivia asked as gently as she could.

"We were still hooking up and Ashlee knew it. I fucked him last night. The fuckhead slept over, and I fucked him last night and this morning too. Then Raquel calls and tells me that she saw C.J. with Ashlee last week, arm in arm near her apartment on Boulevard East. I asked him about it. And he admitted it like it wasn't a big deal. He said, 'Yeah, I hang out with Ashlee sometimes.' So, I said, 'Did you fuck her too?' And he was like, 'Yeah, you and me, we're not exclusive, man. You knew that. What's the big deal?' Like he didn't even care about me."

Tears flew out of Petal's eyes. Becka poured her a shot of vodka, lit a cigarette, stuck it in Petal's mouth. "Here. He's a total douche." Becka said in a mild voice.

"What did you say to him after that?" Olivia asked.

"Nothing. I hung up on his dumb ass and smashed my phone into pieces."

"We got her a new one already." Becka gave an uncertain smile.

"He's a loser." Olivia said.

"What do you think, Justin?" Petal sniffled, then took a long drag off her cigarette.

"Whatdaya mean?"

"He's your friend. He must have said something to you." Her eyes pleaded at Justin.

He shifted on the couch. "No, man. Me and C.J. hang out sometimes through Travis, but we don't talk about stuff like that."

"I don't understand." Petal cried. "What more did he want?"

"Listen. C.J. isn't relationship material. He's always been a player. Right? This isn't about a problem with you, it's a guy who wants to have his cake and eat it too." Olivia rubbed her back.

"Oldest story in the book." Becka threw back a shot.

"You always think you're the one that's gonna change him. You know? I always want the guy that no one can hold onto. I want to be the girl that he wants. The one he changes for."

"It's askin' for trouble if you think you're gonna change someone." Becka took another shot.

Olivia thought she seemed more anxious than Petal. "You alright, Becka."

"The whole day has been emotional, that's all. She's been crying all day. Got me charged up."

Petal eyed Olivia and Justin. "I want what you guys have."

"Someday you'll have it. But you've got to stay away from guys like C.J." Olivia said.

Petal moved closer to Justin. "How did you know, Jus? How did you know that you loved Liv?"

"When all I did was think about her."

Justin and Olivia shared an admiring look.

"What did I do wrong? Why wasn't he thinking about me?"

"I'm sure it's nothing you did." Justin touched Petal's shoulder. "Sometimes things just don't work out."

She leaned against Justin. "I hope you're right."

The buzzer rang. C.J., Travis, Cory and Manny were downstairs. C.J.'s voice bellowed through the intercom static. "Let us up."

Petal screamed, "No. Do not let that bastard in."

Becka's eyes scanned from Petal to Justin to Olivia.

"Tell him to go away," Olivia admonished.

"Um. It's not a good time," Becka said into the intercom, mildly.

"C'mon, Becka. Let us up," C.J. bellowed.

Olivia walked over. "Watch out." She scooted Becka over. "She doesn't want to see you. Understand. Go away. You're an ass, C.J.," she hollered into the intercom. Satisfied, she returned to the couch next to Justin, arms folded. "What an asshole," she huffed.

The buzzer sounded again. And again.

Justin took a heavy breath. "I'll get rid of him."

"Dude," Justin spoke into the intercom. "She doesn't want you here. Have some respect."

"Fucking Steeler. Whose side are you on? I didn't do anything to her. She's acting psycho."

"Have some fucking respect, C.J."

"*You* have some fucking respect."

"*Dude.* I'm not letting you up. You need to leave her alone. She doesn't want you here."

"Fuck you. And her."

"Let's go," they heard Travis say. Justin kept his finger on the "listen" button. Muffled voices, then static. "They left." He plopped back down on the couch, took a long sip of his beer.

"Good. He's a total dick." Olivia said. Petal sniffled, then took a long drag off her cigarette. "I wish I was a strong as you, Liv," she said, releasing tendrils of smoke.

"You are. You just don't know it. Give me one of those."

Petal handed her a cigarette.

"I thought you were quitting?" Justin looked at her.

"I am. Just one."

Petal plopped back onto the sofa, wedging herself into the small space between Olivia and Justin. "I love you guys." She rubbed her hand back and forth along the leg of Justin's jeans.

FOREVER AND ONE DAY

He put his arm around her back, tentatively. "It's all gonna be alright. You're beautiful, fun, smart. A good guy will come along soon."

She rested her head on his shoulder. "I hope so."

"Petal always goes for the jerks." Olivia said to Justin later that night at his apartment.

Justin went to say something, but hesitated.

"What is it?"

"Nothing. It's just... maybe C.J.'s not into Petal."

"Well, if that's the case, he shouldn't be messing around with her."

"He's a guy, Liv. If she's putting it out there on a platter, he's gonna take it."

"It's not the girl's responsibility to make sure the guy acts respectfully." She put her hands on her hips.

"I agree. But that's not who C.J. is. You know that. He's always messed around. And Petal always gives in to him."

"I've talked to her about that. She thinks she loves him. I don't how she could. He's not loveable."

"I think Petal's afraid to be alone. Maybe she thinks C.J. will take care of her 'cause he's got such a strong personality. You know, save her from her house and her mother."

Olivia sat on the couch and put her hands between her knees. "I feel like when I left for college, everything got worse. Like I filled that void and now that I'm away, she keeps looking for someone else."

Justin sat beside her. "She's got to figure it out on her own. I know she's your best friend, but you can't hold up your life because you're worried about hers."

"You should talk to her more when you see her out with the gang while I'm away. She listens to you. I think it's because she sees how you treat me."

"You know that I listen to her stories when you're not home to listen them."

"Maybe you need to listen less and dish out more advice. Like telling her to stay away from C.J. and any other guy who acts like him."

"I'll try. This actually relates to something I wanted to talk with you about."

"Oh?"

"I was thinking. If you get into Rutgers for graduate school, maybe you can live back here and commute, instead of me moving there."

"I don't know, Jus. The curriculum is going to be demanding. I thought we agreed that you would move to New Brunswick."

"I know. It's– this is home. Know what I mean?"

"This will *always* be home. But don't you want to spread your wings. Experience new people and new things? Besides, we have to be prepared to move further. I don't know where I'll be accepted, yet. I've applied all over the country. This is why I thought maybe we should wait to be engaged until I was done." She looked at her ring. "But I don't want to wait anymore."

"Me neither."

Olivia noticed his far-off look. "What?"

"I dunno. Maybe you could wait a year before you start graduate school."

"Wait? I've been working my ass off. This is what I want. What we both want, right?"

"Of course."

"I have big aspirations."

"I know you do. It's one of the things I love about you." He took a heavy breath. "My band's here, Liv."

"Jus, you're the talent. You. You'll find another band. Maybe it's time for you to send some of your own music off to an agent. Anything can happen after that."

"You make it sound so easy. Finding a band that you click with is *not* easy. And finding an agent, no matter how talented you are, is even harder."

"I know that, but I believe in you. And you haven't even tried. Besides, do you want to stay living in North Bergen for the rest of our lives? I want to live in a few different places. I want to see things. This town, that life, it wouldn't be enough for me. I thought you wanted that too. We always talked about living other places."

"I do want those things. I just… I feel at home with Furious Whiskers. And I have mixed feeling about pursuing music on my own."

"How so?"

"It's a cut-throat world, Liv. You know how I tell you that the writing is the deepest part of who I am?"

"Yeah."

"It's not easy for me to put my work out there to agents or other bands. Putting my art out there for judgment feels like a big risk."

"Sweets, it's scary to take chances, to put yourself on the line. But you're not alone; I will always be here to support you. I am your biggest fan and I believe in you."

He pulled her close. "I know you do." He kissed her cheeks, then her lips. "We'll figure it out."

Olivia melted into his arms. But again, she had that gnawing concern that he wasn't sure what he wanted to do with his life.

We'll figure it out. Together. She tried to reassure herself.

Two weeks later, Justin came to Rutgers for the weekend. Smith stayed with her boyfriend Damien Jones, so Olivia and Justin had the small dorm room to themselves. Smith's boyfriend went by his surname, Jones, which made Olivia laugh. "Smith and Jones. You sound like a company." Olivia had remarked when Smith started dating him.

Jones was a track star and had the strongest legs Olivia had ever seen. Whenever he sat in Smith's desk chair, Olivia wondered if it would crack under the sheer enormity of his quads and hamstrings.

Before Justin arrived, Olivia mentioned her concerns to Smith and Jones. "I'm a little worried that Justin's not sure what he wants to do in his career. I think he's afraid to move out of North Bergen and move forward with his life. With our lives."

Jones said, "Guys take longer to figure stuff out. My sister knew what she wanted to do with her life at nine. Me, I'm still not sure."

Smith elbowed him. "Yes, you are."

"Having a general idea is different than having a definite plan."

Smith looked at Olivia. "I don't think it's a gender thing. I think it's a personal thing."

Jones nodded. "She's got a point. The guy loves you. I can tell from how he is with you. And he's asked you to marry him. Sounds to me like he knows exactly what he wants. A life with you. Maybe your priorities are different than his."

Smith giggled. "How did you ever get so smart, Jonesy?"

Olivia shook her head. "Our priorities are the same. We want to spend our lives together."

"Then what are you worried about?" Jones smiled at her.

"Right. Nothing. I'm just thinking too much."

Justin arrived, a small package in hand. "I got you something."

"What is it?" She took the package. "It feels like a book."

"Open it."

Olivia unwrapped it. "My gosh. Where did you find this?" It was a first edition copy of *Love and Will* by Rollo May, one of her favorite existential writers.

"Last week when we played in Manhattan, I found it in a used bookstore. I know it's one of your favorites."

"This is so awesome." She squeezed the book. "I can't wait for us to have our own place and to grow *our* book collection together." She kissed him.

"Speaking of books, I decided I'm going to look at graduate schools. As soon as we know where you're going, I'm gonna look into a master's in music education."

She sighed. "I'm so glad to hear you say that. Honestly, I was a little worried after our last conversation."

"Sweets, I wish you would stop worrying so much." He plopped down on her bed. "C'mere."

She lay next to him and he kissed her face, her cheeks, her lips. She rested her head on his shoulder while he stroked her hair. They were so close. There was no way this couldn't work.

Thinking about Petal and Becka and the tribulations they dealt with when it came to men, she couldn't believe how fortunate she was to never have to go through that. Justin and she began dating at the beginning of their senior year in high school. Once they got together, it was easy right from the start.

Justin wasn't like the other guys. Although sometimes he acted cool in front of them, she knew who he was beneath his swagger of self-assuredness: a warm, sensitive, artistic type who dreamed big and loved hard. Unlike other guys, like C.J., who fell in and out of love so easily, going from one girl to the next, tossing around *I love you* casually, Justin didn't love easily; but when he did, it was with everything he had.

Exactly like her.

Funny thing, she knew Justin since their freshman year in high school, when he started hanging around C.J. and Travis, who Olivia and Petal knew since elementary school. Tall and lean, with brooding dark eyes and a quiet manner, Justin seemed softer than the other guys, almost dreamy. Curious about him, one night she struck up a conversation. Justin barely responded to her, nodding with a cocky-edge, making her feel like he was doing her a favor by talking to her. Olivia didn't like him in the beginning.

"He makes you feel like a bug, a nuisance he wants to swat away." She had said to Petal one night when Justin first started hanging out with them.

"You got him all wrong. He's nice. You know how guys are with their attitudes. They have to act cool around each other. I like him."

"You always like the cocky guys."

"No, I don't. I'm just not picky like you. Sometimes, you don't give people a chance."

"I do so. I gave him a chance, and he made me feel like I wasn't good enough to talk to. Screw him. If the guy's not kissing the ground you walk on, then he ain't worth your time."

Petal laughed. "Look at Liv. So tough."

For nearly three years, Olivia hung out with Justin in crowds of people. She didn't talk to him that much after that first time. Though they shared a few words on a number of occasions, the casual exchanges held no significance. Justin's coolness turned her off, but sometimes she would catch herself watching him. Girls dangled on Justin, Petal included, but he always seemed standoffish. A guy like that was trouble.

Petal insisted that he was likeable. "Adorable *and* sexy," she would say. "I would go with him in a heartbeat." Olivia never trusted Petal's judgment when it came to matters of the heart.

Then one night, early in their senior year, the tides turned. While hanging out in C.J.'s garage drinking beer, Justin and Manny strumming guitars — nothing out of the ordinary — Justin's lyrics caught her attention. He sang so casually, like he made up the words as he went along, his voice barely a mutter under the din of the drunken talk that filled the garage. The lot of them — C.J., Travis, Joel and Cory, Olivia, Becka, Ashlee Lynn, Deidra and Petal — hovered around the keg blabbing to each other in loud voices.

Justin sat on a metal garbage can that had been turned upside down, and sang:

> *Her smile belied her intensity and passion,*
> *Her red wavy mane and natural compassion.*
> *She bared a beauty he was dying to know,*
> *A bright light, a countenance with an intoxicating glow.*

He couldn't tell her, she'd never know,
Words in his head would not flow.

Olivia looked up at him as he sang. She wasn't even sure what made her look. But when she did, their eyes met. He sang those lines, staring straight into her eyes with a piercing, intense expression. It gave her a shiver. Petal looked at Justin, then Olivia, then back. She elbowed Olivia, whispering, "Is he singing to you?"

"I dunno." She sipped her beer, nervously, her eyes glued to his with a naïve inquisitive gaze.

What was he doing? She wondered, with a knot in her stomach. No one had ever looked at her like that before — so completely. He had barely paid her any mind for the last three years and here he was singing to her? Or was he?

Justin continued singing, never unlocking his eyes from hers.

A girl with a manner that made you believe,
Things you would otherwise never conceive.
Like a lone ray of sun on a gloomy day,
He'd relished her warmth from miles away.
He couldn't tell her, she'd never know,
Words in his head would not flow.
Damn words in his head would not flow.

She looked away. When she looked back, he still looked at her, penetrating her with such intensity it was impossible to ignore. And then it hit her, she had completely mis-understood Justin. He wasn't arrogant, he was shy. And she was a bitch for deciding that she didn't like him after that first conversation, never giving the guy another chance to really talk to her.

God, the way he looked at her felt magnetic. She chewed on the edge of her cup, tried to continue hanging out with the gang without making it obvious that she wanted to kiss Justin — bad.

Someone, maybe Justin, she wasn't sure, flipped the stereo on. The garage filled with Pearl Jam, one of Justin's favorite bands. It was probably Justin.

Justin came next to her, his arm so close to hers she could feel the brush of his skin. She gave him a shy smile. He smiled back, making her whole body quiver. It was unexpected and exciting and romantic.

As the night continued, the gang drank more, talked more and laughed more. Another ordinary night in North Bergen, except for Olivia. She sensed the intimacy swell between the two of them. The graze of his arm along hers made her stomach flutter. She had never felt anything like it before. She wanted to feel his arms around her. Wondering how the night would end distracted her. But she did her best to act casual and ordinary, even though excitement coursed through her like an electric current.

"Come with me to the bathroom?" Petal asked.

Caught up in her reverie, Olivia didn't notice Petal.

"Liv?" She tugged her shirt a little. "Come to the bathroom?"

"Huh? Oh, sure."

As soon as they were out of earshot from the others, Petal gushed. "What is going on with you? Is it Justin?"

Olivia felt her face burning. She wanted to blurt out her excitement to Petal, but it sort of felt like she would ruin the private bond she now felt with Justin. Besides, nothing had happened — yet. "I thought he might be singing to you." Petal giggled. "But then I realized he wouldn't do that. Why would he do that? I mean, you guys are barely friends."

"Right." She drifted off. *Was Petal right? No. Justin had sung to her and he did it in a way that she would know, but the others wouldn't.* "Right. Go in and pee. I have to go really bad." Olivia jumped up and down. Petal went into the bathroom.

She wouldn't mention a thing to Petal unless or until something happened. As much as she loved Petal, her *bestest* friend, the girl had a loose tongue. If she told Petal, Becka would know, and probably Ashlee and Deidra too, before the night ended.

Petal came out of the bathroom. "If he was singing to you, if Justin is into you, I think you should go for it. Hook up with him. I would. Justin is *hot*. Besides, you never hook up with anyone. Soon we'll be graduating. Don't you want to have at least one high school boyfriend to look back on?"

"Hooking up and boyfriend aren't the same thing."

"I just want you to have fun."

"I do have fun. Now go. Let me pee before I go in my pants."

She fantasized that when she walked out of the bathroom Justin would be there waiting for her, but he wasn't. She went back outside, stood back where she had been, next to him.

The night winded down. She hoped that he would offer to walk her home or ask if he could call her, something.

"Night," he said to Petal and her as they walked out. He gave her a long look, but said nothing.

Nothing.

Petal lived around the corner from Olivia. They walked to Petal's first. "Wanna sleep over?"

"Not tonight. Call you in the morning, though."

"'Kay. Night."

When she reached home, she found Justin in front of her house. His long legs spilled out along the stairs, a bottle of wine beside him.

"Hi."

"Hi." He held up the wine. "So, you want to share this with me?" Even with his intense gaze, his expression had a bashful quality.

"Yes." Never had Olivia felt so certain about anything. "Let's hang in my backyard."

He took her hand, weaving his fingers through hers.

His hand felt warm and secure.

After that night, the two were nearly inseparable.

During the tense weeks of waiting for her graduate school interview invitations — hopefully, she'd get at least three — Justin called with disappointing news.

"I'm not going to graduate until next year."

"What? I thought you said you would be graduating this spring?"

"And I thought I would be. But when I met with my advisor, he looked over my courses and said I was two classes short. One of them is only offered in the fall, so I can't even finish in the summer."

"How could you not know that?"

"I don't know. I guess. I had other things going on and didn't think to check."

"*Justin.*"

"Listen. It's not a big deal. I'll be done by next winter. It's only one semester. We can make it through that. We've made it through nearly four years of you living away at college. Right?"

"Yes. But it's the point. I worry that you don't pay attention to these things."

A piercing silence hung on the line for what seemed an eternity.

Justin broke it. "*Liv.* I was busy trying to save for the ring, working extra hours at the guitar store. Busy with my music. I have dreams too."

"Dreams are good. And I love that about you, but real life has demands that need to be met sometimes. But you're right, it's only a semester. Sorry, I'm being hard on you. I just want everything to be the way we planned."

"You know, life throws curve balls sometimes. It's how you react that makes the difference."

"I know."

Turns out, Justin couldn't have been more on-the-nose about their future. Life isn't a straight path. It's a crooked one, filled with twisty turns, many abrupt and unexpected.

When Olivia looked back on the events of her life, the demise of two of the most important relationships from her youth, it was hard to know when things started to go wrong. Retrospective reveries provided no satisfying answers. And she had been left with a big hole in her heart, and a daunting question about how things that seemed so right could end so wrong.

9

Friday night happy hour. Downtown in the East Village. Date two with Adam. Olivia sat outside enjoying the breezy evening air. The atmosphere pulsed with the subversive individualism that permeated the streets of downtown Manhattan. People strolled along, talked, laughed. An elderly woman clacked by in four-inch platforms. She sported pink hair and was walking a tiny dog on a pink leash that matched her hair. Olivia smiled at her as she sipped a dry red and waited for Adam. The beat of the city energized her. Life always seemed large in downtown Manhattan.

Adam had said that the *Vine Bar*, their date location, was one of his favorite happy-hour locales. She could see why. Attached to the bar was a large independent bookstore where people could bring their drinks and peruse books, sit and read.

Adam had called exactly as he said he would and asked her out for Friday. Immediately after hanging up she had opened an Internet search, proceeding to hunt for details about Adam's life. For someone with a reasonably high-profile career, there wasn't much available. The only things she learned through her search were things related to his writing, things she basically already knew. Nothing about his family, nothing about his financial situation or previous relationships.

If she wanted to know, she would have to ask.

"Hey, you." She felt his hand on her shoulder and stood up.

"I like this place."

"I thought you would. You look great." He wrapped his arms around her and kissed her. The familiarity of his body from their previous date sent a slight shiver down her spine.

"What are you drinking?"

"Merlot."

The server came over, a tall man with long fingers and a thin moustache.

Adam said, "I'll have the same as her."

"And water, please."

"Make that two." That first moment when she sat face-to-face with a practical stranger that she had been physically intimate with always felt mildly awkward. Bodies familiar and yet plagued with the question: *Who is this person that I allowed inside of me, whose body penetrated mine?*

Adam smiled warmly, and she recognized genuine affection in his eyes. Again, something about the whole-hearted way he looked at her sent a rush of warmth through her body. She sipped her wine, smiled back. "Tell me about your life."

"Spoken like a true shrink. Is that derogatory? Shrink?" He laughed.

"No. We say it all the time. So?" She raised her eyebrows.

"What do you want to know?"

"Have you ever been married?"

"Wow. Right to the good stuff. I came close once about ten years ago, but– " he trailed off.

"What happened?"

His eyes turned pensive. He sipped his wine.

Olivia's head tilted with a curious look.

"She passed away."

"Oh, my gosh. I'm sorry."

"Breast cancer. It was terrible. We had been together for three years, and then she got sick. She was only thirty-three. Life is cruel and unfair sometimes."

"It is." She met his eyes and thought of her mother. *Should she?* "My mother is in remission from breast cancer. It's been a rough year for my family. I really understand how hard it is to watch someone you love be sick and feel completely helpless." She put her hand on his.

"Sorry to hear about your mom, but glad she's in remission."

"I'm grateful. Just sort of always worried that it will come back. Every time the phone rings at an odd hour, I wonder, will this be the day that she calls to tell me it's come back? I brush these things off, but they always lurk beneath the surface."

"I hear that. Since Zara passed away, I've tried my hardest to push myself every day to live to the fullest. It's one of the reasons I left journalism and began writing novels. It was always something I wanted to do, but kept putting it off. After Zara, I realized there was no waiting. All we have is the moment." He sipped his wine and looked at her. "It's one of the reasons I took a risk by giving you my number at the signing. There was, *is,* something about you that captured my attention. I needed to pursue that. Typically, though, I am not one to approach women."

"I'm glad you did."

"Me too."

"Have you ever been married?"

"No." He had been so honest, and she felt tempted to dish out her Justin story, but she held back. Meanwhile, she was quietly distracted by the parallel between Zara and the Tamara character in his most recent novel. Tamara had breast cancer. The question of if she died or not remained open at the end. But now that Olivia knew there was a plot connection that mirrored his real life, a bigger question about the book popped into her head. The male character, who the protagonist Penelope falls into a torrid affair with, is named Marshall Clive Drake. His parents were both murdered in the Hamptons.

If that had really happened to Adam, it would have shown up on an Internet search she told herself. *Besides, the book is fiction, not a memoir.* She certainly wasn't going to ask him about it anyway. The night had already started off on a serious note. No need to drag more death — or murder — into the conversation.

After another drink, they strolled through the bookstore, lingering in the philosophy section, both salivating over the used copies of Camus and Dostoyevsky, Nietzsche, May. There was an ancient-looking, disheveled copy of *Being and Time.* The pages were dogged-eared, marked up with a pink highlighter, and the cover was half missing from the back. "I have to buy this for my friend Sebastian. He's one of those folks who reads Heidegger for enjoyment."

Adam laughed. "I have a couple of buddies like that."

"Sebastian is a philosophy professor. I told him he was sadistic. He relishes in watching his students struggle through Heidegger. But truth is, he's passionate about him. Passion is always a good thing."

"Sure is." He kissed her.

"I think I need to eat." She said.

"Great. Do you want to eat down here or uptown?"

"Let's go there." She pointed to an Indian restaurant across the street.

"I like how you always seem to know what you want."

She blushed. "Not always."

"Ok. Not always, but a lot of the time." He wrapped his arm around her as they ambled across the street to the restaurant.

Back at Adam's after dinner, he popped a bottle of Champagne. "What's the occasion?" Olivia asked, perched on a kitchen chair.

"Tonight is the occasion. Life is the occasion."

"Perfect."

They clicked glasses and sipped.

There was a loud *BOOM,* then a flash of light.

"A thunderstorm. I love thunderstorms. Come on."

He guided her up the spiral staircase toward his private space: his bedroom and writing room.

The floor opened up into a large area with a long desk, one desktop computer, two laptops, papers strewn across the desk, unorganized. Books sat piled on the floor next to the desk. Mostly new releases, a couple of classics. There was a long bookshelf. So many books — again, no pictures. More artwork on the walls that had the same amorphous splatters of color as the ones downstairs. One reminded her of a Rorschach card. She laughed to herself thinking that she should ask Adam what he saw in the painting to learn more about the way he interpreted the world. The adjacent room had a king-sized bed, a large steel dresser and a big-screen TV. Again, no pictures, just obscure artwork.

BOOM.

"Look." He opened a door in the bedroom onto another balcony overlooking Central Park. The sky covered with black clouds, the air so heavy it seemed tangible. And right as she took in the expansive darkness, the whole sky lit up with a crackling zigzag of white light.

Another *BOOM*.

"Wow. Adam. This place is amazing."

"Thanks." He took her hand and brought her outside. They sat on two chairs underneath an awning on the balcony listening to the soothing cadence of pouring rain. The smell of moist grass and fresh flowers filled the humid air. As they sipped their champagne enjoying the meditative noise of the storm, Olivia again had the unsettling feeling that if she let herself go, she might never want to leave Adam's side.

The question was: Was this man worth the risk?

More disconcerting, did she even have control over her heart's wild abandon this time?

10

The world opened up with possibility when Rutgers contacted Olivia in the middle of January offering her an interview. Following that phone call came a series of other offers from desirable choices: Duquesne University, Temple University, University of Miami and University of Boston. She set up her interviews immediately.

The semester was busy and stressful. Besides interviewing and her courses, she was dealing with the emotional vexation of transitioning into a new stage of life. She was an adult now. Her decisions would influence the path of her future.

Meanwhile, Justin and she saw each other every weekend, even if he only came for one night or she went home to North Bergen for one night. Having his support meant everything.

Then upheaval occurred when Petal left a message on Olivia's cell phone. Hysterical crying, her breath catching between words, she blurted, "Liv. Where. Are. You. Call me. It's urgent."

Urgent. Olivia rushed back from the library to her dorm room to call her, wondering with every step what could have happened.

As soon as she opened the door, Smith asked, "What's wrong?"

"I'm not sure. Petal called crying."

"It's probably nothing. You know how she loves drama." She said, cavalierly.

Petal did love a bit of drama, but it annoyed Olivia to hear Smith say that about her. The tension between Petal and her had grown over the last year or so, but Petal was still her best friend. "I dunno. Sounds important."

Olivia kicked her boots off and hit the call-return button. "Liv." Petal picked up.

"What happened?"

"Becka." She heaved. "She…"

"What?" *Something bad had happened to Becka.* Suddenly, worst-case scenarios flooded Olivia's thoughts.

Petal blew her nose, then sniffled. "She's fucking C.J. Has been for over a month."

Olivia sighed, relieved that Becka didn't end up in a worst-case scenario. Now Olivia had to turn on her concerned voice for Petal despite that Smith was spot-on. Petal was overdramatizing. She and C.J. had been over for a year, now it was only an occasional hook-up. Still, girl code stated that Becka should have steered clear of C.J. Olivia braced herself, then stepped into the drama. "No way. That's crazy. Who told you that?"

More heaving, tears and sniffling, then, "She did."

"Wait. What? Calm down and tell me exactly what happened."

"I don't fucking know what happened," she hollered. "All I know is that Becka, my roommate and my second-best friend, was — IS — fucking the guy I have been fucking and trying to pin down for the last two years. She's been doing him behind my back. And they are in love. Supposedly. Per her, C.J. told her last night that he loved her. C.J. had been making her keep it a secret. And you know Becka. She does whatever she's told. Fucking follower. So, she kept it on the down-low. Then he– " a series of tears and sniffles. "He told her he loves her and supposedly wants to be her boyfriend. And everyone knows. Becka wanted to tell me before everyone found out and I heard it from someone else. But when I called Raquel and Deidra, they already knew. C.J. supposedly told Ashlee Lynn after she called him up to hang out two nights ago. Ashlee told them."

Olivia shook her head. "Wow. I'm sorry. I thought it was over between you two. Not that it makes what happened right. I'm just trying to understand."

"You know how things were between me and him. It was over for like a week after I found out about Ashlee. Then, he kept calling and calling. I gave in after about the tenth phone call and we started hanging out again. I'm a totally idiot."

"You're not an idiot. He's the problem, not you. He's not a nice guy. I know it's hard to see now, but this is a good thing. And he'll do the same thing to Becka — eventually."

"No. You're wrong. He didn't love me. No matter what I did, how well I treated him or how much attention I paid him, he didn't love me. He loves her. And WHY? She's not special. And now I have to move, too. I can't stay here with that two-faced whore."

"Come down here. You can stay with me and Smith for a few days."

Smith waved wildly and shook her head. *No,* she mouthed.

Olivia held her hand up, *OK.*

"No, I can't. I have school and work. I can't miss any classes. I'm already just barely scraping by." Petal said.

She can't. Olivia mouthed to Smith.

Smith placed her hand on her chest. *Good.*

"Will you go to your mom's?" Olivia asked Petal.

"I ain't got no other choice. Where else can I go? Not that I want to stay with her. She's dating that new guy, Harold. The guy drinks and smells. But she said I could stay in my old room, with the treadmill she's got in there now, until I figure something else out. Come home." She said in a whiny voice. "Pleeeeze."

Olivia brushed her hair off her face.

Smith mouthed, *are you alright?*

Olivia nodded, *yes*. "P, I wish I could, but I have classes and then this weekend my final interview. I'll be in Pittsburgh."

"I know you're busy." Her small voice brought out pangs of guilt in Olivia.

"Let me see what I can do. Where are you now?"

"Still at the apartment. The whore's place, packing my shit. She's at C.J.'s."

"Give me a few minutes. I'll call you back."

Olivia hung up the phone and released a long sigh. "What's going on?" Smith raised her eyebrows.

"The guy Petal was hooking up with is now with Becka. You know my other good friend. The–"

"The one Petal lives with."

"Yep."

"That's fucked up." Smith shook her head. "Becka's obviously not a real friend."

"Yeah, I guess. But the guy, C.J., he's a total bastard. It's his fault too."

"Is it? Girls got to stick together. If he's a bastard, then he was just doing what bastards do. Your friend Becka acted duplicitously. That's worse."

"Maybe. Petal's a wreck. And I feel bad. I can't be with her. I'm gonna call Justin and ask him if she could stay with him for a few days."

"Yeah?"

"Yeah." She said, tentatively. "I don't want her to be alone."

"She has other friends."

"But the gang is all intertwined. The girls are all friends with Becka too. Maybe she needs to be with someone not close with Becka for a few days. Someone she can really talk to with no worry that it will get back to Becka. I worry about Petal. She can be impetuous."

"And you trust her alone with Justin in his apartment."

"I'd trust them both with my life."

Smith gave an uncertain smile.

When Olivia told Justin the whole story, he said, "I'm not surprised. I sort of suspected they were hooking up."

"What? How? Why didn't you say anything?"

"I didn't know for sure. And it was none of my business. You know I hate gossip."

"What made you suspect?"

"One night when we all hanging out, I saw Becka coming out of C.J.'s room while on my way back from the bathroom. Then, a few minutes later, I saw C.J. walk out. What else would they be doing? I didn't know it was a regular thing. No one said a word to me. Probably because they knew I'd tell you and you would tell Petal."

"Can Petal stay with you for a few days?"

"Why?"

"She has to leave her place. She can't stay with Becka."

"What about her mom's?"

"She'll probably go there for a while, but she sounds really devastated. She asked me to come home, but I have my interview this weekend. I feel bad. I haven't been there for her this last year. Not the way a best friend should be. Please. Just for a few days. For me, Sweets."

"You know I hate getting caught up in the gang's drama train. And then more gossip will come down the pike when people find out she's staying here."

"But there's no gossip. Just you helping out your fiancée's friend. That's all."

"C.J. and the guys will be asking me what she said and shit."

"And you'll tell them she said nothing. Screw him, anyway."

Justin took a heavy breath. "Alright, Liv. But only because I love you so much."

"Thanks, Sweets. Can I tell her she can come now?"

"The place is a mess, but yeah. Only for a few days."

"Only for a few days."

"Love you."

"Me too. So much. I'll call you before bed."

Olivia called Petal and told her that she could stay with Justin for a few days.

"My God, you and Justin are lifesavers. I really don't know what I'd do without you."

"It's only for a few days, so you're not alone and have someone to talk to. But then you're gonna have to go to your mom's. I'll come home the following weekend, and we'll look for a new apartment for you."

"You know I can't stay with my mom for long. We only get along now 'cause I don't have to deal with her on a regular basis."

"We'll find you a place."

"Why didn't C.J. love me? I just want to know WHY?"

"It's nothing wrong with you. C.J. didn't choose to be with Becka; it just happened. When it comes to love we don't always have control over our choices."

"You chose to be with Justin and he chose you."

"No, it just happened. Love is inexplicable."

"Well, whatever it is, Ms. Philosophical, you are very lucky. My life sucks."

"It'll get better. I promise."

"Liv?"

"Yeah?"

"I can't stay with my mom for too long, but I've never lived alone either. What if I can't do it?"

"Don't be silly. Of course, you can do it. You're stronger than you think. And I'll help you as much as I can. It's going to be OK."

"I hope so."

11

The thunderstorm finally ended. Adam wiped down an outside chair and put a sheet over the cushion. The moisture from the rain left the air sultry. Adam took his shirt off and pulled her close. Kissing him on the balcony overlooking the lush flowers and emerald pastures and thriving trees in the park felt romantic and sexy and stirring. Adam slipped the strap of her sundress down her arm and kissed the top of her chest. Electricity coursed through her. The newness of him exploring her body aroused her, but Adam's touch also had a familiarity to it.

She breathed heavily into his ear. "Let's go inside. I want you to take my dress off."

"Out here. No one can see."

She looked around quickly, but almost didn't care if anyone could see or not. Her body felt hot. She wanted Adam to undress her. Now.

She motioned for him to take her dress off. He gently guided her onto the cushioned chair, while removing it. Moisture from the rain still lingered; her bare back felt wet as soon as she lay down. He drizzled champagne along her naked torso, then licked it off slowly, his tongue circling around her stomach and just above her panty line. She shook.

"That feel good?"

"Yes."

He pulled her panties off, bent down between her legs and kissed her inside. Watching the subtle stir of his head between her legs aroused her. Heat coursed through her. She felt herself letting go, giving into the pleasure in a way that she hadn't in a long, long time. Soon, Adam slipped out of his pants and mounted her, running his hands down her torso and through her hair, slowly driving in and out, gradually increasing the speed of his thrusts until she released. He quickly followed.

Laying naked outside on his balcony, a quiet nook in the busy city, they wrapped their bodies around each other. No words for a few minutes; the cars swooshing along the wet ground, the only sound.

It was peaceful and comfortable — she could get used to this — and… her eyes flipped wide open. A sudden restlessness.

She needed to go.

She wiggled out from his embrace and stood up, quickly slipping her dress on.

He looked perplexed. "You alright?"

"Yeah." She said, distractedly. "Where are my panties?" She scanned the balcony with her eyes, then began a frenetic search, under the chair they had been on, under the other chairs She moved the table legs, looked underneath. "Where could they be?"

Adam, clad in boxers, his dark hair tousled, a perplexed look, pulled her panties from right on top of the chair they had been on. "Here. They were right in front of you. Sometimes when things are obvious, we don't see them."

She took a sharp breath. "Thanks." She slipped them on.

He braced her shoulders, gently. "Please don't lie to me? Are you married?"

The way he touched her, calmed her down enough to reflect on what she was doing. She looked straight into his eyes, said nothing.

"What is it? You look like you're going to cry. What aren't you telling me?"

"I'm not married."

"Then what is it? Talk to me. No filter is what you had said. Right?"

His eyes had a look of vulnerability — of complete exposure. The intensity was too much.

"I'm sorry."

"Liv."

"I'm sorry." She grabbed her things and hurried down the spiral staircase toward the front door; Adam came up behind her. When they got to the front door, he looked at her through heavy eyes, said in an even tone, "When you're ready to tell me. Give me a call."

He looked annoyed, maybe.

She didn't care, or maybe she cared too much. Either way, she had to go and fast.

"I'll call you and I'm sorry." She turned and left.

By the time Olivia made it from the Westside to the Eastside, she berated herself. What the hell was she doing? She liked him, and he seemed to genuinely like her. Not since Justin had she felt so drawn to a man, and it was different with Justin. They had already known each other and because of that, the trust was there before they even got started. Besides, they were young, blinded by the innocence of youth. This was different.

Fear. One word, four letters and she knew, deep down, that that's what this craziness was about. She was afraid to feel comfortable or vulnerable, to give of herself completely. And she could see in Adam's eyes that that's what he wanted. Her. Completely.

Fear. A four-letter word starting with F that needed to be eliminated from dictionaries and thesauruses throughout the world. Like *closure*, fear was another superfluous word that had no business on the planet. Or at least in her vocabulary. She debated lying. She could say she had lost her keys, then she'd have a reason to go back to Adam's. *I'm sorry. I had to come back. I can't get into my apartment until tomorrow morning when the landlord comes.*

She cringed at her own lack of courage. Jettisoning that thought, she took her phone out of her bag and called him.

Brriiiing. God, if he didn't pick up, she'd really feel like an ass.

"Hey." He said, warmly.

"Hey."

"You ready to tell me what's wrong?"

"I freaked out," she gushed. "I'm sorry. It won't happen again. Can I come back over?"

"I told the doorman to let you in when you came back, and my front door is unlocked for you."

Her face burned up. "H – How did you know?"

"I had a feeling. I'm glad I was right."

"I'm embarrassed."

"Don't be. I take it as a compliment. People only freak out when they have something to lose."

His accuracy caused a flush across her face. She hailed a taxi and hurried back over, promising herself that she would give this a chance.

As if she had a choice.

12

Justin picked Olivia up at the airport on Sunday afternoon. She was halfway down the escalator to the baggage claim when they met eyes, smiling at each other. Olivia loved when Justin and she shared a smile, a private world of unspoken understanding, more powerful than any words, more intimate than any sexual experience. She hurried toward him. "I missed you so much," she said, squeezing him tight.

"Me too." He squeezed her back.

Coming home to Justin after the anxiety of the interview was reassuring. His arms felt like a blanket wrapped securely around her. She melted into the embrace.

Petal waited for them at her mother's. Staying with her mom turned out to be more stressful than Petal had ever imagined. She had told Olivia that Harry, Ms. Taylor's new boyfriend, was a drunk — and not a nice one. The first night Petal had stayed there after she left Justin's, Harry had had a conniption over nothing and threw things at Ms. Taylor. Petal screamed for him to stop. He had flung a glass at Petal, which shattered against the wall, spraying shards of glass that got embedded in the rug. They all had to wear shoes as they couldn't be sure they had gotten all the pieces up.

Petal had told Olivia that the next morning was even worse. As soon as Harry had woken up, he demanded coffee and breakfast. Ms. Taylor had doted on him, hovering over the oven like a desperate lunatic trying to create a perfectly shaped pancake. He had wanted tiny silver-dollar ones, not the regular size. When she had served him one that looked too big, he had hollered, "You could make the goddamn effort to cook me what I asked for. I am supporting you. And now, her too." He pointed a thick finger at Petal.

When Petal told Olivia the whole story, she had said, "My mother makes me sick. How can I respect her when she lets a man treat her that way?"

"She's probably afraid to be alone."

"That's a lame excuse. It's better to be alone than be with a man like that. My father was a loser. He left, right? And then she chooses one loser after another. You'd think she'd learned her lesson. I need to get the fuck out of here. I've only been here two days and one night, and already I have a permanent stomach ache."

"I'm gonna come straight to North Bergen after I land from Pittsburgh. Justin's gonna pick me up and

I'll come home for a few days and help you find a new place."

"What about classes?"

"I can miss a few. This is important."

"Justin was good to me, Liv. He let me stay for three days like we had agreed on and he listened to me bitch and complain. He listened to all my pathetic woes. I felt like he really understood why it's been so hard for me to get my shit together. And he talked to me about why it's important to be more independent. He really is different than the other guys. I hope one day I find someone as nice as him."

"You will. First, focus on school and work. That will help you be more independent. When you don't need a guy, you will be more selective."

"Justin said the same thing. Did you two talk about this behind my back?"

"No. It's just the truth. And we both want you to be OK."

"I'm going to try."

"So, it went well?" Justin drove north on the turnpike.

"I think so. It'll be a challenging program, but I think I could be happy there. There's a good music scene in Pittsburgh. I think you'll like it. We should go visit."

"Shouldn't we wait and see where you get in first?"

"I'll know soon. Not soon enough, though. I'm anxious. What if I don't get accepted anywhere?"

"Impossible."

"Not impossible."

"Look at me." He briefly looked away from the road and straight at Olivia. "You will be accepted somewhere. You will probably have your pick. Stop doubting yourself."

"It's the not knowing, the anticipation, that's hard."

"It is hard. But not knowing can be exciting too, as long as you have faith that it will all work out."

"I hate not having control over outcomes."

"When we don't have control, we have to have some faith that things will work themselves out. And this will." He squeezed her thigh.

"I don't know what I'd do without you." She kissed his cheek.

Pulling up to Petal's mother's house depressed Olivia. It was a small house off Bergenline Avenue on 80th Street. A nice block near Hudson County Park, but the house was run down. The paint was chipped everywhere. The roof looked cockeyed, almost like one side was going to pull the other side right off if the wind hit it too strong one day. There had been a wire fence around the whole house from when they had had a dog, but it was bent and mangled, and there were pieces missing. Olivia went to open the front gate, and it swung like a loose tooth. It hung on by two small latches.

Justin beeped the horn a few times as Olivia went up to the house to get Petal. Thankfully, Petal walked out before Olivia got up to the door. Dark crescents shadowed her under eyes and her face looked pallid. "How you holding up?" Olivia put her arm around Petal.

"Hanging in."

"There's a basement apartment in Justin's friend's building. It's off Boulevard East."

"I'll never be able to afford that. I'm living off student loans and a part-time waitressing job."

"Al, Justin's friend, knows the owner. He's gonna cut you a deal. Only $550 a month. You were paying more than that with Becka, right?"

"Yes. Oh my God. Thank you, you two." She took a heavy breath and plopped back into the car seat. Her voice caught as she said, "I– I don't know what I'd do without you guys."

Petal took the place, even though it smelled a little of mildew. The walls were recently painted, and the floors were wood, which Petal liked. The kitchen and living room were basically the same room, but there was a separate bedroom, a door separating the living room/kitchen from the bedroom.

Olivia spent the next two days helping Petal move in. The second day, Justin and Scully helped get Petal's bed out of Becka's place. Olivia went in with Justin and Scully. Becka stood, hand on hip, tapping an anxious foot on the tiled kitchen floor. "Are you not talking to me either? I didn't mean it."

"Didn't mean what? To be messing with one of your closest friend's boyfriends."

"He wasn't her boyfriend. And I didn't mean for it to happen. It just did."

"She loved him. Whether it was a committed relationship or not, she loved him. You took her feelings for granted and did what was good for you."

"I didn't mean to. I loved him too. What was I supposed to do? I loved him, and he loved me. I never wanted to hurt her." Becka lit a cigarette and took a long drag.

Olivia considered what Becka said. How could someone fall in love with a close friend's love? Wasn't that like falling in love with a cousin or something? On the other hand, like she had said to Petal: Sometimes there is no choice when it comes to love, it just is and there isn't a darn thing that can be done about it. Maybe Becka and C.J. couldn't help it. Either they came out with the truth or remained captive in a clandestine relationship forever.

"Give it some time, Becka." She gave her a tight-lipped smile, turned and left.

Rutgers acceptance letter came a few days later. This was one of the most important moments of her life: the day she was invited to develop her scholarship at the program that was her first choice. "Rutgers graduate student" sounded sophisticated rolling off her tongue, as she said it softly to herself.

Justin and she would be living together within the year, and together they would go hand-in-hand into their adult lives. She read the letter three times, before running back to the dorms from the student center.

She had planned to call her parents and Justin as soon as she got back to the dorm. But by the time she got in, she decided to drive home and tell them all in person. It was Friday. Justin was supposed to come up the following day, anyway. Filled with excitement, she quickly packed an overnight bag while bellowing out the beat to "Pomp and Circumstance."

13

The doorman greeted Olivia with a knowing glance as she walked back into Adam's building. Mortification burned through her skin. Adam must have mentioned something about her freak-out to him. Worse yet, she tripped over, what? The edge of the area rug on her way toward the elevator. She wobbled, then steadied herself, her platforms making a bang against the tiled floor. She craned her neck. The doorman gave a bright smile, "You alright, Miss?"

"Yes," she hurried around the corner to the elevator.

Adam opened the door, shirtless, right as she was about to knock. Her breath caught. Dashing, charming, intense, whatever it was — did it even matter — she was drawn to the man. With a teasing glint in his eyes, he said, "I'm glad you came back."

She smiled through tight lips, hoping he wouldn't want to discuss her display of craziness, her freak-out, and they could simply go on as if it never happened.

"We don't have to talk about it if you don't want to." He said, as if he read her mind.

"Thanks. I don't want to." She said, without making eye contact.

He held her hand, "You can always talk to me. Even if it's something that could be hurtful. I'd rather know the truth about how you feel, then be sheltered by silence. OK? I will never fault you for your feelings."

"'Kay." Boy, did she know what he meant. Being sheltered by silence or a lie was something she knew too well. She would do her best to be open with Adam.

Still, there were things about him that were mysterious. Since openness was on the top of his early relationship priority list, she decided to dive right in.

But first, a drink. "A glass of wine?"

"Coming right up."

He poured two glasses of Merlot. They walked up the spiral staircase into his writing room. Both of them plopped down into the cushy black leathers chairs, which faced each other.

Olivia leaned forward. "Since we are talking about being truthful, I have to know: Why don't you have any pictures anywhere? Not one."

"I'm not hiding anything if that's what you're thinking." He gave an easy smile, but his eyes looked pensive, maybe sad.

"I don't know what to think. There's nothing in your apartment, besides the books and Tucker, that tell me anything about who you are. That's a little... interesting."

He rubbed the scruff around his face, parted his lips as if to say something, then stopped.

Olivia rested her hand on his knee. "What is it?"

"I have had some hardship. It's something I don't normally tell people."

"You don't have to – "

"I want to."

"OK."

"Both of my parents died in a car accident when I was twenty-three. I was traveling in Asia at the time. My brother finally reached me by phone. I was alone with strangers in a foreign country when Daniel called and told me what had happened."

She squeezed his hand. "Oh my God, that's awful. I'm so sorry."

"Thank you. A few months after the funeral, Daniel and I had a huge falling out. It was inspired by his wife, Verona. She wanted the house in the Hamptons, which was left to both of us. She wanted me to sell my share. When I refused, she started a war between us. Dan was never a strong person. He kept pushing me and arguing with me to sell. Instead of working together to make sure our parents' wishes were carried out, he stood by Verona and what she wanted. In the end, I gave up the house. I couldn't take the fighting. I was exhausted and grieving. She wanted their boat; I gave them that too. After that,

I became reckless and then reclusive; I couldn't let anyone close. I had all this love trapped inside with nowhere to go. It was when I met Zara, fourteen years later, at a fund-raiser, that I finally opened my heart again. She breathed life back into me. Then. Well. You know the rest of the story."

She reached over and squeezed him. Her heart broke for him.

"I don't like pictures, especially not on display. It probably seems strange to you, but the snapshots of pleasant and happy moments in life seem like lies. A few memories dispersed upon a backdrop of loss and suffering. Of pain."

"But pictures are real moments; moments of pleasure, however fleeting, are still real. And they should be treasured."

"I can't look at them. I can't look at the pictures of my parents, young, happy, vibrant. Or Zara, healthy and happy. It's too painful. And this," he motioned his arm around the room, "everything I have is from my parents' money. My father made millions as a banker and my mother came from old money. I have more money than I know what to do with. I didn't even want it; it made me feel like I won something for losing them. But an aunt, my father's sister, convinced me that it would make my life easier and that my parents left it to me to make sure I would live on and be happy. So, I have these *things* and I miss them like crazy.

"I understand. I — I don't even know what to say. Your life has been hard and unfair."

"I'm not a miserable bastard, so you know."

"I didn't think you were."

"I haven't dated too much since Zara. There were a few women, but none that I felt I wanted to share the truth with. I hold my feelings close."

She kissed his hand; the more he said, the more she felt pulled toward him. "I'm glad you told me."

"It's hard for people to accept tragedy sometimes."

"It is. But it takes courage to live and the harder your life, the more courage it takes. You're a survivor. That's attractive and admirable."

"See, I knew there was something I liked about you." His eyes twinkled. "Anything else you'd like to know, Dr. Watson?"

"You know I don't do any clinical work. I teach and do research, write. I'm not a 'sit behind the couch and listen' kinda shrink."

"I just like teasing you. You're easy to tease and I like when your cheeks turn red."

"Oh, is that so." She kissed his lips.

He pulled her close, hugging her and kissing her. Within minutes, he slipped her sundress down her body. She pressed against him. His arms felt strong around her, but the pain he had shared made him feel soft and vulnerable. She caressed him, feeling his sadness, kissing away his brokenness while trying to heal her own. He guided her toward the bedroom. A few minutes later, they were naked, rolling around, fierce desire swelling between them, a desperate attempt to heal the wounds of loss through the connection with each other. He mounted her. She shivered and shivered, allowing him to take her — completely.

This time while cuddling afterward, Olivia nestled into his body and relaxed, before drifting off into a sound sleep.

She did really like him.

A lot.

The sun shone through the slits in the blinds, making a maze on the floor. Where was she? She spread her arm onto the opposite side of the bed. *Adam's*, she smiled as she remembered. Where was he?

The subtle smell of syrup arouse from downstairs, a clanking noise, a cabinet closing. Adam must have been making breakfast. She took a T-shirt from the back of a chair, threw it on. The scent of his aftershave lingered on the shirt. She held the banister as she stepped quietly down the spiral staircase into the kitchen.

"Hey." She hugged him from behind. "Smells great."

"Morning." He turned and kissed her. "I hope you're hungry and like French toast."

"I am, and I do."

Over breakfast, Adam asked her some questions about her life, her family, her important experiences. Her life had been easy, extremely easy, compared to his. She was almost embarrassed to share her experiences. With the exception of her mother's cancer, which thankfully was in remission, and her father's brief affair, which her parents seemed to completely resolve, everything else was the usual disappointments and frustrations that happen in life. Sad, when Abbee got divorced — she had really loved her brother-in-law — disappointed, when she didn't get the teaching job at Columbia, and then the serial disappointments that come from dating and not finding the right guy.

One thing she purposely didn't share was her fear that she might never be a mother. She didn't want to scare him away by making him think she was on the hunt for an immediate husband and father for her children. She wasn't. If she never found a man to share her life with, she would accept it, maybe, hopefully, adopt.

Then there was Justin. There was always Justin — the tragedy of her life. Compared to Adam's story, even that seemed, or was, insignificant.

But when he asked, "so you've never been married, ever been engaged or lived with someone?" she felt she needed to be honest. He had been so open; it seemed unfair to cover herself.

"There was a guy. But it was a long time ago."

"*The* guy?"

"At the time he was '*the* guy,' but since it didn't work out, I suppose he wasn't."

"The guy who broke your heart." He said it as a statement. How on earth did he know?

Her face flushed. "He did. How did you know that?"

"I could tell by the way your eyes looked pained when you said it, then your voice trailed off before you finished your sentence. I know heartbreak when I see it. Plus, if he was *the* guy, it's likely that it ended in heartbreak. I was just playing the odds." They chuckled. "So… what happened? Do you want to tell me?"

"I'm that transparent?" She looked disgusted with herself. "Anyway, should we really be discussing our relationship histories? It's not so sexy."

"Backstory. It helps me understand you. Same as you wanted to know why I didn't have pictures up. Without the backstory, it didn't make sense or it seemed unusual, and now with my backstory– "

"It makes sense. It gives me context. I was engaged to the guy. He was my high school boyfriend, my first love. We dated all through college and became engaged our senior year." She went to tell him the truth, but stopped herself. Even though it wasn't her fault, the fact that Justin betrayed her and the way he did it, still hurt. She hated thinking about it, never mind telling the story. It was the dark cloud that hung over her otherwise spirited nature. She would tell Adam the truth, just not so soon. "We were so young and so stupidly in love, the way you can be when you don't really know much about life. What made sense in high school and college, didn't make sense going into adulthood. And I was leaving for graduate school. He broke it off. I was devastated. But like I said, it was a long time ago. I'm not even the same person now that I was then."

Adam reached for her hands across the kitchen table. "You look sad when you talk about him."

"I get nostalgic, not sad. Mistakes we make in the past sometimes keep us connected. Heartache sometimes keeps us connected."

"I know what you mean. Pain can keep you connected. In the case of my parents and Zara, this is a good thing, because it keeps me connected to them for the rest of my life. But with someone who broke your heart, it's different. You want the past to be forgotten and yet, it's always there, because somehow it has defined a part of your life. A part of who you are."

"Exactly." God, he was insightful and articulate. The way he described her feelings unnerved her. But she did not want to spend the afternoon enveloped in nostalgia. "Now let's drop discussions about our past and focus on our present. It's Saturday and sunny. Let's go do something."

"I'd like that."

"I'll run home and take a quick shower and change. Then we can meet up."

"Or you could shower here. And then we can both go to your place and you can change."

She nodded. "Sure."

Adam put the water on in the shower, set two towels onto the hook. He went to clean up from breakfast. Olivia lathered up the loofah; the soap smelled like Adam and she smiled thinking of how attractive he was in both mind and body.

The water cascaded over her body; she made it hotter, relaxing as it pounded along her shoulders. She put more soap on the loofah, taking in the crisp aroma, enjoying the steam that accumulated in the shower.

Adam knocked on the opened door. "You want company?"

She stuck her head out from behind the curtain and nodded, *yes*.

Their eyes met, and she swallowed. The intensity in his eyes, the way he took her in, again, for a moment, reminded her of the way Justin used to look at her — with complete abandon.

She watched him take his shorts and T-shirt off, desire wedged in her throat. A thin layer of steam accumulated in the bathroom. As he stepped into the shower, his eyes wandered along her body, penetrating her with the intensity of the passion she saw in them.

It would be late afternoon before they left his apartment.

14

Exit 14. Exit 15. The split in the Turnpike. A merge toward 16E.

She was close to home. Pearl Jam blasted out of the car stereo. Her mind raced, as she went over how she would present the good news to Justin. He would be thrilled. And imagining the look on his face, the way his eyes would light up when they shared a smile, had her accelerating a little past the speed limit. Telling him would be something the two of them would remember for the rest of their lives.

Her parents would be thrilled, too. Both of her parents had gone to Rutgers for their undergraduate degrees, her father for business administration, her mother for sociology. Although they had encouraged her to spread her wings and pick whatever program she wanted, deep down she knew they were hoping she wouldn't veer too far from home.

Justin had worked it out with Scully and the other guys. They had all agreed that Justin could stay with Furious Whiskers if Olivia got into Rutgers. It was close enough for him to make it back to North Bergen for the practices. Besides, Scully had told Justin, "The band would not be the same without you, dude. You've got the voice. You're the writer."

Justin applying for his master's in education would be great. Deep down she believed Justin's real calling was playing and songwriting, not teaching. But it was always good to have an alternative plan.

God, she could not wait to be living with him.

Twenty-one, and her life was about to start.

Her black Toyota zoomed down the hill at 79th Street. No parking in front of Justin's, which wasn't unusual. He lived in an apartment building along Hudson County Park, 79th Street between Broadway and Boulevard East, a congested area. She drove around the block, her anticipation growing by the minute. Finally, she found a parking spot around the corner.

Hurrying out of the car, she nearly went flying over a crevice in the sidewalk. *Whoa*, she steadied herself, then walked quickly while looking in her handbag for Justin's key. Normally, she would give a call first, but she wanted to surprise him. She had the envelope with the acceptance letter in her hand. She'd open the door and hand him the envelope before words were exchanged. They would share a smile. Justin would squeeze her, a Champagne toast, then they would go tell her parents, together.

"Yippee," she squealed, as she slipped the key into the front door of his building and ran up the staircase to the second floor. Outside of his apartment, the sharp smell of cigarette smoke pierced her nostrils. Justin didn't smoke. Maybe it was from the apartment next door. As she opened the door, the odor grew more pungent and there almost seemed to be a thin fog of smoke lingering in the air.

"Justin?"

She put the key and her bag down on the small table in the hallway. Justin's keys lay there, so he was home. She held the acceptance letter in her hand.

"Justin?"

The silence felt solid and disquieting.

Maybe he was napping. Strange, at a little past 7:00.

"Jus, sweets, you sleeping?"

Past the kitchen, through the small living room, to the bedroom. The door was closed. Mad rustling and hushed voices sounded from behind the door. What? Her heart plummeted into her stomach; an ominous feeling washed over her.

In a loud, harrowed voice, Justin hollered. "Liv. Wait. One minute."

"Justin?" The door creaked as she opened it.

"Liv. NO."

Whaaat? Her eyes must be mistaken. She scanned the room, confused, horrified.

The visual information wasn't real.

Petal naked on top of Justin, her legs spread across his.

Petal naked on Justin. It didn't make any sense.

Whaaat? A determined lump wedged in her throat; she couldn't speak. Tears pierced her eyes with a burn so intense it felt like they were being licked with flames. She felt disembodied. This wasn't her. This wasn't happening. This wasn't true. Her jaw hung open.

Justin, naked, eyes wide, a look of devastated panic, pushed Petal off him. In a hurried craze he threw his shorts on.

"Liv." He said, his voice cracking. He stumbled toward her, his balance wavering.

She needed to move, but felt paralyzed. Her eyes glued to the scene. Still, unbelievable.

Justin and Petal? Tears gushed down her face.

Petal covered herself with the sheet. Her long blonde waves cascaded over her shoulders. Her cleavage obvious, as the sheet hung right at the top of her bare breasts. She said nothing.

Nothing.

Olivia glared at her, then at Justin.

Justin pulled Olivia. "Liv. Please." She smelled alcohol on him, something strong, maybe tequila.

Nausea overwhelmed her, her stomach, queasy. "Oh, my God!" She screamed, then put her hand over her mouth.

He pulled her arm. "Please. Liv."

"Get. Off. Of. Me."

"Let me explain."

"I said, get your fucking hands off me. You lying, cheating bastard."

Horror, pure horror, splayed across Justin's face. Tears streamed down his cheeks.

Olivia and Justin both gushed with tears, a heavy wordless gaze between them.

Petal still lying under the sheets of Justin's bed, like she belonged there, said nothing.

Nothing.

"You're a fucking bastard. And you. YOU," she looked right at Petal with pure disgust, "are a fucking whore, just like your mother. And I never want to see either of you ever again. EVER. Have a nice life."

Justin went to pull her close. She glared at him one more time, her mouth tight, her eyes livid. "Get your hands off me. I never want to see you again. You broke my heart. Both of you."

She ran out, dropping the letter of acceptance. It waved slowly in the air before landing on the floor of his hallway.

It was all over. Nothing would ever be right again. In one minute, everything had changed.

Justin with shorts, no shirt, no shoes, chased her out of the bedroom.

She grabbed her bag, flung the key she had to his apartment at him. Right at the front of his door, he wrapped his arms all the way around her, pulling her tight. "I love you. Please. Let me explain. Just give me five minutes."

Her arms swung viciously as she struggled with him to release her. "Explain?" She finally got him off her. "You've got to be fucking kidding me! There is nothing to explain. Your actions told me everything I need to know." Tears blurred her sight. Her nose ran over her lips and down her chin.

"Liv." He bawled.

"Here." She flung the engagement ring at him. It ricocheted off his chest, landing on the hallway floor in a loud *clang*.

She ran down the stairs and out of the building, gasping for breath with every step.

As she stepped outside the cold air bit her, freezing the tears on her face. She hurried to her car, calling Smith as she walked. Her mind spun. She still didn't understand what happened or how it happened. How could Justin be involved with Petal and she never have suspected it? How could he do that to her? How could Petal? Nothing was what Olivia thought it was. Her life as she knew it was over.

Smith answered as Olivia slid into her car.

"Hey girl. How did Justin take the good news?"

Olivia cried, heaving as she tried to get the words out. "Justin, he– "

"What? I can't understand you? What happened?"

"Justin and Petal are sleeping together." It felt surreal coming out of her mouth, like it wasn't true, like it wasn't real.

"WHAT? NO."

"I caught them in the act. Oh, my God, I saw them. Both naked. Petal on top, in a fucking straddle. My best friend from childhood, naked and straddling my fiancé." She cried, but her voice grew stronger, angry.

"What did he say?"

"He didn't have to say anything. I saw them together. There's nothing for him to say."

"You didn't ask what happened? You don't want to know?"

"I do know. He's sleeping with someone else. My best friend. I hate them both. I don't know what to do with myself right now. I feel confused. Where should I go? To my parents?"

"Can you drive?"

"I'm shaking." She looked at her hands quivering along her legs. She sniffled, took a heavy breath, "I can drive. I have to leave North Bergen. I can't be here right now."

"Promise me you'll pull over and call me if you feel too upset to drive. I'll have Jones come get you wherever you are."

"I'll be OK. But, yeah. I promise."

"And Liv, I'll be here waiting for you. Play music, sing, think about something else until you get here."

"'Kay."

"You need some sort of explanation. Some sort of closure. You have to hear him out. Once. You were engaged to him." Smith said over a jar of peanut butter.

Olivia had arrived at their door safely. Tears hung in the crests of her eyes the whole ride, but a fury had developed on that ride back to Rutgers, which seemed to dry most of the tears, at least temporarily.

Justin had called fourteen times, leaving messages on five of the calls. "Please. Call me. Let me explain. It was a mistake. I love you," were four of the messages. On the fifth one, he sang the song he had sung to her the first night they kissed, the night he told her through his lyrics that he wanted to be with her, but was too shy to tell her. Normally, that song melted her heart. This time it left her with a sour taste in her mouth and sent a fierce rage coursing through her.

Closure was a word used when someone couldn't let go: an excuse for the hopelessly forlorn.

"There's nothing he could say to fix this. And he doesn't deserve my ear."

"Really?" Smith raised an eyebrow. "You loved him. I'm not saying to forgive him. What he did was terrible, inexcusable. But for the love of God at least find out how it happened. You're never gonna let go if you don't know. Hear him out, at least. Not for him, for you."

Olivia nodded. "Maybe."

The phone rang again. Justin again.

Smith gave her a steely look. "You gonna take it?"

"I'm not ready."

This time his message said, "I just found the Rutgers acceptance letter on the floor. Congratulations, Sweets. You came home to tell me. I know you did. Please. This is our plan together. Call me."

After Olivia let Smith hear his message, Smith said, "Call him when you're ready. What an ass he is making a mistake like that."

"We don't know that it was a mistake."

"Sounds like a mistake, Liv."

"Not all mistakes are undoable."

"Agreed." Smith said, then continued with, "let's do something to take your mind off of him for a little while. How 'bout a run? I'll go slow."

"No running tonight. Justin likes to run. How about a walk?"

Smith wrapped her arm around Olivia. "A walk it is."

Justin showed up at the dorm the following afternoon. The winter sun was bright that day. Olivia would never forget that. The sun juxtaposed with the darkness of her mood felt starkly incongruent as Smith and she ambled to the Saturday brunch. Olivia wore sunglasses to hide her swollen eyes.

An hour back at the dorm and the knock came.

Olivia was curled up on her bed, Smith answered. "It's Justin."

"Tell him to go away."

"Liv." She heard him cry from the other side of the door.

Smith gave her that steely look again.

"Alright. Let him in." Olivia sighed.

"I'm gonna go to the library. I'll call when I'm on my way back."

Olivia gave her a pursed-lipped smile, nodded.

Justin walked in, looking disheveled. Shirt out on one side, tucked in on the other. His eyes were bright red, dark heavy circles underneath. "Liv."

Staring at him, those brooding dark eyes with that intense expression he always had when he looked at her, made her breath catch. How could she still love him? She was so angry. But looking at him, she felt her heart beating rapidly; as angry as she was, she loved him with everything she had.

And she desperately wanted him to say something that made it OK for her to forgive him.

"I love you. Please," he pleaded. Kneeling beside her bed, he took her hands in his.

I love you, three words, eight letters, so simple and yet, indubitably the most universally complex string of words in verbal communication. Those three words wouldn't be enough.

"There's no excuse for what you did, Justin. None. Telling me that you love me isn't ever going to erase what you did!"

"Please. Liv. Please. Just give me five minutes, that's all I ask."

"Fine." She sat up on the bed.

He tried to pull her into an embrace.

God, she wanted to melt into his arms, but at the same time she felt sick when he touched her. She pulled away. "Go ahead. Explain why the hell you slept with my best friend!" Tears dripped out of her eyes.

Olivia's heart bled with every word he spoke; with every glare in his eyes, her heart bled. She loved him to absolute pieces. "I – I don't know, Liv. There is no excuse. It was a mistake. I don't love her. *I love you.*"

She listened, but the words felt empty. *It was a mistake* didn't explain how he got to the point that Petal and he were naked, and he was inside of her. The visual image made her sick. The thought made her sick. Justin had been naked with Petal, had been inside of Petal. Justin and Olivia had shared intense intimacy; Olivia had been the only one who knew Justin in that special way, in that private way. Now he also shared that experience with Petal, destroying, in one action, their exclusive bond. Tears continued to stream down her cheeks. How could he do that? How could he kiss someone else, touch someone else, his long fingers feeling someone else's skin, his breath breezing through her hair, laying with her, bodies exposed and merged together, how could he? And he allowed her to touch him, to feel him. Petal felt him — close. She felt Justin's arms around her. She felt his body underneath hers, the brush of his hair along her face. Looking at him, she wanted to die. How could he? She felt tired. Exhausted. Sick. She didn't think she could live with him knowing what he did. And yet, she didn't want to live without him. "What do you mean it was a mistake? How did it happen?"

Please, she thought, dying inside, *please say something that makes me forgive you.* Her heart broke in half while she watched him fumble for words. "I— I don't know. We were drinking, and she came onto me."

"And you didn't stop it?"

"I tried. She was persistent and I— I gave in. I don't even know why. I think I blacked out. I don't even find her attractive. I'm sorry. Liv. Please." His dark, intense eyes pleaded.

God damnit, say something that lets me forgive you. Say something that makes what you did make sense to me. Fuck, Justin. Please say something.

He said nothing. He stared into her eyes, tried again to pull her into an embrace.

Tears continued to pour out of her eyes. She stared back at him, pulling away from his grasp.

"Say something, Liv. Please say we can talk about this again."

"Was this going on for awhile? Did it start when she stayed with you?"

"No. NO. It only happened once. I swear to God."

"I can't believe you. I don't know what to believe. I want you to leave — now."

He bowed his head.

"Now." She pointed a finger at the door.

He nodded reticently, shoulders dropped.

She walked him to the door. Looking into his eyes, she wished with every ounce of her body that he would say *something, something* that made her able to forgive him.

"I love you, Liv. I always will. Forever and one day. And I am sorry. I will be sorry for the rest of my life." He stared at her, his pupils huge, his gaze heavy.

"Don't ever call me again. I mean it." Her lips dropped into a quivering frown.

"I'm calling you tomorrow. I hope you will take my call."

"I won't. If you really love me, which I don't believe you do, but if you really do, then don't ever call me again. Have a nice life with Petal." She said, furiously.

She slammed the door behind him, ran onto her bed and cried so hard she could barely breathe.

Justin tried again. He called the next day and the day after that and the day after that. Olivia didn't take the calls. She heard his voice and her whole body ached, still hoping he'd say something, whatever that something was, that would allow her to be open to trying again.

There was nothing.

Petal called a few times. Her voice whiny and creaky, like she held tears back in her throat: "Please, Liv.

Please. Talk to me. I'm sorry." Her voice made Olivia sick. Furious.

I'm sorry, two words, seven letters. No matter how many times she heard it, it meant nothing. Nothing.

The empty language of false contrition. Nothing could undo what had been done. No amount of Justin or Petal's litany of apologies could give her back what had been taken: her untainted love and trust for both of them.

Justin continued to call through the summer, up until she moved to Pittsburgh. A few times, hearing his voice, she nearly broke down and called him back. With her finger suspended right above the return call button, she would stare at the phone, thinking of him. Missing him. God, she had loved that boy with all her heart. She had given him all of her and he threw it away. She would close her phone. There was nothing he could say.

A few months after she was settled in Pittsburgh, Justin started sending emails, then letters. She deleted the emails without reading them. The letters, seeing his handwriting, knowing he had touched the envelope, caused a wave of messy emotions. She missed him too much, more than she wanted to, but she was so hurt, so angry. She couldn't read his words. There was nothing he could say to erase what had been done. She sent every single one of his letters back. After the first year, they didn't come often, only every four months or so. Sending them back became perfunctory over the years. After five years, he stopped writing.

When she let her mind wander down the Justin path, she wondered why he had stopped trying and what he was doing with his life. Sometimes she thought of him wistfully. Never in a million years could she have imagined not knowing Justin. To avoid dwelling in the nostalgia for too long, she kept moving forward, pushing for the future she wanted, to be scholarly, to be in academia. She did her best not look back on what had been lost.

The image of Petal on top of him entered her dreams. Even when she wasn't thinking about it, it would randomly pop into her head. She would never be able to erase that. She would never be able to forget what had happened. And she would never understand why on earth Justin slept with her.

In the end, it didn't matter.

It was over.

Weeks merged hazily together in the aftermath of the breakup. She pushed herself to classes, to the library, even out to the bars a few times with Smith and some other friends. Nothing felt exciting or meaningful. Smith provided a ceaseless supportive ear and plenty of peanut butter. Peanut butter was Smith's remedy for just about anything. Broken hearts, included.

When anyone from the gang called, saying things like *'please let us know you're OK,'* or *'Justin made a mistake, give him a chance, Liv,'* she'd listen to the message, then delete it immediately. She turned her back on all of them. Every single one of them connected back to Justin.

She couldn't deal. One day, maybe she would see them again. Or maybe not.

The acceptance letter from Duquesne came and she felt numb, then the one from Boston came, still numbness. All her hard work, yet she read those letters like they were a list for the grocery store. She called her mother and cried. "I'm not going to grad school. I'm going to take the year off."

Lily Watson, her mother, an even-tempered woman with the same auburn hair as Olivia, responded, "Liv. Honey. I know you're upset. My heart is broken for you, but are *you*, my strong, proud baby-girl going to let this man or boy define who you are becoming? Are you going to give him your future, too? Haven't you already given him enough?" Her mom's vehemence made Olivia snap out of the fog of misery she had been walking around in since the breakup.

Her mother was right; she wasn't a victim. In this case, she had choices.

Olivia blew her nose. "I know you're right. I'm just so angry and so disappointed. Everything I had planned — or that *we* had planned — is done."

"So, you start over on your terms. It's your life, not his."

"I can't go to Rutgers, mom. That was *our* plan. If I am going to do this on my own, my terms, then I need to follow a different path."

"So where will that be?"

"I'm going to go to Pittsburgh. To Duquesne."

"Good. You have no idea how happy I am to hear that. Your father will be thrilled. We both love you so much. Someday you will find a man who will love you for the rest of your life. I know you loved Justin. We all did. But you two are so young."

"Love isn't limited by age."

"Of course not. But we change as we age and what you want now will change with time and life experience. Someday you may look back and see that Justin wasn't right for you. That there were things wrong that you couldn't see."

"Well, I can't *see* what you're saying now. As I *see* it, he left me when he decided to betray me with my best friend. I will never understand why, even though the why doesn't matter, that will always bother me. I loooved him."

"I know, baby. I wish I could take the pain away. You could– "

"What?"

"Well, you could give him a chance to explain. You could work it out. Maybe. You could at least try. I know he really loves you. There must be some reason. Something maybe he's going through that he didn't know how to explain."

"What? *Him* going through something. There's no excuse for what he did. I can't get past it."

"Have you really tried, honey?"

"This isn't like with you and dad. You forgave him because you had to; he's your husband."

"I forgave him because he made a mistake and he deserved another chance."

"I don't know how to forgive Justin. It feels like I can't. It's done, Mom. I have to move forward. At least I made a decision about grad school. That makes me feel a little better."

"Focusing on your life and your education is a great step forward."

Feeling empowered after the phone call, she called the salon. She needed a radical change. So, she did something she never thought she would do: She had her hair colored. She walked in a redhead with long hair and walked out a brunette with hair that rested on her shoulders.

When she walked into the dorm room following her metamorphous, Smith through wide eyes, said, "Wow. I almost didn't recognize you. What gives?"

"Justin loved my hair. He loved to sing, *'Liv, with your long red hair.'* I needed to change it. It takes me another step away from him, and closer to my recovery."

"Nothing like a change to cleanse the mind. I think it looks sophisticated. You already look like a grad student."

"Thank you. I feel like one today." Olivia smiled, the first genuine smile she felt across her face since the day it happened.

15

"The weekend with Adam went well." Olivia blushed, trying to hide her excitement.

"Oh, give it up, Liv. We have known each other for ten years and I have never seen you glow after a weekend with a man before. Do tell." Sebastian gave her a shrewd look.

Monday afternoon. Olivia could still smell Adam's aftershave, despite the fact that she had showered at home before work. "I don't know what to say. I like him."

"Since no man thus far has been able to woo the strong, proud Olivia Watson, I'm thinking he's got to be rather exceptional."

"Yeah. He's sexy in an effortless, rugged sort of way. Intelligent, charming and sensitive, but he also has an edge. I think the main thing is, he's really easy to talk to. And not pushy, I like that."

"And the sex?"

She blushed. "Amazing. And just for the record, he's not emotionally unavailable. So, don't even start with that. He's actually open and warm."

"And you still like him? Hmm. Sounds serious."

"Maybe." She batted her eyelashes in a coy fashion.

"Glad I pushed you to go to the book signing. I'm guessing you have a date for your reunion, now."

"I haven't asked him yet. The reunion's almost four months away. I'm gonna wait a month or so, and if all's still good, then I'll ask him. Hopefully, he'll come, but even if he doesn't, I feel better about going."

"I see. Like I said at the signing, I guess all we needed to relieve your existential crisis was a handsome stallion." He gave her a smirk. "And some hot sex."

"Ha. Ha. Ha. For your information, it feels good to like someone."

"I'm in the wedding. Just remember."

Wedding. She felt her cheeks burning, then Justin flashed through her mind for a moment. *Stop, he's not important.*

"Let's not jump ahead. It's only been a week."

"You sound different this time. And, you're blushing again."

Justin wasn't important anymore. Although in 2010 when she had signed up for Facebook and learned that Justin married Petal, it was shocking. And painful. Ten years had passed. Her life had moved forward. She was a strong, independent woman, a doctor with an exciting life in the city. It shouldn't have mattered that they had married. And she had been angry with herself that it did.

She wondered how he had the power to hurt her again. She was over Justin, and still he had some sort of pull over her feelings. Like a shadow that would disappear and then spontaneously reappear if the light was angled just right, the feelings associated with the memory of her time with Justin would re-emerge when she least expected it.

Ugh, that day ten years earlier when Becka had reached out through private message as soon as they had become Facebook friends. Becka had married C.J. and they had a baby, Christopher John, Jr. Petal and she had made up. The gang missed Olivia. Blah, blah, blah...

And then she wrote: *You know Justin and Petal are married, right?*

No, I didn't. Olivia had lied. And seeing the sentence spelled out made her eyes water. *And, one word, three letters,* and it connected the two of them, Justin *and* Petal. How could such a small word be so significant? Her nose burned, but she was not going to allow herself to shed one more tear over the two of them. She swallowed those tears and wrote: *Good for them. Things work out the way they're supposed to.*

Maybe you'll come visit soon. We all miss you. Justin and Petal too.

Becka wasn't too bright. Justin *and* Petal too, really? *You were always an airhead, Becka,* she had thought, but wrote back: *Sure. Yeah. Sometime. I'd like that.*

Olivia and Becka had stayed in touch through Facebook over the last seven years, Happy Birthday, Merry Christmas, stuff like that. Nothing too personal. Olivia didn't post much on Facebook, but she looked at her friends' posts. And she often saw pictures of her old friends, all hanging out together, even vacationing, Justin and Petal included in some of those photos.

So yes, it hurt. It still felt strange. But eventually, she got used to seeing them together. It was what it was.

Becka sent another Facebook message after she noticed that Olivia was going to the reunion. *So glad you're coming this year. We can't wait to see you.*

We, like the gang was an entity unto itself.

It kind of was, so many of them were still friends, good friends.

Excited to see the old gang too. It's been too long.

Waaay. Are you bringing anyone?

Of course, she'd ask that. Olivia had debated ignoring the question, but wrote: *Not sure.*

Are you dating anyone? I can't tell from your pictures. And you left your relationship status blank.

I am dating someone. I don't think my relationship status needs to be public information.

Oh, right. LOL. Liv. You always were a private one. I look forward to meeting him. It is a him? Right?

My most recent relationship is a him. Talk to you soon. Gotta go.

She had giggled thinking of Becka in front of her computer trying to figure out if Olivia was a lesbian or bisexual.

Within one month, Olivia had a drawer full of clothing at Adam's. By the second month, she had three drawers of clothing and was spending almost every night at his place. Things had moved quickly, but it all felt natural. It was passionate and easy, serious without being serious.

Then one evening they took a stroll through Central Park. Late July, a gentle breeze blew through the trees. The flowers in bloom made a magnificent landscape in the park: orange, yellow, red, purple. The sweet smell of summer swirled through the air in the breeze.

Adam wrapped his arm around Olivia's back and pulled her close. She had felt it before when he squeezed her tight, the security of his arms. It was a different feeling than she had had with other men. His arm wrapped around her back felt like a safe space. That feeling of running away from the possibility of permanence she had had with every other man since Justin, wasn't there with Adam.

For a millisecond, she remembered that feeling with Justin, the security, the trust in their love. She pushed that thought aside, like she always did when Justin entered her mind. She relaxed into Adam, feeling the words *I love you* on the tip of her tongue. Her knees felt a little wobbly at the thought. Those three words, those eight letters, she hadn't exchanged those with a man since Justin. She never said them frivolously or carelessly; she knew how momentous they were.

"You alright?" He noticed.

"Yes. Fine. Why?"

"You suddenly seem distant."

"Just thinking, I guess."

And then, as if he read her mind, "Me too, Liv." He guided her toward a bench. Olivia's mind spun as she wondered what was on his mind. "I want to say something." He looked deep into her eyes.

"What?" she whispered.

"I love you, Liv. *I love you.*" He kissed her lips softly and searched her face.

Her stomach did a flip. "I– I love you, too. I do." And she did, more than she had even realized. As the words came out of her mouth, the truth of them felt solid. She loved Adam. And he loved her. Her face flushed thinking about it — in love.

Walking back to his apartment, arms around each other's shoulders, she felt a stronger bond between them. Adam brushed a few wisps of her hair from her forehead. "So, I'd like you to meet my brother."

"I thought you didn't talk?"

"There's still tension, but we talk. I think we both want a relationship with each other, despite our differences. He's coming in from Miami for business in early August. He'll be here for a few days and I'd really like to introduce you. If you're up for a family gathering." He peered over his glasses.

"I'd love to meet him. And while we're doing invites, I was wondering if you would escort me to my high school reunion. It's in September." She blushed.

"High school reunion. I didn't know they had those anymore." He joked.

She elbowed him.

"So, I will get to meet your childhood friends?"

"Yes. I haven't seen any of them in a long time. And they are all an important part of my past."

"And our past makes our present. You know, back-story." He gave a teasing elbow.

She smiled. "I thought it would be nice to see some old friends. I'd love to have you come."

"And I'd very much like to be your date, Dr. Watson." He kissed her as they walked. "I can't wait."

16

As Adam walked, Olivia flowed along, her slight frame tucked under his arm. Central Park was beautiful in the summer. The flourishing greenery and flowers made him feel so alive. And then there was this promising new relationship with Olivia.

He kissed the top of her head as they strolled along. The smell of her hair entered his nose, coconut mixed with something almost sugary from her shampoo, then a touch of a scent that was unique to her. It was surprising the first day he laid eyes on her. There she sat in his audience, a face of anonymity among the other anonymous faces, at his book signing. When she stood up and asked her question, he felt his breath catch. Her hair, auburn, with soft, easy waves and that penetrating look in her eyes, like the question she had asked demanded an answer that was life or death, she reminded him of Zara.

Eight years had passed since he lost Zara. There had been women, probably too many women, warm bodies to fill the aching, empty spaces. The women were enjoyable, soothing for a night or a few weeks, sometimes even a month, but he never felt anything.

His heart seemed impenetrable.

He found solace in his writing. It filled a void. He spent most of his time in his imagination, finding comfort in experiencing the lives of his characters. But sometimes the emptiness would creep in, enveloping him like a large, tormented wave.

There at the signing came this sublime creature who reminded him of Zara, bringing back in one moment a rush of feelings — good and bad. She looked at him with those questioning eyes, demanding, wanting, serious. He felt himself smile, genuinely, almost affectionately, as he addressed her. This stranger. He wanted to know her. After their first night together, he knew he felt something with Olivia that was different than with the other women he'd met since Zara. There was something impenetrable about her, something she buried deep within herself that she didn't speak of. He could feel it, her pain, and it reminded him of his own impenetrableness.

Amazingly, things with Olivia had progressed quickly and easily. Saying I love you was something he thought he would never utter again and mean it. Shamefully, he had said it to a few women he had dated. Sometimes during sex, he felt it, fleeting, in a rush of passion – love.

Afterward, to his vexation, he would realize it was only lust, nothing more, and break it off.

One woman who he dated for almost two months, Ginnifer, had pin-straight blonde hair and a devilish smile. He had genuinely liked her. Liked, not loved. Big difference. When he broke up with her, she went ballistic, shouting, "But you said you loved me. YOU said you loved me. And I believed you. How could you?"

"I'm sorry, Ginny. I meant it when I said it, but things aren't working out."

"What more do you want? We get along great. We have so much in common. We have fun together. The sex is fantastic. What is it?"

"I don't know. It's me. I'm just not sure I am capable of loving anyone."

She went into the library, hollering a litany of obscenities. She pulled books off the shelves and flung them around the room. Adam let her get it out of her system, but watched anxiously, hoping she wouldn't break anything. With a satisfied huff and a look of triumph, she observed the mess of books on the floor. She stormed toward his front door, glared at him one last time, screamed, "Fuck you," as she opened it, then slammed it with a *BANG* behind her.

He needed to be more careful with his words.

When he felt himself wanting to say it to Olivia, he waited. He held those words in for over a month. But he knew he loved her. When he wasn't with her, he thought about her all the time, and not only her naked and their bodies entwined in sex. He thought about things he wanted to share with her, activities he wanted to experience with her, ideas he wanted to talk to her about.

Before Zara, he had been *the guy who wanted too much.* That's what the guys in college had called him, *Adam Siegfried — his old name, before they changed it — Adam Siegfried, the guy who always wanted more.* If he dated one girl for a month, soon he found something not quite right and would look for whatever was missing in someone else. Spoiled and on top of the world, he thought he had everything, looks, charisma, money, intelligence, an excellent career path. When his parents died, he realized that he was just like everyone else — vulnerable. And if he didn't make changes, he would wind up alone.

Liv had something special. Sure, the long red waves and serious, wanting brown eyes reminded him of Zara. Maybe that's what made him take notice of her, but it was more than that. Liv thought about things, important things. She lived with an intensity he didn't find with most women. It enthralled him. It excited him. It practically breathed life into him.

Saying I love you when it was true was harder than saying it when it wasn't, interestingly. He sat with her on the bench in Central Park, the words hanging on his tongue as he studied her face.

Then finally, he said it: "I love you, Liv."

Her eyes filled with emotion, her whole face with an expression he had never seen on her before — honest abandon, love. The impenetrable wall around her disintegrated.

Then she said, "I love you, too."

When he pulled her against him, he felt the intimacy swell. As they walked back to his apartment, he was preoccupied with getting her upstairs and taking her clothes off. He wanted to feel her bare body next to his. He wanted to penetrate her. He wanted to fill this sublime woman with ecstasy.

17

Daniel Summers strolled into The Café, a rolled-up newspaper in a swinging hand, a bag flung across his chest. Adam waved him over. Daniel stood tall like Adam, with a similar lean, muscular build. He had leathery skin, and beady eyes.

"Hey, brother." He went to shake Adam's hand.

Adam pulled him into an awkward hug instead.

"And you must be the famous Dr. Liv Watson," he extended a hand toward Olivia.

"Not famous, but yes, I'm Liv. Nice to finally meet you." His hand felt sweaty when she shook it.

"If Adam talks about you, then you're famous in my book."

She blushed.

Daniel, clad in khakis and a white polo shirt, looked fresh and polished. When he sat down, she got a whiff of his cologne. "Verona, didn't come?" Adam asked.

"I didn't want to say until it was finalized. We're getting a divorce." Olivia noticed the big white patch of skin looping the base of his ring finger.

"Sorry to hear that, man. What happened?"

Daniel sighed. "Things hadn't been going well for a while. She's obsessed with her appearance. Always has been. But after she turned forty-five, she became certifiably insane. She sees a plastic surgeon almost weekly. She spends two to three hours at the gym. More than that though, we were fighting all the time. And... "

Adam squeezed Olivia's hand. "You didn't tell me any of this."

"We don't exactly talk about... stuff," Daniel said with over-controlled animosity.

"Dan. You know you can always come to me. No matter what."

"You never liked her."

"I respected your decision to marry who you wanted to marry, but no, I wasn't Verona's biggest fan. But I was always cordial."

"What is it you called her? A money-sucking barnacle?"

Adam took a heavy breath. "Listen. There was a lot of stress after — after mom and dad. I thought we said this was behind us."

"It is."

They shared a hard look; Olivia felt the unresolved conflict that hung between them.

"Are you doing OK?" she asked Daniel, trying to make the brunch atmosphere more amicable. Maybe she could help them get along better. "With getting divorced."

His eyes softened when he looked at Olivia. "I am." He turned toward Adam and, in a scathing tone, continued, "She's taken on a lover. Her trainer from the gym. Some young muscle-head. What a fucking cliché. I suspected it. So, I hired a private investigator. And he got some snazzy shots of the two of them. Good ammo for the divorce settlement. Once that bitch knew that I had her on infidelity, she backed down. Sometimes being cheated on, as it turns out, can be an advantage."

"You need anything?" Adam asked.

"No, man. It's all good now," he said, not masking the sour feelings he had. "So, what are we going to eat?" He opened his menu.

Olivia asked Daniel some questions about his business. He was a financial advisor, something she didn't quite understand. But she tried to establish some sort of rapport by talking about what was comfortable for him. He was Adam's brother. For Adam, she thought it would be nice if they could have more of a relationship.

Daniel was a bit of an ass, though. Unlike Adam, he felt entitled to all the money he inherited and even more, the money he seemed to exploit from his clients through business finagling. He name-dropped. Funny, because Olivia didn't know any of the names he dropped and she didn't care. She only knew that the names where supposedly important because of the pointed expression he used when he said them.

Adam shifted in his chair, played with his omelet more than he ate it. Olivia squeezed his thigh under the table, trying to be comforting.

"I might as well tell you before you see it plastered across magazine covers. I've been hanging out with *the* Monique Finnis."

"Who?" Adam squirmed in his chair.

"Monique Finnis. The model that made that salacious sex tape that went viral. Gorgeous." He held his hands, palms up, in front of his chest, suggesting big breasts. "There're not real. She told me."

"Um, couldn't that affect your divorce?"

"No. Not since we were legally separated. But just in case, we're simply hanging out as friends until the divorce goes through."

"How old is she?"

"Thirty. Don't you know who she is? Don't you two pay attention to the world around you?" He chuckled haughtily.

Olivia felt Adam tense up. She responded, "We do. Sometimes. You know writers and academics; we live with our heads in books and things."

"Apparently. You two will come to Miami and stay with me. You can meet her then."

"I don't–" Adam went to say.

"We'd love to." Olivia chimed in. Even though the last thing she wanted to do was spend a week with this man. Still, he was Adam's brother.

Another half hour of superficial talk, then Daniel left for his business meeting, finally. The air thinned as soon as he got up. Adam released a long, frustrated breath. "Is it me? You seemed to have an easier time with him."

She hesitated. "He's your brother."

"And a complete dick."

"Well there's that." She gave a sympathetic smile.

Later as they walked through Central Park, Olivia brought Daniel up again. "You and your brother are very different?" She probed, wanting to know more about Adam before he lost his parents, who he was, what his family was like. Whenever she asked, he would get a far-away look in his eyes, a slight wince. She would change the subject.

"Yeah. Dan and I — we have always had differences."

"It's worse now? Since your parents? And the conflicts with their money?"

He contemplated. "It is. He looked like he was going to elaborate, but in a measured tone, repeated, "It is."

"What was it like? Growing up wealthy? You never talk about it."

"I don't want the money or the luxuries the money has afforded me to define who I am. Especially to you." He gave her a heavy look.

"I would never see you for your money. But it has to have influenced you. Your *backstory*." She nudged him and smiled. "I just want to know, to understand your life. Because I love you."

He squeezed her hand and slowed their pace. "I grew up privileged. Around other kids who were privileged. It's not something I am particularly proud of now, as a man looking back."

"It's not a lack of virtue to grow up with money."

"But people abuse it. I've seen people abuse money and power simply because they could. That's always been the contention between Dan and me. He uses the money to get things – like young women, or expensive cars, things to impress others. Inside, he's vacuous. We've never had a conversation of any depth. It's always about things. External things. Me, I was the dreamer of the family. I thought about things. I looked for meaning outside of the wealth, the fancy cars, the posh parties. Sometimes the money made me angry. It always seemed to be all that mattered. Dan gave me shit for it. In fact, my parents, a few times, accused me of not appreciating the things they gave me." He winced.

"It's hard for me to talk about this. The last conversation I had with my parents was an argument. They accused me of being frivolous, using the money to play around in Asia like a kid, rather than focusing on my career. I was furious. But after the accident, I knew they were right. I was subversive, reckless, living in the moment. Thinking nothing of my future because I came from money and I didn't have to worry about anything. I could do whatever the hell I pleased. I was angry. Maybe even entitled. I abused the money on purpose because part of me hated it. Losing them changed me. For the better. It made me realize that the money didn't make me or my family any different." He took a sharp breath.

"Regrets are awful, but at least you learned something, right? You gave the pain meaning. You changed for the better."

"I know." He wrapped his arm around her. "I still get emotional when I talk about it. The importance of giving pain meaning was one of the ideas that drew me into a deeper study of existentialism. The reading helped me through the worst part of the grief."

She searched his face. His pain was palpable. "Who you were before, doesn't matter to me. All that matters is who you are now. I just want to know about your life." She kissed his lips softly. They strolled back to his apartment in a comfortable silence.

Daniel called the next day and cancelled their dinner plans. He was heading back to Miami a day early. Adam acted disappointed while on the phone with him, but Olivia saw his face and shoulders relax. He had told Adam that he enjoyed meeting her. *Tell Liv it was a pleasure*, were the words he used. Olivia felt positive that Daniel was appalled by her extra few pounds of body fat, lack of dazzle and obliviousness to the latest celebrity gossip. He was probably sizing up her flaws and imagining what a few nips from a plastic surgeon could do for her.

Honestly, she hadn't been looking forward to another meal with Daniel, but she was still disappointed. She thought spending more time with Daniel would let her know more about Adam's past. Adam was so discreet about it. It made her wonder what he didn't want her to know.

Later that night, Adam slept soundly next to her while she tossed and turned. She tried counting backward from one hundred. She tried imagining sheep jumping over a fence as she counted. She tried hopelessly to clear her mind. No luck. Her thoughts vacillated between Adam's painful past and her own.

Not that they remotely compared. Adam knew a type of loss that no one person should have to endure in a lifetime. And still, miraculously, he seemed to pull something gainful from it. Clearly, he was an extraordinary man. And she trusted him as much as she was able to trust a man, but still... she felt he was concealing something from her.

The other concern interrupting her sleep was Justin. *Justin.* Seventeen years later, finally in love with another man, and thoughts of Justin still troubled her. Maybe it was the reunion, knowing she was going to see him. Well... Petal and him. She hadn't told Adam that Justin would be there, because telling Adam meant that Justin still mattered. And he didn't — not really. She worried that it would be awkward seeing him, them, for the first time since they betrayed her. This was what preoccupied her mind. The initial awkwardness. Nothing more.

It will be fine, she told herself.

She ambled her way into Adam's writing room using her iPhone screen to light the way. She flopped down into the cushy chair, hung her legs over the side, and ran a Goggle search on her phone. It was the same Goggle search she had run nearly ten times: Adam Summers. Nothing could be found that she didn't already know.

So, she tried Daniel Summers.

Pictures of Daniel popped up. He wore the smug expression that was on his face the day they met. He was nestled in a loveseat next to a long, lanky brunette who was overly tanned with lips that looked like two red bananas pursed together into an artificial smile. A few of the photos showed the two of them on a big white boat called, *The Verona.* They held champagne glasses, along with two other couples, equally as tanned and sharp smiled. A few links popped up about Daniel's business: *Summers & Horowitz, Financial Planning.* Nothing too interesting on those links. Then another headshot of Daniel, looking polished and self-satisfied and older than his 48 years.

Feeling dissatisfied, she went to her *New York Times* Crossword app on her phone and started a new puzzle. Trying to figure out words relaxed her, and the more obscure the hints, the better. She dozed off within a half hour.

After Daniel's visit, she started thinking about introducing Adam to her parents. What on earth was she waiting for? Olivia had told her mom about their relationship back in June. Her mother had responded with, "He sounds wonderful. Will we get to meet this one?"

"I think so."

Olivia hadn't brought a man home to meet her parents since Justin, except for a male friend from graduate school and Sebastian.

Her mother had said, "Sounds like this could be serious."

"Maybe. But it's still early. Anything can happen."

"Be positive, honey." Neither of them had mentioned what happened with Justin, but Olivia could feel the unspoken six letter word — *Justin* — lurking in the silence. The J-word, as her mother had taken to referring to him in the few years following their breakup.

Adam meeting her parents seemed monumental. She had built the whole thing up in her head, like if he met her parents, it meant that the next logical step was marriage. Finally realizing that was ridiculous, one morning as they sipped coffee after breakfast, she said, "So, I'd like you to meet my parents."

He looked up from his book, and nodded. "I'd like that."

"How about one night over Labor Day weekend? Since we're staying in the city."

"Invite them here. I can cook."

"I thought we'd go there. Then you can see where I grew up."

"But your parents moved out of your childhood home."

"Edgewater is very close to North Bergen. I can take you to my old neighborhood."

"OK. Let's do it."

Later that week she called her mother. "What are you and dad doing Labor Day?"

"Dad's taking me to Cape Cod for the long weekend."

"You didn't mention that last time we talked?"

"We just made the plans. I've been feeling tired. You know how your father is. Always insisting that I do too much. He's taking me somewhere to relax. Why do you ask?"

"I was thinking that maybe I would bring Adam to meet you. When you get back then."

"Oh. Now I wish we hadn't made those plans."

"Don't be silly. We'll make a plan when you get back. For a weekend in September."

"What about next weekend?"

"We're going to a show Saturday and Adam has a big deadline. When you get back. After I've settled into the new semester."

"Don't change your mind between now and then. We can't wait to meet him."

"I won't." She smiled. "You're going to like him. I'm bringing him to my reunion."

"Oh? I didn't know you were going."

"I must have forgotten to mention it."

"Uh, huh."

"I just forgot."

"I didn't say anything."

"You didn't have to."

"I'm glad Adam's going with you. And honey, go out and get yourself a new outfit."

"I have clothes."

"I want you to go there feeling spectacular. Go shopping. Have Sebastian take you. My treat."

"Thanks, mom. You don't have to treat. I have money for an outfit."

A few days later, Sebastian took her to purchase a new outfit for the reunion. "I'm glad your mother said something before I had to."

"I have a closet full of clothing."

"I'm well aware of what's in your closet, which is why you need something fabulous. You're going to your high school reunion and will see your ex-fiancé and his wife, your traitorous ex-bestie. You need to dress to kill. Besides, your mother won't invite me for Thanksgiving this year if I don't take you. I say this is an excuse to splurge. Let's go to Michael Kors."

"Um, a little out of a professor's price range."

"That's why we should go there. C'mon. Let's put you in something striking. Make your old friends' heads turn and Adam's heart melt."

"Did you and my mother talk?"

"No. We both know you."

"Since when did you become so interested in fashion? Heidegger not stimulating you enough these days and you decided to enter the real world?"

"If Heidegger had been a gay man living in downtown Manhattan, he would have been interested in fashion too."

"Um. I don't think so."

"Me neither."

They both laughed.

Once in Michael Kors, she found three dresses she liked, two black ones and one red one. Before she got to the dressing room, Sebastian stopped her. "No black. It's too safe." He handed her an elegant, silky, navy blue sleeveless dress.

"Really?"

"It's outside along the Hudson River. Sexy. This is perfect and will look great on you."

"It's sort of a statement kind of outfit. Long, silky and clingy. It almost looks like lingerie. You know I enjoy a more tailored look."

"Why be a wallflower when you can be the centerpiece? Try it on. Live a little."

The dress felt smooth along her skin. It didn't cling too tightly, either; it hugged her body just enough and in all the right places. She stood tall, sucked her stomach in, and observed herself in the mirror. She ran her hand over that small area of her lower abdomen that made her self-conscious. As long as she stood straight, it looked good."

"Let's see it." Sebastian called from outside the dressing room.

She opened the door. "I hate to admit it. But I like it."

"You look gorgeous." He smiled.

"It needs a scarf or something. Maybe a wrap." She said.

"Don't ruin it by dangling some arbitrary piece of fabric over it to cover yourself." Sebastian huffed.

"I'll need something in case I get cold. It *is* sleeveless, and the fabric is silky."

"So, you're worried that if a September breeze passes through, your nipples will be hard and noticeable. I say that's a good thing."

"Bash." She blushed, then said, "I wasn't thinking about *that*. I was thinking more about goosebumps. I hate being cold."

"You have that navy scarf that your mother gave you. It would be perfect."

"How on earth did you remember that scarf?"

"I was there when you opened the box. Remember? Last year on your birthday."

"Oh, right. I love that scarf, but it may not be big enough, you know as a wrap."

"Liv. You are too modest. It's perfect."

"Alright. Alright. I guess I can bring a light coat and leave it in Adam's car just in case I get cold."

"A coat?" He rolled his eyes. "Are you worried that there's going to be an arctic cold front in September?"

She smirked. "Ha. Ha."

"Fine. Play it safe." He teased her.

They both laughed.

18

Adam navigated the traffic on the Harlem River Drive. The smooth September air flowed through their open windows. Music hummed softly in the background. Olivia played with an imaginary string on her dress, then twirled tendrils of her hair, then reapplied her lipstick.

Adam turned briefly from the road. "You alright?"

"Yeah. Fine. Why?"

"You seem nervous."

His precision unnerved her more. "Do you talk to any of your high school friends?"

"Never." He teased. "Yeah, I still talk to one or two people from that time. You're nervous about seeing your old friends? I thought we were doing this for fun?"

"We are." *I should tell him about Justin.* "I don't know what's wrong with me." Part of her wanted to tell him, but her words were stubborn. *IT doesn't matter. HE doesn't matter.* It was the initial awkwardness that was on her mind. Once that was over with, it all would be fine.

"You look beautiful."

"Thanks."

Adam wore dark denim jeans and a white button-down shirt. His dark hair and gray eyes stood out against the stark whiteness. She took a long breath, inhaling the fresh scent of his recently showered skin and deodorant. As he drove the black BMW up the ramp to the George Washington Bridge, Olivia looked out the window, noticing random stars twinkling against the dark sky. Having Adam beside her eased her mind... a little. "Follow that sign. Turn right." She directed him toward River Road. "Right here—"

"Liv, the GPS is working fine. Relax." Adam drove through the parking lot all the way to the edge of the river. The reunion was at Pier 115, right on the Hudson River. Expensive cars lined the reserved spaces for residents of the nearby buildings along the water. "This place looks nice. The view. Wow."

"I told you. Wait until we get out and you can see the panorama. We have the best view of the New York skyline anywhere."

She smiled as she got out of the car, feeling a little anxious, but actually more excited to see everyone. A light, balmy breeze blew over the Hudson, a few clouds scurried through the sky. Otherwise it was clear, making the bright lights of Manhattan vivid. They could even see cars driving in the streets of the city. Adam took the valet card. Strolling into the restaurant, he weaved his finger through hers.

Olivia's eyes scanned the room, looking for people she knew. Becka had said that they weren't able to rent the space out for a private party, but that they held a reservation for 75 people, the amount who responded that they were coming. There was a bar inside and one outside, seating in both areas. A large menu. The D.J. agreed to play some music from the 90's.

She felt an arm on her back. The sharp smell of heavy perfume entered her nose and mouth. "Liv," she heard Becka's mild voice.

Olivia turned. "Hi." She said with a huge smile. "Oh, my gosh, it's so good to see you."

"You too." Becka squeezed her.

Becka was still thin and curvy and perfect as ever. Her brown hair was to her shoulders now and her eyes had a few thin lines when she smiled. Other than that, she really looked the same.

"God, Liv. You look great." She screeched, touching the ends of Olivia's hair. "I always loved your hair. And this must be your date. Hi, I'm Becka. One of Liv's best friends from high school." Becka looked Adam up and down, shot Olivia a nod of approval.

He shook Becka's hand. "Adam. It's a pleasure."

"Most of the gang is at the outside bar. C.J.'s back there, Ashlee, Deidra, Cory, Travis and... Petal and Justin." Becka's expression looked uneasy when she mentioned the infamous couple. "Everyone is excited to see you."

Olivia's stomach tossed, but she made sure to stand tall and proud. *It will be uncomfortable for the first few minutes, and then it will be fine,* she reassured herself.

"Oh, there's Felicity and Brenda." Olivia noticed two friends at a table inside, with a wave of relief. "I'm going to go say hello. We'll be outside soon."

Becka hesitated, looking like she had more to say.

"We'll be outside soon." Olivia repeated and kissed her cheek, hoping Becka would not say something about Justin and Petal.

It was then that she realized that she should have told Adam. Not because Justin mattered that much, but because inevitably it would come up. And she almost felt dishonest for not telling. She hunted through the Internet to learn more about Adam's past and despite that, he had told her so much. She, on the other hand, had told him nothing of the baggage she carried.

And there they were, about to confront it.

She debated pulling him aside, when she heard C.J.'s voice come from behind. "Liv Watson!" he bellowed with his thick Hudson County accent. His chest was so thick, it protruded as he walked. He outstretched his arms to hug her and she quickly realized that he seemed different, warmer. Not arrogant. He actually looked happy to see her.

"Hey there." She hugged him.

"This is Adam. My boyfriend."

"Hey, man. Good ta meechya." He shook Adam's hand with a thick, sturdy grip. "What have you been up to? It's been forever. Come outside. Let me buy you a drink."

"We're going to have one in here first. I want to say hi to Felicity."

"I'm going to take a piss. Come outside. The whole gang's out there."

"We'll be out soon."

Adam gave her a curious look. He suspected something.

"My ex-boyfriend from high school is out there." She whispered. "You know, the one I was engaged to. I would have told you, but I didn't think it was a big deal."

"I figured."

"You're not mad. Are you?"

"Why would I be?"

"I don't know. I should have told you. It won't be weird. It was a very long time ago. He's married now."

"Backstory is always important. A heads-up would have been nice, though."

She nodded. "You're right."

"I can deal. I'll get us some drinks." Adam went to the bar.

Olivia said hello to Felicity and Brenda and a few other people that sat at their table. Everyone felt so familiar, like no time had passed. The chitchat was smooth and easy. And even though lives had changed and people had moved on, it still felt like home.

It was home.

Adam came behind her and handed her a glass of wine. She enjoyed the way she felt with him next to her — secure. His quiet strength was reassuring. Olivia introduced him to everyone at the table. Felicity giggled and shook his hand. Long, thick eyelashes circled her big brown eyes. "You look familiar." She said to Adam.

It was then it occurred to Olivia that perhaps people would know who Adam was from his books. Adam smiled at Felicity. "I get that a lot."

"Are you from around here?"

"No. Long Island."

"I used to work in the city as a marketing representative for Coach. What do you do? Maybe we met at some point."

"I'm a writer."

"That's interesting. What do you write?"

"I used to be in journalism, now I write romance novels." He went into his wallet to grab a business card.

Felicity swung her gaze between Adam and Olivia, batting her long eyelashes. "A romance novelist. Wow." She smiled at Olivia and said, "That's sexy."

Olivia smiled and nodded. "You should check out his new book. It's excellent."

Adam wrapped his arm around Olivia and handed Felicity his card.

"I definitely will." Felicity said. She then told them about her two young children and how busy she was being a mother. And how much she loved it.

After another ten minutes, Olivia said to Adam, "Let's get another drink and go outside."

He nodded. They said goodbye to Felicity and Brenda and walked over to the bar.

"Two more Merlots." Adam ordered from the bartender, then turned to Olivia. "Ready to go outside? Or are you going to procrastinate seeing your ex-fiancé all night?"

Her cheeks flushed. "C'mon."

Olivia's heart raced. As they stepped outside, the smooth September air enveloped her. The Hudson River lay expansive: dark, mysterious, solid looking excepting the faintest ripples from a mild breeze. Stunning reflections from the New York City skyscrapers stretched out, shimmering across the water. Red and blue lit the top of The Empire State Building. The whole city seemed large and brilliant and close enough to touch.

"It's quite the view."

"Yeah. We used to drink beer overlooking the skyline when I was a kid. I never realized how magnificent our view was until I moved away from it. I could stare out at it all night."

"I can almost hear the cars beeping and the hum of the traffic; it's so close."

"I know what you mean."

To the right, on the fringe, the gang hung around the bar. C.J. stood out, then Becka sidled up to him. Ashlee's hair was down to her waist and straight now instead of curly. Olivia was about to suck in her stomach, but as she ran her hand over her abdomen, she felt the flat torso beneath it. She gave a silent thank-you to Sebastian for making her wear the Spanx. It really did give her more confidence. She walked toward her former classmates, head held a little higher than a moment ago.

Everything seemed to move in slow motion as Adam and she ambled toward them. They all turned and looked at her. For the briefest moment, everyone stood still, frozen in the awkwardness. No one spoke. Even though the music blasted, Olivia's world became soundless.

Then… everyone gushed at the same time, chiming in synchrony with: "Liv. Oh. My. God. It's so good to see you."

Her eyes brimmed with tears and she was glad it was dark outside. She hoped no one would notice.

Justin and Petal stood toward the back of the crowd. She saw them out of her periphery as she greeted all her old friends with warm hugs and kisses and spilled out numerous introductions to Adam. She wondered if her ex-friend and ex-fiancé were going to talk to her. It hadn't occurred to her until right then that they could survive the night just by ignoring her, stewing in the silence of their original sin.

C.J. was buzzed already, but warm and friendly. He talked with Adam like they were old buddies. And although Olivia would have thought the two had nothing in common, quickly they discovered their shared passion for motorcycles. Adam appeared to salivate as C.J. told him about his new Harley. Travis came over and dove into the conversation. Olivia stood in a haphazard circle with the three men.

She felt Justin looking at her. She turned without thinking. And there were Justin's dark eyes staring right into hers. The gaze was intense and unmoving. She gulped.

Petal sat next to him, her hair cascading over her shoulders in a blonde waterfall. She looked at Justin looking at Olivia. Petal suddenly tensed up as she witnessed Justin come to life. "Liv," Justin said in an uncertain voice. Seventeen years of unspoken words, broken promises and unanswered question connected Olivia and Justin in that moment.

"Justin." She stared at him, feeling gripped by his gaze.

"Hi, I'm Adam," he came up behind her. *Perceptive Adam to the rescue,* Olivia thought as she felt his strong presence next to her. Adam reached his hand out to Justin.

Justin shook Adam's hand. "Justin. And this is Petal."

"*His wife.* Petal. Nice to meet you." She shook Adam's hand.

"I went to high school with Justin and Petal."

"I assumed." He kissed Olivia's cheek. "Did you see the pictures of C.J.'s bike? Man. We'll have to go looking next weekend."

Then to Justin, Adam asked: "You ride too?"

"No. Well, I did in Asia decades ago. I'd like to again. I like the rush. Maybe someday."

Petal said. "You get your rush from running." She turned to Olivia and Adam and said, "Jus is big into long-distance running now. He ran the New York City Marathon last fall."

"No kidding." Adam said. "I run too. I've never run the marathon, but I've done a few 10Ks in Central Park. It *is* a rush. And good for the mind."

"Jus is good at it, but I still don't get it. Why put yourself in pain on purpose?"

"I told you, it's not about feeling pain," Justin turned to Petal.

"It's about transcending it." Justin and Olivia said at the same time.

Justin and Olivia looked at each other. An awkward silence settled in.

Justin used to run two to three miles a few times a week back when they were together. He would talk about the rush of transcending pain. Marathons, though. That was impressive.

Adam broke through the discomfort. "Are you running this year?"

"Nah. Running New York City was a once-in-a-lifetime experience. If I train for another one, I'd like it to be smaller and less hilly. Really test my pace on a fast course."

"There's one on Long Island. It's a flat course. You should check it out."

"Thanks, man. I will." Justin turned toward the bar. "I'm getting another drink. You guys want anything?"

Adam looked at his almost empty wine glass. "Not now. I'm driving. Maybe later."

"Liv?" His voice pierced her.

"Merlot."

When Justin returned with the drinks, he and Adam engaged in more casual small talk. She assumed Adam knew who Justin was. There was no way to miss the awkwardness. Yet, he seemed confident without any discomfort. She couldn't figure out what she felt. Part of her wanted to run away. All of the unresolved questions and feelings she had been able to avoid dealing with rushed over her in a tangled web of emotion.

Part of her wanted to touch Justin. He looked handsome; his dark, thick hair still had a restless tousle, and his eyes, two deep pools, dark and haunting. She was pretty sure she recognized sadness in them when he looked at her, or maybe it was her own sadness she saw in them.

While he bullshitted with Adam, she felt him watching her on and off out of her peripheral vision. She acted oblivious to Justin, while trying to make conversation with Petal. She wanted to forgive her. Or she did forgive her. Maybe. Deep down, she really wanted to talk to Justin. As much as she hated admitting it, feeling his eyes on her felt good.

"You're a doctor now. It's what you always wanted, and I'm so glad for you." Petal's blue eyes searched her face. Olivia wondered if she really meant it. She kept noticing Petal noticing Justin glance at Olivia. The attempt to chitchat over all the unspoken words made her feel verbally constipated. She didn't know what to say and the little she did say felt forced.

Petal grabbed her hand. "Liv. I'm sorry."

Justin looked over at the two of them talking.

"Let's go over there." She pointed to an area outside with large standing ashtrays, people smoking around them.

"I don't smoke anymore."

"Come with me. I'll have one."

Olivia nodded, turned to Adam and said, "We're going right there. Petal wants to smoke."

Adam kissed her cheek.

Large curls of smoke spiraled through the air as they stood along a metal fence right on the river, an area where smoking was allowed. Petal lit up, inhaled, then released a long exhale. Smoke tendrils escaped from her mouth and twirled in the river's breeze.

"Adam seems nice. You guys live together?"

"Not officially. Not yet."

"You're serious, though? It looks serious from the way he looks at you."

Petal's questions annoyed her. Of all things, why was she asking about her relationship status? "It's going well. He's wonderful to me and I'm happy."

Petal wore a tight-fitting dress, which kept hiking up, exposing most of her thighs. Olivia watched as she pulled it down so it rested right above her knees. Her silhouette was perfect, small waist, rounded hips, full breasts.

"Listen. Me and Justin, we never meant for anything to happen," she took in another long drag.

"It was a long time ago." Olivia tried to sound nonchalant. How many times had she envisioned confronting Petal, yelling at her, telling her that she was always a whore and that Olivia never should have trusted her? But those angry inner tirades were a long time ago. They were back in her past when it still hurt every day, when she missed Justin every day, when she still felt broken. Back when she was still a girl. She was a woman now. This didn't matter to Olivia Watson, the woman.

A pinch of irritation coursed through her though; unplanned words spilled out. "Why Petal? Why Justin? Never mind. It doesn't matter anymore."

"No. It does. Of course, it does. What happened was – is inexcusable. I betrayed you, my best friend. I have wanted to explain since the night it happened."

"Go on then."

"When you left for college, you know it was hard for me, right? I mean we had spent all of high school glued at the hip."

"It was hard for me too."

"But Liv, you always had your shit together. You always knew what you wanted. Me, I always felt like I was scrambling trying to hold things together. No matter how hard I tried, I just couldn't stay focused. You were away at Rutgers, and me and Justin were at local universities, still living in North Bergen. When the whole gang hung out, he would go on about you. And when I would talk to you, you would go on about him. Then on school breaks when you would come home, the time felt so short. It's selfish-sounding now, but I always wanted things to stay how they were. And you — you had moved on. You were moving on."

"I knew all this." She said with a pinch in her tone. "We talked about this. And what does it have to do with anything anyway? I helped you. I got Justin to let you stay with him when you had your breakdown over C.J. This feels ridiculous coming out of my mouth. It was so long ago."

"It was. But we never talked about it, so it's still hanging over our heads. Or at least mine. But I have no right to ask you to listen if you don't want to know."

"I just don't want to hear excuses."

"There's no excuse. But there is reason."

"Go on." She gave her a sharp look.

"Justin had his music. He was so passionate about it. And he would play out in Hoboken. We'd go sometimes to see him, you know that. With Becka and Tory and Ashlee. Sometimes the guys came, C.J., Travis, Cory. Justin would listen to my problems with C.J. And I knew he did it for you. Because I was your best friend and he loved you. I never had anyone do anything like that for me. It made me really see how lucky you were. Maybe it made me like him. I dunno. I never did anything about it. It was a feeling. A passing feeling. But he was your boyfriend, so I pushed the thought to the side. I don't even like admitting it to you or even to myself, but I want you to know the truth. You deserve the whole truth." She dropped her cigarette on the ground, smooshed it out with her sandal.

Olivia stood tall and glared at her. "You're right. I do." She felt exasperation arising in the pit of her stomach. What was Petal trying to say, that it was Olivia's fault because she had someone who had really loved her, and Petal didn't? Or at least she thought Justin had really loved her. "How long were you two hooking up before I caught you? I want the truth," she said sharply.

Petal lit another cigarette, took a long drag. "That was the first time we hooked up. But–" she blew out a long spiral of smoke, watched it rise and hang in the air.

"But what?"

"But. I'm sorry, Liv. I have to admit that I had been hoping something would happen for a while. I didn't want to want that, but deep down, I did. The truth is: While you were moving forward with your life, I fell for Justin. And, I think he felt that we — me and him — were more compatible. You had this wanderlust, this need to be independent. He wanted someone less... unpredictable."

"Unpredictable? I was *never* unpredictable or impulsive. Ever. Like you said, I always knew what I wanted."

"Let me say this better." She took a long drag off her cigarette, then blew it out. "After you left for college, he felt you weren't predictable when it came to him. He wasn't your priority anymore, you wanted too much for yourself. He wanted someone who needed less from the world and more from him."

Olivia's heart sank. Petal was right, that is who she was. She had thought Justin loved that about her. Maybe she had just imagined that he did. Maybe the real Olivia flourished in college and Justin and she wanted different things, but tried to preserve the love they felt would sustain them.

But still, something didn't add up. Justin and she were so close. In fact, she had felt closer with Justin than anyone else in her life, before or after. How could he keep that from her? He would have said something? Wouldn't he have?

And then she wondered if she had been so caught up in her aspirations that she missed what was going on. Maybe she didn't really know Justin at all.

"You loved him, then? You loved him while I was still with him? You loved him while pretending that you were my best friend? I'm not mad, I just want to know. To understand."

"Yes. I loved him." Petal's eyes were wide with consternation; her brow furrowed. "I didn't want to love him. In fact, I tried anything I could to talk myself out of loving him. But I did love him. And I am so sorry for that. If you never forgive me, I understand. I probably wouldn't forgive me."

Olivia gave Petal a hard look. Her words stung, but she wanted to be able to let it go. Years of wondering why, too proud to listen to the answer; in the end, there were things that she missed. *Sometimes,* she thought, *we only see what we want to see, and we don't see what we don't want to, even when it's staring us in the face.* Justin had talked to Olivia about being different after her first couple years in college. She had imagined he enjoyed her coming into her own; in reality, Justin felt left behind.

Now the worry and pain in Petal's eyes revealed the truth: Justin and Petal had developed a bond over Olivia's absence. Her moving away brought them together. She had felt so betrayed. But they didn't mean to hurt her, they were following their hearts and that hurt like hell; but if it was the truth, she couldn't be angry anymore. She wanted to love them both enough to want them to be happy. And in that moment, she did.

Petal had a pained look, "Can we start over? Can you ever forgive me?"

"I'd like to try. That's the best I can offer. It will never be the way it was. But we can try talking."

"That's more than I had hoped for." A few tears rolled down Petal's cheeks. She pulled Olivia into a tight hug. "I have missed you so much over the years. So much has changed and there were so many times I wanted to call you and share things with you, but I knew you wouldn't answer."

A few tears trickled down Olivia's cheeks. The tears weren't for Petal though, and she knew it as they spilled out of her eyes. Those tears were for Justin. She stopped paying attention to what was important to Justin, and she lost him because of it.

Petal looked at Olivia's watering eyes. "You're still a crier, huh?"

"Yeah. Some things really do stay the same." Olivia cleaned up her tears. She didn't want Adam to know she had been crying, because then he'd know she was crying over Justin.

Petal laughed through her tears and put her arm around Olivia's back, as they walked toward the gang. Justin looked at Olivia with his intense gaze, a hint of curiosity gleaming this time. He must have known that Petal had apologized, and that Olivia had forgiven her.

Olivia smiled at him. A small, but generous smile, telling him that she understood now and that she forgave him. He smiled back, warm and munificent, and she saw a man that she didn't really know, not the boy she had fallen in love with. There was recognition of who they once were in that smile and a gratitude and respect for what they had shared, love gained and lost — first love. She felt warmth course through her as she shared that smile with him.

Turns out, Justin and she could still smile at each other across a crowded room, communicating something deeper than any words. There was something there between them, something that could never be taken, something that kept them connected over time. Someday she hoped that they could talk about their past. She wanted to hear him explain what had happened and to offer him her forgiveness. She wanted to apologize for the mistakes that she may have made, too. But in that moment, all they had was that shared smile.

And it was enough.

The night continued. More food, more drinks, more laughter. As the drink consumption increased, loud boisterous chatter echoed at the bar. It was strange how familiar everything felt and how much things had stayed the same. C.J., although with tempered superiority, still led the conversations with his large personality and deep resolute voice. Instead of Petal dangling on his every word, it was Becka now, flipping her hair casually as she laughed at whatever he said. Ashlee still acted proper until she was suitably drunk, then she hung on the guys in a friendly, but overly solicitous manner.

Travis, who was single, twirled Ashlee's long blonde hair through his fingers, watching her with a detached curiosity as she swayed back and forth in front of him. Olivia wondered if they were hooking up. Cory was in a relationship, but hadn't brought his girlfriend. Deidra and Raquel, both dressed in tight minidresses and looking strikingly similar to each other, danced on a makeshift dance floor in front of the bar and along the river.

Adam mingled easily with the gang. He spoke with Justin and Petal for quite a while. She heard Justin laugh a few times while they spoke. The sound reverberated in her memory, nights when the two of them shared inside jokes while surrounded by their friends. She moved next to Adam after she heard him laugh, curious about their conversation. She listened, said very little.

She learned that Justin wasn't pursuing his music anymore and hadn't been for years. He gave Olivia a heavy look when he conveyed this information to Adam.

Petal hung her arm across his shoulders. "He knew he wasn't gonna make it. Not because he wasn't good enough, but because few people even with great talent, do. We discussed it at great length and he decided he needed to pursue a more secure path."

Justin looked at Olivia through the chatter, a gaze that had a thousand unspoken words. He gave her that smile again. And she smiled back. She wanted to talk to him, but knew tonight was not the time. What Petal had explained left her with more unanswered questions, questions that she realized she had never let him answer.

She felt sad thinking that he had given up on his music, and she hoped that he didn't have regrets. Adam asked, "So what do you do now?"

Petal responded for him. "Carpentry. He's excellent if you ever need someone."

Justin looked at Petal. "I enjoy it. I've worked on some amazing real estate down here along the river."

"His clients loooove him."

Adam nodded generously. "That's the best, man. Knowing you're good at what you do is priceless."

Petal still had an affinity for being a messy drunk, slurring words and sloppy mannerisms. It was particularly stark in contrast with Justin's cooler, more reserved manner. She gossiped about some friends who weren't there. Maple Ruiz was now a single mother of two. Petal had seen it coming. No one liked Laurence Fishman, their friend Holly's husband. They lived in a big condo right on the Hudson; everyone thought Laurence was involved in shady business deals. Holly didn't love him, but liked the money. Petal whispered in a careless voice. "Travis has hooked up with her a few times. She told me. Don't say anything. No one is supposed to know."

Olivia nodded, though suspected a few of their classmates had just overheard the secret.

Justin wrapped his arm around her tight. "Stop gossiping. Especially here." He shot an uncomfortable look over at Travis who danced nose-to-nose with Ashlee, their hips moving in a side-to-side synchronized wave.

"Holly was always a gold digger."

Justin glared at her. "I don't think Liv and Adam really care who Holly's having an affair with or her views on the value of financial security."

"OK. OK. Sorreeee. It's only Liv. She's not gonna say anything. Right, Liv?"

"Right." She said with a pinch of discomposure.

Justin, still with his arm around Petal, had an uncomfortable expression on his face.

Adam changed the subject. "Do you two live along the water? I wouldn't mind leaving Manhattan for this view."

"We live up the hill. Not far, but we don't have a view from our apartment. It's a nice area though." Another look at Olivia.

"And you two?" Justin asked, casually.

"I'm on the Upper Westside." Adam looked at Olivia.

"I'm on the Upper Eastside."

"Nice."

"Let's dance, Jus." Petal pulled on him to get up.

"Nah. You go."

"Liv? C'mon. Just like old times."

"There's not really a dance floor."

"That nevah stopped us before." Petal pulled at her hands.

"Maybe later. OK? I need to use the bathroom."

"Alright." Petal huffed, then went and joined Deidra and Raquel.

"Be right back." Olivia said to Adam. She gave Justin a polite glance and went inside.

The music soared out of the stereo. Loud talking, feeble attempts to converse over the music, created a cacophony. She ambled toward the bathroom through a thick sea of people.

Once inside the ladies' room, she looked at herself in the mirror. She reapplied her lipstick. Her eyes looked glassy from the alcohol; she put a new coat of mascara on.

Her thoughts kept returning to Justin, the glances between them, the smile they shared, the story Petal told her. *Not now, you can think about it tomorrow.*

But while inside the stall peeing, she couldn't stop her musings. The way he looked at her, she knew he wanted to talk. Same as her. Petal seemed to hover

over him in a domineering manner. Olivia wondered if Olivia's presence made her nervous. Also, and perhaps most importantly, she could not believe Justin had given up on his music. At the very least, she couldn't believe he wasn't teaching music or writing. But he wasn't her concern. And why was she making him and his choices a concern, anyway?

She thought of Adam outside mingling with her friends. She washed her hands and exited the bathroom. Her eyes popped open as soon as she was out the door.

Justin stood in front of her, arms crossed, a small smile on his lips, a heavy look in his eyes.

They locked gazes.

"Justin. Hi."

"Hi."

A wordless moment passed between them, eyes glued to each other's.

"It's good to see you, Liv."

"You too." Despite the uncomfortable circumstances, she liked standing there with him.

"How've you been?"

She swallowed. The unspoken words from the past made her feel awkward, but a feeling of intimacy swelled between them. "Good. I've been good. Busy. You know." She shrugged her shoulders.

"You always kept busy. You haven't changed a bit." He said, warmly. "And congratulations on your doctorate."

She smiled. "Thanks. So – carpentry? Marathons?"

"Yeah. I guess life doesn't always go as planned." His eyes turned sad. "Right?"

Lost in his eyes for a moment, she thought: *I wish we could talk about what happened. Maybe there were things wrong in our relationship that I missed, things that I didn't see, that we didn't see. Gosh, you look so handsome.* "Right." Olivia finally said.

She touched his cheek without thinking. "You look good, Justin." Her eyes wandered across his face. "I'll see you outside." She turned to leave.

"Liv?"

"Yeah?" She turned back toward him.

"I'm sorry."

"I know you are."

"Maybe one day we could talk. You know. About... "

She nodded. "I'd like that. One day."

His eyes grazed the floor, then came back and met hers again.

They shared a long, loaded look. She wanted to feel the warmth of his skin. She wanted to run her fingers through his hair, cry hysterically on his shoulder. All the years they missed being together rushed over her. It almost felt like no time had passed at all.

"I'll see you outside." Olivia said again. Before he could speak another word, she hurried away from him, navigating the heavy crowd of people.

The air felt light and relieving when she got back outside. Her face felt hot. She meandered toward Adam, slowly, giving her heart a chance to return to a normal rhythm.

"Let's go." She weaved her arm through Adam's.

"Sure. You're ready?"

"Yeah. Let me say goodbye to everyone."

Saying goodbye when people were drunk wasn't always easy. Becka hung on her like Olivia was a life raft in the middle of the ocean. "Stay, Liv. Pleeeeze. It's been sooo long. And we miss you."

"Miss you guys, too. We'll get together again soon. Maybe you can come into the city one night." She kissed Becka. "Adam has to drive. It's late."

"It's not *that* late." Ashlee chimed in, weaving an arm through Adam's.

"We'll come back soon. I promise."

"You promise you promise?" Becka asked.

"Yes." Olivia laughed. Becka was the same as ever and Olivia loved her for it.

Adam and she said goodbye to Justin and Petal. Justin gave her one last look. Petal talked in her ear, like she whispered, but her voice came out loud. "I'm so glad we talked, Liv. Let's meet up next week. I'll come to you in the city. 'Kay?"

Olivia felt awkward. "Call me." She said, knowing full well she hadn't given Petal her phone number.

"OK. Love yoooou."

She kissed her politely on the cheek, whiffing the heavy smell of alcohol and cigarettes.

As Adam and she walked out toward the valet, she felt a wave of relief.

"I like your friends. Did you have fun?"

"It was great."

She pulled him close, kissing his lips, hard. "Thank you for coming with me."

"Of course. I love you. I wouldn't have missed it." He squeezed her tight, lifting her feet off the ground.

When Olivia looked up, she thought she saw Justin watching them from behind a large beam in the garage. She blinked a few times and he was gone. *Maybe it was a shadow,* she told herself.

19

Olivia gazed out her window as Adam drove toward the George Washington Bridge. Feeling wistful, she watched the bright lights of the skyscrapers, which created New York's own nighttime constellations in the midtown and downtown skylines, morph into the sleepier, tree-dotted view of northern Manhattan. Finally, as the car tires hit the noisier bridge pavement, Adam broke the unintentional silence. "So that was fun. I enjoyed meeting your friends."

"It *was* fun." She said absently. The moon, bright and almost full, held her gaze. She looked up at it admiringly, trying not to let her thoughts go toward a replay of her conversation with Petal or the one with Justin outside the bathroom.

"You want to talk about it?" He rested his hand on her leg.

"About what?"

"About what happened between you and your ex and his wife? We don't have to if you don't want to. But I saw the way he looked at you."

She looked at him, surprised and uncomfortable.

"Come on, Liv. You'd have to be completely obtuse not to pick up on the tension between the three of you. You were engaged to him. And what? You broke up and he wound up married to a close friend?"

"Best friend." She whispered. "That was a long time ago. It was awkward because I haven't seen either one of them since." She swallowed. "You don't miss a trick."

"It's looking beyond the words. Eye contact and actions tell their own story. When you look beyond the words, you wouldn't believe the things you notice."

"And what, then, did you notice?"

"I noticed him looking at you in a way that a man looks at a woman when he has a lot to say but feels like he can't say it. Petal hung on him like a watchdog. I figured she felt insecure or threatened by you. Or that he was pulling away and she was afraid she was losing him"

"I don't think that's it. They seemed happy to me."

"Maybe — want to tell me what happened between you three?"

"Not really. It's all in the past. Distant past."

"Backstory always influences the present story."

"Not always."

"Always." He turned, giving her a quick glance. In a warm voice, he continued. "But you don't have to tell me about it if you don't want to."

She inconspicuously wiped a tear from her cheek and rolled down her window halfway, letting the air hit her face. The buzz of the traffic on the bridge drowned out a deep sniffle.

"As I had mentioned, Justin was my first love. We were together in high school and all through college. We became engaged toward the end of my fourth year. I thought we had the perfect love, but I was young and naive. There were things — problems — that I... I wasn't paying attention to. At that time in my life, I was very focused on getting into graduate school. I think Justin felt he took second to my work. And truthfully, he probably did, although I was too young to realize it at the time. I guess he and Petal grew close as they both felt me grow distant in some way. It still doesn't totally make sense to me. But love, feelings, they aren't rational. We don't choose who we love. Anyway, it was strange seeing them together, but it seems things worked out in the end." She smiled at him. "Right?"

He squeezed her hand as he drove. "Yes. It seems that way."

It did work out, she thought, but felt a small knot in her stomach.

The closer they got to Adam's apartment, the better she felt. The nostalgia had mostly dissipated, replaced by more of a detached curiosity about Justin's career decision. She did feel something when she saw him. Something she wished she didn't. Some kind of love, a lingering connection. And that shared smile, wow, that felt intense, almost the way it used to. But it wasn't romantic love that she felt. It couldn't be romantic love; she loved Adam and Justin was married. No, not romantic love, more of an old-friend love, one of care and compassion. And forgiveness. She felt forgiveness.

Adam talked about how much he liked Edgewater, that he never thought of leaving Manhattan, but that he wondered what some of the large condos on the Hudson River looked like. "Maybe we could call a realtor and have a look sometime."

"Yeah." She said, casually.

"Liv, I know we haven't been together that long, but I've been thinking. Would you like to move in with me? We practically live together already."

She watched his profile as he drove. He talked about redoing the apartment with her and how much he would enjoy waking up to her every morning. She observed the way he sat, so straight, proud, distinguished. The few grays that peeked through the brown hairs along his sideburns, the scruff around his mouth, over his chin, the way his lips curled at the corner as he talked, he really was handsome. She kissed his hand. "I'd love to." She said, without really considering her answer. But once it was out, it felt like the right one.

He squeezed her hand. "I'm glad you said yes." She could see from his profile that his smile turned wide.

"Can you break your lease? Maybe you can be in before the winter."

"I can and I will. No one wants to be moving in the middle of winter. I'll talk to my building manager on Monday."

"Excellent."

When they got back to Adam's apartment, soon to be their apartment, he asked if she wanted a nightcap. Olivia looked around the place, thinking about where some of her belongings would go. Moving in with Adam was a big step. Really big.

Tucker meowed loudly, stretching his front legs along Adam's lower leg as Adam fed him some dry food. "Hey buddy." He rubbed his back as he ate. Olivia heard him purring from across the room. "Cognac?"

"You asking me or the cat?" Olivia chuckled as she stepped onto the balcony.

"Tucker is more of an Irish Cream kinda cat." He walked outside with two snifters. Olivia followed.

The streets were quiet, except for the hum of the light traffic along the park. Looking up at the sky, the dark, mysterious, endless black, she thought about how strange life was. A long time ago, she had imagined one life, a life she had difficulty unimagining. Things hadn't turned out the way she had planned, but they seemed to work out. Maybe life had to be lived flexibly, bending and curving with the unexpected shifts and twists. Justin may have been her past, but Adam was her future.

Adam lit some candles. They flickered, proffering soft, almost ethereal light. She felt peaceful sitting out there with him. A light rain developed, pattering along the outer balcony in a delicate tempo. He had one hand wrapped around hers as he sipped his cognac with the other. *It really did work out,* she thought. *Soon she would be taking a big step forward by moving in with Adam.*

20

Liv's hair flowed down her back, a thick, wavy auburn mane. He had always loved Liv's hair. As soon as he had laid eyes on her that night, he wanted to touch the long tendrils, letting them stream easily through his fingers, the way they used to.

Instead, he watched another man squeezing her, lifting her feet off the ground as he planted a kiss on her cherry lips. Justin hid behind a thick beam on the periphery of the parking lot, gazing out longingly. He could still remember exactly how her lips felt when he kissed them. A woman like Liv could never be forgotten.

Seventeen years had passed, and he wondered where the time had gone. He had thought of Liv a lot over the years, missing her. Going over what he would say if he ever got the chance to talk to her. The way it ended was awful. So many words left unsaid. So many feelings left unresolved. He never got to explain.

He had believed that she hated him. And he couldn't blame her.

But that wasn't true, he realized as soon as they met eyes that night. The closeness they had shared was still there. And when she touched his face outside of the bathroom, he wanted to rest his hand over hers. The desire to feel her physically close nearly overwhelmed him, as the memories washed over him. It was one of those moments he wished he could hold on to for as long as he could, to let the moment absorb into his pores before he had to let her go again.

Regrets haunted him. And he had desperately wanted to call her over the years. He wanted to hear her voice. He never thought he could miss hearing someone's voice so much. Some nights he would lie awake, willing himself to remember her exact intonation, the gentle stream of words flowing out of her mouth, graceful and raspy. "What do you think about that, Sweets?" she would ask while pondering ideas about life. Her eyes, curious, her head tilted as she waited for him to answer.

They would talk for hours, too, sipping wine or beer or coffee, sometimes milkshakes. Justin wasn't much of talker. Although he had a lot to say, words often felt awkward leaving his mouth. Ideas and feelings used to pour out of him when he wrote, though. With Liv, he had talked effortlessly. She shared herself so honestly, so courageously. It made him want to tell her things he felt deeply in his soul, things he never told anyone else, things that felt clumsy leaving his mouth. People always seemed to think he had nothing to contribute in conversations because he was quiet. But Liv knew better. He held things so close to his heart, he didn't want to reveal them easily.

For five years, he waited for her to come back, wrote emails and letters explaining, asking for forgiveness, hoping she would eventually talk to him. Their love had been so pure, so complete; he really thought she might return. How could he be so broken and Liv just turn her back on everything they had shared?

Travis had said it, Becka had said it, hell, even his older sister, Ronnie, had said it: "*You betrayed her; she caught you in the middle of fucking her best friend; she saw you naked with another woman; she's never going to come back.*"

People don't recover from that shit.

Petal hollered when he walked back toward the gang. "Where were you?" She pushed her lips together in a pout. He hated when she got drunk.

"Bathroom."

"The bathroom's that way." She pointed.

"I came around this way."

She shot him a suspicious look, but thankfully let it go. When Petal got on something that pissed her off, she could be relentless. Liv was always a bit of a sore spot. When Petal noticed that she was attending the reunion, she hounded him, asking questions like he was in a deposition. Every answer he gave led to another question. She twisted his words, tried to get him to say that he still loved Liv. He would never say that to Petal, even though it was the truth. Petal was his wife.

The alcohol made her even more impetuous than she was when she was sober. Sometimes she would say things that were malicious, then regret them once she sobered up. Tonight, she was drunk, but nowhere near as wasted as he worried she'd get. He had brought up the "maybe we need time apart" conversation again earlier in the week. It was at least the twentieth time he had attempted to gently broach the topic with her. She had gotten drunk every night since, and begged him to stay. And again, he promised that he would give it, them, a little more time, like he always did.

Petal scooted toward Deidra and Ashlee and joined them in their drunken dance. Justin sipped his beer, watching them but not watching them. The shimmering lights from the city glimmered on the water. The river was just shy of a mile wide, separating New York City from New Jersey. Though the city looked large and close enough to touch, the river looked vast and dense, putting the city out of reach. He looked across the water to the lights of the big city, thought about Liv living there. It's where she belonged. She had big dreams and she seemed to be living them. He had always admired her tenacity, almost like a wild horse, beautiful, intense, and galloping fiercely toward what she wanted.

Petal came over and leaned into him. A thin layer of sweat covered her brow.

He rested his hand on her shoulder. "You having fun dancing?"

"Yes. Don't I look good?" She laughed loudly and gave him flirty eyes. Her dress was hiked up to the top of her legs. Petal's body was rock solid and curvy.

He put his arms around her narrow waist. "You do." And she did. Petal was gorgeous. He had grown attracted to her over the years.

"Liv seems real happy." She sat on a stool next to him.

"Yup."

"Adam's nice."

"Yup."

"Maybe we can all put the past behind us now. Be friends."

"Yup."

"Can't you say something besides, Yup? You must have felt something seeing her after – everything."

"I don't have anything to say. It was nice to see her. She's an old friend, and I'm glad she's made a nice life for herself."

Petal bit her lower lip. "You felt nothing?"

"Nothing other than it was nice to see an old friend. You're not gonna bring the whole Liv-thing up again, are you?"

"No." Petal said, weakly.

Justin sipped his beer. "Let's go soon. I'm getting tired."

"Yeah. Ok." She played with strands of his dark hair.

When they got home, Petal nagged at him. "You're in one of your somber moods. I hate when you get quiet."

"I'm tired, babe." He said, trying to sound sympathetic. His introverted nature drove her crazy sometimes. She didn't understand his need to revert to quiet places in his mind. She took it personally and would nag at him to talk to her when he had nothing to say.

Tonight was different. Tonight, his mind wasn't quiet, it was restless and preoccupied. It felt cliché to think it — and he tried to get the thought out of his mind, but it was relentless — Liv, was the one that got away, the girl who stole his heart and still held a piece of it. "I'm going to take Jules for a walk." Jules their precious chocolate Labrador.

"She went on the paper."

"I know. But she likes to walk. It's good to take her out."

"It's three in the morning." Petal looked drunk; her eye makeup was smudged, making dark circles under her eyes.

To avoid an argument, he said, "Come with me," knowing she wouldn't feel like going outside, but his invitation would assuage her.

"Oh, babe. I don't feel like going back out." She kicked her shoes off. "Don't go. Come to bed." She pulled her dress over her head, exposing her bare flesh and curves in a white lacy bra and panty set.

"I'll be right back."

"Fine. Hurry." She walked into the bathroom, unfastening her bra before she closed the door.

Outside, the air was still and quiet. Jules bounced next to him as he strolled down the block toward the skyline. Above the hill, the view was further away than down on the river, but still brilliant and vibrant. He thought about the moment Liv and he met eyes and how he felt they communicated through their eye contact all night. Heavy gazes filled with an unresolved past. Something that kept them connected. Liv was the only person he ever had that type of bond with, someone who could read the silences within him and between them. She knew him before he even knew himself.

Maybe she still felt it too.

The longer he was outside and the deeper his contemplation, the more he realized he was foolish dwelling over these shared moments with Liv at the reunion, as though they meant something significant. Liv had moved on. And so had he. Whatever they had had was in the past. He had made an irreversible mistake. He had learned to live with the consequences. They both had learned to live with the consequences.

He shook his head and huffed. He could really be a dreamer sometimes, a causality of being a frustrated artist. As he turned back toward their apartment, a breeze blew off the river, gently nudging him from behind. Thin drops of water released from the sky. He picked the pace up, hurrying home, Jules quickly striding next to him.

His hair was damp when he got back inside. He took his shoes off, towel-dried Jules and went into the bedroom. Petal lay under the covers, the television on low, her eyes closed.

"You sleeping?"

"No. Almost. C'mere."

He took his shirt and jeans off, got under the covers. She pulled him to nestle against her naked body. This was the way they stayed close. When they were physically intimate, they weren't fighting and the problems between them temporarily abated.

"You feel good." She whispered.

"You too."

She turned toward him, pressed her breasts firmly into his chest. A fury of mixed emotion overwhelmed him: love, anger, guilt, desire, regret. He pushed himself into her. After they finished, Justin rolled onto his side and, his back to Petal, thought about Liv. This would happen sometimes after sex with Petal: He would think of Liv. This night, the thoughts came with more emotion. Regret and longing, mostly.

As much as he wanted to talk to her, as much as he wanted to explain the truth, as much as he wanted to apologize, he decided that it was best not to. There was too much that remained between them. The past held them together in some way. He didn't want to wreak havoc in his present — or hers, by dwelling in the past. He didn't want to make more bad choices, choices that would leave him haunted by regrets.

She seemed to forgive him. That would have to be enough.

21

Adam made blueberry pancakes the next morning while Olivia laid in bed enjoying the sweet aroma as it seeped up the spiral staircase into the bedroom. Tucker snuggled next to her, purring, and rubbing his head along her arm. She smiled, thinking that this soon would be her home.

She scrolled through Facebook on her phone. Becka had tagged her in two photos, one of the two of them, one of Becka, Adam and Olivia. There were a few others on Becka's page; two had Petal and Justin in them.

She enlarged the photo. Looking at them together, arms slung over each other's, an *and*, she felt a sense of reconciliation. She loved Justin, probably always would to some degree, but they clearly weren't right for each other. Their pasts may have been similar, but their visions of their futures were vastly different. And now, finally, she was with a man who she felt a more mature connection with.

"Liv. Ready." Adam hollered from downstairs. Hearing his voice, Tucker hopped off the bed and pattered down the stairs.

Olivia stretched her arms above her head and pulled the comforter off of her. She was on the stairs when her mother called. "Hi, mom."

"Hi, honey. What are you up to?"

"Adam's made breakfast. We're just about to eat. Can I call you back?"

"What are you two doing today? Want to come over for dinner?"

"Tonight won't work." She suddenly realized there was something hesitant in her mother's tone. "What's wrong?"

"Nothing, honey – uh, how about tomorrow after work?"

"I know something's wrong. I can hear it in your voice."

She heard a murmured sound, rustling, then her father's voice, "Honey. Liv. The cancer has come back. It's bad. Come home. Please."

"How bad? Come home now, bad?" Her heart plummeted into her stomach. Tears brimmed her eyes.

Adam came to the foot of the stairs. He looked at her curiously, his expression quickly morphing into concern.

"It's everywhere. There's nothing they can do." Her father said.

"How long?" she cried. Adam walked toward her and placed his hand on her shoulder.

"A month, maybe less. Come home and spend time with her. With us."

"We'll be there soon." It was her worst nightmare. Her mother's cancer returned, and this time with a vengeance.

Adam drove her to her apartment so she could pack a bag. She kept dropping small cosmetics as she attempted frantically to pack.

"Let me help you. Tell me what you need." Adam's presence was steadfast. "Take some deep breaths."

"I don't know what I need." She cried.

"OK. Here, I'll grab some stuff I know you use regularly. We can come back tomorrow, or I can come back tomorrow."

"Oh, my gosh. I feel like I'm going to have a heart attack."

"Come here." He hugged her. "I'm here for you. This'll be hard. Probably the hardest thing you'll ever go through, but you're not alone."

She squeezed him, desperately. He quickly packed her bag and they left.

Her eyes watered the entire ride to her parents. Adam put some classical music on, planted his hand firmly on her thigh. They didn't talk much, but his presence was both soothing and appreciated.

She dreaded the first moments when she would enter the house: looking into her mother's eyes, while her mother tried to look brave for her, her father running around trying to distract himself from the reality of the situation. That was how it was the first time. But the doctors had given a cautiously optimistic prognosis then. This sounded completely different. Her mind spun. What had happened? Had her parents known and not told her? One moment, and her life went from contentment to terror and devastation.

The hue of the sky turned darker as they drove, going from white clouds into silver-gray and now a few black ones. A downpour foreshadowed. The leaves on the trees rustled as a stern wind developed. She was almost glad a storm loomed. It matched her mood and the feeling of utter doom she felt inside. Olivia muttered to no one in particular. "Happiness is a frightening state of being."

"What do you mean, babe?" He shot her a warm glance.

"If we let ourselves be happy, then there is something that can always be taken from us. In one minute, one second, everything can change. Has changed."

He nodded as he drove. "Happiness is transient. I truly know how you feel. I never thought anything could touch me until I lost my parents. And once I did, nothing was ever the same. I knew then that life was random and things could change in a second." He entwined his hand with hers. "I know you're scared and that's exactly how you should feel."

Tears rolled down her cheeks. "I need to pull myself together before we get there. I need to be strong."

"You are strong."

"I don't feel very strong."

"Having an emotional reaction to a devastating experience isn't a weakness. It's called being human. You, Liv, are a strong woman. I know you will make it through this. Cry, if you feel like crying, scream, if you feel like screaming, break something, throw something. Do whatever you have to do to get the feelings out. Acting normal in this situation would be abnormal. Right?"

She gave a small, sad smile through her tears. "Yes."

The sky opened up and released a heavy rain. Huge drops of water hit the windshield, thumping like a mallet against a bass drum. Adam flicked the wipers on. They moved quickly back and forth, *click, click; click, click*. She watched the rain land and then be wiped away. More huge drops fell, only to be swiftly eliminated. It was the constant ebb and flow of life, manifesting on the windshield: something developed, existed briefly, only to be gone in a smear. The cadence of the hammering water mixed with the click of the wipers felt hypnotic as she tried to avoid the reality of what she was going home to. She watched this process of birth and death on the windshield, almost numb, until Adam pulled up at her parents' house.

Adam and she hurried toward the front door with coats over their heads, trying to avoid getting soaked. Her father greeted them as soon as she opened the front door. His eyes had a heavy look, but he smiled warmly at Olivia, then pulled her into a tight hug.

"This is Adam, Dad. I hope it's OK that he came," she said, wiping her eyes, when they released the embrace.

"Of course. Your mother has been anxious to meet him."

"Gregg Watson. Please call me Gregg." He extended a hand toward Adam. They shared a sturdy shake.

"I'm very sorry to meet under these circumstances."

Her dad nodded. "It's OK. Come. She's been waiting for you."

"What happened? I didn't even know she was sick again and then on the phone it sounded dire. What can I expect?"

He took a heavy breath. "It happened so quickly, honey. She fainted. So, we went to the ER. They ran a series of tests."

"Why didn't you call me?"

"We didn't want to worry you, unless there was something to worry about."

"I talked with mom a few days ago."

"This all just happened. The tests, honey," her dad wrapped his arm around her back, and gave Adam a grave look, "showed that the cancer has spread to her brain and lungs. It's everywhere. There's nothing they can do."

"There's always something. We need to get a second opinion. Even a third. There are trials happening every day. New treatments being developed. There's always something."

He looked at her hard and serious. "It's too advanced, baby. It's at the end. Your mother's wish was to come home and spend her final time at home with the family."

"It can't be. How does this happen? How does someone go from being well to being sick so quickly? It doesn't make sense."

Adam put his arm around her and squeezed.

"You're right, honey. It doesn't." Her father said.

"Come. You're sister's on her way. Your mom wanted us all to have dinner while she's still strong enough to sit up."

"I don't know what to say when I look at her. Or how to act."

"Honey, you're her daughter. Just be who you always have been."

"You go. I'll be right in." She hurried into the downstairs bathroom to throw water on her face. She stared at herself in the mirror, noticing the lines around her jaw, the sadness in her eyes, the overall strain on her face. This would be one of the saddest, but most important times in her life: the final days she would have with her mother. Even thinking of it, it seemed hard to grasp in any real way, intellectually. But she felt it, through her bones, in every organ, she felt it. Grief.

There was a hospital bed in the den. Her mother sat in a large chair next to the bed, a quilt over her body. The heat blasted and a whiff of sweat mixed with antiseptic overwhelmed Olivia's nose. Her mother looked small under the quilt, but her face was bright and she smiled wide. "I guess I had to get sick in order for you to bring Adam to meet us." Her mother, always the humorist. Even under these circumstances she was joking.

"Mom." Olivia gave her serious look.

"Oh, honey. Have a sense of humor. Humor is medicine. You must be Adam."

He walked toward her mother. "Yes. It's so nice to finally meet you. Liv talks about you and her dad all the time."

"Nice to meet you, too." She pointed to her cheek, indicating that she wanted a kiss from Adam.

He obliged.

Olivia's heart broke looking at her mother, smiling at her, at Adam, acting like everything was normal. She wanted to know what her mother felt, what she thought. She wanted to know what was behind the visage she portrayed. Unlike Olivia, her mother wasn't one to disclose feelings. Olivia wanted to crawl up on her lap and cry hysterically, as she watched her mother engaging in chit-chat with Adam.

"I loved your book." Her mother said to Adam.

"Thank you. Liv didn't mention that you read it."

"I didn't know."

"Well, I figured, or I had hoped, we would get to meet Adam, eventually. I had to read his work."

She adjusted the quilt on her mother. "So, how are you doing, really?"

Her father said, "Adam, come with me to pick up the dinner. We ordered in. To make it easier."

"You got it." He smiled at her mom, kissed Olivia's cheek and walked out behind her dad.

"I like him." Her mother smiled, with a glint in her eyes. Olivia noticed the sadness behind the spark.

"Mom. I... I... "

"I'm OK, Liv. You are my beautiful baby. I'm OK; it's you I worry about."

Her eyes welled. Despite her best effort to hold her tears in, they hung at the brink of her eyes and then streamed down her cheeks. Dread sat in her throat, in her stomach, in her bones. She felt like she was going to fall apart, her body fragmenting from her core into pieces. But she had to be strong.

"Are you scared?" She had to know.

"Only of what I'm leaving behind. I am only scared that you all will suffer. And I don't want you to. I want you to be OK. I want you to continue living. I am going to be OK. I know that. Look at me."

She raised her eyes to meet her mother's. It was a moment she would never forget. A look of such strength, such resoluteness coming from her mother and she wished she had even half the fortitude her mother had.

"I want you to listen to me. This is important to me."

"Yes. Of course."

"You are a beautiful, strong, independent woman. But your pride has been a downfall, sometimes. It's good to be proud, but when it comes to love, sometimes we have to sacrifice our pride in order to be open and vulnerable. I know you don't like talking about it, but we don't have the luxury of time anymore. Justin broke your heart. I know he did. And I know behind your strength and dignity, you have never fully recovered. If you don't risk your heart again, I fear you will never find the love you deserve. Give Adam a chance. Instead of controlling your desire with your mind, let yourself feel. Let your heart guide you. If you get hurt again, you will survive. Promise me you will open your heart." Her mother wrapped her hands around Olivia's.

She sniffled. "I promise."

Olivia and her mother sat sipping tea when Abbee arrived ten minutes later. "I came as fast as I could."

Abbee worked as a chemist in a lab. Ever since her divorce, she spent almost all her time there. "I took time off. To — help." She pursed her lips, gave Olivia a steely look.

Abbee and she were different in terms of their emotions. Abbee was more like their mom, reserved and stoic. Olivia was more emotional and more forthcoming when it came to her inner thoughts about things. Abbee came in and started with the logistics: Did they have a nurse? What palliative care had been offered? What were her mother's most important concerns in terms of comfort?

Of course, these were imperative questions, but Olivia couldn't even think past what was impending, weeks away: the loss, the emptiness, the nothingness that would exist in the chair her mother now occupied. Terror that she would fall apart, sat defiantly in her stomach.

Adam and her father returned with dinner, chicken, vegetables and pasta from her mother's favorite local Italian restaurant. Her mother walked into the kitchen with her father's help. Watching her weakened stature made Olivia's heart ache. She couldn't have ever imagined the level of utter helplessness she felt watching her mother at dinner pick at her food, eat very little. Her mother smiled and talked, listened and laughed, but Olivia could see how fragile she was, the winces of pain she tried to conceal from them. Minutes after they finished dinner, she asked her dad to walk her back into the living room. "I'd like to lie down for a bit before dessert. Don't worry. I'll be ready for the chocolate cake in just a little while."

While her mother rested, Olivia discussed her plan to take a family leave from work. Her father tried to convince her otherwise. "I'm here. Abbee's here."

"Dad, really. If she only has a short time left, I want to be here every day. I want to spend every single second that I can with her." She put her hand across her forehead, frowned.

Her father came around and hugged her around her back.

Adam stayed, an unwavering presence, until around 11:00, when he asked, "Will you be OK, if I go home now? I've got a deadline this week. I want to get up early and write, but I'll come back tomorrow evening."

"Of course. Go home. You have to work. You don't need to be here every day. I know you're here for me."

"You have a wonderful mom, Liv. A wonderful family."

"I feel so helpless. I don't know what to do."

"Just be here. Just love her. Make sure you don't leave anything unsaid."

She nodded at him, knowing that that was a luxury he had not been afforded.

"I'll call you in the morning. But call me any time, even the middle of the night if you need me. Love you."

"Love you."

Olivia slept upstairs in the guest bedroom. Her night was restless. She had a dream where she was stuck in a tunnel which kept getting narrower and narrower, until her body was squeezed into a small space and she couldn't go forward anymore. She woke up choking for air, feeling suffocated. Every time she dozed off, she'd wake up, gasping. Finally, she took a sleeping pill from the prescription her father had been given by his doctor.

The next morning, she spoke with the dean about family leave and was awarded the privilege without any hesitation. She was given the entire fall semester off, which was more than she had requested, but seemed like a good idea, regardless. She would need time, afterward. She didn't even like thinking about that and it almost seemed unreal when she did.

She had meant to call Sebastian, but the day sort of blended into a haze. In the middle of the afternoon, he called after hearing what had happened from another professor.

"Are you alright? Do you need anything?"

"I am. I don't need anything right now, but thanks."

"Please let me know what's happening. And I can always rent a car and drive out there."

"You? In New Jersey? Thanks for making me laugh."

"For you, I will cross the river. Anytime. Seriously, let me know and I will be there."

"I know you will."

The week blurred. She didn't even shower most days. Family and friends came by, keeping her mother busy and animated. But Olivia could see the pain wearing on her. In one week, she looked like she had lost twenty pounds. Still, her mother sat up for guests, made casual conversation acting as if everything was fine. Adam called and texted every day. Olivia had told him to come after he met his deadline. There was nothing he could do and knowing he was there for her was all she needed. Truthfully, she worried that being around her family during such a difficult time would remind him too much of his own tragic past.

On Friday, the nurse, a late middle-aged woman with dark hair pulled up in a high bun and a warm, sympathetic manner, said she didn't think it would be long, but added, "Your mom's a fighter, so it's hard to say. I have seen people last weeks when I thought it would be days. But she's weakening."

Soon after the nurse left, the doorbell rang. Her father and Abbee had gone to the grocery store. Her mother slept. She thought it was a friend of her mother's as she ambled toward the front door, pulling her hair back into a ponytail.

She opened the door.

And there he stood. His dark, thick hair, damp and tousled, dark jeans, black windbreaker. Chin down and eyes up, heavy, dark, broody, "Hi," he said, looking sheepish.

Justin.

She stared into his eyes, confused, overwhelmed.

He winced.

"Justin." she said, almost inaudibly. "Wh– what are you doing here?"

Even as she said it, she knew she was glad he was there. She wanted to grab him, squeeze him, hold him, cry, but she simply stood, lost in his heavy gaze, waiting for his answer.

22

One hour earlier

Justin ran toward Boulevard East, hoping to clear his mind. Petal had come home from work about a half hour earlier and said, "Liv's mother's dying. Becka just told me. Cancer, I think."

News always trickled down at lightning speed when it was bad.

"I got her number from Becka. You think I should call her?"

"Dunno."

"I can't stand when you give one-word non-answers. This is important."

"I really don't know. Maybe wait. If her mother's really dying, then maybe call her or go see her afterward. She's probably dealing with enough now."

"Good point. I might call her anyway."

"Why ask me my opinion if you're not going to take my advice?"

"I like hearing your thoughts. It helps me figure out what I want. I'm taking a shower."

"OK."

As soon as Justin had heard the water running, he took Liv's number from Petal's phone.

"I'm going for a run." He had hollered into the bathroom.

"OK." She had yelled back.

Justin made a right on Boulevard East, and ran along the river. His mind felt split. He wanted to call Liv, but thought he shouldn't. Lily was dying. *Jesus Christ.* He ran his fingers through the front of his hair. He had always loved Lily. She had almost been his mother-in-law. And now he wasn't Liv's husband and Lily was dying. It was a lot to take in.

Looking across at the city, there was a thin mist creating a haze across the skyline. The dim sun leered at the left, just above the horizon. Dusk was falling. He stopped his run and looked out as the sun slowly sunk, disappearing along the edge of the sky. Memories brought a wave of melancholy.

It was the same story, the same regrets he used to go over and over in his mind years ago. He had thought he had beaten it to death and somehow let it go, but now it came over him as fresh as the day it happened, like the scab of a wound that had been ripped off. He had made a colossal mistake that changed the course of his life — permanently.

He got wasted and slept with Liv's best friend. *That* was only the surface mistake, though. After sex with Petal, he came to understand what caused him to hurt Liv so thoughtlessly.

He was afraid of Liv's dreams. And he did things to try and quell his insecurities.

That was the mistake that cost him to lose Liv. He chose what was safe, hung around Petal for some kind of twisted feeling of security from a woman that dangled on his every word, instead of rising to Liv's level and meeting the challenges set before him.

Unfortunately, he didn't understand any of this at the time.

He shook his head, trying to will the thoughts of the past out of his mind. He eased back into his run. He wanted to call Liv and see if she needed anything. He wondered if Liv would let him see Lily. There had been a time when he felt close with Lily.

Lily understood him. Maybe because she was also reserved when it came to how much she shared. Society always seemed to value the extroverts. The people with big personalities, like C.J. The life of the party. The people who engaged easily in big crowds. He respected that in people. But the only time he could share in large crowds was when he had a guitar or a microphone in front of him. When he was onstage, it was like he became another person, confident, daring, certain.

He stopped running again, took his phone off of his armband, and looked at Liv's phone number. It was as if those numbers connected him to her; one push and he could hear her voice on the other end. Reminiscing, he heard her say, *hey, sweets* or *hey, Jus,* the way she used to, soft, warm, loving. He even heard her smile when she said, *hey, sweets.* He had known every nuance of her mannerisms back when they were together.

He was thinking too much. If he was gonna call, he needed to just fucking call, stop pussyfooting around it because he was afraid. He needed to see if she was OK. A surge of adrenalin coursed through him. He would do it. Yes. He straightened his shoulders, hit her number.

He quickly hung up.

He shouldn't call.

His energy deflated, like a balloon that had been popped; the fullness of the moment escaped him.

He took a frustrated breath and started running again. This time he ran fast, taking long, quick strides, concentrating on his breathing and cadence instead of his tangled thoughts and emotions.

When he was done, he inhaled the evening air. Running always made him feel better. No doubt it's what had helped him regain control over his life when he realized Liv was never coming back. Running, and helping Petal through school.

Walking into the apartment, he heard Petal talking on the phone. He listened to her side of the conversation and surmised that she made plans with Becka and

Ashlee. "Happy hour." "Girl's night." It wasn't too often that she went out with the girls.

"Hold on." She said into the phone. "Mind if I go down to Hoboken to hang with the girls for happy hour? C.J.'s home early and is gonna watch Christopher. You know that's a big deal."

"Go. Have fun."

"What are you gonna do?"

"Don't worry about me. You know I can keep myself busy. Or I'll call up one of the guys and head out for a bit."

"Great."

She walked out onto the balcony, lit a cigarette, and continued her conversation. He heard muffled words through the balcony door. None were clear, other than *Liv*. It was like she purposely said the word louder.

As he watched Petal get ready to go out, the back-and-forth of "should I or shouldn't I?" started again; volleying to-and-fro in his mind, giving him a dull headache. Petal went into the bathroom to apply her makeup. He lay on the couch staring up at the ceiling, pushing his temples in with his thumbs. Then the decision came into his head fully formulated. Although it seemed insane, it felt like the correct choice. He wouldn't call; no, he would go to Liv's parents' house. He would ask if there was anything he could do for her, for Lily, for their family. If Liv didn't want him there, he would accept that. At least he would know he had reached out to her.

Driving over to Liv's parents' house, the various scenarios that could play out went through his mind. Her boyfriend could be there. Liv could take one look at him and insist that he leave. She could politely ask him to leave. She could invite him in, but be cold and unreachable. Or she could be happy to see him. Reminding himself that she had alluded to having forgiven him outside the bathroom the night of the reunion, the softness in her eyes, reassured him that at the very least she wouldn't be angry that he came.

Or maybe when it came to Liv, he was a fucking fool.

He made the right turn onto her parents' block. His heart bounced a little as he parked and looked up at the house.

Was he making a mistake? Would Petal find out? Would Liv hate him?

The questions plagued him, temporarily. But at the same time, he felt strongly that this is what he needed to do. Liv had been one of the most important and influential people in his life. Time had passed. He truly wanted to offer support and friendship. Maybe get to see Lily too.

He walked toward the house looking up the stairs and at the front door. A rhythm entered his mind, then some words. This used to happen to him all the time when he wrote music and poetry, but it hadn't happened in years. Words, lines, a melody swarming around formulated without any effort. He heard it in his head at first. It went round and round a bunch of times, then he sang it softly.

Spanning an inch and crossed with a finger,
Echoes of words in the air that would linger.

Then he continued it.

The distance remains in the space in between,

And loneliness courses with promises dreamed.

He let himself feel the words in his mind. When poems, lyrics, melodies would emerge in his head like this, he knew it came from the deepest part of who he was, his heart, his soul, his unconscious. He took his phone out, typed it into an email and sent it to himself. The melody went around in his mind as he made his way up to the front door. Before he rang the bell, he looked around, sort of checking to see if anyone saw him. As if the *National Enquirer* was doing a story on him: *Justin Steeler surreptitiously visits ex-fiancée and family during time of tragedy, leaving wife in the dark about his whereabouts.*

He shook that craziness off, rang the bell. His palms moistened with sweat. Liv answered, looking strained.

Her expression morphed from confusion and apprehension into something he couldn't quite make out, something warmer. "Hi," he said, feeling awkward as she stared at him.

Then her eyes turned sad. And he wanted to pull her into a hug, never let her go, kiss away the pain.

"Justin. Wh– What are you doing here?"

Oh, God, Liv, what am I doing here? I don't fucking know. I can't stop thinking about you. I want to be here for you. I love you.

"I heard about your mother. I'm here as an old friend, to offer any help or support.

She stared at him, his heartbeats marking the seconds of that eternity.

A discomfort burned through his skin. "Jeez… I'm sorry, Liv. I – I don't know what I was thinking coming here. I'm a fool. You know, always have been." He shook his head and turned to leave, muttering under his breath.

She took a heavy breath. "Wait."

He turned back toward her.

"It's OK. Come in."

23

J ustin was in her parents' house. Being near him felt hauntingly familiar; Olivia felt him deep in her bones, the memories, the old feelings — him. She shook it off. Of course, she had remnants of feelings. Justin had been her first love, her first everything, which, despite his betrayal, couldn't be denied or taken. Now, he was just an old friend. An estranged friend. At best. Yet, as much as she hated to admit it, the familiarity of his presence soothed her.

His dark, intense eyes looked into her hers. "What happened?"

She explained her mother's cancer history and the sudden rapid decline of her health that week. His face looked pained as she spoke. It was strange to be sharing such an intimate experience with him after all these years. As they talked, she felt the unspoken words from their past hovering between them. Elusive, inarticulate feelings swirled around filling the pauses in their conversation with glances and heavy gazes. "I'm sorry, Liv."

She looked at him curiously, not knowing if he meant about her mother or what he had done to her. A mix of emotions coursed through her; a few tears trickled down her cheeks.

An awkward second passed, then Justin pulled her into a tight hug. She cried in his arms.

Filled with emotion, she wasn't sure if the tears were only about her mother or if some of them were for him, for what they had shared, for what she had lost. Perhaps, she thought, as she let herself feel his arms around her, warm and sturdy and familiar, it was her forgiveness.

He felt good, but she wiggled out of his grasp. "You want a drink?" She sniffled.

"Sure. Where's your mom now?"

"She's sleeping. Dad and Abbee went to the grocery store. They will be back soon. And I'm sure surprised to find you here."

"Do you want me to leave? I don't want to add to your family's distress?"

She considered. "It's OK. Nothing could make this worse. And the only thing that seems to bring any relief right now is having other people around."

"It's good to be here."

She looked at him hard. She wanted to know where Petal was and if she knew he was there. But she didn't want to hear an answer that caused her to feel he needed to leave. For just a little while, she wanted to forget everything that had happened and be with Justin, uncomplicated, a close person from her past, someone who knew her and her family before all of this, someone who knew her mother and all that Olivia was losing.

"You want a beer?"

"You having one?"

"I'm going to have wine?"

"That's fine."

"Merlot?"

"Sure."

She poured two glasses, handed him his glass and sat across from him at the kitchen table. "So... no more music?"

He diverted eye contact. "I see you still dive right in when you have a question." He gave an uncomfortable smile.

"It was so much of who you were. I was surprised to hear you didn't play at all anymore."

"Yeah. Lots of things have changed."

She tilted her head. "What happened?"

He rustled in his chair. "Maybe this isn't the best time for this conversation."

"Something bad happened?"

"Something." He sighed and looked down at the floor. "After I lost you, I couldn't play anymore. It was always something I wanted to do. My professional aspirations all had to do with pursuing the music, playing, writing, teaching. When I lost you, I guess I lost the inspiration, the motivation." He looked back up at her. "The courage."

She looked at him. She didn't know what to say or how she felt.

"Truth is, Liv, and I don't expect anything from you now, but you should know that you always made me rise to your level. It was something I didn't understand until I... until I lost you. But you pushed me to be the best version of myself. When we, um... when it ended, I stopped trying."

"And Petal? How did that happen?"

He looked around the room. "This is a conversation I've envisioned hundreds of times. But is now the right time for us to have it?"

"Probably not, but tell me anyway." She sipped her wine, looked at him hard.

"I was a complete idiot. I could tell she was interested. And when I felt... I dunno, insecure, doubtful or that I would never measure up to your expectations, I found comfort in her attention."

"I never expected you to be anyone other than who you were."

He shook his head. "I know that now. You were so full of life, so driven. You always saw the world as full of possibility for you and for me. As much as I loved that about you, my younger, foolish self was afraid of it."

"So, Petal, she– "

"It happened once. And it was a mistake. A mistake made by a foolish, immature boy who was scared of how much he loved you."

As he looked at her, she noticed the love in his eyes, the yearning, the abandon. She shivered.

"You married her, Justin. Married."

"What was I supposed to do? I tried to get you back. I waited for you to come back. But you didn't want to talk to me, and I was forced to accept the reality. You were gone, and I had to move on with my life."

"Why her? It makes it seem like you wanted her the whole time."

"No." He winced. "That's not what happened."

"Then tell me what happened."

He nodded, slowly. "I don't want it to come out wrong. I don't want to hurt you more than I already have, and I certainly don't want to make this time any harder for you."

"As long as you tell me the truth, I can accept it."

"OK." He paused. "We were drunk the night you found us. It's not an excuse. I just want you to know that it happened impulsively. And it meant nothing. Nothing happened between Petal and me for five years after that. I was a mess. I was lost without you. And I kept hoping somehow, I could reverse my mistake. Petal wanted us to be together, but I didn't feel anything for her. My heart was with you." They held eye contact, then Justin's eyes grazed the table before he continued. "She was a good friend, though, listening to me go on and on about losing you. About missing you. But she was a mess too. She could barely hold down her waitressing job and school. She almost lost her apartment. Her mother was no help, of course. So, I helped her. She had no one else. I paid her rent for over a year, so she would finish school. I helped her with school assignments. I made sure she stayed focused. I did all of this as a friend to her, because she was a supportive friend to me." He paused, searching for the right words. "Her needing me gave me a sense of purpose that I needed to regain control over my own life. A companionship grew between us over time." His eyes searched her face.

He looked so vulnerable. She put her hand over his without thinking. "Do you love her?"

He placed his other hand over hers. "Liv," he said in a weak voice.

"I shouldn't have asked that."

He looked away, then looked back at her through intense eyes. "I'm always looking for you in her."

Their eyes locked. God, how she wanted to feel his arms around her. "I don't know what to say."

"There's nothing to say. It's life, right? We make choices, sometimes bad ones, sometimes good ones. Each opens up some paths, closes off others. We have to learn to live with the choices we make."

"Very true."

"I don't want you to think I'm a total dick. I'm not here to try and convince you to come back. I just… I want to be here for you."

She smiled at him. "You are here for me."

He cupped her hands and squeezed. His palms felt warm and comforting.

"I'm sorry too. I'm sorry for never listening to what you wanted or taking your calls after it happened. For sending all those letters back unread."

The front door opened. She heard her father and Abbee speaking in hushed voices, the crinkle of bags from the store. They walked into the kitchen, saw Justin and her sitting at the kitchen table. They looked at them, then at each other. Silence. Olivia looked up at them through wide eyes.

Abbee finally said, casually, "Hey, Justin. Good to see you."

Olivia looked on as Abbee and Justin carried on a conversation. Justin said that Becka had learned about their mom from Abbee through a Facebook message, and Becka had told Petal. She watched Abbee talk to Justin with a comfortable ease as though no time had passed at all. She wondered if Abbee had purposely told Becka, knowing how gossip trekked quickly within the gang. Maybe Abbee wanted him there.

"Staying for dinner, Justin?" Her dad asked.

"I probably should get going soon."

"Let me see if my mom's up, so you can see her."
Olivia went into the den. Her mother's eyes were closed,
but she softly said, "Liv."

"You're up?"

"Yes. Can you get me some water, honey?"

She went to the pitcher, poured her mother water.
"Here. How do you feel?"

"I'm OK. Here help me raise the bed up."

Olivia propped the pillow behind her, moved the top
of the bed forward so her mother sat up.

"Mom."

"What is it, honey?"

"Justin is here. He came to see you. But only if you're
up for it."

Her mother raised her eyebrows with interest.

"He's an old friend, mom. There was a time when
we were very close and when he was close with the
family."

"You're explaining the obvious, dear. I'm not the
one you need to convince why you let him in."

"It finally feels good to forgive him."

"Music to my ears."

Olivia kissed her mother's brow.

"I would love to see Justin."

Justin sat next to her mother's bed for a half hour
while holding her hand. Olivia checked on them peri-
odically, but mostly stood outside the den eavesdrop-
ping, wondering if she was the topic of conversation. She

heard her mother laugh a few times. Olivia was grateful that he afforded her the luxury of laughter in a time when she desperately needed it.

Justin's eyes were moist when he walked back into the kitchen. "I love your mother. Thank you for letting me see her."

Justin looked like he belonged, standing there in the kitchen with her family. She admired him. He took the risk and came over. That was a bold move. He offered comfort despite the inherent awkwardness of the circumstances.

And she was glad he did.

Her father asked once more if he wanted to stay. He politely declined, but said he would come back.

Olivia walked him to the door.

Standing at the front door, Justin took both of her hands in his, gave her a warm, generous smile. Again, she saw the genuine love in his expression. It gave her the shivers. God, she wanted to kiss him.

"Thank you," he said.

"You're welcome. It feels good and right. I need to ask, though. Does Petal know you're here?"

"No. She's out. I didn't tell her I was coming, but I intend to tell her I was here."

"She'll be upset?"

"I'm not sure. But we've done nothing wrong. Friends. Right?"

"Friends."

He pulled her into another warm hug, then said, "I'll stop by again, but take my phone number, so you can call me if you need anything."

"'Kay. One sec." Olivia grabbed her cell phone. Justin gave her his phone number and then left. Olivia watched him drive away from the window. She gazed out at the empty space where his car had been for a few minutes afterward.

"Justin looks good," Abbee said with raised eyebrows, as soon as Olivia walked back into the kitchen.

Her father nodded, said nothing. He prepared a plate of food for her mother.

"He stopped by as a *friend*." Even she could hear the defensiveness in her tone.

"Of course. Why else would he be here?" Abbee said, sarcastically.

"Abbee." She gave her sister a piercing look.

"C'mon, Liv. Justin. A friend? I saw the way you were looking at each other."

"Um. He's married. I'm involved and happy, and we haven't been together in like seventeen years. We are grown adults, you know. We have put the past behind us."

"Good for you, honey." Her father said, then walked into the den with her mother's dinner.

"Why did you tell Becka about mom?"

"We chat sometimes on Facebook. She had written to me the day after we found out, so I told her."

"Really? You chat with Becka? I didn't even know you two were friendly outside of me." Olivia considered the stoic look on Abbee's face. "I don't believe you. I think you told her on purpose."

"For what reason?"

"So that Justin would find out. And maybe he would call. Maybe he would try again. You must have been pretty freaking elated when you walked in and saw him. Mission accomplished."

"Liv. Why would I do that? I know you're upset. We all are. But that sounds crazy. I just told Becka. She's your friend. You're being ridiculous."

Olivia took a heavy breath. *What am I thinking? I must be losing my mind.*

"So?" Abbee raised an eyebrow. "How was it seeing him anyway? You guys looked cozy."

"Abbee."

"I think you still love him. Mom says no, but I don't agree."

"You talked behind my back about this."

"Mom's worried. She wants you to be happy. She's worried your heart is closed."

"Then, she should be worried about you too. You're the one with the ugly divorce who works all the time."

"The divorce was hard and disappointing. But I know I'll find someone again. I *am* dating."

"I'm dating too. Adam. Who you will meet tomorrow."

"I know about Adam. I'm not saying I thought you and Justin would wind up together or anything like that.

I just always liked Justin. Even though I was furious at what he did to you, deep down I always thought there had to be some sort of reason. He tried so hard to make amends. And you never gave him a chance to tell you. I always thought a piece of you was still with him because you never resolved what happened. I was happy to see him here, because I thought maybe you finally cleared something up from your past."

"You were always a meddler, Abbee. Seriously. You *did* tell Becka on purpose."

"*I didn't.* But I'm not going to deny that I was glad to see you two looking cozy when we came in."

"Justin is married. *Married.* And just like you think I'm too proud, too private, I always thought you were too easy on people. Too forgiving."

"Maybe I am. But Liv, who are you trying to remind that Justin is married? Me or you?"

She felt her cheeks flush. She stuck her head in the refrigerator, pretending to look for something to drink, so Abbee wouldn't see. "Not that it matters anymore, because it doesn't. But Justin did explain what led up to the betrayal. I understand it now." She turned back toward Abbee. "And it does feel good to know and to forgive him."

"See." Abbee put her hand on Olivia's shoulder.

"It's disappointing that it didn't work out. I think if we had been older, more able to communicate, maybe we would have wound up together."

Abbee put her arm around Olivia. "Timing sucks sometimes."

"Yeah. It does."

"You still love him, don't you?"

She contemplated, shrugged her shoulders. "I will always love Justin in some capacity. But he's married, and I'm invested in this new relationship with Adam."

When the lights were out at night, Olivia felt panicked. She laid in bed; the streetlamps casting thin streams of light into the guest room. All week, she had tossed and turned, wondering what was going to happen to her once her mother was gone. What would her life be like? She thought about her dad? How was he going to survive without her mom? Would he break down? She thought about her own mortality and the fragility of life.

A few times the light streaming into the room seemed ethereal; she'd sit up startled, wondering if she had seen a presence. She felt like she was losing her grip on reality. As a flurry of questions raced through her mind, she thought of Justin, then Abbee's statement-question: "You still love him, don't you?"

Abbee, being her older sister by two years, always had this idea that she knew things about Olivia's personality that Olivia didn't know about herself. She had brushed Abbee's statement-question off all night. But there in the room, alone with her thoughts, already feeling emotionally vulnerable, it entered her mind and wouldn't go away. *Did she still love Justin?*

She would always have something for him. But did she love him? She thought about the way his arms felt around her body, the way his cool edge veiled his sensitivity, but how easily she could feel how deeply he felt things. Particularly, how much he felt about her. For a moment, she became lost in thoughts of how good she felt when he looked at her. Like a beautiful flower being touched by the sun, she bloomed in his gaze. She imagined a kiss between them, him running his hands through her hair and down her back, gently, the way he used to when they kissed. She rubbed her lips with her finger, remembering the feeling.

No! He married Petal. He IS married to Petal, the woman he betrayed me with. She sat up, flicked the desk light on and opened a new crossword puzzle on her phone.

She loved Adam. She would never have the feeling of falling in love the way she had experienced with Justin. What she had with Adam was calmer, but steadier, more solid. Exactly, what she had envisioned for her future.

Adam arrived the following day in the late afternoon. Her mother was weakening, but was still awake. She insisted that Adam and Olivia go out and do something *fun*. Fun, like she could fully enjoy anything knowing her mother was dying. She felt like she needed to be there every second. But her mother, father and Abbee insisted that they go out. To assuage them, Olivia finally conceded.

"How are you holding up?" He asked, as she moved the food around on her plate.

"I'm holding it together by a thread, but it's a sturdy thread."

He peered over his glasses. "I understand that."

"I didn't think it was possible to feel so helpless."

"I know."

"Watching her deteriorate, and so quickly, I…"

"I know."

She wanted to go on, but she saw a sadness gleaming in his eyes. "How's the new book coming?"

"The draft is shaping up. My editor likes how it's coming along."

"My mother said she recommended your book to a lot of her friends."

He smiled.

"Are you ready for me to read the manuscript yet? It would be a welcomed distraction."

"Not quite yet. A couple weeks. I'm ironing out some of the characterization. We could start another game of scrabble if you're up for it."

"That might be helpful. You know, you're one of only a couple of people who have beaten me at Scrabble."

"And you're one of only a couple of people who have beaten me."

"I'm going to win the next game."

"You are a closet optimist."

She chuckled. "Maybe I am."

Her mother was already asleep when they arrived back at her parents'. Adam stayed for another couple of hours. They had some wine, chatted with her dad and Abbee.

After Adam left, Olivia watched her mother as she slept, holding her hand. Under the blanket, she looked so small, almost childlike. Tears rolled down Olivia's cheeks. Her mother rustled and opened her eyes. "Hi, honey." A frail smile emerged across her lips.

"How're feeling? Can I get you anything?"

Lily shook her head. "Did you and Adam have a nice dinner?"

"Yes."

"He's a nice man."

"I know."

"I meant to ask you, did you and Justin talk when he stopped by?"

"Yes."

"That makes me very happy. Honey?"

"Yeah."

"Oh, never mind. It's probably just my imagination."

"Well, now you *have* to tell me."

Her mother took her hand. "Adam reminds me of Justin."

"What? How?"

"The way he looks. Both are tall and handsome, with broad shoulders and intense eyes. They have some of the same mannerisms too."

"They look nothing alike. They *are* nothing alike."

Her mother looked at her warmly. "Maybe it's just me."

Olivia kissed her cheek. "I think so."

"I love you."

"I love you too. So much." She fixed her mother's sheet.

On Sunday, her mother's sister came over. Aunt Betsey wore a tight bun and a button-down shirt; a long gold necklace hung down her chest. She had come a few times during the week. Today, she came with Jack, her husband.

Aunt Betsey fussed over her mother, moving things around the den, bringing her food that her mother had no appetite to eat. When she wasn't helping her mother, she was in the kitchen, cooking or moving items around in the refrigerator.

"Leave it. Come sit already. You're making everyone anxious." Uncle Jack insisted.

Her uncle was tall, with a large build and thick extremities that gave off a formidable presence. But, his big, warm smile melted everyone's heart. You couldn't help but like him.

Aunt Betsey continued her quest to dispel her nervous energy.

"Bets. Leave it." Uncle Jack said again.

Her aunt burst into tears. "I don't know how else to do this."

Uncle Jack draped his thick arm around her. "Have a drink. You're going to have a nervous breakdown." Aunt Betsey had had at least one nervous breakdown that Olivia knew of. Maybe there had been more. Uncle Jack poured her a shot of whiskey. She threw it down in one gulp. He poured her another. She plopped on the couch, nursing the drink while she crossed, uncrossed, re-crossed her legs, squeezing that gold pendent like it had the power to keep her still.

Her father talked about the arrangements that her mother wanted. Aunt Betsey poured another shot and paced with it in her hand. Olivia watched her go back and forth while her father spoke. Once her father finished discussing the arrangements, they commenced with the small talk, which Olivia was in no mood for.

Olivia excused herself. She went upstairs to bury herself in a new crossword puzzle. The truth between the spaces of that superficial talk was unbearable.

Before she even opened the puzzle, Justin's phone number rolled across her screen. She hesitated, then picked up after three rings. "Hey."

"Hey." A pause, then, "How's your mom today?"

"Same."

"How are you?"

"Same. My aunt and uncle are here. They were discussing the arrangements. I can't bear it."

"Do you want to get out for a little bit?"

"Whadaya mean?"

"You want me to pick you up? We can go for a coffee or drink, maybe a short ride? If you feel like getting out. I don't want to take you away from your mother for too long."

He said it so ordinary, almost like it was seventeen years ago and he was making plans to pick her up at her parents' while she was home on a school break. He sounded so sincere, too.

"Justin. Where's Petal?" She almost didn't want to know, but she had to ask.

"Working. She was put on a later shift for the next month or so." Petal was a radiology technician at Holy Name Hospital.

The invitation was loaded and deep down she knew it. *A coffee or drink, maybe a short ride?* They hadn't spoken for seventeen years and now she would see him three times in one week. And twice, alone, without his wife.

She did want to see him, though. "Can you come now? I don't want to miss dinner."

"I'm on my way."

She plopped back onto the bed, stared at the ceiling. *Friends,* she told herself. *Justin is a friend.* But something stirred in the pit of her stomach, something vaguely familiar that she hadn't felt in a long, long time.

When she went toward the door to meet him, long sweater fastened around her, knit hat pulled down passed her ears, they all looked at her.

"Where are you off to?" Her dad asked.

Abbee raised suspicious eyebrows. Olivia's stomach tossed when she saw Abbee's face, like she recognized that Abbee knew exactly where she was going.

Or maybe not.

"Stepping out for some air."

"Oh. Alone?" Abbee asked with an accusatory tone.

"What's your problem, Abbee? I'm going for a long walk. I do that sometimes." She glared at Abbee. "And yes, alone. I need to clear my head."

She wanted to insult Abbee; she could be so snippy with her sometimes. But she knew everyone was suffering; nothing could have been more stressful.

"I'll be back before dinner." She said more gently.

"OK. Enjoy your walk." Her dad said.

"Are you sure that sweater is enough. It's getting cold."

"I'm fine, Aunt Betsey. I've got my hat on."

The air had a bite to it when she stepped outside. It was the first night that she could feel fall in the air. A few leaves swirled in a light wind, and the chill felt good. Justin sat across the street, window rolled down, his elbow resting along the edge. She nodded toward him. He smiled, his eyes wide and practically glued to her as he watched her walk toward the car. She had to divert his eye contact. It was too intense.

"Hey." The car smelled fresh when she got in, a crisp and pleasing aroma. She quickly recognized it: the way Justin used to smell after he had showered. One whiff and the memories of lying with him after he had showered came back to her, how much she had enjoyed those times. She noticed that the ends of his hair were damp.

"Heeey," he said with that casual ease she remembered so well.

She leaned back into the seat of the car, feeling inappropriately contented.

"Want to go sit down by the river? I brought this." He had a bottle of red wine and two cups.

"Sure."

It seemed so ordinary: Justin and her sharing a bottle of wine outside. It was something they had done all the time, something she used to love doing. She hadn't realized how much she had missed it until they were on their way to share the bottle.

"How're you holding up?"

"Honestly. I'm a wreck. But there's nothing I can do except be there."

"I feel selfish taking you away."

"It's good to get out for a little bit. I– I'm glad you called."

Justin's arm looked oddly stiff as he held the steering wheel.

"You are?"

"Yeah." She crossed her arms across her chest. A heavy silence developed between them. Justin flipped the radio on.

Some pop song played in the background, filling the silence. Justin tapped his fingers along the steering wheel to the beat of the music. She looked at his long, lanky fingers. She still remembered every inch of his hands. He wore a black windbreaker that fit snug around his broad shoulders, the extra fabric hung loosely around his torso, same body, same posture. His jeans had a small tear near the knee. She figured he had done it on purpose. That was his thing back when they dated:

take a new pair of jeans and make them look worn. He pulled the car down behind Whole Foods in Edgewater. The skyline was lit up, and the buildings made long, thin reflections off the water. "Wanna get out? Or is it too cold?"

"Let's see." She opened the door. "It's chilly, but nice."

He uncorked the wine. They both walked over a hump of grass and sat on a bench overlooking the city. A few random people walked passed, one runner and a couple walking holding hands, then a woman hustling to catch up to a small boy on a bicycle.

He poured them each a substantial cup of wine.

She looked at him willfully. "Justin, what are we doing here?"

"Can I be honest?"

"Please."

"I– I can't stop thinking about you."

"It's because we just saw each other for the first time since — you know."

"I've never stopped thinking about you."

His remark left Olivia speechless.

"Have you thought of me at all? Was there ever a time when you wondered 'what if'? I have been driving myself nuts thinking *what if.*"

"There was never a 'what if' for me. You slept with my best friend. I'm not upset about it anymore, but it's the reality. I did think about you. I missed you, but I wouldn't let myself feel it, not deeply, at least. The pain. When it came on, I pushed it aside. Then ten years passed. And

I find out you married her. Married. If there had ever been a 'what if,' it was taken away when I found out that you were married." She put her hand over her mouth. That last sentence spilled out. She didn't even know that she thought it until it slipped past her lips. *Would there have been a second chance if he hadn't married Petal?*

And for the first time, she admitted to herself, perhaps, *yes.*

Now she looked at him and felt the *what if* washing over her. The desire to touch him, to remember how his lips felt kissing her mouth, her skin, her hair, felt irresistible. She gulped.

He stared into her eyes and she felt a kiss coming. Their faces hovered in an awkward dance as their mouths drew closer. She could feel the warmth of his breath against her lips. *My gosh*, she shivered, leaned in, then quickly pulled back. She broke the eye contact. Trying to shake the sensation, she gulped down some wine. "Justin. We can't."

"I know." He responded. But she could see the longing in his eyes. And the love, she could feel it, enveloping, like she was immersed in a deep sea surrounded by Justin's feelings, by their feelings. She ached for him to touch her. As much as her words said *we can't,* and as much as she was saying *no* in her head, her heart was saying *please kiss me.*

Please just grab me and kiss me before I can say no. Make me remember, bring me back to that time, before the hurt, before my mother got sick. Please.

Justin put his arm around her and kissed the top of her head. "You must think I'm a total dick."

"I don't. I should, but I don't. I think I know who you are. We both made mistakes. And now we have to live with the consequences."

He took a heavy breath. "I know."

She sipped her wine, trying to drink away the feeling of wanting him, but the longer they sat there, the more her desire for him grew.

Maybe if they kissed, she would be able to let go of this. Of him. Or perhaps being friends with someone she had been so close with was a mistake. Her body knew him intimately; she could remember the way his fingers felt wandering across her breasts, between her legs, how he felt laying with her, blowing into her hair after they made love. *My gosh, Justin. Kiss me.*

She looked up at him, his arm still draped around her shoulder. His face was nearly on top of hers. Her whole body tingled. He rubbed his lips against hers, this time more completely and she moved her lips slowly back-and-forth with his.

She pulled him in tight; his broad shoulders wrapped around her whole back, his chest warm against hers. In the moment, time suspended. She was alone with him, none of the complications of their lives muddying her thoughts. She pushed her lips into his and they kissed fiercely. The years that had separated them — the hurt, the pain, the longing — created a desperate yearning that felt boundless. She wanted to crawl under his skin, merge with him, forget the consequences of what was happening. For an instant, she wondered what the hell she was doing, but she couldn't stop it. In that moment, she wanted nothing more than to be merging her lips with this man who she had fallen for so many years ago.

A horn honked, making them both jump. Behind them, two cars vied for the same space. Olivia looked up at Justin and they shared a smile. Justin kissed her lips, then pulled her body next to his. They sat side-by-side looking across the Hudson at the skyline, the buildings alive with lights that contrasted the darkening sky. "I'm sorry. I made you—"

"I'm a grown woman. You didn't make me."

"It felt… right."

"Yeah," she whispered, staring straight ahead, a concerned look on her face. *Too right.*

"What is it?" He turned her face, so she looked at him.

"We can't do this. You're married. I'm involved. We both have totally separate lives now. What we had was in the past. And I'm not denying that I still have feelings, but they are old feelings, remnants from our time together. Feelings I didn't confront until yesterday. You were such an important part of my youth. I will always hold something for you." As she said it, she had the vague, nagging feeling that she was trying to convince herself more than him.

"You're right." He squeezed her hand.

"I need to go home."

They stood and faced each other. Lost in his eyes, she leaned into his chest and they hugged.

Driving back to her parents, Olivia could not stop thinking about that kiss. She looked at him as he drove and wondered about those letters he wrote to her, the ones she sent back. What did they say? Maybe they could help her reconcile all of the mixed emotions swarming around in her head.

"Hey, Jus. What happened to the letters?" In a soft voice, "The ones you sent me in Pittsburgh."

"Open the glove compartment."

"OK." She opened it.

"There's an envelope in there. That's for you. It's all the letters. I saved them."

"And you carry them around in your glove compartment?" She pulled out a manila envelope, peeked in and saw a bunch of smaller white envelopes.

He chuckled. "I brought them and planned to give them to you because I want you to understand. I want you to know how sorry I was. *I am.* But then I thought that now wasn't a good time with everything you have going on with your mom. Take them. They're yours." He smiled at her.

"Thank you. Jus?"

"Yeah."

"I wish I would have read the letters."

His shoulders slumped. "You were angry. And rightfully so."

She looked at him. She had hurt him, too. Maybe she had wanted to make him feel the same abandonment that she had felt. The emptiness, the loss. But now sitting there with him, she couldn't believe that she hadn't even opened one letter, not one. She had loved him so much, yet she had never even given him a chance.

When he pulled down her block, the reality of her life washed over her, the doom of what she faced in the near future. "The street seems so quiet."

He pulled over. "Life is so hard. You never realize it when you're younger. You know, when you look at your parents, you think they'll be around forever."

"We try to tell ourselves that because acknowledging the reality is too much to bear. But the possibility is there, every second of every day, the fragility of life. And right now, I'm dealing with it. And it's worse than I ever imagined. The helplessness, especially."

He pulled her into a hug. "I wish there was something I could do."

"You still have your guitar?"

"Yeah. I've got a couple guitars. Why?"

"An acoustic?"

"Yeah."

"Pick it up. Practice."

He gave her a confused expression.

"I wanna hear you play again. I want you to play something for me." Olivia appraised his doubtful grimace. "Soon."

"Um... OK."

"Thanks for the letters." She kissed his cheek and got out of his car. When she got to the top of the stairs, she turned around and waved at him before going into the house. *I want you to play something for me. Soon?* She thought to herself.

Maybe this was the *after.* The after he betrayed her, and she, stubborn, with too much pride, waiting too long to forgive him, realized that she could and did. And now she was experiencing feelings that she didn't want to feel. She stowed the envelope under her heavy sweater, then braced herself and opened the door. When she walked in, she immediately felt like her family could see the guilt written across her face.

"Long walk." Abbee poked at her.

"Yeah. I was talking on the phone and lost track of time."

Aunt Betsey hung her hand around her pendant. Abbee gave Olivia a knowing glance.

Her father said, "Well, you're back in time for dinner. We're going to eat in the den with your mom."

"I figured."

She ran upstairs and quickly changed into pajama pants. She was halfway out of the bedroom door when she turned back and looked at the letters sitting on the bed. She wavered by the door for a second before plopping down on the mattress. She dumped all of the letters out.

Looking at the dates, she opened the first one he had sent. Two pages written on spiral notebook paper, she unfolded the pages. She quickly scanned the first page, then the second. A tear dropped down her cheek. She went back and read it slowly.

Dear Liv,

I know I have no right to ask for you to hear me out. There is no excuse for what I did. I don't know what else to do. If I thought you would see me, I swear to God, I would drive to Pittsburgh and stand outside your door and wait for you. Even in the freezing cold. Whatever it took. Just to explain.

I have called and called. I have called over one hundred times. I know you're angry and you have every right to be. I'm lost without you. Nothing means anything. And I see you everywhere, even when my eyes are closed, I see you. I hear your voice. Calling out to me. I reach for you in my mind, but I can't touch you. And it's all my fault. Our whole future, destroyed, and it's all because of my fears.

I understand now why I made the mistake that I did. I know that when I said I was sorry, it wasn't enough. It was foolish of me to even consider that a simple apology would be enough. You need to know why or how I could have ever done something so hurtful to you when you trusted me. You were going to be my wife.

So here it is.

You saw me, Liv. You are the only person I have ever known who truly saw me. The parts of me that hadn't been developed yet, the parts of me that were still evolving and becoming. You, my beautiful sweets, you saw those parts of me and you tried to bring them out. You believed in everything I did.

The problem was that I was so stupid. I was foolish. I was immature. A boy, trying to be a man. I couldn't see that at the same time that you believed in me with everything you had, I didn't believe in myself. I was afraid I would fail you.

I was in the process of becoming the man that you saw. I wanted to be that man more than anything. I wanted to rise to your level. I wanted to be strong enough to take care of you. You were always such a strong-spirited girl and you were becoming the most exquisite independent woman.

I was terrified that I would fail you. I know this probably sounds crazy, because you never asked anything of me other than to pursue my dreams. But I felt insecure and afraid. I felt unworthy. I acted in a moment of insecure immaturity and I made the biggest mistake of my life. I will always regret that I didn't understand what I was doing. I still can't believe we aren't together. It feels like a bad dream that I started

and can't stop. I wish I could press rewind and
start the story over. There is no excuse for what
I did. But please, I hope when you read this,
you might consider talking to me. Maybe there
is something we can do to try and fix this. I
know how proud you are. I know you don't
like to compromise your principles. I love how
strong your resolve is. But. Please. I hope you
consider talking to me. I love you.
Love, forever and one day,
Justin

Tears dripped down her cheeks. Scanning through a few other letters, she saw pages and pages of Justin's inner turmoil, explanations of why he hurt her, pages of regrets and I'm sorrys. Letters written and sent back from Pittsburgh. The last letter was five years after the last time she saw him in the college dorm. She had never considered how hurt he was. She was the victim, Justin the perpetrator. But there on the pages existed the anguished world of Justin Steeler, the boy who crushed her heart and inadvertently shattered his own.

"Liv. Dinner's ready." Her father called from downstairs, snapping her back into reality.

"Be right there." She hurried into the bathroom, sniffling and wiping the tears off of her face.

Adam had called while she was out. What on earth was she doing? Adam was her present, Justin, her past. But even as she thought it through, she still tasted Justin.

She could still feel the sensation of his presence, his arms fastened around her. His freshly showered scent lingered on her sweater. She sniffed it, taking it in, thinking for a moment of how electric that kiss was. She brushed her teeth and washed her face, told herself *no, no, no.* Two letters, one word, *NO,* but even as she said it over and over, her heart whispered a delicate but determined, *yes.*

She texted Adam: *We're about to have dinner. Call you right afterward.*

OK. He quickly responded.

She sniffed the sweater once more, then took it off, throwing on a flannel shirt. The only thing that mattered was spending time with her mother. She was probably thinking about Justin as a distraction from the abyss of grief she was enduring. She hurried downstairs to be with her family, still trying to rid herself of the feeling of Justin wrapped around her.

24

Justin tapped the steering wheel in a steady, anxious cadence. Liv and he kissed. A long, passionate kiss. It was unexpected. It was wrong. And he wanted it. When he went to see her, it was just as a friend. He would just support her through this difficult time. If he separated from Petal, then maybe he would see if something reignited with Liv. But sitting there with her on the bench, he felt it right away, the mutual connection, powerful, passionate, unbreakable. He wanted Liv. And she wanted him too. He was a dick. He had betrayed the only woman he ever loved, and now he was cheating on the woman he had cheated on her with. If he were watching this unfold in a movie, he would hate him. What he wouldn't have understood while watching the movie play out was that he didn't want it to be like this. It was the unfortunate truth of his feelings. He had never stopped loving Liv. She would always be the one.

JACQUELINE SIMON GUNN

His thoughts had been ricocheting all around since he had stopped by Liv's parents' house. He wanted to be there for her as a friend. Even though he still loved her, he didn't want or mean for anything to happen while he was still with Petal. He hadn't told Liv the truth about Petal and his marital problems or how many times he had tried to separate from her.

Petal needed him and, as much as they fought and as dissolved as their marriage was, he felt obligated to try to work it out. He had made a commitment. His parents had been married for almost forty years. Besides, when Petal begged him to stay, he recognized that look of panic in her eyes. He knew that feeling: the terror of losing the person that you love. Knowing how that felt made it so hard for him to leave. Petal had no one else.

He drove around aimlessly for over an hour thinking about that kiss, about how she felt in his arms, about what it meant. Liv had been his first love. From the first day he had laid eyes on her their freshman year in high school, he loved her. He was too cool to admit to her, or even to himself. But he had thought about Liv all the time. Her long, red hair; those intense eyes, always curious; her perfect posture; the way she laughed with her whole body. Finally, he had conjured up the balls to show her, to sing to her. It only took him three whole fucking years. As it turned out, having a guitar in his hands; had given him the confidence he needed.

He had wanted to love Petal with the same authenticity that he loved Liv. And he had tried. But he couldn't make himself feel something that he didn't.

For years he had buried his love for Liv in the back of his mind and tried his hardest to make his life work. But like a dam that had ruptured, being near her flooded him with feelings, making him remember not only their love, but who he was when he loved her. He knew then what he had to do. He had to make the changes he had been trying to make for years. He had to separate from Petal no matter how hard it was. Regardless of the outcome of the kiss with Liv, he knew that had to have the courage to separate.

When he got home, he poured three fingers of Scotch. Petal would still be at work for another couple of hours. He was grateful for the alone time. For the first time in he couldn't remember how long, ten years maybe, he picked up his guitar and preferred pick and began strumming the opening chord progression to Liv's favorite song.

25

Olivia heard muffled voices coming from the den. They all sat in there with paper plates on their laps. Her mother sat up in her bed, a fragile smile on her face. With her hair pulled back, Olivia could see the gray hairs poking out at the roots; her skin looked pallid and aged. She didn't say much, but her gaze dwelled upon whomever spoke.

Aunt Betsey kept adjusting Lily's pillow and blanket. She tried to spoon feed her mother when she noticed that her mother wasn't eating. They all looked at each other, grave, distressed faces, when her mother said weakly. "Bets. I'm not hungry. Really. Stop fussing."

"You have to eat." Aunt Betsey said, pleadingly.

"No, I don't."

Uncle Jack looked at her dad with a sad expression. "Come, Bets. Leave Lily be. Don't make her eat if she's not hungry."

"Jack. I can still defend myself." She released a short, thin laugh, then winced.

"You need a painkiller?" Abbee asked.

"No. Not now."

The small talk was excruciating. Pretending that her mother wasn't sick and that she wasn't noticeably deteriorating felt like living a lie. She could feel the truth in the heavy, sick air in the den, but they all ate, trying to talk like it was a regular night. The worst part of it: the long harrowing, collective wait. Olivia could feel the loss coming, quickly, and they all sort of sat and waited for it. Her mother, included.

After dinner, Aunt Betsey went into the kitchen and began cleaning, everything. They had eaten on paper plates and used plastic cups. What on earth did she find to clean? Uncle Jack and her dad were in there with her. Their voices muted under the clamor of whatever Aunt Betsey was doing. Maybe polishing the china or silverware.

"What on earth?" Olivia said to Abbee.

Her mother piped up. "My sister could never sit still." She motioned to Abbee and Olivia. "Come closer. You girls have to promise me you'll be OK after I'm gone."

Tears immediately streamed down Olivia's face. Abbee's eyes were red and her face looked distressed, but she didn't cry.

"We will." Abbee said.

"Liv?"

Olivia nodded.

"And please make sure your father's OK. I worry he'll fall apart. Your father needs a woman. If he dates, let him. Don't give him a hard time just because of his past mistake."

Olivia and Abbee looked at each.

"And I worry that both of you are beautiful, loving women who are single, alone."

"Single and alone aren't the same, mom. We're fine." Olivia said, nodding at Abbee with widened eyes, prompting her to agree.

"I know. It's... Abbee, you can be cold sometimes, and I fear that it affected your marriage. I know you feel things deep inside, because you are like me. And I know I've spent my whole life nurturing other people's feelings without sharing my own. This was maybe a mistake. Tell people how you feel, especially when you love them."

Her mother and Abbee shared a long, endearing look. "I will." Abbee hugged her, still no tears.

"And you, my baby." She turned to Olivia. "You are so soft and gentle on the inside. You always feel like you need to act strong to protect yourself. And that pride of yours, it's gotten in your way more than once. If you love Justin, it's not a weakness to give in to that. When I forgave your father, it wasn't the weakness you saw it as. It was a strength. I had the strength to forgive him and not let his mistake define who I was or who we were together." Her mother grimaced, then sunk down into her pillow, like her testament had zapped all of her strength.

Olivia looked at Abbee with a bite. "Were you and mom spending these last... these days talking about Justin and me?"

"Only because he stopped by, honey." Her mother said, her eyes closed. "I'm not saying you love him. Seems to me you're happy with Adam. I'm just saying if you do, I want *you*, my baby girl, to follow that big heart of yours. Don't waste it." Her mother's breathing sounded labored now.

"I love you so much." She laid her torso gently over her mother's and squeezed her.

Her father walked back in. "I hope you girls want dessert. Aunt Betsey's making cookies."

"Cookies?" Abbee said with a raised eyebrow.

"Yeah. Cookies."

That must have been what all the clanging was.

When Olivia peeked in the kitchen, Aunt Betsey, clad in a yellow apron, rolled dough back-and-forth with an old wooden rolling pin. On closer inspection, Olivia's heart sank. It looked like the rolling pin her mother had used when Abbee and she were kids and they all had made cookies together.

"Is that," she looked at her dad, "the one from when we were kids?"

"Yeah. Think so." He smiled warmly, but she could see the tension in his jaw, the flinches of deep sadness.

"She kept it?"

"Your mom kept a lot of things from when you were kids."

Thinking of them all in the old house in North Bergen, laughing, rolling cookie dough, flour on their faces, felt heartwarming and heartbreaking. How could two such incongruent emotions exist contemporaneously in her mind? She felt nauseous.

"I'm going to step outside for a few minutes. Get a little air."

"Again?" Abbee raised a suspicious eyebrow.

"Right in front. I'll be on the steps if you want me. I'm hot."

Abbee nodded as Olivia opened the door. Once she was alone on the front steps, she rang Adam.

"Hi." He answered.

"Hi. How's your night? Miss you."

"Miss you too. Getting the writing in. How's it going with you? With your mom?"

"She's not doing so well. Today's been difficult. This sitting and waiting is absolute torture and yet, the thought of not waiting anymore is worse."

"Maybe try not to look at it as waiting, but more as moments together. Precious moments."

A few tears rolled down her cheeks. She inhaled the chilled air, then released a long exhale. "That helps a little."

"I'll come out tomorrow."

"Let me see how tonight goes," she said.

"Whatever you need. This is about you. I do– "

"What is it?"

"Oh, nothing."

"Tell me."

"It's nothing, babe. I just wanted to say that I know how hard it is."

"I don't know how you survived losing both of your parents. And so suddenly."

"Sometimes our only choice is to find a way to keep going. Life takes courage. And I see that courage in you. You will make it through this."

"It doesn't feel that way, but I know you're right. Besides, I promised my mom."

"Liv." She heard Abbee calling her, then the door opened. Abbee's blue eyes looked harrowed.

"Whaaat?" Her stomach dropped.

"Her breathing's become more labored. We called the nurse. Come inside."

"I– I– "

"I heard. Go be with her."

"I– " She felt breathless.

"I'll come right out."

"Wait. I'll call you first."

"Are you sure?"

"Yes. I gotta go." Her hands trembled. The phone slipped from her grasp. She went to pick it up and banged her head on the edge of the door. She stayed scrunched down, letting the tears flood her cheeks. She felt a small tender spot where she hit her head, every part of her ached.

Everyone stood around her mother in the den. Her father held her hand. Aunt Betsey paced. Her mother released wheezing, labored breaths. "Is she in pain?"

"I had just given her a painkiller," Abbee said, her eyes wide and frozen looking. "I hope not."

Her father stroked her mother's arm. "We're all here. We love you. And we're OK."

This was her mother's biggest concern through her entire life, that everyone who she loved be well and happy. Olivia sniffled. She had to pull herself together and give to her mother in her last days or last day, what she knew she needed in order to let go. She needed to hear that they were all OK.

Olivia needed to be OK. The tears streamed down her cheeks. She took a tissue, wiped them away and pulled from every emotional reserve she had.

Standing beside her mother, she said, "You were always the strong one. Let us be strong for you now. We are all here, with you and for you." She leaned in and kissed her mother's cheek.

Abbee and Aunt Betsey walked around in circles. Aunt Betsey, still wearing the yellow apron, held her hands to her cheeks. "What's taking the nurse so long?"

"She'll be here any minute," her father said.

"Aunt Betsey, did you shut the oven off?"

She pressed her lips together, exasperated. "Damn it." She turned and went into the kitchen, muttering under her breath. Tears hung in her eyes when she hurried back into the den.

A few minutes later, the nurse arrived. After checking Lily's vitals, she turned to Gregg and said with gentle empathy, "It won't be long now."

"Is she in– in pain?"

"I gave her a mild sedative. She seems peaceful. Talk to her. I believe she can hear you."

"She can?" Olivia's lips quivered.

"I believe so, yes."

"Do you want some tea?" Aunt Betsey asked the nurse.

"I'll make it. You stay."

Time went by. She didn't know how long, everything felt hazy except for watching her mother as she struggled for her last breaths. They all stood around her, each waiting, fighting off the tears, already grieving. Olivia struggled to stay steady, a few times her legs felt weak. But she told herself that she needed to hold it together for her mother. Her mother had given her a wonderful life, a loving home and family. In her last moments, she needed to give her mother what she needed: a sense of peace in her transition.

Nothing in her life had ever been so painful. She didn't even know how she was still standing. But she realized this was one of the most significant moments of her life: her final moments with her mother. And it seemed unreal.

Her mother passed peacefully with them all beside her. Even Aunt Betsey stood still, showing her mother that she was with her in her last moments. Olivia would never forget how her mother looked as she released her last breath. Stillness washed over her. The tension in her face relaxed and a look of tranquility replaced it.

A whole life ended in one final breath.

26

When Adam heard her voice, he knew immediately. "Hey," was all she said at first. Even with only one word, he heard the tentativeness, like she couldn't believe what she was about to say. After a long pause, in a hollow voice, she told him: "My mother's... gone."

Then, no words, only the sound of abundant, anguished tears.

He knew that feeling, the trauma, the surreal feeling that followed immediately. A fog of confusion and disorientation, combined with a pervading and yearning emptiness that swallowed you. He knew this from losing Zara.

Losing his parents had been different because of the abruptness of their passing. And then, the scandal that followed. He still hadn't recovered from it, especially because there was still tension between Dan and him.

Dan didn't care about maintaining their anonymity, but Adam didn't want to be associated with the whole ugly situation.

He had let it go, though. And then he saw it, like a slap in the face: the cover of *Choice Magazine*. On the bus earlier that day, the woman next to him had had it conveniently placed on her lap. His jaw had dropped when he saw Dan's tanned face, his arm dangling over a busty brunette in a string bikini, both smiling on that magazine cover, their teeth as white as cotton.

The headline: *Does Monique Finnis' New Boyfriend Have a Secret?*

He had hung his head over the woman's shoulder without realizing it. She had given him a sharp look, like she thought he was a creep.

"Sorry." He had said, absently. As soon as he had gotten off the bus, he ran to the newsstand and bought a copy. What a complete ignoramus Dan was, leaving himself vulnerable to any sort of scandal that might pique the interest of the vultures. Hadn't they suffered enough?

Dan simply didn't care. Never did.

The exposure made Adam uncomfortable, particularly because he had a reasonably high- profile career. He had been so painfully scrupulous about keeping his past a secret. Now Dan may have blown it.

More important, he needed to tell Olivia. He was about to on the phone when she had called earlier, but then it sounded like her mother was in her final hours.

It wasn't the right time. Now, her mother had passed and it definitely wasn't the right time.

Olivia had asked him to come spend the night. She had been distant over the last week, not wanting him to come out and be with her. He suspected she was trying to protect him from her grief. He packed a small bag, trying not to worry too much over the Dan thing. Olivia wasn't big into media scandals and salacious Hollywood bullshit. She never read the tabloids. When he went into his drawer to pull out a heavy sweatshirt, he looked at one of the old newspaper clippings.

Investigation into Siegfried Deaths Continues.

He stuffed it in his bag. If the timing felt right he'd show her the article, then explain the truth of his past.

After that, he would wait a little while and then, he would ask Olivia to marry him. He had considered proposing before her mother passed so that her mother would know of the engagement, but everything happened so quickly. He knew for certain that Olivia was the woman he wanted to spend his life with.

He felt pretty certain that she felt the same way about him.

27

Olivia's eyes burned. With her hands wedged under her pillow, she turned toward the window. The muted light seeped through the blinds, suggesting a morning sun. As wakefulness emerged, she had a moment of calm, then a vague, ominous feeling settled in. What happened? *Oh, no.* She bunched her body up into a ball.

Her mother was gone. Long streaks of tears dribbled down her cheeks, soaking her pillow.

It was her third night without her mother. The only peace she had was during sleep. And that was only because she drank a sizeable glass of whiskey to knock herself out. Then there was that brief moment in the morning, before she was fully conscious, when she wouldn't recall her tragedy. When she remembered, an ache rose in her heart, then a feeling of emptiness enveloped her.

The mattress moved. Someone stirred next to her. Adam, she remembered. He had come the night her mother passed and had stayed since then. He reached for her, pulling her from behind and against his body. He wrapped his legs around her.

She nestled against him, letting herself be soothed by the warmth of his body. The tears fell harder.

"Anything I can do?" He whispered.

She shook her head, *no*.

It was the morning of her mother's funeral.

Her mother had left meticulous details of how she wanted the funeral arrangements. She was as organized about the ceremony of her death as she was about living her life. The social worker that came for a visit had said, "Death is simply a stage of life. Same as birth. People transition into their death in the same way they had lived their life." That was true of her mother: most concerned about everyone else, stoic, brave and loving; shedding last wisdoms on everyone, giving each one of them something they could hold onto for the rest of their lives.

She had asked that her funeral be as soon as possible. Instead of a wake, she wanted a day of celebration after the memorial service. She also wanted to be cremated. Aunt Betsey nearly had a conniption when her dad had shared her mother's wishes with her. "Cremated. Her body will be… burned?"

Uncle Jack had put his sturdy arm around her. "Bets. She won't feel it. And she wants her ashes spread along the Jersey Shore. We will all go to Sandy Hook and honor her wishes."

She leaned into him and nodded, no words.

There were a lot of wordless moments following her mother's passing. And when there were conversations, much of it had to do with making phone calls and preparing the ceremony to be the way her mother had envisioned it.

Adam stayed with her the entire time leading up to the funeral. He had a quiet strength about him and it comforted her. When she cried, he held her, didn't offer too many words. That was exactly what she needed: not words of comfort, because in the immediate days she wanted to feel the pain of the loss; she didn't want some proverbial Band-Aid, only the feeling of knowing that she wasn't alone. Adam provided that and tenfold. He reminded her of her mother in that way, who was always the solid, stoic, backbone of the family.

The morning of the funeral was no different. Adam got up and made breakfast. Abbee, her father, Adam and she ate together. Conversation was sparse, the air heavy with grief.

Her father looked exhausted. Now in his late 60s, his hair had mostly grayed. Gregg flashed the same brown eyes as Olivia, warm and intense. He wore wire-rimmed glasses. He usually looked much younger, maybe even mid-fifties. When Olivia looked at the wear in his face, the deep lines around his eyes and the hollow look of his cheeks, she thought he had aged ten years in a week.

Aunt Betsey and Uncle Jack came at 10:45; the limo arrived at 11:00. When Olivia saw the long, slick car pull onto the quiet block, her eyes welled again. Abbee, as always, held it together. A few tears dripped down her cheeks and she looked tired, but for the most part she was undemonstrative. They piled into the limo. Small talk was made on the ride over to the funeral home: a few comments about the rest of the family who would be there; the old friends who said they were coming; the arrangements for afterward when everyone would join them at her dad's house for food and drinks. Olivia heard the sound of words, but she wasn't listening. Sitting between Adam and her father, she spent most of the ride playing with an imaginary string on her shirt.

She knew some of the old gang would be there. Becka and Petal and Justin had called. She didn't call any of them back. They all offered condolences and said they, along with some other friends, would be there. Abbee had posted the details on Facebook, so they knew where to go and when.

She wanted to call Justin back. After reading the letters — she still hadn't read all of them, but she had read enough to know how he truly felt — and after they kissed, something had been reopened. She wasn't sure exactly what she felt. Something, though. She knew they needed to talk. And her mother's wisdom and wish that Olivia follow her heart, not be afraid, not waste the love she had, whirled around her mind, jumbled in with all of the other life considerations that this major loss was kicking up.

But Adam was there, a constant, supportive presence.

Justin would have to wait. All said, this new development was too much.

Sebastian would be there with another professor friend. He had gushed on the phone when she had called to tell him. "Liv. I'm so, so sorry. I'm so, so sorry." He went on for so long, she almost began consoling him.

Smith would be there too. She hadn't seen Smith in over a year, even though she lived in New Jersey. For some reason, although New Jersey and New York were only separated by the river, crossing over in either direction seemed arduous. Smith and Jones had broken up and reunited more times than Olivia could count. Finally three years ago, the two of them eloped to Vegas.

Olivia looked forward to seeing Smith and Jones, and so many other people that would be there that she hadn't seen. And after just losing her mother, it felt incongruous that she would be looking forward to seeing anyone.

By the time the limo pulled up at the funeral home, Olivia had gone through nearly a whole package of Kleenex. Granted, it was one of those small packages, the kind you throw in a purse. But still, she couldn't get the tears to stop.

As they walked in, she saw her mother's name on the door to the memorial room, *Lily Watson*. She felt disengaged, like an outside observer looking in. Her mother's name on the door didn't seem right or real. It must be a mistake. Maybe she was having a nightmare.

But then they spoke with the funeral director, a nice man, stout with full cheeks and a generous smile. And she knew that it wasn't a nightmare. It was really happening.

There were magnificent and abundant floral arrangements in the front of the room. Her mother loved flowers, especially red and yellow roses. Red and yellow colored the room and it felt wrong, all the color, the vibrancy of life juxtaposed with the reality of what they were doing there.

There were pictures of her mother, spanning her life: a baby picture; pictures of her with her own parents; a wedding photo of her mother and father; then pictures of mom, dad, Abbee and her; one of mom and Aunt Betsey sledding in a park, red cheeks, smiling faces. So alive. Looking at the pictures broke her heart. It was a brief glance into her mother's life, and the idea that she was no longer living seemed unbelievable. In front of the flowers sat a small, steel box with her mother's name engraved in thick curvy letters. Her mother's ashes. The only physical manifestation left of her mother's body. She grabbed Adam's hand and steadied herself, feeling dizzy.

He squeezed her hand back. She felt hot and then cold, and she wondered if she might pass out.

Soon, family and friends began arriving, and she realized she needed to pull herself together. Courteous introductions were made. Relatives she hadn't seen since she was a little girl came. Her mother's cousins, old friends, people who said things like "I remember when you were just a little girl, all eyes and that beautiful red hair, just like your mother." She smiled graciously, though each introduction tore a little more of her heart out.

Smith and Jones walked in. Both tall and athletic, they stood out looking like two Olympians ready for a track race. "Liv." She pulled Olivia into a tight embrace. Olivia balled in her arms.

Choked up, Smith said, "I'm so sorry, Liv. I loved your mother."

Olivia smiled at her through glassy eyes. "Thanks for being here."

"Of course."

As she introduced Adam to Smith and Jones, a hand touched her shoulder from behind. Smith's eyes widened. Olivia turned and saw it was Petal — with Justin right beside her.

Petal gushed, "We're so sorry, Liv. I couldn't believe it when I heard. It happened so fast. I called you. Did you get my message?"

"I did. I wasn't up to returning calls, but I appreciated the message." Olivia and Justin shared a long, heavy look. Everything fell silent for a moment. He looked handsome and sad and uncomfortable all at once. They exchanged an awkward kiss on the cheek.

"Sorry." He said.

"Thank you," she said, addressing him and Petal at the same time.

Adam exchanged informal greetings with them, some perfunctory conversation.

Olivia wanted to look at Justin again, but didn't. Instead, she tried to hold the eye contact more toward Petal. She thought for sure if she looked at him, someone, maybe Petal, maybe Adam, maybe even Smith, would see her unresolved feelings for Justin. Their unresolved feelings. When Becka, C.J., Ashlee and Deidra arrived their presence widened the circle, breaking into the mechanical conversation and making it more fluid.

Olivia turned away from the gang to go toward her family. Smith whispered in her ear. "Justin and Petal?"

"I'll explain later. Are you coming back to my dad's?"

"Yes."

"Good." She kissed Smith's cheek.

Sebastian came from behind. "Liv."

She turned, "Hi. You. Thanks for coming." She gave a sad smile.

He nodded, then pulled her into a hug. She fought off more tears, but a few streamed down her face despite her best effort.

Sniffling, she introduced Adam and Sebastian.

"Ah, Liv talks about you all the time." Adam said. "You're a Heideggerian scholar?"

"That's very generous. Knowledgeable of Heidegger. Yes. Infatuated with his ideas. Yes. A scholar of his work? Let's just say I'm working on it."

The room was roasting. She took off the sweater she wore over her blouse, pulled her hair off of her neck, letting what little air was in the room hit it.

Her father nodded for her to come toward the front of the room. She could tell by his stiff mannerisms and the grave look on Aunt Betsey's face that the service was about to start. Her mother had told her dad how she wanted it, short, succinct and ending with her favorite song, "The Rose," by Better Midler.

Olivia sat between her father and Adam. A minister directed the service. He spoke of the celebration of her mother's life: her dedication to her career as a community college professor of sociology; her forty year marriage to Olivia's father; her love of raising Abbee and Olivia and watching them grow into beautiful, fine women; her love of the ocean and the feeling of sand between her toes; rainy days when she could bake bread and cookies without feeling guilty for not leaving the house; her secret, guilty pleasure of daytime soap operas, and how her laughter was contagious.

Tears streamed down Olivia's face the entire time. She saw her father hanging on every word the minister said, like if he held on to his words, he could hold on to her mother a little longer. He nodded a few times as the minister described, rather laconically, as per her mother's request, the highlights of her mother's life. A few times her dad even smiled.

Then, the minister asked their family to come in front and stand beside her mother's ashes. He spoke to the guests. "Lily Watson believed that life needed to be lived with love and courage. The two weren't mutually exclusive for Lily, who felt that loving took more courage than anything else and was life's greatest adventure. She believed that life needed to be lived with purpose and passion, chasing dreams that seem unreasonable, taking chances. Most of all, she wanted you all to know how much she loved you. As she came toward the end of her life, she reflected. When she reflected, she feared that although she loved deeply, she had been unable to express in words the depth of her love. She wanted me to tell you all how much she loved you, and how much each of you contributed to her life. She asked that you not mourn her life, but celebrate it. And to commemorate her memory, here today, she asked me to play this song."

Olivia stood in front with her dad, Abbee, Aunt Betsey and Uncle Jack; together they made a semicircle around her mother's ashes. She sweated under her blouse, and her eyes and nose burned from struggling to fight off the tears. A pianist sat to the right. The minister nodded to her and she began to play "The Rose."

As the first few chords rang from the piano, Olivia's eyes watered. She kept it together, but she kept seeing memories of her mother playing "The Rose" on her piano when Olivia was a little girl. Abbee and mom and she would all sing together, always making their voices louder and more forceful in a steady crescendo, trying their best to mimic the way Bette Midler sang it.

Looking out at the guests while the song played, she noticed so many old faces. She didn't make eye contact with anyone; she sort of skimmed heads and looked at noses. But she saw many people with Kleenex, tears dripping down people's cheeks, a few faces down, people resting their heads on loved one's shoulders. Everyone felt it. The power of her mother's final message. The love. The loss. The fragility of life.

The pianist's voice was strong and bellowed in a steady upsurge. Olivia could feel the intensity of the music in her body. The pianist sang lines about fears of loving and fears of taking chances, being afraid of heartbreak. Justin and she met eyes. She had looked into no one's eyes, but his eyes gripped hers and wouldn't let go. The song continued. She couldn't release the gaze. It almost seemed as though the rest of the guests faded into blurs of color while Justin stood out as the only recognizable person. The power of the song, her mother's words, and Justin's gaze all coalesced in the pit of her stomach, a nagging, aching feeling as the climax of the song came. The last line, her mother's favorite part, was about the seeds of the rose blooming. It made her shiver. Her mother had always said that that last line meant that when there was love, there was always hope. As the piano stopped, her father wrapped his arm around her. She pried her eyes from Justin's.

And the ceremony was over.

28

Thank God he had been able to convince Petal that they shouldn't go to Olivia's parents' house. "We went to the funeral. That's enough."

"We've all made up. She was my best friend."

"*Was* is the operative word. I don't want our presence to cause her any added stress."

"You're always thinking of *her.*"

"This *is* about her. Jeez, her mother just died. This day is for Liv and her family."

"You still love her. Just say it."

"Stop it. Please."

"Say it."

He took a heavy breath. "No."

He wasn't even sure that going to the funeral was fair to Liv. They had shared that kiss, and now, on the worst day of her life, he showed up with the person he betrayed her with.

"I'm going whether you're coming or not," Petal had insisted, her lips scrunched up to the side, annoyed. Justin finally decided that letting Petal go alone would be worse than he and Petal showing up together.

Turns out, Liv was at the funeral with her boyfriend, which made sense. She *was* going out with the guy. He stuck by her too, and from the looks of it, he really loved her

Part of Justin thought that if he really loved Liv, he would leave her alone. Adam seemed like a good guy, had a solid career. And she seemed to like Adam, maybe even love him. But Justin could tell by the way she looked at him, that she still loved him, too. And *that* made it nearly impossible for Justin to let it, or her, go.

Everyone deserves a second chance. Take a chance. That was the message he took from the wisdoms of Lily Watson. But he had other people's feelings to consider. Risk wasn't always as simple as it sounded.

He had married Petal. He had made a commitment. Petal had been so loyal too, waiting for him to come around, waiting for him to finally let go of Liv. For five years, while he was broken and depressed, still hoping Liv would come back, Petal had remained a source of support, reminding him that she wasn't going anywhere.

"You should never have to work so hard to be with someone." She would tell him when he would be crushed after Liv returned another one of his letters.

One day, while hanging out in his apartment, she had said, "Jus, Liv's always been hard to reach. Can't you see it? You would have been working your whole life to keep up."

He looked at her pensively. Liv did make him work. Maybe they wanted different things. Maybe this was never meant to be, and he couldn't see it.

Petal's blonde waves cascaded across her shoulders, her skin, pale and flawless. Her cleavage peeked out of her V-neck shirt. He thought maybe he had been looking in the wrong place all along. There was something to be said for Petal's tireless patience with him, for her unconditional love. And having helped her through school created a closeness between them.

He pulled her close and kissed her lips. At first, he kissed her apprehensively. They had hooked up only that one night, the night Liv found them together so many years earlier. Petal had tried to be with him after that, but he couldn't touch her. It felt wrong.

That night he had kissed her tentatively, trying to let himself feel something. She slipped her tongue into his mouth, pressed her breasts against him. Slowly the kissing felt smooth. He settled into the kiss and desire burgeoned, nothing forced. He wanted to feel her naked and close. To his surprise, it felt natural.

Two years later they were married. She kept asking for marriage and he kept putting off, until one day he decided it was time. What was he waiting for? She wanted it and he wanted to make her happy. Their relationship, their connection, was nothing like he had imagined he would settle for. Nothing like it had been with Liv. No overwhelming excitement, but rather kind of just doing what he thought he should. After only a year into the marriage, he realized that he had married her for all the wrong reasons. He had married her because he felt broken. He had married her as half a man, a man searching to heal, to fill in gaps that Liv had left empty. He had confused his need to feel needed for love. He confused Petal's unwavering attention and adoration for intimate understanding. But still, he had tried to find what he needed — a deeply loving relationship — in his life with Petal. He had felt he owed it to her, to them. But it was pointless. They had fought all the time. Justin grew more distant and Petal drank more.

The thing that really gnawed at him now was that he had been trying to separate from Petal on-and-off for the last nine years, and he hadn't had the strength or the heart to do it. Now, because he thought he might have another chance with Liv, he felt like a fire had been lit under his ass.

"I saw the way you looked at each other. I know you still love her. And I want to hear you say it."

"No."

"Well, I'm going to her father's house whether you're coming or not. Maybe I'll ask her if she still loves you, since you're not giving me a straight answer."

"Don't do that. What's wrong with you? Today is not about you. It's not always about you. Have some consideration."

"You have some consideration and tell me the truth. You still love her."

"Yes." He said sharply, then paused. Looking at her softly, he continued. "No. I mean. I love her as a person."

"And that's all."

"Yes." He said, trying to sound convincing.

"I don't believe you." Tears welled in her eyes. "I will never let you leave me."

"I hate when you threaten me."

"And I hate when you say that we need time apart. You promised to always be there for me. Every time you bring up time apart it reminds me of what my loser-father did. Leave me."

Justin's faced turned red with rage. "I have always been here for you."

"Helping me through school and helping me financially is only a part of being here for me. I want all of *you*. I shouldn't always feel like you have one foot out the door."

"And I shouldn't always feel that nothing I do is good enough."

"I hate when you say that."

Justin calmed himself and in a measured tone said, "I don't want to have the same fight again. Can we talk when we are both calmer?"

She took one of his hands in hers. "Please don't leave me." Her eyes pleaded with him.

"Let's grab something to eat." He placed his hand on her shoulder. "We can talk more later with clearer heads."

"Fine. But you're not leaving."

They went to the diner, ate sandwiches and drank coffee. Both read on their phones, intentionally avoiding the unfinished conversation.

Justin wanted to call Liv, but he'd wait a few days. He needed to iron this out with Petal first. Seeing the desperation in Petal's eyes an hour ago, he realized a breakup would not only be hard, but ugly. Very, very ugly.

When they got home, he picked up his guitar and strummed. He sang softly. Petal looked at him askew. "You haven't played that thing in like, forevah."

"Yeah. Thought I'd pick it up again."

"What song are you playing?"

"Nothing specific. Just fumbling around. Letting my fingers remember the chords."

She nodded as she bit her lower lip, then went out onto the balcony to smoke.

He must think I'm a complete idiot. Petal took a heavy drag off of her cigarette, let the smoke linger in her throat, and then blew it out in a furious stream. *I saw how he looked at her.* After ten years of marriage, he never once looked at her that way.

It made her stomach sick. Liv stole Justin from her in high school and now she was doing it again. And effortlessly. What was it about her that he loved so much? It made no sense. Petal treated him better. She paid more attention to him. She loved him better. And still, he loved Liv more.

She exhaled another fierce gush of smoke. Justin was married to *her*. She got him. Although, he hadn't made it easy, in the end she did get him. And now, he was committed to her. She would never let him go.

Besides, knowing Liv, too-tough, too-much-pride Liv, she'd never take Justin back after what he did to her. She seemed happy with Adam, anyway. If anything, Justin would try to win Olivia back; she'd brush him off, just like Liv did to everyone; he'd come running back to her. Because *she* genuinely loved him and, deep down, Justin knew it. Petal loved him more and better than Liv. Always had. Always would.

She knew he was in there playing — or trying to play — "Glycerine" by Bush too. Right after he and Liv broke up — before he stopped playing his guitar — and he tried to get her to forgive him, he would play that song over and over, staying especially fixated on three lines that had to do with wanting to change but being afraid to. She knew it had something to do with Liv and how he felt. It made her nuts.

"That song reminds you of Liv? Those lines?" She had asked.

"Nah. I just love the song."

She knew he was lying.

Justin wasn't overly generous about sharing his thoughts and feelings. Sometimes she felt like she didn't know him at all. He always had this far-off, dreamy look in his eyes. But when she asked him what he thought and felt about things, he gave her almost nothing. "What are you thinking about?" she would ask him when she noticed that pensive expression in his eyes.

"Nothing, really."

Justin expressed himself best through his music. When he was with Liv, he used to write his own lyrics. Liv had said once when Justin and she first started dating, "It's hard to see it on the surface because he's so reserved, but Justin's really sensitive. He puts it all into his writing and playing."

Petal had listened to Justin sing for years. Many of those songs were either about Liv or inspired by his feelings for her. She had never told anyone, but Petal used to imagine Justin writing songs about her and singing to her. Why should Liv have that and not her? Liv's parents were together. Petal had only her mom, and her mom was drunk most of the time and obsessing over some loser. Liv's parents had encouraged her to get her education. They had believed in her. Petal had received none of that. Her mother's biggest concern had been that Petal be able to pay for her own apartment and food after high school. Liv had a sister. Petal had no siblings.

And Petal knew Liv wasn't as beautiful as she was, but somehow Liv got everyone's attention. Something about her drew people to her. Liv didn't even realize her allure; she just walked around doing whatever she wanted, and people liked her. Why should she get the guy that sang and wrote songs about her?

When she finally had gotten Justin to pay attention to her, to sleep with her, she thought maybe he would write about her, be inspired by his feelings for her. But soon after Liv and he had broken up, he had stopped playing. He had stopped writing too.

"Play something for me," she had asked him one day.

He had responded, flatly, "Nah. I'm giving it up."

"Giving it up? You love your guitars. Your music."

"Not anymore."

"Because of Liv?"

His eyes morphed into that deep, reflective gaze he got when he went to a place in his mind and she couldn't reach him. "Nah."

"Talk to me. Please."

"I guess it's time to grow up and choose a responsible career path. Something stable and predictable."

"That makes sense," she had said. She had tried to convince herself that it was a reasonable decision, and it had nothing at all to do with Liv. But why couldn't he have a responsible career and continue to play his music on the side? Couldn't he just play guitar for the pure enjoyment of it?

Now out of the blue, Justin was playing that... that *thing*. And right after he saw Liv for the first time since they had broken up.

She could hear him playing through the door, muffled sounds of "Glycerine." Liv would never take him back. She had that handsome writer-boyfriend. Why would she leave him for Justin after what Justin did to her? She released a cloud of smoke from her nose and mouth, watched it circle around in the air.

She had always sort of known that Justin never loved her the way that he had loved Liv. But he did love her and had helped her when no one else did. He had been the most supportive person in her life, ever. That had been enough. But seeing him look at Liv that way, intense, almost helpless to take his eyes off her, made it impossible to ignore the fact that whatever he had felt for Liv never truly went away.

It made her sick to her stomach.

She would never let him go, regardless of his feelings. Regardless of Liv's feelings. No. She would never let him go. Ever.

29

People packed themselves into Olivia's parents' house. Food and drinks and conversation, laughter and recollections of fond memories of her mother and her life, filled the house. Exactly how her mother would have wanted.

It was the little things that people remembered the most. When people spoke of her mother, it wasn't necessarily some monumental event or accomplishment, it turned out to be the subtle, everyday things that mattered to people. Her mother's laughter, the way she could rattle off recipes from memory, how generous she was with her time, helping her students and friends and family, listening. "Your mother made the best banana bread," was a statement she heard from a handful of different people. "She could nurture a plant back from near death," Lori, her mother's college roommate said, squeezing a smile from her sad expression.

Olivia grinned when Lori said it, thinking about how many plants her mother had miraculously nursed back to health. There were so many little things that touched other people about her mother. Olivia relished hearing so many stories about her mom from her old friends.

Becka and C.J. and Ashlee came back to the house and stayed for an hour or so. She wondered where Justin and Petal were. It was better that they didn't come. At the same time, she found herself looking for him. She didn't ask Becka where they were, and Becka didn't bring them up.

Smith finally got her alone. "Justin and Petal?"

"Let's go for a walk outside. I need fresh air."

They went into the backyard and sat on a bench that her father had built next to her mother's rose bushes. "Remember I mentioned that I was going to a high school reunion?"

"Yeah."

"Well, I saw them there. It was awkward at first, but we talked." Olivia fought off a smile. "And it was good. I realized I wasn't angry anymore."

Smith raised her brow. "I see."

"What?"

"What else?"

"Nothing." Olivia said, unconvincingly.

Smith shot her a "gimme a break" look. "Come on. I know you."

Olivia took a deep breath. "We– we talked. Me and Justin. And I don't know, I feel something. I'm not sure what, but something. And… we kissed."

"Wow. I didn't expect that."

"Me neither."

"So, what now?"

"I dunno. It's all too much. Dealing with the past, my feelings. And now with my mother."

Smith nodded.

"How could I be in love with him after all this time? I couldn't. Right? It's just the residuals from our past. The old love lingering because he was my first. I mean, I don't even know him anymore. And he's married."

Smith contemplated. "He is married. That's true. But love is love. You loved Justin with your whole heart. I was there. I saw it. Some loves make sense, some don't. You have to ask yourself what you really want. If it's Justin, then you need to talk to him about it."

"And what? Break up his marriage? No way. I'm not a home-wrecker."

"I'm not suggesting that. I'm saying just talk to him. Be honest with yourself and with him."

"How can I be honest if I'm not sure what I'm feeling?"

"Do what you have to in order to figure it out."

"My mother told me to follow my heart, to take risks in love. She said I've been closed off."

"Good advice from Lily, as always." Smith smiled warmly.

"I don't know who I'm supposed to take the risk with. Is it Adam? Or is it Justin?"

"That's a tough one, Liv. And maybe now's not the best time to be trying to sort through a complicated love life."

"Now is the only time." Her eyes welled. "My mother got sick and died within a week. Time is an illusion. All we have is now." Tears streamed down her face. She placed her face in her palms. Her shoulders shook.

Smith took a tissue out of her bag, handed it to Olivia, then put her arm around her shoulders. "I can only imagine how hard this is for you. Maybe give yourself a week or so, then if you're still thinking about Justin, spend time with him. See how you feel. And I don't think you should feel guilty doing that just because he's married. I say that as a married woman. I say Petal meddled in your relations. You owe her nothing as a woman."

Olivia blew her nose. "But he did it too."

"Yes. But I truly believe he made a mistake. An awful one. But a mistake. Liv. That man called and called, and how many years was he writing emails and sending letters."

"I know," Olivia took a sharp breath. "He gave me those letters a few days ago. And we spoke about it. I never let him back in. Never gave him a chance. Now it may be too late. If I even want it."

Smith raised her brow again. "Liv. Sounds to me like you still love him."

"I don't know. I love Adam. I'm going to have a future with him. We have more in common, and he's never hurt me. It doesn't make any sense, Justin and me."

"It doesn't have to. Not everything can be reasoned through or philosophized. If you love him and he loves you and you want to be together, then it does make sense, even if you can't find some rational reason why you still love him."

"I have a lot to sort out."

"I'm here for you whenever you want to talk."

"We need to see each other more."

"We do."

Jones poked his head out the back door. "Is this a private talk?"

Smith squeezed Olivia across her back, pulling Olivia close to her.

"No. Smith was trying to convince me to take up running, as usual. We'll be right in."

"Now that you mention it. Running would help you."

"Remember that time that you got me out running and I fell in front of that group of lacrosse players?" Olivia smirked at the recollection.

"Haha! Yes. I have to say that was one of the most graceful falls ever. You definitely have a talent for it. And made quite an impression on the lacrosse players."

Olivia dried her eyes as they laughed and rejoined the crowd in the house.

Later that night after everyone left, an empty feeling permeated the house. The absence of her mother felt large, like a big gap that would never be filled in. Adam stayed the night. He would return to the city the following afternoon.

"I think I'm going to stay here with my dad for a few weeks. Since I have the whole semester off. He may need help and I hate to think of him all alone in this big house."

"Good idea. And, whenever you're ready to come back into the city, we'll make the arrangements for your move. I know you're going through a lot of difficult emotions right now. I want to take care of you."

She looked up at him. "I'm all over the place emotionally."

As she lay with him in bed that night she felt the security and stability of his presence. Moving in with Adam was the right decision. He was her future.

Adam left early the next morning to go home and write. The wind blew in strong bursts, sending a squall of howls through the house. It felt even more vacant than it had the day before.

Olivia smelled the rich aroma of coffee as she ambled toward the kitchen. Abbee had already made a pot. Heaviness washed over her as she remembered the smell of morning coffee from her childhood and her mother cooking breakfast.

Now it was Abbee in the kitchen, coffee and toast, a bowl of cut-up fruit. Her brown hair was pulled up in a high ponytail, exposing the wear on her face. "Morning. Want some toast?"

"Not yet." Even though Abbee needled at her sometimes, Olivia was glad she decided to stay for the week too.

Her dad spoke on the phone with Aunt Betsey. She wanted to go through Lily's belongings, but her father wanted to wait. "It's too soon," Gregg said. "We need the reality to settle in first. Maybe next week. Yes, Liv will still be here next week. I'm not sure about Abbee, but she can come when we decide to do it."

A long pause as he listened to whatever Aunt Betsey said. Then, "I'm sorry, Bets. I know she was your sister and this is hard for all of us. But I just can't this week. OK?" His "OK" had a forcefulness that was uncharacteristic of her father's usual docile nature. Olivia and Abbee shared a sad, knowing look.

Aunt Betsey conceded. Gregg thanked her and hung up. "It's a cold morning." He said.

"Yeah."

"I'm going to the gym. You girls want to come?"

They both shook their heads.

"An old friend of mine, Karl, asked us to go to lunch with him. That sound OK for you girls?"

They both nodded.

The time ticked by slowly that day and the next one. Abbee and she played at lot of gin rummy and watched too much television. Other than lunch with their dad's friend and grocery shopping, they stayed home and in their pajamas. Gregg tried to keep himself busy. He called old friends, fixed loose doorknobs, painted a wall in the living room that didn't need painting; they all acted like it did.

She hadn't brought up the move into Adam's or her confused feelings about Justin. But then Abbee asked, "Did you talk to Justin at the funeral?"

"A little."

"Were you OK that Petal came?"

"Yeah. I guess."

"I know you still have feelings for him. It must be hard seeing them together," she said, the compassion in her voice catching Olivia off guard.

Olivia couldn't talk about it. She tried to ignore the pesky feelings about Justin that kept intruding into her thoughts, whirling around in a complex mess with her intention to move forward with Adam.

"It's alright. It was a long time ago. I'm happy with Adam."

Abbee gave her the one arched eyebrow look, but let it go.

Thankfully.

But not talking about Justin and not thinking about Justin were two totally different things. She kept looking at her phone, hoping he called. She had read through two more of the letters, but it was too much: the loss, her lack of any acceptance of his desperate attempts to discuss what had happened, her own responsibility in the chain of events. What on earth could she ever have been thinking? She had loved him more than anything and still, she wouldn't even listen. Even after four then five years had passed, she still had been so stubborn. And for what? In the end, it worked against her.

She thought about her mother's comment that her pride was to blame. Was she still allowing her pride to get in the way? Was she denying her true feeling because Justin was married? Because he had hurt her?

Feeling chilled, she went upstairs to grab a sweater. When she put the sweater on that she had worn the night she and Justin kissed, it still held the faintest scent of him. She held it up to her face and took a light sniff. Maybe she should call him?

She lay on the bed feeling wistful. She longed for a time when her mother was alive and well, when she was younger, when she thought Justin and she would be together forever. Her life had seemed organized and made sense back then. How could life become more confusing as she got older? Wasn't it supposed to make more sense?

She dozed off into a light sleep and was awakened by the phone. When she looked at the phone and saw Adam calling, she admitted to herself that she wished it had been Justin. "Hi." She answered.

"Hi, babe. How's your day."

"Same. Abbee and I hit the rock bottom of afternoon television today. We watched *Days of Our Lives*. We tried to play Scrabble, but I just can't. It reminds me too much of her."

"I noticed you hadn't taken your turn in our game either. It's going to take time."

"I know."

"I'll come out tonight and stay."

"I miss you. But come out on the weekend instead."

"What is it?"

"I just want to be with Abbee and my dad." Her words quivered.

"Is there something wrong, Liv?"

"I'm just tired."

"Alright." He said, hesitantly. "I'll come Friday." He then recommended a few books to her for healing and grief. He told her a funny story about Tucker getting locked in the laundry room. "Cats. They love to go where they're not supposed to."

When they hung up, she stared at the ceiling thinking that she had lied to him. She asked him not to come because she wanted to see Justin. She scrolled through her phone and stared at Justin's number. Smith was right, if she was ever going to figure this out, she needed to see him. She called.

"Heeey," he answered.

She felt her face flush. "Hi."

"How are you? I've been thinking about you."

"I'm hanging in there. So, you wanna go for a walk along the river or something this week?"

"What are you doing now?"

"Nothing."

"How 'bout I pick you up? We can go for a milkshake."

A milkshake. Justin and she used to go to a place on Bergenline Avenue that had the best milkshakes. They would sit there for hours, talking, sharing a chocolate shake.

"A milkshake? Where?"

"I know a place."

"Come get me."

"I'll leave now."

They sat at the counter of an old-fashioned ice-cream shop off 9W, both sipping chocolate shakes. Olivia beamed as she swallowed a cold, creamy sip. "Where did you find this place?"

"I did some work for the owner."

"Ah." She looked around and noticed some wood pieces carved with meticulous details. Two rocking chairs off in a corner, a hand-carved table between the them, a stack of newspapers and magazines on top. The legs of the table had intricate swirly designs. Behind them, she noticed two big, wood-carved tables, Baroque-style etchings on the legs. She went over to look more closely. "This is your–"

"Yes."

"Wow. You're very talented. Who knew you could do all that with a piece of wood."

He looked at her.

"What is it?" She tilted her head.

"Nothing."

"Jus. C'mon."

"You used to always say things like that to me."

She smiled.

"I'm sorry about the funeral."

She gave him a curious look.

"That I came with Petal. Honestly, I didn't know what the right thing to do was. Go with Petal or not go at all. I really wanted to be there for you. And pay my respects to your mom."

"It's fine. I'm glad you were there."

"How's it been? The last few days? I wanted to call sooner."

"It's been hard. It will be hard for awhile."

"Can I do anything?"

"I don't think so."

"I wish things were… easier."

"Me too." They shared a heavy look. "So, have you picked up the guitar again?"

He nodded. "I've been practicing."

"That makes me happy."

"It felt great. Once my fingers got warmed up, it came back quickly."

"You know. You underestimate your artistic ability. Look at what you've done here. With wood. For your music and songwriting, it's not too late, you know."

He gave her a pointed look. "It's not too late?"

Their eyes met. "It's not too late to pursue your music, your songwriting. I really think you have something special."

"You always made me feel like I was capable of more than I thought."

"I know. I read that in one of your letters."

"You read them?"

"Not all of them. I will. It's just been hard with my mom."

He put his hand over hers. "I loved her. You had the best mom."

She smiled sadly and nodded. His hand felt warm over hers and she wanted him to pull her close. The intensity between them unnerved her. As good as it felt to be with Justin, it was difficult too.

"Let's go." She said.

"Yeah." He nodded, seeming disappointed. He looked like he had a lot on his mind, but said, "OK."

They exchanged no words the entire ride back to her father's house.

Justin tapped his fingers on the steering wheel as he drove. She watched his long fingers. Her eyes moved across his dark hair, wandering down to his broad shoulders, then along his legs. A mix of emotions washed over her. Subtle at first, but with each mile closer to her dad's, they became more powerful and messier. She wanted to touch him, kiss him, run her fingers through his hair. She wanted him so badly, it hurt. She felt furious with him, too. Furious that he didn't tell her the difficulties he was having in the relationship. Furious that he slept with Petal in a moment of weakness. Furious that he still loved her. Furious at herself for wanting him. Furious at herself for not listening to him when he tried to explain.

"You alright?"

"Fine."

But the heaviness swelled in the car. When they reached her dad's, she hurried to get out without even saying goodbye. He got out on his side. "Liv." He stood, arms out, palms up. "What is it? C'mere."

When he called her name and it echoed in the air, she felt the familiarity, the way she used to beam when Justin said her name. She went toward him and yelled. "Why. WHY didn't you talk to me after we got engaged? We told each other everything. If you only had told me how you felt, we could have worked it out. How does sleeping with — fucking — my best friend fix our problems?"

"You're right. I didn't know. I didn't understand it until afterward. I was so afraid of how much I loved you."

"BULLSHIT. Just bullshit." She couldn't believe the ferocity of her voice as it came out. She was overcome with years of bottled-up emotions. "If you loved me that much, you would have talked to me. I felt closer to you than anyone. ANYONE. And you didn't feel close enough to me to tell me how you really felt? We could have worked it out."

"It wasn't like that. I didn't totally understand it when it was happening. If I did, I would have told you. Now I know that I was afraid. Afraid that I wasn't strong enough for you. Afraid that if I revealed my weaknesses,

I would lose you forever. Losing you was about the worst thing I could imagine. And in the end, I fucked up so badly that I *did* lose you. Being afraid was the real weakness. I will regret that for the rest of my life. I love you. I loved you every day since I first met you. No matter what, that will never change."

His admission caught her off-guard. It diffused her rage. She could see the passion, the anguish, the wanting, the love, all of it in his eyes as he said with undeniable vehemence that he would never stop loving her. And as she looked into his eyes, she knew that she would never stop loving him either.

And it hurt to love him.

"I have to go." She turned, tears streaming down her cheeks. The wind blew, pushing thick strands of her hair across her face.

"Liv."

One word, three letters. Don't look at him. Don't.

"No." She said without turning.

"Liv."

Her lips quivered. Feeling helpless over her impulses, she turned and went toward him. She slapped his cheek and stared into his eyes. Justin pulled her close. She tried to wrestle out of his embrace, but even while squirming she knew she would give in. Quickly, she loosened the tension in her body and let him hold her. Their lips merged in a frantic kiss. Justin had his back against the car and she pushed into him, feeling his chest against hers. She kissed him passionately. She pulled him as close as she could. He wrapped his arms around her back, holding her so tight it almost hurt.

Desire overwhelmed her; volatile and precarious, and she felt helpless to stop it.

"Take me somewhere." She whispered between kisses. "Now."

He grabbed her face, softly, looking at her with helpless abandon. "You sure? Maybe we should talk–"

"Shhh." She placed a finger over his lips. "Take me somewhere."

He kissed her. "OK."

As they drove toward the Marriott, the intimacy between them grew, filling the empty space in the car, connecting them with an invisible bond. They didn't talk. It was a time of desperate anticipation that they didn't want to spoil with words. It was one of the things she could never find with anyone else. She could be with Justin without uttering a word, and feel the intimacy, the love, the connection. In the car, it came back to her. She knew him in a way that she had never known anyone else. A wordless way. And he knew her similarly.

She ignored the implication of the hotel room: Justin being a married man. Right then, he was the man who used to be the boy who she had given her heart to. Selfishly, she didn't care who she hurt. She disregarded Petal. Worse, she disregarded Adam. She felt swept away. It was impetuous and emotionally dangerous and she didn't care.

It was Justin and her, and nothing else and no one else.

When they opened the door to the room, the kissing began again. Slower kisses accompanied by a burning exploration of each other's bodies. Justin guided her toward the bed where they fell into each other's arms. "Take my shirt off," she begged him.

He pulled her shirt over her head, removed her bra and kissed her breasts. She pulled his shirt off, so she could feel his bare chest against hers. She wanted to feel him as close as possible.

When they finally laid naked and he entered her, she knew she loved him as much as she always had, maybe more. She dug her fingernails into his back as he penetrated her, pushing back and forth, going deeper and deeper. Allowing herself to finally feel the intensity of her love for him, she let him take her completely. The same way he used to.

30

Olivia rested her head in the crook of Justin's neck after they made love. Lying with him, she felt as if she had found the missing piece to a puzzle she had been trying to solve for years.

"I love you," he whispered in her ear.

"I know."

"You don't have to say it back."

"I can't."

He kissed her head. "I'm just glad you're here with me."

"Me too." The warmth of his breath danced along her cheek in a delicate ballet, echoing so many intimate memories. *I love you, Justin,* she thought, but couldn't say it. She meant it too much to let it go. As their bodies rested against one another, perfectly snug, two parts of one whole, she knew that Justin knew that she still loved him. She pushed her breasts into him and kissed him. He pulled her close, making love to her again.

Night settled in, turning the room dark except for the dim light from a small lamp. When she looked at the time, it was 10:00. Her sister had called, leaving a concerned "Where are you?" message. Adam had texted that he went to a movie. Looking at his message made the reality of what she was doing impossible to deny.

Justin read it on her face. "Your boyfriend?"

She nodded. "This is very messy."

"I know."

"I should tell you, I told him I would move in with him." They lay face-to-face, bodies together under the comforter.

Justin propped his head up on his arm. "Do you love him?"

"I think so. *This* is confusing me."

"I don't want to cause you any more pain. Especially right now while your grieving."

"Maybe the pain was already there, and I have been running from it all these years."

He brushed wisps of her hair away from her face. "You love me too. I can read it on your face."

"Yes," she admitted in a whisper, "but it's complicated with you. It's easy with Adam. It's not just that you hurt me, you're married. And until you are unattached, I can't consider this as anything serious. Love alone isn't enough."

JACQUELINE SIMON GUNN

He hooked strands of her hair behind her ear. "I – I want to tell you something."

"OK."

"I have been trying to separate from Petal on and off for many years."

"Why didn't you say anything?"

He contemplated. "I didn't want to make it your problem. It's mine. Honestly, I was hoping to have separated before I told you."

"What's keeping you from leaving her?"

He winced. "It's… it's been. He sighed. "I feel guilty that I made a commitment that I want to back out of. My parents are married almost forty years. I always believed that when you married someone, it was for better or worse. But I can't do it anymore. Seeing you, remembering what we shared, made me realize that I need to do this."

"You can't leave her for me. You need to do it for yourself."

"I know that. I'm telling you because I love you. If there is a possibility of a second chance for us, I don't want to lose it."

"Jus." She touched his face and looked at him admiringly. "Even if you leave her, I can't guarantee that I will be able to go back to how it was."

"Because I hurt you?"

She contemplated. "Yes. And I'm involved with someone else. I made a commitment to him."

"But what we have is once in a lifetime. Even after all this time, I know you feel it. The love is exactly the same."

"We need to think and not just act on our feelings."

He took a heavy breath. "You're right."

"Let's take it one step at a time."

"When are you going back into the city? When are you moving in with him?"

"I'm not sure. I want to see how my dad's doing. But soon. Couple weeks."

"Can we see each other again?"

"I'd like that."

They reminisced about her mother on the drive back to her father's house: the occasions when her mother used her wooden spoon for a microphone while she sang, the high notes she could reach, the way she folded in half when she laughed, the time she tripped over something in the yard and Justin tried to stop her from falling and the two collapsed together. "Oh, my gosh, yes, I remember that." Olivia laughed, tears of joy welling in her eyes.

"Your mother was the best. I always felt like she understood me better than my own parents. She had a quiet way about her, but you could tell that she felt things deeply. She said something to me that last night I saw her."

Olivia looked at him with eager eyes, relishing every opportunity to hear stories about her mother.

"She told me that she always felt like she knew me better than she actually did. The same way I felt about her, like she understood me. She could see how much I loved you, and how scared I was to let you down after our engagement. She thought of talking with me. Maybe she could have helped me understand what I was going through. The fears I had. After what happened, she said she wished she would have said something."

Olivia contemplated. "I wonder why she didn't tell me that." She looked down at her fingers. "Actually, maybe she did, and I refused to listen." She sighed.

"This isn't your fault. It's mine."

"It's both of ours. It's not just that though, I really miss her. It comes in waves, but it's there all the time. I don't know that I'll ever feel whole again."

"A part of you will always be missing. But that doesn't mean you won't go on living. Right?"

"I promised her I would. And I will."

"Remember forever and one day?" He pulled into a parking spot across the street from her dad's and looked at her.

"Of course. I would never forget that. Those were our special words for each other. For our love."

"Forever isn't a time; it's a place."

"You always said that. Gosh. I remember you singing about it. Singing to me." She smiled warmly at a memory of Justin singing those lines.

"Remember when I told you that the words *forever and one day* came to me from out of nowhere one day while I thought of you. You know, the way words and poems and lyrics would just pop into my head."

"Of course." Feeling the intimacy between them, she weaved her fingers through his.

"I've thought a lot about it over the years. We can't understand anything eternal if we think in terms of time, because time has limits. Beginnings and endings. Forever crosses time and physical space; it's a place where we go when we no longer experience the limitation."

"I've thought about that too. I even wrote a paper in graduate school about the way our own thinking limits our understanding of anything beyond beginnings and endings."

"Love is limitless. I have felt you in my heart, even when it hurt like fucking hell. You have been with me, even when you were gone because *I love you*. And when we love someone we share a place. Your mother is with you right now and always will be, even if you can't see her physical body. Your love created a shared place, your *forever and one day* with her."

She contemplated. "I do feel her. I even feel her in my body, the parts of me that are like her. And I feel her love all around me." She squeezed his hand. "Jus?"

"Yeah."

"I've missed our conversations."

"Me too."

"You have been with me over the years too." She shook her head. "I tried to deny it, but you were." He looked at her with that wild abandon in his eyes, the love.

"I had a nice time." She said.

"Me too. I'll call you."

She kissed him one last time, and got out.

Abbee and her dad were in the living room watching a movie when she walked in the house.

"You missed dinner." Abbee snipped. "You didn't even call or text. We were worried."

Olivia looked at her dad, who said, "We were a little concerned because it's so unlike you to disappear."

"I'm sorry. I lost track of time."

"Where were you?" Abbee raised a suspicious eyebrow.

"Um. I was… with Smith. She picked me up and we went for coffee."

"Doesn't Smith live in Paramus? She drove awfully far for a cup of coffee."

"Jeez. It's not that far."

"Come watch with us, honey."

"I'm going to make some popcorn. You want some?" Olivia asked.

"Sure." Her dad said.

"I'll help you." Abbee followed her into the kitchen. "You were with Justin, weren't you?"

"Whaaat? Where would you get that from?"

"It's written all over your face."

"How so?"

"You look flushed and dazed and happy."

"Fine. But I don't want to talk about it."

"You still love him. I knew it."

"I– I do, but he's still married. Besides, I told Adam that I'm moving in with him. Don't say anything to dad yet. I'll tell him next week."

"Moving in with Adam? Riiight. Didn't you just fuck Justin?"

"Abbee!"

Abbee gave her a shrewd look.

"We were intimate. Yes."

"If you could have seen your face when you said that. All lit up. The only time you ever light up like that is when it's about Justin. That's how I knew when you walked in."

"I don't know what I'm doing. I'm afraid I may fuck up with Adam, fuck up my whole life."

Abbee nodded. "I have always liked Justin, you know that. But right now, aren't you doing to Adam what Justin did to you?"

Olivia sat and folded her hands between her knees. "I know. I'm a terrible person. A hypocrite. And yet, I feel like I can't stop myself. I'm so drawn to Justin. I just don't know if it's for the right reasons. I have a more mature connection with Adam."

"Liv. I have to say this." She paused. "Adam resembles Justin."

"What? Did mom tell you that?"

"We both thought it. Dad said it too."

"They look nothing alike."

"They do, Liv. But even more than physical features, their mannerisms are similar. They hold their shoulders exactly the same. They both have an edge. Both are reserved, but you can see the depth in their eyes. They even have a similar gleam in their eyes when they smile."

"*Abbee*, that is the most insane thing I have heard in a while."

Abbee tilted her head. "I don't know why you can't see it. Whatever you do, Liv, be careful. I don't want to see you hurt."

"If I've learned anything, it's that no matter what, we can't protect ourselves from being hurt when we allow ourselves to love. We loved mom, and we are in pain now because of it. It's the price we pay for loving." Her lips quivered as she fought off a frown. "I miss her."

"Me too." Abbee hugged her.

Justin watched Liv walk up the stairs to her dad's house and open the door; she turned and waved before she disappeared inside, her red mane like a halo framing her face. As soon as she was gone from sight, he wanted to see her again. He could look at Liv all day. She was the most exquisite woman he had ever seen.

They had just made love for the first time in seventeen years. He almost couldn't believe it. All those years separated from her, all the pain he had endured after losing her, the guilt, the regret, the lost time, none of that matter once she was in his arms.

Her skin felt soft to his fingers. Liv was sensual. He could see his affect on her, in her eyes, the way her body quivered when he touched her, the sounds of pleasure she whispered in his ear. Her naked body danced under his fingertips, more honest than any words.

Liv had always had a gorgeous body and still did: rounded hips, full breasts, slender, but not too thin. She had this little bit of extra skin around her lower abdomen that used to bother her when they were younger. It was nothing really. And he loved that part of her body. It was only noticeable when she was naked, which made it special, a private part of her only he knew. When he had slipped her pants off that night, he saw the spot immediately. Like no time had passed, Liv's body looked almost the same, a little curvier. He kissed her stomach over and over. He missed that spot. And every other inch of her.

He drove away from the house. The car seemed to *putt-putt*, slowly, regretfully, matching his mood. When he turned off the quiet street and hit River Road he pushed the gas, feeling the rush of the acceleration. He opened his window all the way to feel the cool autumn air rush into the car. He felt a wave of adrenalin. A woman like Liv could do that: make you feel high, on top of the world, and like anything was possible.

That's what being alive was all about.

His thoughts raced, playing back the evening's events. He thought of the moment he penetrated her, the feeling of being close to her in that way. He had missed that. He thought about how much he enjoyed watching her talk, the depth of her expressiveness, the way her big, brown eyes held that intensity, especially when she looked at him. He thought about their unspoken understanding. Liv could still read him, same as she had always been able to.

She had said, "I know what it means when you get that look," while they lay face-to-face after they had made love.

He had responded teasingly. "Really?"

"I know all of your looks, Jus." She had smiled warmly. "This one means that you didn't quite get what I was saying. I know sometimes my thoughts are dense. Sometimes I'm not even sure what I'm saying."

He had felt embarrassed, but didn't say.

"Don't be embarrassed. It's cute. I'll repeat it. It helps me flush out my own thoughts to go over it again."

"I could listen to you all day."

Her eyes had gleamed, and she kissed him. He had blown gently in her ear and made love to her again.

With Liv, it wasn't two bodies engaging in physical intimacy. It was a deep and powerful emotional connection. She opened herself up, allowed him to be absorbed deep inside of her, to penetrate her, closing any gaps between them.

Regret began to creep into his consciousness, usurping some of his excitement. Regret was one of the worst emotions. Regret meant that the pain was the person's own fault. That if they hadn't done something that couldn't be undone or they didn't do something they wished they would have, there would be no pain. Justin had many regrets. And now, he had done something else that he had promised himself he wouldn't do: He had slept with Liv before he had been honest with Petal.

He had broached the topic again with Petal the previous evening. As usual, his words felt clumsy because he didn't quite know how to express what he wanted. "Um. So. Um. Let's talk."

Petal's blue eyes had turned anguished. "Don't say it. Do. Not. Say. It. Pleeezzze."

"You're not happy either."

"I *am*. You are the only thing that makes me happy. I have no one without you. Pleeezzze." She had grabbed at his arms to hug her.

He had wrapped his arms around her. "We can't go on like this. Neither one of us are happy. You aren't getting what you need from me. I don't know what else to do."

"All I want from you is *you*. I want you to give me yourself. To stop holding back."

"I'm giving everything I can. See. This is what I mean. I want to give you what you want, and I've tried, but it's not enough. You have been unhappy with me because you have needs I'm not meeting. And I'm sorry for that."

Tears had flown out of Petal's eyes. "Justin. Please. I don't know what you're talking about. You are the most important person in my life. Sometimes I just feel that you have more to give and I want it. I want you to give me everything you have. You can't leave. Ten years of marriage and you want to throw that away? What the fuck? Whatever you're going through we'll work it out." A look of desperation had splayed across her face.

He had hugged her and whispered. "Calm down. OK." As he held her, he knew he was going to have to be firmer, but in the moment her desperation worried him.

The thought of Liv with her boyfriend and now taking the step to move in with him sent panic coursing through him. But he could see it in Liv's eyes, her desire to be with him, not her boyfriend. Liv needed him to convince her that he could be the man she needed. And not with his words, with his actions.

The fact that she even still loved him and admitted it was a miracle.

He arrived home before Petal got off of work. He quickly took a shower, tossed some bread crumbs on a plate and put it in the sink. He erased the text exchanges between Liv and him. By the time Petal walked in the door, he had his headphones on and was carving designs into the legs of a table in the den.

"You're still working?" She stood in the doorway, taking her arms out of her coat.

"Nah. This is a gift for my mother. It's her birthday next week. Remember?"

"Right. It looks nice." She said without even really looking. "You wanna go for a drink?"

"It's after 11:00."

"So? You act like we're old or something."

"I have an early client meeting."

"Well, I need a drink after the stress of work. You want one?"

"Nah. I'm good."

She inspected him from the doorway. "What is it?"

"What do you mean?" He tried to sound nonchalant.

"You seem different."

"How so?"

"I dunno. Different."

"I'm the same as I always am." He said without looking up. If she saw his eyes, she'd know he lied. He didn't want to start the conversation again this late in the evening, especially when she was exhausted from work and drinking. It made her less reasonable.

Within an hour, Petal was buzzed and sloppy. She pulled at his shorts, initiating sex.

"Not now, you're drunk. You know I hate when you're drunk."

Her face turned red. "It's always on your terms. I'm so fucking sick of that. It's like I don't even know who you are anymore. What man turns down sex? You can be such a dick."

"You're a mean drunk. Go to sleep."

"I'm sorry. I didn't mean it. C'mere." She pulled him down onto the bed. "Come lay with me. Please."

"I'll be in in a few."

"No, now. I need you."

"Let me brush my teeth. I'll be right in."

She huffed. "OK."

He went into the bathroom and threw water over his face. Looking at his reflection in the mirror, he tried to convince himself that he was doing the right thing by leaving Petal.

When he went back into the bedroom, she was breathing heavily. Thinking she was asleep, he slipped under the covers, carefully, trying not to wake her. As soon as he settled in, she wrapped her body around his. He spent the night restless in her embrace, trying to quell his angst.

You will wait for the right moment and then be firm, he promised himself.

31

Justin and Olivia spent time together the next day and the day after that. Petal's hospital schedule made it easy for him to slip out in the early evening hours after he finished work. By the following week, Olivia was balancing Justin and Adam, teetering a line of uncertainty that she felt helpless to stop. When she talked or spent time with Adam, his steadfast nature, his ambitions, their similar intellectual curiosities, being with him made sense. She would think: *Moving in with Adam is the right decision. Absolutely.*

Then she would hang out with Justin and feel this unspoken closeness, the pull toward him that words failed to describe. Justin touched the deepest part of who she was. Her heart felt connected to him and she wondered if she could ever really let go of him. Or if she wanted to.

The following Thursday, the weather was temperate, almost summerlike. Justin suggested they go to Hudson

County Park like they used to. A balmy breeze stroked the leaves of the colorful autumn trees, making the foliage dance in an easy to-and-fro. They stayed on the interior paths, avoiding spots where traffic passed in case someone they knew drove by. Until Justin officially separated from Petal, they needed to be careful.

Justin brought his acoustic and a bottle of red wine. They parked themselves behind the lake, right on the edge of a short dirt trail. Trees were dense in that area; they found a nook where they thought they had privacy.

Justin and she used to go to the park and drink beer or wine when they were together, sometimes with the gang, but a lot of times just the two of them. He laid down a thin blanket and uncorked the wine, poured some into two paper cups. "Cheers." They smiled easily at each other, clicking their cups together. A groundhog scurried out of a burrow, looked at them and then waddled off into the thick of the trees.

"I always loved it here," Olivia said, admiring the surroundings.

"I know. We had a lot of good times here."

"Sitting here it seems like yesterday, but it was a long time ago. So much has happened since then."

"I know." They sat side-by-side, legs spilling out in front of them. He placed his hand on hers. "You thinking about your mom?"

"I'm always thinking about my mom. Even when I'm not thinking about her, she's there in the periphery of my thoughts."

He put his arm around her, and she rested her head on his shoulder. They sat quietly for a few moments, sipping wine, each in a private reverie.

Olivia broke the stillness. "Play something for me."

"Whadaya wanna hear?"

"Surprise me."

Justin playing the guitar used to be one of her favorite things to hear. And as soon as he rested the acoustic on his knee and began strumming, she felt giddy. That edge he possessed, which was sexy given that she knew underneath he was a gentle person, radiated prominently when he played. She gazed at him as he strummed and felt herself smile.

He played "Black Balloon," by Goo Goo Dolls, then "Good Riddance," by Green Day. He sang. Olivia swayed, enjoying the feeling of him and his music all around her. "Come on. Sing with me."

"I'm awful. You know that."

He laughed. "No, you're not. Besides, that never stopped you before. Don't be shy." His eyes glistened.

"Play 'Wonderwall.'"

"Only if you sing."

She nodded.

He started the song. Olivia sang softly at first. As the song went on, she felt the freeness of the moment, Justin strumming as they sang under the twilight in the park. They sang louder and to each other, smiling. She hadn't remembered how good it felt to let herself go, to not be self-conscious, to be in the moment. Justin had been the one who was good at that. She had been the planner, always two steps ahead. And then it hit her: Justin had offered a side of life that didn't come naturally to her.

As much as she focused heavily on their futures, Justin was able to enjoy the moment, to be spontaneous. She bellowed that song, louder and louder, remembering a side of her that had disappeared long ago. A feeling of fullness enveloped her. Justin put the guitar down after the song finished, emotions swirling between them. He pulled her close and they made love under the trees.

"We never did that before." He said, when they lay staring up at the sky afterward.

"I don't know why not." She smiled.

After that night, it became nearly impossible not to think about Justin all the time. Still, she remained torn, because she had made a commitment to Adam and she did love him. In reality, Adam was better for her in the long term. At least that's what she tried to tell herself.

Adam came over on the weekend. He asked a few times, "Everything alright? You seem lost or distant."

"I'm just tired from everything, you know."

"Right. Of course." He said each time, but he held a look of uncertainty in his eyes. Adam was perceptive. How long was she really going to be able to pull this off? And what on earth was she doing anyway?

"So, you're coming back next week?" He asked before he left on Sunday.

"Or the week after. Let me see how it goes."

"Alright." He said, looking a bit disappointed.

Within only a couple of weeks, a rhythm had developed between Liv and Justin. After he left work, they would go for something to eat. They took long walks along the river or in Hudson County Park. They went for long drives, admiring the autumn foliage. They spent time at the Marriott. The more time they spent together, the more he felt an unspoken commitment burgeoning. But when he had asked Liv, she had said that she still planned to move in with her boyfriend. Again, she emphasized that she couldn't consider him as any sort of long-term possibility until he left his marriage.

"I feel it though. Us. I know you do too."

"What we feel and what we do about it are two different things."

"How can you fight this?"

"I'm not fighting it, Jus. I'm not capable of fighting it. I'm here with you. But I'm not going to change my life until you make changes to yours."

"I will. I plan to tell her this weekend."

Liv nodded, said nothing.

That weekend, he tried to tell Petal, but his words wouldn't come. All weekend, he played the conversation over and over in his head. But when he looked into her eyes, he felt so guilty because no matter how he sliced it, he had married her out of weakness. Now he would be hurting her as a result of his mistake. *How do you tell someone you care about that you want to break the promise you've made?*

Sunday night they went out to dinner. "You're distracted," Petal said, sipping her third martini.

He hoped to get her home before she started slurring. He had planned to tell her that evening, but he knew better than to do it when she was drunk. "So, I thought I'd call Liv next week. See if she wants to get together." She said, antagonistically.

"Oh." He went to say more, but stopped himself. This conversation would lead nowhere good.

"You want to see her too, don't you? Or maybe you already have." She said it like she knew something; he felt a flash of warmth.

"Let's get the check and go home and talk about this."

"*This.*" She raised her voice. "*This.* So, there is something to talk about? I knew it. You saw her. Becka and C.J. said it. I saw the way you two ogled each other at the funeral. You must think I'm a real idiot to miss that. And you've been different since then. More distant. And happier! Happier because of *her*. How could you?"

"It's complicated. Please. Lower your voice. I want us to talk. Privately." He scooted his chair over and placed his hand on her arm. "I care about you."

"Care about me? I thought you loved me. You fuck. I'm the one who stuck by you no matter what. Not her. She's selfish. Liv only cares about Liv. Have you forgotten that?"

"Petal. Please. I do love you." He hailed the waiter for the check.

"I want another drink. I'm not ready to leave yet."

"You've had enough. We can't talk if you're wasted."

"Fuck you." She said to Justin, then hollered toward the waiter, "I'll have another. The same."

A few people looked toward them.

Petal's blue eyes looked wild when she said, "If you have something to say, say it."

"One minute." He got up, went to the waiter, apologized and paid the bill. He went back to the table and reached for Petal's hand. "Let's go."

She got up with a furious look in her eyes, pulling her purse from the chair with a violent tug.

Justin drove; Petal punched his shoulder a few times. "Say what you have to say, you fuck?"

"Stop it. I'm driving. We're going to have an accident. Wait 'til we get home."

When he parked, Petal looked livid. "So, talk. *Justin.*"

"Let's go inside."

"No. Not until you say what you have to."

He took a deep breath. "I'm leaving. And I mean it this time."

Her jaw tightened. "No. You. Are. Not."

"I know you haven't been happy for a long time. I can't give you want you want. What you deserve."

"You're not happy because you still love HER! Just fucking say it. I want to hear you fucking say it."

His eyes looked heavy as he looked deep into hers. "I'm so sorry. I tried as hard as I could to make this work between us. To give you the love you wanted and deserved. I have been weak and selfish. But this isn't about her. It's about us."

"You never loved me."

"I do love you. We just… we're always fighting. We don't work together."

"Because of HER."

"I don't know what to say."

"You love her more. Always did."

"This isn't about *her*! It's about us. I'm not leaving for her. I'm leaving because I finally realized that this is not good for either of us. I wanted it to be. But it's not."

She looked at him, her face bright red. "So, you've been with her. TELL ME."

"I have spent a little time with her. But it's not about her. It's about us."

"You slept with her?"

"No."

"I'm not letting you go, you fucking dick. I am never letting you go. I waited for you and waited for you. I earned the right to have you love me. And you made a commitment to do that."

"I know. And I'm sorry to break that promise."

"You're not breaking it, because I'm not letting you go." Tears gushed out of her eyes and she pounded his chest with her fists. "You understand. You aren't leaving me."

He tried to grab her fists and pull her tight and soothe her.

She kept flailing. "I hate you." She punched his arm.

He grabbed her hand. "Stop hitting me."

She shot him a long, furious look, then lit a cigarette.

He rolled down his window.

She blew smoke in his face. "You can't leave me."

He waved the smoke away and looked at her, his face long.

She rolled down her window and puffed smoked out. "I can love you better."

He took a heavy breath. "It's nothing you did. I promise. It's not you."

"Can we talk more upstairs? Please. Pleeeeze."

"Why?"

"Because we have been married for ten years and I think you owe me more than a brief discussion in our car."

"Don't say that. We have been talking about this for years."

"Pleeeeze." She pulled at his arm.

He stared at her with a look of confusion and consternation.

"Pleeeze."

"Alright."

As soon as they got upstairs, Petal cracked a beer open. She drank and cried, vacillating between telling him she hated him and begging him to stay. She flung a few beer bottles across the apartment; one hit his arm before shattering against the wall, leaving shards of glass all over the living room. Finally, she wore herself out, passing out on the bed with a beer bottle in her hand.

He lay wide awake on the couch the whole night. He would pack some of his things tomorrow in the late afternoon, after she left for work. He would stay at his sister's until he got an apartment.

At 5 a.m. the next morning, he looked for paper to leave her a note. She came up behind him, "Can we work this out?"

"I don't think so," he said softly. "But I want you to be OK. You mean a lot to me."

"Maybe I can change your mind."

He looked her right in the eyes. "No."

"You know you never told me what you were thinking. I feel like this might be the first time you have ever been honest and open with me. Do you have any idea how that feels?"

"I know I can be closed off. And I'm sorry that's hurt you. But it's another reason this isn't right. I need to go to work. I'm going to come back while you're at work to get my stuff? Is that OK?"

She gave him a hard, anguished look. "None of this is OK. *Justin.* But you were always the one making the rules. I'm tired of trying." She threw herself on the couch. "You will regret this. Liv's never gonna be with you. Evah."

He looked at her once more, said, "Bye," as he left. A wave of relief washed over him as soon as he walked out the door.

That night, Liv and he walked through Hudson County Park holding hands. "I told her."

She stopped walking and looked at him. "You did?"

"Yes. She didn't take it too well. But I think she'll be OK."

"She's got no choice."

"Yeah, 'cept she's not strong like you. It's one of the things that has made it hard to leave."

"Sometimes, the right things are also the hardest things."

"True. But no great things come easy, in my opinion." He looked at her and smiled.

She elbowed him. "You know, I have to be honest. Part of me doesn't feel bad for her at all. I know this wasn't all her fault, but if she wasn't willing to sleep with her best friend's fiancé, this might never have happened."

He squeezed her hand. "Can I change the subject?"

"That's a good idea."

"Where do we go from here?"

She searched his face. "I don't know, Jus. I– I, need time."

"You're afraid."

"Of course, I'm afraid. You hurt me. It's hard *not* to be afraid."

He looked deep into her eyes. "Maybe you were always afraid."

She crossed her arms. "Your fears were the ones that caused this whole mess to happen."

"I *was* afraid. I was a foolish, insecure boy totally in love with a strong woman. And it caused me to fuck up. I'm afraid now. I'm afraid to lose you again. But I am not going to let those fears stop me from loving you completely. You could crush me right now if you walked away, but I would survive because I would know that I gave it everything I had." He considered something. "Maybe, you–"

"What?" She glared at him.

He took a deep breath. "Maybe you were afraid — *are* afraid of how much I love you."

"Why would that scare me?"

"Being with me means giving up some of your independence." He leaned his head closer to hers. "I think you're afraid to give up control. I think you're afraid of losing yourself."

"That's not it," she crossed her arms tighter. "I'm afraid that you will hurt me again. I'm afraid that I can't move past what happened."

"I would never hurt you again." He uncrossed her arms and took her hands in his.

"I trust that you believe that, but no one can make that promise and know for sure."

"So? What? You don't take a chance on us? You stay with someone else?" He raised his voice. "Someone who's safe?"

"Jus." She gave him a hard look. "You just told Petal you were leaving tonight. You can't expect me to just turn my life upside down because you finally decided to leave your marriage. I need time to figure this out."

"Right." He took a heavy breath. "You're right. It's just hard to be patient when what you want is staring you right in the face."

She touched his cheek and smiled. "Can't we just enjoy the night?" She searched his face. "Please."

"Yeah. Yeah. Of course."

"Let's go back there. And…" She laughed.

"You sound like your mother when you let yourself laugh loudly."

"That's sweet. And thank you."

"Come on." He grabbed her hand. "This isn't as inconspicuous as the spot last week."

"We can use my coat." She leaned against a tree; leaves still remained on the branches, a menagerie of red, orange and yellow. They hid behind a large boulder.

"This is so unlike you." He put his hand along her cheek. "And twice in less than a week."

"Maybe it's a step toward not playing it safe."

"I like that." He laid her coat down. "The ground is colder than last time."

"I don't care. Take me."

Right there in the twilight, in the middle of the park, he made love to her.

They lay nestled together afterward, looking up at the darkness, sounds of squirrels crunching leaves along the trail. A breeze buzzed through the trees. He felt sure that soon they would be able to be together. Really, together. The way they had always planned.

"This may be one of the craziest things we have ever done." She chuckled. "Let's go for a drink?"

"I know a place."

He took her to a small local bistro along the river. They sipped red wine and ate cheese and crackers and olives while talking about movies they saw, books they read, laughing about some of their friends' social media posts. Then without any forethought, Justin asked, "Where would we live?"

"Whadaya mean?"

"If this works out. Us. Would you consider moving back to Jersey or do you have your heart set on staying in the city?" The question echoed the old issue of Liv wanting to leave the neighborhood, and Justin feeling attached to it. He'd move, regardless.

"I think it's premature to have this conversation. It's the artist in you, always dreaming big and fast. There are lots of other things to consider before where we would live."

"Sure. But it's good to dream, Sweets. You got where you are with your doctorate by following a big dream. Right?"

Her eyes turned pensive. "Take risks in life, but not in love. Hmm."

He put his hand over hers.

"It's hard to say as a hypothetical, but if things worked out between us and you wanted to stay in Jersey, I think I could do that. Would do that." She looked at him intensely. "I still need time."

He nodded, but he knew she was lying to him, maybe even to herself. He saw the hope in her eyes. Liv just wasn't going to give in until he was fully separated and he could give her what she needed. And he would.

Later, he went back to the apartment to pack a suitcase. When he walked through the front hallway, he heard "Glycerine" blasting from the living room. *What the?* He ambled toward the sound. Petal wasn't supposed to be home yet.

He scanned the room. Panic coursed through him. Petal was on her back on the couch, one arm limp and off to the side. White pills were scattered along the floor next to her, along with an empty bottle. Her mouth hung wide open. It looked like she wasn't breathing.

"Oh my God, oh my God, no, no, no!" He ran to her while calling 911.

32

Olivia felt dizzy from the evening, from her life. She had just made love with Justin behind a boulder in Hudson County Park. There were a few trees, but the foliage wasn't thick over there. If someone had walked their dog along the grass, they would have seen them.

Justin brought out the freer side of her, making her feel awake, excited. She had always worried that he wasn't responsible enough, but that's not what it was. She understood now. In retrospect, she realized she was too structured and anxious about what was coming instead of living in the now. He tried to get her to enjoy the moment, their relationship, the love they shared. That had been enough for him. She always wanted more and more and more.

She knew Justin was right too. She *was* terrified. Being with him meant risking her heart entirely. She had never realized it until he said it and it resonated: Justin wasn't the only one who had been scared after their engagement, she had been too. And it made her run toward her other pursuits too fervently, pushing him away in the process. That she could work through.

The bigger problem was that the closer she felt to him now, the more troubled she was about his marriage. She had seen Petal and him naked together, which still remained a vivid imprint in her mind. She had forgiven him, but she couldn't help but wonder what it was like when he was intimate with Petal. Did he lay with her the same way he laid with Olivia? Did he share deep private parts of himself? They had been married for ten years; that's longer than Justin and she had been together. And the thought of them even spending time together, laughing, traveling, talking, pained her to her very core if she let her mind go there. As much as being with Justin healed something, it left the remaining wounds wide opened and vulnerable. She could not stop thinking about him, though. She could feel Justin in her bones, under her skin, in her heart. The taste of his breath lingered in her mouth, the scent of his skin rubbed off on her.

She got her MP3 player out, flipped through the songs, found "Wonderwall" and hit play. Memories from the night Justin proposed emerged, when he sang that song while looking into her eyes, then memories from the other night when they sang together. The song played in her ears. She could see the reflective gaze in his eyes, the way his lips turned up at the corners just enough to look like a smile. Until he looked at her, and then that resting smile would transform into a wide grin. She longed for the time behind her, for the uncomplicated past she shared with Justin. Even more, she missed her mother. She rolled over, tucked her knees under her, and pulled the thin blanket over her.

Her phone vibrated. Adam. She had just made love with Justin. Now the person she had made a commitment to was calling her. Perhaps this whole thing with Justin was just a way to ease the hurt of losing her mother, an attempt to remember an easier time in her life. She sniffed the top of her shirt and inhaled Justin's scent.

Or maybe not.

"Hello." She picked up.

"Hi, Babe. How's it going?"

"It's getting there."

"There's something I wanted to tell you. I was trying to wait until you came back into the city, but it can't really wait anymore."

She sat up. "Is everything OK?"

"Yes and no." He took a deep breath to fortify himself. "You know my brother is dating that model; remember the one he told us about."

"Monique something, the one who made the sex tape. Finnis. Monique Finnis. Right?"

"That's her." He took another long breath. "My brother has become a source of interest for these tabloid

FOREVER AND ONE DAY

reports looking for a good story and willing to twist facts in order to get it."

"No one believes the tabloids."

"Some people do, or they wouldn't sell. Anyway, it doesn't matter. Once it's out there, it gets people talking and thinking. It affects people's privacy. Dan is never one to be concerned with his privacy or anyone else's for that matter. But I care. As you know."

"Are they coming after you?"

"Not yet. But… there's something I haven't told you. Not because I don't trust you, but because it's so horrible that I don't tell anyone. I told Zara when we were together. And I promise, I had planned to tell you before you moved in. But with your mom and everything–"

"What is it? You can tell me anything."

"My parents' death was investigated. There was evidence suggesting that the brakes of the car had been manipulated. Dan had been considered a suspect. His motive was the money. He hated my parents and he couldn't wait for them to die to get his hands on the money."

"My gosh, Babe. That's awful. I'm sorry."

"He was never arrested. Lack of evidence. And he denies it. It's hard for me to believe that Dan, as much of an ass as he can be, would be capable of something so evil. My father's sister and her husband suggested that we take their last name so that this wouldn't follow us for the rest of our lives. Summers is their last name."

"I see."

329

"Are you upset that I didn't tell you?"

"Not upset. More... surprised."

"Our last name had been Siegfried. Anyway, I fear the tabloids will rip this old wound open, just to get a good story. And now that I'm an author, I'm really vulnerable to public exposure and humiliation at the hands of irresponsible media."

"I understand. It's actually a lot to wrap my head around. But I'm here for you. Is there anything we can do? Maybe talk to Dan."

"Ha, there's no talking to Dan. He's probably basking in the attention. In his mid-forties, on the cover of magazine with a young model. I mostly wanted to tell you so you wouldn't see it on the cover of a magazine. I wanted you to hear the truth from me."

"I appreciate that. I never look at those magazines, though."

"You never know, I saw the story while on the bus. Someone next to me was reading it."

"I can't believe that happened to you. As if losing both of your parents wasn't enough, to have your own brother suspected of murdering them."

"Like I said, I don't think Dan did it. I think when people have money, other people enjoy making up salacious stories."

"You sound upset."

"I'm pissed at Dan. But even more than that, it really forces me to think back to that time. How irresponsible I was, Dan calling me in Asia, my never having any resolution with my parents. The two of them dying while I wasn't talking to them."

Olivia had never heard Adam with such a heavy voice; he was always so reserved. She felt sad for him and guilty, too. Guilty, that she was doing something behind his back, and something else that could hurt him. She had been the only woman he let close since he lost Zara, and now, he potentially could lose her too. What on earth was she doing? Someone was going to be very hurt, and this time it wouldn't be Justin or Petal's fault. It would be hers.

"Want me to come into the city. Stay with you tonight?"

"It's late."

"It's not that late."

"I could come there."

"Don't you have to write in the morning?"

"Yeah, so, I'll drive back in after breakfast."

"No. I'll come to you. Maybe stay a few days."

"When are you moving in?"

"Not sure. My dad still needs me. But I'll come be with you tonight."

"Love you, Babe. Can't wait until you get here."

"Me too."

Abbee had offered to drive her to the Upper Westside, but she didn't want to endure a conversation about what she was doing. She could tell by Abbee's piercing gazes that she knew Olivia had being spending a lot of time with Justin. She decided against an Uber too. A bus ride would be longer, affording her more time to wash off the feeling of being with Justin. She sat on the bus lost in her thoughts. The stores along River Road were blurs of color, nothing formed or definite, matching her mood and thoughts.

Adam needed her. She couldn't do to him what Justin's betrayal had done to her. Adam had never hurt her. He had lost more than anyone she had ever known. She couldn't let him lose her too. Yet, she ached for Justin. As much as she tried to focus on Adam, her thoughts kept circling back to Justin. But could she really be with him?

She didn't know.

When she walked through the Port Authority, she caught a glimpse of a magazine headline at the newsstand: *Monique Finnis Seen Topless with New Beau Dan Summers.*

Her breasts were blurred out, but there Dan stood, overly tanned, muscled and bare-chested with an arm draped around Monique Finnis' long, thin body. Olivia looked closely. It almost looked like Dan's hand was cupping her breast, but it was hard to tell. *Yikes.* She couldn't believe she actually had met someone who was on the cover of *Choice.*

Poor Adam.

The doorman greeted her when she walked into Adam's building. She smiled, "Nice to see you."

"You too, Dr. Watson."

Her shoes tapped the tile as she walked confidently toward the elevator. This was who she was, a city girl, Adam's girlfriend. Her stride developed a certainty as she continued to walk. Maybe she wasn't confused at all. Maybe this was where she was supposed to be. She pushed the elevator to the penthouse floor.

Adam opened the door shirtless, looking handsome and dignified, as always. Adam could be wearing a ripped T-shirt and look distinguished.

"Were you working out?"

"Yeah. Just finished up. Best stress reliever. I need to hit the shower." He peered over his glasses with a devilish glint. "Want to join me?"

"I'm not dirty." She said teasingly, but she felt dirty. Guilty. He would be washing the remnants of the sex she had had with Justin off of her. But looking at him and knowing what he was going through, she had to say yes. She took her shirt off and gave him a coy look as they walked toward the bathroom. After they made love in the shower, they retired to the balcony for a glass of wine. Olivia was exhausted, but didn't say.

"You alright?"

"Yeah. Why?" She heard the defensiveness in her tone.

"You seem distant. You've seemed distant since your mother's funeral. Is it because of what you're going through, the grief? Or is it because I asked you to move in? Maybe it was the wrong time."

"No. It's not because you asked me to move in. You're right. It's my mom."

He nodded. She saw him eyeing her out of her periphery. She changed the subject. "How are you doing with the situation with your brother?" She didn't mention that she noticed him on the cover of *Choice*.

"Pissed at Dan. He's so careless in life. He's my only family. Everyone else is gone and I've always wished we could have more of a relationship, but this kind of crap just proves that that will never happen."

She finally looked at him and saw the disappointment in his eyes. "You have been through more than any one person deserves."

"I do have you now. I'm so glad you're here." He took her hand in his.

Jesus Christ. She needed to stop seeing Justin. She squeezed his hand and smiled.

Soon they went upstairs. Before she got into bed, she shut her phone off.

The night was restless. Adam fell asleep easily, his somber breaths stepping into a gentle rhythm that should have soothed her. Instead, she laid awake, watching shadows scurry back and forth across the ceiling. *There's a bird; there's a dog and a cat; there's a squirrel, no that's not a squirrel; it's a groundhog. Shit.* She slipped a sweatshirt on, took her phone and walked downstairs.

She plopped on the couch and turned her phone on, admonishing herself. She tried to tell herself that she wanted to work on a crossword puzzle until she got sleepy, but the truth was she wanted to see if Justin had called. Adam had said, "I do have you now. I'm so glad you're here." He had been so good to her. How could she risk hurting him?

That all made sense rationally, but the impulse to put the phone on superseded any control she had. She watched the phone light up. A smile stretched across her face when she saw he had left a voicemail.

"Hey, Liv." Justin's voice sounded unsteady, making her heart skip a beat. A long pause, and then, "I'm in the ER. Petal took a bunch of pills. Liv, she tried to kill herself. Call me whenever you get this. No matter what time."

Shivers ran up her arms and back.

33

Justin's phone rang and rang. No answer. She called again. No answer. She took a glass of water and a flannel blanket, went outside and sat on Adam's balcony. The streets were nearly vacant. A few taxis whizzed by along the park, a few people hurried along in the chilly air. With an overcast sky and no moon to cast a glow, the darkness of the night felt thick. While most in uptown were fast asleep, here she sat wide awake and anxious.

What on earth had happened? And where was Justin?

And what was she doing sitting on her boyfriend's balcony with his flannel blanket slung over her body, calling her ex-fiancé — and current lover?

She pulled her knees up against her chest. She called again. No answer. She nibbled on the inside of her cheek. She looked at her phone screen, looked back, looked away. Did Petal actually try to kill herself? Or was it an accident? What if she died? Would she accept any of the blame? Could she?

The concern quickly turned to anger. Petal always used drama to manipulate people, to get attention. She couldn't see it when Petal was her best friend. But when she looked back years later, she realized that Petal frequently did things to get attention. Was this a way to keep Justin close? A way to get between them again? No. No. No. That's crazy. She was about to call Justin again, when his number flashed across her phone screen. "Jus. Hello." She said loudly. "What happened?"

"She's OK. She took a bunch of Valium, but she's going to be OK."

Olivia released a long exhale. "Where are you?"

"I'm still at the hospital. She's resting. I'm going to stay here overnight."

She knew he was doing the right thing. Petal was his wife. It broke Olivia's heart, though. Imagining him there with Petal, supporting her, helping her through her chaos, tore at her insides. It wasn't his fault. She let Justin close again. Too close. And again, he was hurting her without any intent to do so. It hurt her. The past hurt her.

"Liv. Are you there?"

"Yes." She said softly.

"You understand that I have to make sure she gets the helps she needs. I feel responsible."

"Yes, of course. I understand."

"You're upset."

"No. Maybe. It's all so complicated."

"It is. But as soon as I know she's getting the help she needs, I'm leaving. Nothing has changed. Can I see you tomorrow? Can we talk about this?"

"I– I'm in the city. I'm at Adam's."

Silence.

"Jus?"

"When did you decide to go there?"

"After I saw you. He needed me. I have a responsibility too."

"I understand." He said, deflated. "When are you coming back?"

"Not sure. A day, maybe two."

"Can we meet then?"

"I'd like that. And please keep me posted on what's happening with Petal."

"I will. I think they'll be sending a psychiatrist to speak with her tomorrow. I'm going to insist that she be sent for treatment. That would be good for her, for her drinking."

"It would. If she complies."

"You sound distant."

"I love you, Jus. So much. But this is all so complicated and confusing."

"I know it is, Sweets. But *I love you* and I will not lose you again."

His voice, the wavy intonation, the affectation she heard made her heart melt. Part of her wanted to leave Adam's and go be with him. But she couldn't. She needed him to resolve his own life. Besides, she had a responsibility to a man who had been nothing but good to her. A man who needed her. "I'll come home late tomorrow afternoon." The sentence spilled out without forethought.

"Great."

What a mess, she thought when they hung up. And she wondered if they could really be together after — everything. Sometimes too much happens and there's no way to turn back.

Maybe it's better to be with someone you don't love too much. Someone you love just enough, but not so much that it could destroy you. She went inside and poured herself a half glass of wine, hoping it would make her sleepy. It didn't. Eventually, she got back into bed next to Adam. She spent the remainder of the night watching those shadowy animals. And she envied them, their ability to frolic, their ability to exist and just as easily not exist, to not have feelings. The safety of lifelessness, the simplicity of being inanimate, those images couldn't be hurt or confused or frustrated. Not disappointed. They would never grieve. She longed for her mother, for a conversation with her. She would give anything to talk to her one more time.

She watched those shadows until slits of daylight illuminated through the blinds, turning the animals into long stripes across the ceiling.

Adam slid his arms around her back and pulled her close. "Morning, beautiful."

"Morning." She said, groggily. She hadn't slept one wink.

Justin paced in the hallway of the hospital. Petal would be fine, thankfully. The doctor had said that she hadn't taken enough Valium to kill herself. Justin wondered if she had meant to kill herself or was just desperate and reckless. The latter seemed likely given her out-of-control drinking. Either way, he knew he had an obligation to stand by her while she got treatment.

Liv was at her boyfriend's. She wasn't supposed to go there. Adam came to *her* on the weekends. He ran his fingers through his hair, released a long, frustrated breath. She had said that she was coming back to New Jersey tomorrow, but Justin could hear the hesitation in her voice. Hesitation in the voice of someone who was already on the fence about a big decision was never a good sign. He had a bad feeling about the way the whole situation was panning out.

He would stay with Petal until he knew she was receiving the treatment she needed. He would have to. Wouldn't he? Yes. He would. She had no one else. Besides, he didn't want to be the guy who would abandon his wife right after she attempted suicide. He would never forgive himself if something happened to Petal. The pacing made him more anxious. He stepped outside. As soon as the crisp air hit his skin he saw Petal's mother walking up to the ER entrance. She looked ragged: her bloodshot eyes; her blonde hair, stringy; her skin, dull; her body, emaciated. Justin smelled the alcohol on her breath as soon as she reached up to kiss his cheek. "Hi, Cutie. I came as fast as I could. How is she? Awake yet?"

Molly had taken to calling him Cutie, which he fucking hated. The nickname made him uncomfortable, especially since a few times when she was drunk and sloppy and uninhibited, she slowly caressed his chest, her long fingernails delicately grazing his neck and shoulders, lingering too long. "*How's my Cutie, today?*" she would say with those same slurry words he heard from Petal all the time. She would lean into him, her breasts touching his body, her breath, reeking of alcohol, blowing hot in his ear. He would back away as gracefully as he could. When Petal would catch such an exchange, her blue eyes would turn fierce. "*Ma, get away from him. You're drunk.*"

"*Sooorry. I didn't mean anything by it. Justin knows that. Don't you, Cutie?*"

Petal would glare at her mother. Justin would try to buffer the tension with something like, "*It's OK, babe.*" He would move away from Molly and wrap his arm around Petal. He had called Molly to let her know what had happened. Now looking at her, he wondered if it had been a mistake. It's not like she came running right over to be with Petal. He had called her a couple of hours ago. She probably couldn't peel herself off her barstool. "She's resting."

She took out her cigarettes. "Want one?" she offered the pack.

"No, thanks." He looked around. "I'm not sure you can smoke here."

"It's the middle of the night. Let them stop me if it's a problem." She lit up, took a long drag. Deep, thin lines surrounded her mouth when she puckered, pulling the smoke in. "What happened? She took too many pills by accident?"

"I'm not sure. I'm waiting for her to wake up to find out. The doctor said it wasn't enough to kill herself. But, even so, her behavior puts her at risk for a suicide. I'm going to make sure she gets help. And I would appreciate you backing me up on this."

"Yes, help?" Molly seemed more annoyed than concerned.

"Help. For the drinking, Molly. For the pills. Whether you want to admit it or not, Petal has a drinking problem."

"Cutie. My daughter enjoys a few drinks. That's not a problem. That's called having a good time. You're always so intense. You need to loosen up." She touched his arm, those long rounded nails, scraping his forearm.

He looked at the chipped blue polish on her fingernails. He was about to blow a gasket. Molly was just like her daughter. No, Molly was worse than Petal. Her daughter had almost overdosed, yet Molly seemed oblivious to the severity of the situation. Looking at her face, her hand holding the cigarette, the purple veins on the hand she rested on his forearm, he felt exasperated.

"Maybe you should go, Molly. I shouldn't have called you." He moved his arm away from her hand.

"I'm her mother."

"Yes, you are. You might try acting like it. She needs help. Understand? Help."

"What she needs is for you to act like a man."

He gave her an angry glare. "What?"

"You're the problem, not the drinking. Come on. She tells me everything. We might fight all the time, but we are very close. And I know you have seen Olivia. That killed Petal. She called me hysterical in the morning. Said she believes you not only still love Olivia Watson, but that you have never stopped loving her. Do you have any idea what that's like for her? Like someone took a knife and stabbed it right through her fucking heart. That's right, Cutie." She placed her hand on his forearm again. "Men can be stupid sometimes. You know I adore you, but you need to step up and be there for her. Make sure she knows you love only her. And that you will not leave."

She dropped the cigarette to the ground, smooshed it out with her foot, lit another. The smoke made him want to choke. "What are you really doing here, Molly?"

"You called me. I came to be with my daughter. To make sure she's alright and that you do what you're supposed to." She sucked smoke in, exhaled a cloud of gray. "She needs her husband to uphold his commitment. Don't be like her father. He left her, us. Got up one day and poof, he was gone. Don't fucking do that to her. Hear me, Cutie?"

"I hear you."

"Can I see her?"

"You can go in. But she's sleeping."

"That's OK. I just want to see that she's OK."

He nodded.

Molly moved to kiss his cheek, but he flinched away. She sneered at him as she walked into the hospital.

"Fuck." He hollered into the cold, dark night air. "Fuck. Fuck. Fuck." *That's pretty fucking articulate, fuck, fuck, fuck. But it does sum it up: You're fucking screwed, Justin Steeler. And you know what? You fucking deserve it.*

He had lost Liv when he betrayed her. And now, he was trying to get back something that was gone. Trying to undo the biggest mistake of his life. The dreamer in him thought that was possible because their love was as strong as ever; possible because he loved Liv, not Petal. But some things couldn't be undone. This, he thought for the first time since they reconnected, might be one of them.

Petal needed him. Her mother wasn't going to help her. There was no one else that was going to stand by Petal and make sure she got help. He had to be the one. And what did that mean for him and Liv? Would Liv wait while he saw Petal through her difficulties? And how long would that take? Liv wasn't gonna wait long. And she had a boyfriend with no baggage.

"Fuck." Best he could do was talk to Liv and hope she understood; maybe she would stand by him. Maybe she would love him enough to wait. Then something occurred to him that punched him in the stomach. If he loved Liv enough, maybe he had to let her go, let her be with the man who could give her what she wanted right now; not have her wait for someone whose life was complicated, someone she had to put her own life on hold for, someone who had hurt her.

But he couldn't bear losing her again.

He would wait to talk to Petal tomorrow. He would talk to Liv too, tomorrow night, when she came back from the city. Hopefully, he would be able to figure out how to help Petal while still having a future with Liv.

He wasn't very optimistic.

Molly came out a few minutes later. "Nurse said she's going to be fine."

"She needs psychiatric help."

"She needs you." Molly said.

Justin looked at Molly, her weathered skin, the deep creases around her eyes and mouth, her skeletal frame. He wondered if this was Petal's future, worn out, the alcohol making her look emaciated, like it ate her from the insides. He didn't want that to be her life; she deserved better. "I'll come by tomorrow after work," she said.

"Call first. She might be moved to a psych facility."

"Or they might send her home."

Justin grimaced. "I'm going to insist she goes somewhere."

"Be good to her." Molly squeezed his forearm and left.

Justin went back inside and sat next to Petal's bed. She looked peaceful laying there. He rubbed her arm. "Please be OK." He whispered, kissing her hand. "Please be OK. It's not that I don't love you. I do. I care about you. It's just not the way you deserve. And I want us both to be able to have something more. I'm so sorry for everything."

He kissed her hand, then leaned back into the chair. He tried to sleep.

Petal felt Justin beside her. The light was bright, fluorescent, painful. She squinted, trying to lessen the pulsing blare of the light and the stark whiteness, the ceiling, the walls, the sheets. She was surrounded by white; it made her head throb.

The buzzing, beeping reverberation of medical equipment echoed, reminding her of work. But she wasn't working. She was a patient in the ER and Justin sat beside her in a chair. She looked at him out of the corner of her eyes, his long body half curled to the side, his dark hair, disheveled. The chair looked too small for his tall frame. She rustled under the sheets, and let out a gentle groan.

He leaned forward. "Hey."

He had a look. *Concern*, she thought. She loved seeing him look at her that way. The pills had done the trick: just enough to get his attention, to remind him of his obligation, but not enough to kill her.

"How're you feeling?" He asked. Justin had a warmth about him. It was veiled by his edgy demeanor, but she could feel it there, covered and protected; underneath his coolness, Justin was a softy.

"I– I'm OK. What happened?"

"You took a bunch of pills. Do you remember doing that?"

"Sort of. I was very upset. I remember holding the bottle. Valium, right?"

"And alcohol. You could have died. Is that what you wanted?"

"I dunno. Yeah. Maybe. I don't want to live without you. In the moment, it seemed like the right thing. To take the pills."

"To kill yourself?"

"To numb the pain. But I knew I might die and I didn't care. I don't want to live without you, Justin."

"I know." He put his hands around her hands. "We're going to get you help. OK? For the alcohol, for the pain you have. It's a long time coming."

"Will you stay with me if I get treatment? Is that what the problem is for you?"

He felt a lie form on his lips, then he took a middle ground. "I will stand by you while you're getting help. The drinking is a problem, yes. But get some rest. There's plenty of time for us to talk about us. I want you to focus on you."

"'Kay." She closed her eyes, but she could still feel him next to her bed.

The worst. The absolute most painful thing about Justin always having one foot out of their relationship was that generally speaking, he was the nicest guy. A "do anything for anyone" type, compassionate, empathetic. He was the only person who ever stuck by her. When she was upset, Justin listened. Justin helped her finish school. He supported her financially when her mother couldn't. Or wouldn't.

While he sat there with her, she could feel his worry. Justin was one of a kind, and she loved him more than anyone. The fact that he did not feel the same made her so desperate for him. She wanted all of him. Everything he kept bottled inside, she wanted him to express those feelings to her, to feel the passion she knew he had for her.

She hoped taking those pills would give her another chance to get that. But she could glean from the non-commitment in his statement about staying with her that so far it hadn't done the trick. Hopefully, something between them would flourish while she was in treatment. She knew he was capable of more; maybe if she got clean, maybe then, she would be more lovable. "Can you get me some water, Jus?"

"Of course. Be right back." She watched him walk out from the privacy curtain into the ER.

34

When Justin re-entered Petal's room with the pitcher of water, two glasses and a cup of coffee, a doctor was talking with her. Justin introduced himself. "Good morning, Doctor. I'm Justin."

"My husband," Petal added.

"Yes. Hello. I'm Dr. Flamingo," she said with a tight smile. She was tall, with shoulder length dark hair and crisp blue eyes. "I was talking to your wife about various options for treatment."

"Are you a psychiatrist?"

"Yes, sir. Once she's cleared medically, I'd advise a 28-day program. I'm concerned about this use of pills combined with alcohol. Even if she didn't mean to kill herself, this is high-risk behavior. As I was telling Petal, she needs to enter treatment somewhere. This isn't a choice." She flipped through some pages on her clipboard. "You understand, right, Petal? The question isn't if you're going or not; it's simply where and for how long."

"Yes."

Dr. Flamingo looked at Justin for his understanding.

"Yes. We both want her to receive treatment. Just tell me what I can do to help."

"I need to make a few calls. Hopefully, find a bed for her today or tomorrow. Because until I find one, she will have to stay here."

"No." Petal whined.

"I'm going to do my best to find somewhere today. I'll be back."

"Thank you, Doctor." Justin said as she walked out.

Later that day, Petal was sent to a 28-day program at Bergen County Psychiatric Center. Justin drove her. She would finish her time there, then her team of counselors would determine if she should go into another inpatient program. Justin wanted her to stay more than twenty-eight days.

"You've been abusing alcohol for way more than a month. Don't you think it would be good to stay in for a while? Give yourself the time and space to be clean and figure out what's bothering you?" He said to her when he dropped her off.

"I'm not saying you're wrong. But even a month is a long time to be away. Maybe I can do outpatient after the twenty-eight days. If they let me. I need you, Jus. More than ever."

He hugged her. "You're gonna do great."

"You'll come for the family visit. Right?"

"Of course."

Petal wasn't allowed to call or see anyone from her outside life until the first family visit, which would be in two weeks. As Justin walked out of the hospital, a wave of relief washed over him. Petal, finally, would get help, and then they would separate. Hopefully, she would be able to accept it once she was in treatment.

When he checked his phone, he saw that Scully had left a voicemail message, returning Justin's earlier phone call. Justin had called him to see what Scully was doing with his music. Justin wanted to get back to playing.

Furious Whiskers had broken up when Justin left the band. Scully, exacerbated, tried to reason with him: *"Dude, do not let a woman stop you from doing your art. Now is the best time to be writing."*

"Man, I can't get any words down. I can't concentrate. I'm so out of it, my fingers are stumbling over the strings. I need a break."

"You're making a mistake, dude. You have talent. Don't throw that away. It's not even about the band. It's about your future as a musician."

"I never needed more than to be playing out. I never wanted the fame, the money. And now, playing out doesn't feel right. I just need time, dude. It's temporary. I'll be in touch."

Last he heard, Scully was playing guitar for a few bands. Justin thought he'd take a chance and see if he could join one of those bands. Or better yet, see if Scully wanted to put Furious Whiskers back together.

He sat in his car and called him back.

Scully answered, his deep voice bellowing over the line. "Dude. Great to get your call. What's up?"

"Hey. How's the music going? How's everything?"

"It's all good. So... what happened to you? It's like you dropped off the grid."

"Shit happened. Life happened. I made some bad choices. I'm trying to get things back on track."

"You still with that gorgeous wife of yours?"

"Things aren't so great there. But I didn't call you to give you my whole long sob story. I called because I miss the music. I wanna play again."

Scully's voice took a serious turn. "When you say 'play,' do you mean futz around? Do you mean jam with us? Or do you mean you want back in?"

Justin hesitated. "Um..."

"Because if you mean 'get back in,' then I, we, would need a promise of commitment from you."

"It's just that my wife–"

"No, Justin. No 'buts.' When you took a break from Furious Whiskers, you left us hanging. You said you'd be back, but then you never called. You never showed your face. We waited for you. We knew you were heartbroken, so we gave you time. But you blew us off. I would love to play with you again. And I bet the other guys would too.

We still talk about the good times with you. But we can't be left hanging again. This is a business for us. If you want in, if you want another chance, we need your assurance that you won't flake on us. We need your promise that you're in it for the long haul."

Justin chuckled. "So how long have you been waiting to get that off your chest."

Scully joined the laughter. "A little while. So?"

Justin wanted in. He wanted to play with these guys again. But he had only just picked up the guitar after years away from it. What if he wasn't good enough anymore? What if he let them down again, like he did to Liv and Petal? Did he have it in him to make the commitment to his former bandmates?

"Justin? Are you there?"

Justin came out of his trance. "Fair warning. I'm rusty."

"Yes!" Scully cheered. "I'll take that as a yes. Justin Steeler is back in the game. Can you come down tomorrow night?"

"Where?"

"Hoboken. We've got a studio there. For practice and recording."

"You've got a spot open in the band?"

"If you can still sing and play the way you used to, we'll make room. We'll figure it out."

"Sounds fucking great, Scul."

"I'll text you the address. See you tomorrow."

"See you then."

He texted Liv before driving home: *Petal is OK and going to rehab. Will you be back in time for dinner? There's somewhere I'd like to take you. Lemme know either way.*

Justin's text came through. Olivia glanced at the message. Adam glanced at her glancing at the message. "It's my sister." She lied. The timing was inconvenient. Adam was actually showing Olivia photos of his parents, Dan and him when they were kids, the mansion in the Hamptons. He even shared a few pictures of Zara. "What's made you show these to me now?" She asked after they were about halfway through the second album.

"We're taking the step of moving in. I want to share my life with you."

Olivia kissed his cheek. A small amount of perspiration accumulated under her neck. Justin's text distracted her. "I'm flattered you're sharing so much of yourself. I have to ask, how much of your family story influenced your book? The family is murdered in the Hamptons in *An Inconvenient Coincidence.*"

"Ah. Good question. None of the events are true, but I used the emotional experience to write the characters' inner narratives. It's something that happens when writing fiction without even trying. I'm sure Dan is innocent, anyway. I feel confident that my parents' deaths were an accident."

"And Tamara?" she teased.

He gave her a playful look.

"Well, I had to ask, since you were sharing so much."

"The truth is, in my mind, it's left open. Sometimes I think she died, and other times, not."

"OK. Fair enough. You're never going to tell me."

"No, I am telling you." He smiled, and his eyes had that boyish glint. "You are tenacious, Olivia Watson. And I love you."

"I love you too."

Four words, eleven letters, and she meant it. She did love Adam. And here he was taking their relationship to the next level of intimacy, sharing parts of himself, parts he shared with very few people. And there she was lying, involved with Justin, carrying on a clandestine relationship with her ex-fiancé. It was messy and confusing and dishonest.

Maybe she would settle for a little less of that abandon she had with Justin, that complete, all-encompassing feeling, and stick with someone she loved a little less but who was able to give her the life she imagined. And give it to her now.

That all made sense, and yet, within less than ten minutes of receiving Justin's text, she found herself in Adam's bathroom responding. *Dinner sounds good. Pick me up at my dad's at 7:00.*

She deleted the exchange, went back into Adam's living room.

"My dad wants to go through my mother's things. I didn't want to say last night, but when I left to come here, he asked me if I could come back tonight. Abbee's going back to work next week. He wants us both there to go through her things with him. I hope you understand."

"I absolutely understand. He shouldn't do that alone. I'll come and help."

Her stomach balled. "No, no. Thank you. My dad loves you, but I think he'd prefer to just do it with us. You know what I mean."

"Yeah." He said, sounding crestfallen. "Liv, is there something else bothering you that you're not telling me? You've been miles away most of the morning."

She tried to perk up. "No. Nothing. I'm just out of it."

She nestled against his body. He kissed the top of her head, a pensive look on his face. "Are you sure?"

"Yes, babe. I'm sure." Duplicity. *One word, nine letters,* and she was guilty of it. *You will make a choice this week.* She promised herself.

When she arrived home, her dad said, "I spoke with your aunt. We are going to spread your mother's ashes this weekend. Saturday."

"OK."

"You doing alright, Honey?"

"Yeah. I'm alright, Dad."

"You want to tell me what's going on?"

"With what?"

"With Justin. With Adam. I know I'm not your mother. But you can talk to me."

She gushed. "I don't know what I'm doing, Dad. I've always known what I wanted. I've always felt so sure of things. But now, I can't make sense of anything."

"Things don't always have to make sense."

"I don't like not knowing what I'm doing or what I'm feeling. I need to figure out what I want. I'm hurting both of them and hurting myself. But I don't know how to stop it."

"Sometimes we know what we want, and we are afraid to admit it to ourselves."

She contemplated. "I *am* afraid. I am afraid that I am in love with two very different men, for different reasons. And I have to make the hardest decision of my life. Adam can give me everything I want right now: commitment, marriage, children, stability. And yet, I cannot stop thinking about Justin. I love him, always have, always will. But life with Justin, at least right now, is precarious." She shook her head. "I don't know what I'm doing. If I go with Adam and put this thing with Justin to rest, I'm afraid I'll never stop thinking about him. If I go with Justin, I'm afraid, I'll never have what I want: a commitment, stability. And I don't know that I can ever truly live with the ghosts of the past: his years of marriage to the woman he betrayed me with."

"We can always forgive when we love someone and sometimes it's hard to separate what we want from what we need. I know you don't like to talk about it, but when I had my affair, it was a mistake. Your mother and I were going through a rough patch. I looked outside for a way to deal with our problems when the whole time the answers were inside of me. I told your mother the truth and we worked it out."

"So, you're saying I should be with Justin?"

"Oh, sweetheart, I wish I could answer that for you. You have to make the decision. It sounds like you *want* Justin, but you're not sure he can give you what you need. At least not right now. I was referring to the part about the past, what he did. I wouldn't want to see you let the past prevent you from getting what you want and need for your future. Maybe give yourself a little more time to figure it out."

"And what? Keep seeing both of them."

Her father placed his hand on her back, gently. "Give yourself a little time and don't put so much pressure on yourself to decide. Stop thinking so much. Love isn't about holding on, it's about letting go. About releasing fears, releasing control. About acceptance, forgiveness, taking chances."

She looked up at him. Her dad's eyes were so warm. He had made a mistake, a big one, and her mother forgave him. Her mother had made the right choice. "Thanks, Dad." She hugged him.

"I don't know that I helped. Your mother was better at this stuff."

"You're doing fine." She smiled up at him through glassy eyes.

Justin came at 7:00 on the dot. He texted: *I'm outside.* But she already knew. She had been looking out her window waiting for him. "Hey, Sweets," he said as she got into the car. His fresh scent filled the air. She inhaled deeply.

"Hi." She felt a wide smile stretch across her face.

He tapped his fingers against the steering wheel as he pulled onto River Road. "I hope you're hungry." He glanced at her and smiled.

"Where you taking me?"

"River Palace. Dark Blues is playing tonight."

"You remembered." Her eyes lit up. She had mentioned their first night together that she wanted to see the jazz band Dark Blues play at River Palace. It was nearly impossible to get a reservation when they played there. The few times she had tried, they were packed.

"I remember everything you tell me."

She smiled, resting back into her seat.

River Palace, a new restaurant along the Hudson River in Edgewater, had an inside and outside dining area, live music in both sections. Even though it was late October, the heat lamps made outside dining comfortable and possible.

Justin had done some work for them and was able to get a table outside, right in front of the band. He escorted her to the table, swinging their joined hands. Night had settled in, making the sky an infinite, solid black. The skyline lit up the river with long reflections in assorted colors. Candles gave off a sultry light in the otherwise dimly lit outside area. The atmosphere felt romantic and sexy, just like she did walking in with Justin.

The band filled the night air with the moving rhythm of jazz. Deep reverberation of the saxophone bellowed under the more delicate keyboards and the sweet sounds of the violin. A tall, thin woman with long, black hair sang, her voice soaring and robust. She hit notes so high and with such intensity, the power made Olivia's heart jump. Justin was an effortless romantic. They sat side-by-side, sipping red sangria, listening to the band against the backdrop of the New York City skyline. "The band's good." He curled a few tendrils of her hair around his finger, then let them gently roll off.

"Good? They're amazing."

He squeezed her hand.

In that moment, the only thing that made sense was being there with Justin. Everything that felt wrong when she thought about him, suddenly felt right. It made her exuberant. She craved a constant physical connection to him.

He reciprocated. He had his hand on hers or his arm around her. He kept leaning in to kiss her, letting his lips wisp along hers. They ordered seafood paella for two and another pitcher of sangria. They didn't talk about anything relating to their relationship. She was dying to know what his thoughts were about Petal being in rehab, how long he planned to support her through it. But trying to take her father's advice, she let the thinking go, the logistics, the reasonableness, the structure and order of the future. She let herself feel. And when she did, there was no doubt where she belonged.

With Justin.

They talked and laughed easily. Justin told her more about his work as a carpenter, some of the amazing buildings he worked in, some of the people he had met through the job. Olivia told him about a few of the journal articles she wrote that had been published, a new one she had considered writing.

They shared a chocolate mousse for dessert. The music helped the night flow along smoothly. Effortlessly. Olivia glanced at the band, then at Justin. "Soon you'll be back at it."

"It sounded good when I spoke with Scully, but we'll see." He said, casually.

"C'mon, Jus. I know you're excited. And you should be."

His face turned a little red. "You could always read me."

She squeezed his leg under the table and chuckled. "That's not a bad thing."

"No, it's not." He laughed. "Help me eat the rest of this thing." He seductively placed his mousse-covered spoon in her mouth.

After dinner, they walked along the river. It was chilly, but still pleasant. Justin wrapped his arm around her. "You wanna talk about anything, Sweets?"

"I dunno. I'm kind of enjoying not talking about anything. Things seem clearer when we don't have to think about our lives."

"I hear you. We don't have to if you don't want to, but not talking is what got us into trouble in the past."

She gave a dismissive wave. "We were very young then."

"But we were also not tied to other obligations. If we are going to make it through this together, talking may be the most important thing."

She stopped in her tracks. "I want you to leave her. Now."

"I plan to. I just– I want to wait until I know she can handle the separation."

"What if that time never comes? What if she constantly keeps you from leaving by being unstable? I can't wait around."

"I just need a little time. I'm hoping that–"

"Why didn't you and Petal have kids? She always wanted kids."

"She had a miscarriage when we were first married. Then a year or so later, when she was ready to try again, her drinking had gotten worse. I had a lot of reservations about the marriage. We started fighting all the time. It didn't seem right to have a child when we were always yelling at each other."

"I want kids."

"Me too."

"I'm thirty-eight. I can't wait much longer. I want two children."

"I understand." He turned and faced her, holding her hands in his. "I want that with you. More than anything. I just don't know how to undo the mistakes I've made. I cannot be the guy who abandons someone he made a commitment to after she nearly overdosed on pills. At least not without giving her a little time to get her shit together. I blame myself for losing you. And I blame myself for hurting her."

"She hurt herself. Don't you get it? She fucking knew how much I loved you and she didn't care. It's time to rip the Band-Aid off and do what *you* want." She searched deep into his eyes.

He looked pained when he said, "God. Liv. I love you so much. Please. Give me a month."

"Things with Adam are progressing. And because you're not leaving, I'm totally confused. I want things for my future. I'm trying to do things differently than I used to. I'm trying to be in the moment, to just love you and let you love me. But still, I'm afraid if I let go of Adam I'll be waiting for you and what I need forever."

"I know what I'm asking is selfish. Part of me thinks I should let you go, but I can't lose again. I can't."

"I'm hurting Adam, even if he doesn't know it yet. I don't know what I'm doing."

"I'm sorry, Sweets. It's going to get better." He grabbed her into a tight hug. She buried her head in his chest.

She wanted him. But the voice of reason told her it was Adam that she should be with. Justin was a relationship from the past. Again, she felt spun around, conflicted, tortured by her own indecision. She thought she might lose her mind before the correct path illuminated itself.

Justin stayed with her at her dad's that night. Before they settled into bed, she excused herself and went downstairs to call Adam.

Adam asked, "Why are whispering?"

She hadn't even realized that she was. The duplicity had become so ordinary. "Oh, was I whispering? I'm in the kitchen. Dad's sleeping."

"Your sister's up with you?"

Shit. Right, she had lied about Abbee still being there. Abbee had gone back home the day before. "Um… she's sleeping too." Lies have a way of building their own momentum. *This is not good.*

Then Adam said, "So, I'll come with you on Saturday to release your mother's ashes." She had mentioned the plan to him before she left for her evening with Justin.

"Um."

"I want to be there for you. Please let be there for you."

"Yes. Of course. I want you to come." The words slipped out of her mouth, but they were the right words.

He *was* her boyfriend. She *was* moving in with him. Most likely he soon would be her fiancé. *Riiight,* she thought with a hint of sarcasm. She was losing her mind, a mind that she no longer felt she could rely on to think clearly or lead her to behave responsibly. As much as Adam's presence would be soothing on Saturday, as much as she wanted him there, a part of her wished it was Justin instead. *Aye-yi-yi. You cannot have it all, Olivia.*

She brought two glasses of Cognac up to the bedroom. Justin sat in the recliner, legs out in front, reading. When he looked at her coming toward him, his cool edge morphed into an admiring, almost helpless gaze.

She curled up in his lap and squeezed him. He carried her over to the bed and they made love. For the first time in seventeen years, Justin and she spent the night together. His body was entirely wrapped around her and hers around him, her head resting against his chest. She fell into a sound sleep beside him.

The sun shone bright into the bedroom in the morning. Justin's arms were around her, his body against her. As he slept, she stirred in his arms. Somehow the illumination of day made the guilt over her indiscretions much harder to rationalize. To quell her angst, she promised herself that she would make a decision, and make it soon. She let the feeling of being in Justin's arms envelope her.

"Morning, Sweets." He said softly in her ear. It sent a shiver up her back. Justin's voice in the morning reminded her so much of the weekends when he would come stay at the college dorms with her.

"Morning." She whispered back, smiling to herself.

He gently turned her face and kissed her. Kissing Justin in the morning brought the memories rushing back. It was something she had never let herself look back on. When she would think about those incredibly close moments with Justin, she would shove them out of her mind with a violent admonishment of, *"It's over. None of this matters. It didn't feel the way you thought it did. It was all an act. He's a cheater and a liar."*

Laying there with him, she couldn't believe how stupid she had been, indulging herself with such rigid denial of how she felt. She had missed him. She had always loved him. Those were some of the best memories of her life. For years, somewhere deep down, she had longed for him or for what she had with him with someone else. That's why she could never find the right guy. On some level, she had always compared them to Justin.

Adam had been the first. *What was it with Adam?* She wondered. How did she let him close, closer than anyone else other than Justin? Her mom, Abbee and her dad saw a resemblance between Justin and Adam, which was absolutely nuts. They were nothing alike other than both being tall, with dark hair and a reserved manner.

Adam had many qualities she liked: intelligent, perceptive, handsome, loving, deep. And she loved the way he looked at her. Or maybe it was because he was broken from his past and trying to heal, same as her. Maybe she saw something in him that reminded her of herself. *Hmmm,* she let that absorb.

Justin kissed her neck, sending a tingle through her body. "What's your morning thought?"

Olivia smiled. "Oh my gosh. You remembered the morning thought."

"How could I forget it? You shared your morning thought with me for years, every time we woke up together." He kissed her neck again, "So?"

"Hmm. This was from a couple of days ago, but it's a good one: If a hole gets filled, it becomes whole."

He let out a small laugh. "That *is* good. I can relate." He squeezed her.

She kissed his face, his neck, his ears. Soon they were making loving again, making sure to be quiet. "I feel like we're kids again, figuring out where to go."

"Yeah." He chuckled in her ear.

Justin had to leave early that morning for an appointment with a new client. Another new restaurant was being built along River Road. They wanted a custom-made bar and bar stools. He reminded Olivia that he was meeting up with Scully in Hoboken at 7:00.

"I'm so glad. You are so talented and besides, I know you love it. Soon you'll be part of a band again. That's where you belong."

He smiled at her. With the bright sun, she could see the hint of lines around his eyes when he grinned. Justin had always been hot, sexy. Now, he was also handsome, and she admired him under the daylight. His looks never seemed to matter to him, which made him even more irresistible.

"Meet me after for a drink or dessert?"

"In Hoboken?"

"Sure. Or I'll come back, and we can meet here in Edgewater."

"What time?"

"I dunno. Probably around 10:00-10:30."

"'Kay. Text me when you're done. Jus?"

"Yeah."

"If it goes late, don't worry. This is important."

"So are you." He leaned over and kissed her before putting his coat on.

35

Justin stayed over again Tuesday night. And Wednesday night.

On Thursday, one of Scully's bands, The Ragged Gems, was playing in Hoboken. Scully had invited Justin to play guitar and sing a couple songs with the band. The two were working on putting Furious Whiskers back together. In the meantime, Justin would jump in with The Ragged Gems. He would jam with them on Tuesday nights and work on some new lyrics. Scully knew a few guys who he thought would work well for Furious Whiskers, especially his buddy, Leo, a fantastic drummer; *the best,* he had told Justin.

Justin invited Olivia. "Won't it be weird?" she asked. "I mean, Scully knows you're married to someone else. And it's not like he doesn't know who I am. Don't you think it could get back to Petal?"

"Scully doesn't give a shit about what I do in my personal life. Besides, the guy's been divorced twice himself. It's not like he wouldn't understand."

"But you're not divorced. You're bringing your ex-fiancée to a show while the wife you are still with is in rehab."

"You worry too much."

"And you don't worry enough."

For a moment, the conversation reminded her of the ones that had made her anxious back in college: Justin thinking everything would iron itself out no matter what; Olivia always worried that he wasn't thinking things through.

Maybe she was too uptight. Maybe she didn't know how to be in the moment without worrying about the future. But as much as Justin could be spontaneous — she found it exciting and loved that about him — sometimes he just didn't think. She wondered if that would cause problems in the long term. You can't fly by the seat of your pants when you've got a couple kids to take care of.

Nevertheless, she brushed the moment aside, because deep down what she really wanted was to go to the show and watch him sing, to be with him as he took this step forward, to share the experience. If there were consequences, which there probably wouldn't be — maybe Justin was right, she did worry too much — she would deal with them as they arouse.

They arrived at the venue, Maroon's, a bar on Washington Avenue. Justin dropped his guitars off with the manager, then parked in a parking lot down the block. The streets buzzed. Justin held her hand as they navigated the loud swarms of people.

"This is exciting. How do you feel?"

"I'm petrified." A shit-eating grin spread across his face. "And I wouldn't want to be anywhere else."

Justin wore a white T-shirt with an unbuttoned flannel shirt over it and jeans. He looked almost the same as he used to, except now his hair was shorter and his arms were more muscular. Just the right amount of toned muscle peeked out of the arms of his T-shirt. Knowing Justin, he'd leave the flannel on, though.

Scully and the other guys were already setting up. "Dude, this is a good night. Glad you're back." He gave Justin a magnanimous smile and sturdy handshake.

"Good to be back."

Scully looked at Olivia with curiosity, then shot Justin a wayward smile. "Liv, nice to see you. It's been forever. How are ya?" He gave her a cordial kiss on the cheek.

Knowing Scully knew something was up made her blush. She couldn't help but smile, though. It felt like she had come home after a long, winding journey, being there with Justin and Scully as they set up. "I'm well, Scully. It's nice to see you too."

Justin introduced Olivia to the other band members, Randy, Vine, Forrest, and Kylie. Kylie, a tall, thin woman with long straight hair and a big space between her two front teeth, sung some of the vocals. She gave Olivia a once over, smiled warmly. Olivia smiled back, hesitantly. Justin hadn't mentioned that there was a female singer. And for a second she felt something: *jealousy,* she thought. She had never been jealous when it came to Justin, but things were different now. He had cheated on her.

Justin put his arm around her and the moment vanished. *I'm a psycho.* Justin would never do anything like that again. It was a mistake. Then she remembered that he wasn't committed to her, really. No, he was committed to Petal.

That was only on paper.

In his heart, he was committed to her.

They sat at a table right to the side of the band, and ordered two beers from a bespectacled, brunette cocktail waitress with huge, pushed-upped breasts. Once she took a few sips of her beer, she relaxed. Justin's leg rested against hers. His foot tapped under the table to the bass.

It all felt so familiar and she kept having memories of the nights Justin played with Furious Whiskers when they were in college. A few images of Petal hanging on Justin entered her mind, him looking uncomfortable as he tried to politely disengage from her physical overtures. Then she remembered one night when Petal had said that she wished she had a guy who would write songs about her and sing to her.

Olivia remembered feeling guilty that she had something that Petal didn't, something special, something that Petal also wanted. Never in a million years, though, would Olivia have thought that Justin would ever be with Petal. In fact, back then, he used to remark that he thought Petal was reckless and drank too much.

It was a mistake, she reminded herself. Justin rested his hand on her leg, tapping his long fingers to the music. She let herself feel his body on hers, the closeness. She pushed those memories out of her mind. It didn't matter. That was the past.

She kissed his neck, and noticed him smile from his profile.

"I'm glad you're here." He kissed her lips.

"Me too. But we probably shouldn't be publicly affectionate." She said, as she could barely keep her hands off of him.

"Don't worry. I understand what you're saying, but no one we know is here."

"It's crowded."

He placed his hand on her shoulder to soothe her. "Stop worrying."

She nodded.

Scully tipped his head to Justin, indicating that he should come up on the stage. He kissed Olivia's cheek. "Love you."

"Have fun."

Justin picked up his acoustic and stood in front of the microphone. Tears pricked behind her eyes as she looked at him. It wasn't sadness. It was nostalgia and happiness and love. He looked so handsome. As much as his standing there reminded her of the boy she had loved, the boy she had been engaged to, she recognized the handsome, sturdy man he had grown into.

She recognized the music the moment it started. She felt a lump in her throat. It was "Wonderwall." She could feel Justin's emotions through his guitar playing and in his voice. His sensitivity. His passion. She felt full of heart in that moment. He sang that song with poignance as he stole intermittent glances of her. She wanted to burst into tears and wasn't sure why.

The band moved into their next song: "Good Riddance" by Green Day. Justin kept the crowd enthralled. Women whispered to each other with coy looks on their faces; men and women bopped to the music. A few people got up to dance in front of the band. Justin was on fire. The more he played and sang, the more dynamic and magnetic he became. She couldn't keep her eyes off of him. He sang to the crowd, but kept returning his gaze to her. As much as she was enjoying the show, she couldn't wait to be alone with him.

Justin sat next to her when he finished, his face flushed from the excitement. She wrapped her arms around him. "You were amazing. How'd it feel?"

"Fuckin great," he smiled. "They have one more set. You wanna get something to eat afterward or go home?"

"What do you want?" She whispered seductively in his ear, then noticed his lips turn upward.

"I'm not really hungry." He looked at her with a cool, mischievous expression.

"Me neither. At least not for food."

He ran his hand over her thigh.

The kissing began immediately when they slipped into the car an hour later. She pulled his flannel shirt off his shoulders. "Sweets, it's too bright in here and the car is too small." He laughed. The car was parked in the crowded parking lot.

"Take me to your place. I don't wanna have to be quiet at my dad's. I want to be able to scream as loud as I want."

He laughed, then hesitated. "Are you sure?"

"Whadaya mean?"

"It won't feel weird for you?"

"No. It's fine."

He hesitated again, looked at her, then with a resolute nod said, "OK, then."

Justin rested his hand right near her panty line. She giggled at him, feeling spontaneous, exuberant, free. As much as Justin said it felt great for him to be back playing his music, she felt even more exhilarated having been there to experience it with him.

She didn't think about anything but being close to him as they made their way into his apartment building and walked toward his apartment.

The apartment door still hung ajar when she grabbed him, kissing his neck, running her hands down his back and along his ass. Justin kicked the door closed and guided her toward the living room where there was a large couch. He lay down, pulling her on top of him, kissing her wildly, passionately. Within minutes they lay naked, wrapped around each other, sweating. He entered her. He felt strong inside of her, and she pulled him closer, as close as she could.

"I love you," he said in her ear.

She panted and groaned as the tension increased. She felt him there with her, their hips thrusting in synchrony, tongues merged in a furious dance. His breath became hers, and hers, his. She was joined to him, completely. The love of her life. Justin.

Her body shook. She screamed with pleasure, long and uninhibited. They came at the same time.

"Wow." She said, catching her breath. She smiled into his sweaty chest.

"Yeah." He kissed her.

They lay on the couch, resting against each other for a few minutes. Then Justin asked, "You want something to drink?"

"Sure. Whadaya got?"

"Beer, wine, scotch, water, juice, coffee."

"I'll have a beer."

Olivia admired Justin's broad shoulders and tight ass as he walked toward the kitchen. She threw his T-shirt on and started looking around.

There was a leash and some dog toys next to a dog bed. "Jus, where's your dog?" she hollered toward the kitchen.

"At my parents'. I didn't know I'd be coming home. They love having her there anyway."

She looked around some more. *His dog? No, their dog.* Being there was a mistake, she quickly realized. Looking around the living room, she saw pictures of Justin and Petal: Justin and Petal at their wedding; Justin and Petal in bathing suits, *on their honeymoon*, she wondered; Justin and Petal smiling, arm-and-arm, in front of a huge cactus. She picked up the picture from their wedding, stared at it. It felt like someone took a knife and split her heart in half. Or maybe it was more like someone dumped cold water over her head, waking her the fuck up.

Justin had a whole life with Petal. A life. And there it sat, on a shelf, in his, or rather *their* — Justin *and* Petal's — living room. What on earth was she doing there? She quickly slipped her panties on. Right as she fastened the clasp of her bra, Justin came back in with two beers.

"What?" His eyes wide with consternation.

"I shouldn't be here."

"What? Why?"

She felt a wave of fury overtake her as she looked at him standing there naked. She loved him with everything she had, but the love ripped her heart right out. She felt so hurt, so betrayed. She let him close and she got hurt *again*, maybe even worse than the first time.

"I have to go."

"Liv, talk to me."

She pulled her pants on. "I can't do this. I look at these pictures and I realize the reality. You and Petal have been married for ten years. You share a life."

"But I love *you*."

"And I love *you*, but it doesn't matter. Because we can never get back that time, the time you spent with her. With HER." She shoved the wedding picture in his face. "I can't do this. I can't be with you."

"What? Liv? C'mon. You're upset. Let's talk it out."

"Justin. I can't. I know this wasn't all your fault. But you did fuck my best friend and then you married her."

"Yes. But, Liv. I tried for five years to get you back. What was I supposed to do? I had to move on. I was just trying to find a way to live without you. I have made mistakes. But I am trying, really trying, to make this right. So that we can have what we always wanted."

Her lips quivered. "Problem is, it can't ever be right. I can't go back. It will always be there. The betrayal, the hurt. I need to go." Her voice caught. "Please let me go."

"No. I won't lose you again."

"Justin. Please. I will always love you. But I can't be with you. I will always feel hurt if I'm with you. You have to let me go. *Please.* Let me go, so I can finally have what I want for my life." She looked deep into his eyes, unyielding. He wrapped his arms around her and he felt good, but she wiggled out of the embrace. She put her shirt and coat on, grabbed her bag.

Justin stood, his face pained, his mouth tight. A few tears trickled down his face. "I love you, but if you leave, please never call me. I know I did wrong. I know that I hurt you, but I can't take it anymore. I can't do this again."

She walked toward the door, her eyes filled with tears.

He followed.

She looked at him through glassy eyes and saw the agony in his gaze. She felt his pain as her own. And she wanted to grab him and kiss him, but admonished herself. This was all wrong. He was married, had been married. It was time for her to let go of him, her first love, and really open her heart to someone else. Adam.

"There's nothing I can say, is there?"

"No." she said, regret in her voice.

They shared a painful look. She stood on her toes and kissed his lips. "Goodbye, Justin."

"Goodbye." He said choking on the word.

An Uber came a couple minutes after she had ordered it, thank goodness. She cried the whole ride home. She tiptoed into the house; she didn't want to explain anything to her dad until morning. She felt disappointed, broken, devastated, but she knew she had made the right decision.

Adam had left a voicemail and a text, asking her to call him back. She was lucky he was even still talking to her after how distant she'd been. She blew her nose and wiped her eyes, then called him back and asked if he could come the next day, Friday. He could stay over, and they would go on Saturday to release her mother's ashes. Her heart felt so heavy while she spoke with him, but she did her best to keep her voice upbeat.

Then she said, without forethought: "I think I'll go back with you on Sunday."

"Back for the night?"

"No, back into the city. Get my apartment in order, get ready to move. It's best to do that before the spring semester starts and I'm back at school."

"You finished going through your mom's stuff?"

"Abbee went back on Monday, sooner than she had anticipated. We'll do it another time. I can come home to my dad's for a few days to take care of it."

"Excellent. It will be great to have you back. I'll text before I leave my place tomorrow."

"'Kay."

"Love you."

"Me too."

She felt strong when she hung up. It was time for her to go back to her real life and stop living in this fantasy where she believed she could recapture something that she had lost from her past. It was time to move forward.

With Adam.

She thought about Justin all night, tossing and turning, old memories and new memories jumbled together. It was going to take some time, she knew that. She did her best to think about moving in with Adam and the life she would be able to have with him, easy, stable, not complicated by a rocky history. She would definitely feel better once she was back in the city and in her regular routine.

She awoke in the morning, tired, her pillow soaked from tears. She took a long, hot shower, trying her best not to think too much about Justin. By the time she finished breakfast, she had already begun to feel better. She would miss Justin — always. But it was such a relief not to feel confused, to have made a choice and to know that it was the right one. Even if it wasn't the easy one.

Justin watched her walk down the hall with long, determined strides until she disappeared. Liv was gone — again. He grabbed his beer and paced in the living room, tears streaming down his cheeks. Glancing at the couch, he could still see the indents from where she had been laying, only moments before, when they had made love.

It was a mistake to bring her there. He had thought that when she asked, but then he believed — he really believed, like a complete schmuck — that they had made it over the hurdle. He had believed that she had faith in their love, and their commitment to work through their difficulties.

He fucked up again. He wanted to run after her and beg her to reconsider, remind her of everything she was throwing away. But he knew it was done. He knew her, and he saw something in her eyes, something different; he saw certainty. Hurt and sadness, but also a resoluteness, an unwaveringness.

The expression on her face in that last moment she looked at him would haunt him. *The silence of the final goodbye,* he thought. She didn't have to say a word. That look told him everything. *Oh, man, Liv. I can't believe you're gone.*

He guzzled his beer, not even tasting it. Tears continued to stream down his face. He felt like he had been run over by a truck, and he knew he'd feel bad for quite awhile. But he had to keep his wits about him. He couldn't let his life fall apart again. He couldn't make another string of bad choices, regretting years of his life. He knew what he wanted: to separate from Petal, to pursue his music. He had to stay focused on those things.

He would. But that evening, and probably for many evenings to follow, he felt devastated. He had tried everything to undo his mistakes, to have a second chance with Liv. In the end, there was nothing he could do.

He had tried.

Everything.

And in the end, she gave him nothing.

Fucking nothing.

His jaw tightened. The tears stopped. Anger, he felt anger. For Liv. A muddled mishmash of emotions swirled through his mind and body. Sad, empty, desperate even, but also anger, or even fury. He had also been hurt. This wasn't just about her. He had tried and tried; he wrote letter after letter, wrote emails and called. She gave him nothing. Sure, he made a mistake. He understood that; it was probably what held any anger at bay until now.

He was the one who fucked up — originally.

But she gave him, *them*, no opportunity for discussion, for reparation, for reconciliation. After five years — which was longer than everyone said he should give her; if he heard one more time, '*Justin, dude, you need to let go already, she's gone,'* he might have hit someone — he did what he had to. She had made it clear that she wanted nothing to do with him, even returning all his letters. Did she have any clue or even care what that was like for him? So, he tried to move on. And then she storms back into his life and upends everything. She revives his love for her. She gives him hope. She says she loves him too. And just when she's got him in her grip, she squeezes his heart, then rips it to pieces.

Well, fuck her, then.

He finished the beer in one long gulp, then retrieved another from the kitchen. He was sick of always having to chase Liv and *her* dreams, to keep up with *her* life expectations. What did she want from him? He didn't need the big city, or the money and notoriety of being a famous musician. She never got that. It was never about the end in sight; it was always about the process, the art, creating the music. Man, there was nothing in the world like creating something from nothing. Writing a song and knowing it came from the deepest part of his soul. That shit was priceless. She didn't get that.

Liv always wanted him to want more. All he wanted was to play with his band, write music and marry her. Be with her. Experience life and all of its possibilities, good and bad, with her. He swallowed that second beer and poured a glass of Scotch. He grabbed his guitar. A final chance at a relationship with Liv was done, and he would miss her. But no more giving up his life to pine away for a woman who clearly didn't really want him. She wanted some sort of superior version. She wanted the Justin who never cheated on her, and that was asking the impossible. Fuck that. Good that he asked her never to call him again.

He would move on this time, really move on, make changes, live the life *he* wanted.

Just not tonight. Tonight, he would drink. And drink. And he did. He drank and played the guitar, wrote a few lyrics down, nothing that would be worth anything in the morning. He strummed that guitar almost violently, letting his hurt, disappointment, anger, frustration out on those strings.

Three scotches later, his words had that slur he hated on Petal. But man, did he feel good, sloshed and carefree. He played, screaming out, *"There and gone/ words are silent/ lost not found/ talk is violent."* Passionate and incensed he continued, *"Angry love/ left behind/ with silent furies/ we can't rewind.* He yelled louder. *"Love and pain/ so sick of the shame. So fucking sick of bleeding your name. So fucking—"*

The neighbor banged on the wall. Looking at the clock, he was surprised to see it was already 2:30 a.m. He went into the bedroom, switched to his electric guitar, put his headphones on and plugged them into the new amplifier he had bought. He played, singing softly, until he passed out with the guitar next to him and the bedroom light on.

36

Friday evening, Olivia, Adam and her dad went for a casual bite at The Brownstone, an old-school diner not far from her dad's house.

Gregg had given her a knowing look when she had said that Adam was coming. "This is what you want?"

She nodded.

"I knew you would figure it out. You're a strong girl. Woman." He pulled her close, kissing her head.

This is nice, she said to herself as the three enjoyed dinner. Adam joined Olivia and Gregg for lively conversation including finance, real estate, even some light history and politics. Adam was well-read like her dad; she found it endearing and comforting that Adam fit right in.

It was easier than she thought to wipe the thoughts of Justin from her mind. All she had to do was think about something else. When her mind went to thoughts of him, she would busy herself with other ideas or activities.

It was a good time to try something new. She should take up running. Everyone talked about how transformative it was. That's what she was going to do. She would be moved into Adam's place as quickly as possible. With Central Park across the street, it was a perfect time to start jogging.

She had called her landlord that morning. Good news: They were going to let her leave her lease a month early. She would be moved into Adam's within the month, probably just after Thanksgiving. What perfect timing! The transition into her new life would be finished before Christmas. She would help her dad go through her mother's things, and adjust to living with Adam all before the semester started in January.

Life could not get any tidier than that.

Friday night, before they went to sleep, Adam mentioned that she could quit her teaching job and pursue her research work exclusively. "You could apply for that private industry research grant you had mentioned. Exploring the death anxiety groups with your colleague. I could easily support us."

This is nice, she thought. Someone she could really depend on to take care of her. "I don't know if I'm ready to give up teaching. Maybe in the future."

"Whatever you want, babe."

Saturday was painful. Having Adam there, his solid, supportive presence, did make it easier. Gregg seemed to really take to him, too. On the ride down to Sandy Hook, Adam and her dad spoke incessantly. In fact, to her astonishment, Adam shared his family secret with her dad. Gregg remembered the Siegfried case, and Dan's being a suspect in his parents' death.

"They ruled it was an accident. Right?" Her father asked.

"Right. I think one of the detectives had it in for Dan. Never liked him. And he couldn't let it go. In the end, they did rule that it was an accident. Recently, my brother has been in the tabloids. He's dating a model who likes attention. Dan likes it too. I just hope they don't start bothering Liv and me."

"We won't let them," Olivia said from the backseat of the car. She was glad that Adam agreed to sit in the front. He and her father seemed to be bonding quite well.

"I'm thinking it won't last very long between Dan and Monique. My brother is not great at remaining faithful."

Neither Olivia nor her dad responded to that comment.

"So, Liv, I'll come help you pack next week, if you want."

"That would be great, Dad. Wait until you see Adam's place."

"Our place." He twisted his neck to look at her.

"Our place." She smiled. *Our place*, she thought. *Our place.*

When they arrived at Sandy Hook, Olivia's eyes welled as soon as she saw the lighthouse and the quaint restaurant next door. Her mother loved that restaurant and the rocky beaches of Sandy Hook.

The waves were wild and huge and the wind, strong. But the sun was full and bright. The entire sky was a clear blue, not one cloud.

Aunt Betsey, Uncle Jack and Abbee were already waiting for them next to the lighthouse. Her father carried the urn with her mother's ashes. The whole thing seemed strange. Surreal. Like someone else's life.

They all took off their shoes and walked down to the shoreline. The roar of the waves, along with the sand under her feet and between her toes, brought back memories of her childhood and the summer weekends at Sandy Hook. Her mother loved to go to the beach after the sun went down when it was quiet and the sunbathers had gone inside. She always said that waves talked. At night, because it was quiet, if you listened closely, sometimes you could hear actual words.

As they got closer to the water and the crashing of the waves grew louder, she listened. And she heard her mother's voice say her name. *Liv,* she heard from the waves, her mother calling her. She bit her lower lip. Tears rushed down her cheeks. She took a tissue out of her bag and wiped her eyes. Adam wrapped his arm around her as they made their way to the edge of the water.

When they got there, they all took some of Lily's ashes and released them into the air, tossing them toward the water. The wind whirled the ashes around in circles before letting them fall into the sand and the water. As

Olivia watched the ashes suspended in the air, floating, floating, then slowly descending, she felt herself letting go of some of her pain.

It was a bittersweet moment. She felt the loss so deeply as she watched her mother's ashes slowly falling into the water — a deep, mysterious place her mother loved. But she also felt the release of some of her grief. Again, she heard her mother's voice saying *Liv* through the waves. She rested her head against her dad. She noticed that tears had fallen from his eyes.

"She loved it here," Gregg said, sounding like he was faraway.

"Her quiet place. She would be very happy with today. We did exactly what she wanted."

Aunt Betsey sighed. "Shall we go eat? That's what my sister would tell us to do."

"Let's." Her dad said.

Olivia looked in the urn before they walked toward the restaurant. "Dad, there are still some ashes in there."

"I'm going to put those in your mother's rose garden. To have her close."

"She'd like that," Olivia said, choking on her words.

"Yeah. Good idea," Abbee added, without dropping a tear. Olivia saw the sadness in her eyes, though. Olivia squeezed her hand. Abbee gave a thin, weary smile, and squeezed Olivia's hand back.

Leaving her dad's on Sunday was harder than she thought. She worried about him in that big, empty house with all his memories, all alone. And as though he had read her mind, he said, "I'm going to be fine, honey. I may go back to work part time. I have lots of friends. I'll keep myself busy. Besides, I'll be coming into the city to help you pack. Right?"

"Yes." She smiled, even though it still hurt.

In the morning while her dad and Adam chatted after breakfast, she went upstairs and took the letters from Justin out of the drawer. She planned to shred them, another step toward letting go of the past. She peered inside the manila envelope, looking at all of the small white envelopes, the letters. She pulled one out, held it with uncertainty. Looking at Justin's handwriting, she felt sad and sorry. Nostalgic. He touched those letters with his hand and his heart. She brought the letter up to her nose and sniffed, as if she could smell him on the 17-year-old paper.

She placed the letter back in the large envelope with the others, planted it back into the drawer, and buried it under a bunch of other paperwork she had kept at her parents'. She wasn't even sure why she kept them. Justin had spilled his heart onto those pages. It seemed wrong to cavalierly toss them out. Once she threw them out, she couldn't undo it. So, she'd leave them there and probably, hopefully, forget she even had them.

This is nice, she thought when they arrived back at Adam's, soon to be *their* place. She was already thinking about small changes she would install to make the apartment feel more like theirs and less like his. He pulled the heat lamps onto his balcony. They made love out there. Afterward, they sipped an expensive bottle of red wine and played checkers. It was a beautiful night. She couldn't wait to go back to her place the next day and start packing for her move.

37

It was a difficult time in Justin's life: transition, loss, change. And yet, things hadn't been this good in a long, long time, maybe ever. Life suddenly fell into place. Liv was gone. Unlike the first time he had lost her, when he held out hope that she would forgive him and come back, this time he knew it was over. During that first week, he had felt like he'd been punched in the gut, but because he knew he had to move on, he found a resilience he didn't even know he had.

He knew exactly what he wanted for his life, and he pushed himself to go after it. He worked hard to get more clients. Edgewater was booming with new real estate. He networked with architects and contractors, meeting new business owners. He had been hired to do some custom designs for a new high-rise that was in the final stages of development. All expensive condos right on the Hudson River.

The building owner, Sam White, owned a lot of riverfront property. As Justin spoke with him about the custom designs he would be doing for a library and a meeting room off the lobby, Justin asked him if there were any properties available in his price range. "A small one-bedroom would be perfect. I need something quickly."

"Oh?"

"Divorce." Justin said, quietly.

"Sorry to hear that. Been there myself." Sam White, a sturdy-looking man with a bush of dark hair, shook Justin's hand. "I've got a few apartments that might work for you. North of here on the west side of the street."

"That could work."

"I'll take you there myself."

"I'll be starting my work here early next week," Justin said. "I'd love to have a look before then."

"How's tomorrow?"

"Perfect."

"One day you might be living in one of these. Your work is some of the best artistry I've seen, son. And I've been doing this for a long time."

"That's nice of you to say."

Putting Furious Whiskers back together with Scully's help went smoothly. They had a band together within two weeks. Parker came back on bass and backup vocals; Scully on guitar and backup vocals; his brilliant drummer-friend, Leo; Kylie, Scully's girlfriend, singing some vocals and playing the keyboard. It was amazing how quickly he could get stuff done when he really put his mind to something.

He started playing with The Ragged Gems, too. After the band had heard him play and sing that first night in Hoboken, there was no way they were letting him go. They made room for him in the band straight away, which felt fucking fantastic. They had shows booked all over New Jersey and even New York City from November through the summer. Scully was going to use his huge contact list to get shows booked ASAP for Furious Whiskers too. When a band gels together, it doesn't take long to be ready to play out. They felt ready almost as soon as they started.

Petal called right before the family visit scheduled the second weekend of her 28-day program and told Justin not to come. He was shocked. It was out of character, not wanting to see him. But even more, he was concerned about why.

"It's nothing bad," Petal said. "It's actually good."

She sounded different, clearer, maybe stronger.

"So, tell me."

"I'm working on some stuff with my counselor here. Important issues. Some from my past. Some about you. Wilma, my counselor, recommended that we not see each other until the twenty-eight days are completed."

"OK," he said, hesitantly. "And then what?"

"I think I'm going to do three months of inpatient. But please come two weeks from Sunday for the family visit and we'll talk more."

"OK. I'm proud of you. I know recovery isn't easy."

"Thanks. I didn't think I had it in me. I think things will get better from here."

He didn't bring up the separation and neither did she. He wondered if when she said "things will better from here," she was referring to their marriage. He wanted to support her through her recovery, but he didn't want to string her along either. He would be honest when he saw her at the family visit in two weeks.

Justin threw himself into his music. It was like he rediscovered a part of himself that had been lost. He was playing almost every night, making all kinds of new connections, receiving all kinds of attention, even more than he used to.

Shy by nature, he was confident while he played, but when people came up to him afterward, he was always uncomfortable. Man, he appreciated that people enjoyed his work, but the adulation made him nervous. He was a humble guy from a blue-collar town. He was raised to be gracious and to treat everyone the same, regardless of what they did or how much money they made or how educated they were. When the audience idolized him, it felt awkward. He wasn't special. He wasn't worthy of such blind exaltation. He was just a regular guy who was lucky enough to have a talent for something he loved.

Scully had told him. "Dude, they love you. Use it to your advantage."

"I dunno how."

"I think they like you even more because you're reserved. A powerhouse onstage, quiet off. They can't figure you out." He slapped his back admiringly. "Man, you really have no clue how talented you are. It's good to be humble. But you gotta have pride too."

"I do have pride. In the work. The music is everything to me."

"I hear that. We need to start sending some of our own music out to agents."

"I'm ready, man."

Olivia's move had gone quicker than expected. Without any responsibility to work, it was easy to pack everything up, get movers and transition into Adam's place, *their* place. She still hadn't gotten totally used to saying it. Their place, their place, their place. She lived in a duplex on Central Park West with Adam. Her dad loved the place, and it was clear how much he liked Adam.

Adam was finishing up edits on his latest novel. He shared the manuscript with Olivia. It was absolutely wonderful. It was exciting to be part of his process, too.

As she had promised herself, she went to the Super Runners Shop, bought a good pair of running shoes and a Garmin, and started jogging in Central Park. It was better than she had remembered it. She could only go for about 22 minutes without having to take a walk break, but Adam said she'd build up; maybe by spring she could run a 5K and 10K.

She tried to run with Adam, twice, which didn't go well. She couldn't keep up, even when he went slowly. He kept pulling ahead; she would try to keep up, breathlessly picking up her stride behind him. "Sorry. I zoned out," he would say as he slowed down to match her pace. She decided she needed to build up her endurance before she could run with him.

Then he surprised her.

The day after she moved in, she heard, "Go ahead, Tucker. Show, Liv." Olivia stood in the library adding some of her books into Adam's collection. The subtle sound of Tucker's paws came from behind. When she turned, she saw it immediately. The ring hung around Tucker's neck, big and glimmering. It took her a minute to register what was happening. *What? Tucker has a ring? The Ring?* Before she even fully absorbed that last thought, Adam got down on one knee and said, "Olivia, I love you. Will you marry me?"

It took her a minute. She swallowed, her eyes wandering across his face; his eyes gleaming as he stared up at her, waiting.

"Yes." She said, a little uncertain at first. Her hesitation only happened because she was so caught off guard. That's all it was — being caught off guard. This was exactly what she wanted. Once what he asked really resonated, she said excitedly — with no uncertainty — "Yes. Yes, Adam. I will marry you."

He stood up, slipped the ring on her finger. They embraced.

It was official. She was engaged.

To Adam.

She, Olivia Watson, was getting married. Adam, handsome, dignified, intellectual Adam, would be her husband. *One word, seven letters* — and she liked the sound of it. *Husband.*

This was one of the most important days of her life: The day the man she would spend her life with asked for her hand.

Everything went so fast, even her thoughts. Her mind had recently become preoccupied with the minutia of her daily life: the move, where she would put the things she brought, what new things she would buy. She shopped online for furniture; maybe they would get a new bed. The balcony should have flower boxes. She ordered some. As soon as April hit, she wanted flowers blossoming. She looked online, read about all different types of seeds, when the best time to plant was. She wanted large standing plants, too. Lots of greenery. She frequented a few of the florists in Adam's neighborhood, no, *their* neighborhood — their neighborhood, their neighborhood — searching for plants that fit the vision in her mind. It was fun. *One word, three letters*, and it was. Putting the whole garden together in her mind took up a lot of time. She started sketching it to make the image clearer. She used to draw and had forgotten how good she was at it. Now remembering, she went to the craft store and bought some drawing pencils and sketch pads. Oh, she also had become obsessed with new running clothes. She looked in stores and online, some days becoming lost on various sporting good websites, looking for the best sales, comparing prices. This took up a lot of time, but she was really enjoying herself.

Now with the proposal, she would be busy planning a wedding. Their wedding. Lists upon lists needed to be made. What kind of dress did she want? She needed to get looking ASAP. A smaller, more intimate ceremony would be nice, maybe down along Sandy Hook. Abbee would be her maid of honor. Adam said he wanted Dan as his best man despite the acrimony between them. Yikes. *He will be family.* Maybe she should take another semester off; there was so much to do. She had stopped thinking about her research, anyway. Maybe she needed a break. It might have been the first time since high school that she didn't have a hypothesis swarming around her head, demanding an exploration. No more cerebral morning thoughts. There wasn't time. Too much real-life stuff to be attended to. Besides, her mind wouldn't stay focused on anything too abstract. Maybe losing her mother made her want to live more in the moment. She was sure that's what it was.

38

Two days after Adam had proposed and she said yes, Dan came for Thanksgiving. He had planned to stay at a hotel, supposedly. At the last minute, he asked — no, he told — Adam that he needed to stay with them. Something about his reservation falling through. Olivia wasn't thrilled about the idea, but he was Adam's brother. When Adam asked if it was OK, she gave an easy, "Of course. He's your brother. Is he coming with Monique?"

"No. I think she's got a modeling gig."

Dan arrived, tanned and wearing all white, except for his navy parka. *White pants in Manhattan at the end of November is a unique choice,* Olivia thought. She observed Dan's presentation and demeanor, wondering if in fact he killed his parents for the money.

That night, Olivia cooked dinner at Adam's — no, not Adam's, at their place. Their place, their place. After dinner, while sipping brandy, Adam brought the whole ugly disaster up. "Dan, you should have been more careful. Our whole family history is now on public display. Aunt Jeanie and Uncle Domino did their best to protect us, you especially. One careless affair with a woman you probably won't even know in a year, and now look."

"What do you care? It's not a big deal. Neither of us did anything wrong. I never understood your obsession with keeping the investigation private." He gave Adam a steely look.

"It's about the media. They're animals. Some will stop at nothing to get a juicy story. And Monique Finnis is the epitome of juicy story."

"Brother, *you're a writer.* Use the media. It could help your career."

"It's like selling my soul, Dan. I'm doing fine without allowing the tabloids to run salacious stories with only a glimmer of truth. You like the attention."

"You better believe it. I love it. If the tabloids want to follow me around and write about my life, well good for them. This is about your feelings of guilt, isn't it? About the fight you were having with them and the lack of contrition, before– "

"That's a horrible thing to say to me. And you're wrong. This is about not having my life exploited for the purpose of entertainment. Don't you get it?"

"I do. And I'm telling you, brother. Let them exploit me. My business has never been better. For some reason people want to do business with the guy banging

Monique Finnis. God, I love it. People are so stupid." He
let out a cutting laugh.

Adam cringed.

Olivia's head went back and forth as she listened
to them banter. Dan was awful and would soon be her
brother-in-law. She took a sharp breath. "Dessert?"

"Sure." Dan offered her a smug smile.

Thank goodness Dan had some business meetings
while he was there, so he wasn't at the apartment the
whole time. They did go out to eat twice, and then Dan
came to her dad's for Thanksgiving dinner. Interestingly,
Dan's demeanor was charming once he was in the company of her father and Abbee, Aunt Betsey, Uncle Jack
and Sebastian.

Dan appeared to show genuine compassion over
their loss, even seemed gracious. He sat between Adam
and Sebastian. Sebastian whispered to Olivia who sat on
his other side, "He's not so bad, Liv. Besides he's handsome like his brother."

She elbowed Sebastian. "Trust me. It's an act."

The whole transformation jarred Olivia. "He can really lay it on thick." She whispered to Adam.

"Yep."

After dinner, Gregg made a toast, "To Olivia and
Adam's engagement." Everyone clicked champagne
glasses. Even Dan wore a generous smile during the
toast. Then Abbee gave her an uncertain look causing
Olivia to wonder what was up her ass now. Later, while
they scrubbed pans and loaded the dishwasher, Olivia

asked her. "You think I'm making a mistake marrying Adam or something?"

"Not necessarily. It was just very fast."

"I'm almost thirty-nine. I know what I want. Why wait?"

Abbee stopped scrubbing the pan and looked into Olivia's eyes. "I just–"

"What?" Olivia snapped.

"I just worry that you're running toward him in order to run away from something else."

"Something else?"

"Someone else." Abbee gave her a hard look.

"Don't even say it."

"Listen, I know I give you a hard time, but I do want you to find happiness and make the right choices for your life. Are you sure about this one?"

"I am. Absolutely."

Abbee's lips parted, like she was about to say something else, but she turned her face toward the sink and began scrubbing the pan again. "I'm glad."

Dan left Sunday, but not before making the announcement. He returned from the deli, carrying a newspaper and magazine. "What complete insanity. Hahaha." Olivia heard the slap of the paper on the living room table.

"What?" Adam asked.

"We're on the cover of *Choice Magazine*. Look. Hahaha. Where do they get this stuff from?"

"*Ménage A Trois?*" Adam looked at the cover, exacerbated. "The ring. How the fuck would they know this. Dan?"

"It would be hard to miss Liv's ring. And they've been following me even when I'm not with Monique now. Don't worry, bro. I'm telling you, this will be fantastic for your writing."

Olivia heard the conversation, but remained unclear on what exactly had happened. She went into the living room, saw Adam and Dan standing in what appeared to be a face-off. A vein on Adam's temple pulsated, and his mouth tightened. "Dan. It's time for you to go. The visit's over." He flopped the magazine onto the living room table.

Dan looked at Adam, then Olivia. "Thanks for your hospitality," he said in a saccharine tone. He kissed Olivia on the cheek and said with questionable sincerity, "Congratulations."

"Thank you." She walked him to the door.

"What happened?" she asked Adam as she walked back into the living room.

"I'm sorry." He showed Olivia the magazine.

What on earth? Her face flushed. "Adam?"

He shook his head. "I don't know how they got that."

"Got what? It's a lie. *Siegfried boys, Ménage à trois?* A picture of me and my ring. How can they get away with this?" She opened to the article, scanned the paragraphs quickly.

"They never say it's fact. They write it as speculation and let their readers assume it's fact." He sighed, plopped on the couch and put his head in his hands. "Fucking Dan. I was afraid of this."

"I just hope it doesn't affect my job. I'm a professor and researcher. This kind of exposure, well, I'm not sure how it will be received by the dean."

"How often do you read this stuff? Or even look at the cover of magazines like this?"

"Almost never. I might not have seen this if Dan hadn't shown us."

"Exactly. I don't think they'll bother us now that Dan's gone back. And the dean will probably never know."

Adam looked so deflated by the whole thing; she decided to let go. Although she felt violated and humiliated, Adam had far worse to deal with. Dan, alone, was like a nightmare. Hopefully, no one important to her would see it. If they did, hopefully they wouldn't believe it. Any attention would probably pass quickly.

Adam and she went out in the early evening to a wine bar near their apartment. They shared appetizers and a bottle of Pinot Noir. They didn't speak about Dan or the article for the rest of the night.

39

Justin stopped by the grocery store to pick up some fresh bakery cookies on his way to the family visit with Petal. He planned to tell her that he still wanted the separation and that he would move out of their place while she was in inpatient treatment. He would still support her during her recovery, if she would let him.

He feared she would flip out, but he had to be honest with her. He had to rip off the Band-Aid all at once rather than lie to protect her feelings. Telling her while she was in treatment would ensure that she had supportive people around her.

Standing in line to pay, distracted by his thoughts, he didn't see it at first. As the line inched up, it sat right under his nose: Liv on the cover of *Choice Magazine*. Whaaat the?

It can't be. It was her profile. Her wavy, red hair stood out, unmistakable. The headline: *Siegfried boys, Ménage à trois?*

There was a picture of Liv, Adam, and some other guy. Encircled at the lower part of the magazine cover was a close up of a huge diamond ring. An engagement ring?

A wave of heat rushed to his face. He took the magazine off the rack and flipped through the pages searching for the story. Unable to concentrate and feeling self-conscious, he bought the damn thing.

As soon as he got in his car, he found the article. *Best-selling author Adam Summers, formerly Adam Siegfried, is engaged. But does his fiancée know his secret. And does he know hers?* Justin's jaw hung open.

The story was about her fiancé's parents' accident; the history of the brother, Daniel, being investigated for tampering with the brakes, but then getting off. And the *pièce de résistance,* Daniel's relations with Monique Finnis, whose picture was inset, was supposedly a cover for Dan really being involved with his brother Adam's fiancée — Olivia Watson, a professor at Hunter College.

Turning the page, he saw another picture of the diamond on Liv's hand. Liv was sitting with Adam at a table, holding a glass of wine. The ring covered half of her finger. Liv was engaged to Adam, maybe having an affair with Adam's brother. Whaaat? He tried to talk himself out of what he read. Those magazines didn't print the truth. *Choice Magazine* was a tabloid. But what was the truth?

For the first time since he saw Liv last, he considered calling her. Not to ask to see her, or try to get back together with her. Clearly, she had moved on; she was engaged. The call would be more about seeing if she was alright and to find out what really happened.

He unlocked his phone and stared at her number in his contact list. Man, he wanted to see what was going on, but what would he say? She had asked him never to call her. And he had asked her never to call him. Fuck.

It was a cold day, and gloomy; gray clouds hovered across the sky, promising precipitation. He pulled a hat out of his glove compartment and walked through the parking lot to the edge of the Hudson River. The wind blew in strong gusts making him pull his jacket tight. Gazing at the buildings across the river in Manhattan, he thought of Liv living there, moving on with her life. She was with a famous author from a wealthy family. She had never mentioned anything about Adam's financial situation or his family's past. He wondered how much was true, and how much she had known while Justin and she were seeing each other.

As his eyes wandered over the tall, proud, buildings, he thought: *Liv chose the life she wanted, a big life in the big city with a man who had money and large aspirations.* His stomach tossed around when he let the reality sink in. Liv was gone. No longer a part of his life. He couldn't call her.

Finally, he was following his own dreams, his own path. As painful as this news was about Liv, he needed to stay focused. Calling her, hearing her voice, if she even picked up — knowing Liv, there was a good chance she wouldn't — it would open a can of worms he didn't think would be good for him to face. Probably wouldn't be good for her either. He exhaled a cloud of frosty air as he walked back to his car. Life was a mixed bag: sad to know that he had really lost Liv; yet, he had never felt clearer about his own path.

When he arrived for the family visit, Petal delivered another surprise. Petal looked great, rested, her blue eyes bright, her skin vibrant.

"Wow. You look amazing." He kissed her cheek.

"You too." She smiled, softly. Her manner was calmer, more relaxed. They chatted for a little while. She told him some stories about her twenty-eight days in rehab. He told her about work and the music, Thanksgiving with his family. Before he even brought up his move into a new apartment and the separation, she said, "I'm sorry for what I did to you."

"To me?"

"The pills. I did it to try and keep you. I know now that wasn't right to do to you. More important, it was not good for me. I've been learning a lot about myself in here. About my feelings of being left by my father, emotionally abandoned by my mother. It's been very hard. But it's good too. I know now that I will get better."

"I'm sorry that I'm another person who's let you down." He held her hand across the table.

"No, you haven't. You have been the only person who hasn't let me down. You have stuck by me at my worst, even when I was mean to you and difficult to live with. Look. Even after everything, you're the one who's here now."

He squeezed her hand.

"But that doesn't make a marriage, right?"

He cocked his head, taken aback by her comment. "Whadaya mean?"

"You're right for wanting to separate. For wanting to leave over all of these years. I kept you trapped because I was so afraid that I couldn't be alone. You gave me the stability I needed."

"And you gave me a purpose when I needed one."

"I always thought if a got a man to love me, I would finally feel better about myself. But Wilma, she helped me understand that I need to love myself first."

"I do love you."

"I know, Jus. I understand things now. Painful things."

"Like?"

"When I found out about Becka and C.J., and you and Liv helped me get my own place, I felt so lost. Confused. Afraid. I didn't know how to be on my own. I– I used you. And I'm sorry. I mean, yes, I loved you. I *do* love you. You are the best person I have ever known. But we are not in love. Deep down, maybe I tried to make you love me because I needed you to take care of me. And Jus," she wrapped her hands around his, "you did."

"I'm sorry too. We both made mistakes."

409

"I was so mean to you."

"None of that matters now. OK? I'm here for you if you need me."

"Good, because I can't depend on Molly, but my goal is to be able to do this on my own."

"Of course. And I know you can do it."

A tear trickled down Petal's cheek. She quickly wiped it away. Justin choked up looking at her, sad that their marriage would end, relieved that their marriage would end, proud that Petal found the strength she needed to make her life better.

Driving home, he felt that urge to call Liv again. This time, he wanted to call and tell her that he was getting divorced and that Petal had agreed to it. He wanted to tell her about the new apartment he found through Sam White and, most of all, he wanted to tell her about the music. He could imagine her face lighting up as he shared everything.

You are a fucking dreamer, he said to himself. That time had definitely come and gone. Seeing Liv living a life separate from him, pictures of her with someone else, made him realize how she must have felt knowing he had a life with Petal.

Like a stab to the heart, that's exactly how it felt.

Life was fucking ironic. He was going to be single and free. Now, Liv would be the one who was married. And the distance between them would only grow with time. That look she gave him in response to his insistence that she never contact him again the last time he saw her entered his mind, reminding him with a stab to the heart that he had known that it was their final goodbye, despite whatever feelings he had that she might ignore his plea. He didn't need the magazine to tell him. Or her engagement to another man. He had already known.

As he drove the rest of the way home, he felt lonely, pensive. He tried to stop thinking about her, but his thoughts were relentless. A poem began to emerge, lines formulated, burning in his mind. He pulled over as soon as he got off the highway to write it down. It spilled out onto the keypad of his phone, a purge of emotion.

> *I knew you best from the silences,*
> *The time and space in between,*
> *The moment before our lips touched,*
> *The way your arms went up in the air before*
> *you laughed,*
> *The smile that we shared before we talked,*
> *The redness on your face before your tears,*
> *The sensation of your arms around me after*
> *you released the embrace.*
>
> *The look you gave me before you walked away,*
> *Nothing had ever been so painful,*
> *No words could say what your eyes told me,*
> *When I wake in the morning without you,*
> *It's the first thing I hear...*
>
> *The silence of the final goodbye.*

Reading what he wrote, a lone tear dripped down his cheek. There was no way he could call her. He took a deep, cleansing breath, pushed the gear into drive and pulled into traffic.

40

O livia awoke to the aroma of coffee swirling through the air. Adam was already up and writing, she assumed. During the week Adam arouse at 5:00 a.m. to write. Interestingly, he said he was able to tap into his unconscious more efficiently when the sun wasn't out.

She let herself enjoy the smell of the coffee and the comfort of the warm bed while going over what she wanted to accomplish that day. Without the structure of her teaching, she had become very good at imposing the order of the day on herself. She had so much she wanted to do before school started again in January.

She planned to go for a twenty-four-minute jog. She wanted to try and push from twenty-two minutes to twenty-four minutes. Then she would go to the grocery story. After that, a few furniture places; she wanted to look at new end tables for the living room and perhaps a love seat for the library. She would go down to The Strand and see if they had a few books that she wanted for her collection — or rather, their collection — then she would make a nice dinner for Adam. Maybe spaghetti. No, not spaghetti. Adam always worried about too many carbs, maybe fish and vegetables, baked potato. Adam tried to be healthy. She should be healthier too. She'd pick up fresh fish and get a few healthy-cooking cookbooks at The Strand. She needed to become a better cook, and now she had the time to practice. Her day would be productive. She also needed to talk with Adam about a wedding date, because she hoped to secure a place before school started. Her mind raced with all the things she wanted to get done as she walked toward Adam's writing room.

He wasn't at his desk. "Adam?"

His voice bellowed from downstairs. She went down the spiral staircase and found him in the kitchen, a big smile across his face. He spoke enthusiastically on the phone. "Yes. Absolutely. Contact them. See what they offer. Almost done. OK. Talk to you later."

He hung up the phone, picked Olivia up and spun her around. Adam seemed thrilled about — something.

"What is it?" She asked after he put her feet back on the ground.

"That was my agent. All three of my books hit the top ten on Amazon overnight. *An Inconvenient Coincidence*, hit number one. It isn't even 8:30 yet, and already my agent's phone is ringing with requests for interviews and appearances."

"That's great." She smiled, but didn't feel enthusiastic.

Her voice must have betrayed her true feelings, because Adam asked, "What's wrong?"

"It's because of the article. Just like Dan said."

"Yeah. I'm sure and so is my agent. I don't like our faces in print associated with gossip, but the damage is done. At least something good came of it."

"But it's not right for them to exploit people. You said it yourself. I thought you didn't like or want that type of attention?"

"True. And I meant it. I still mean it. But now that the truth is out there, I have been forced to confront my past. Things are different now."

"Different? How?"

"I don't feel like I have to hide who I am. Suddenly, I feel liberated from my past."

"I don't get it."

"It was mistake, I think, for my aunt and uncle to have us change our name and not tell anyone where we came from and what had happened to us, especially Dan. It made it seem like we did something wrong because our parents were wealthy, because we grew up privileged, because they died tragically, and we were alone, because the detectives hated Dan since we were teens. They tried to pin it on him. But now, I see I have nothing to be ashamed of. And I want to tell my story."

Adam's whole manner seemed different. The quick metamorphosis made her uncomfortable, but she reminded herself that she had never lived with anyone else. Adam, obviously, had a private self, one that she would get to know with time. He seemed elated, that's all that mattered, so she hugged him and congratulated him on the new opportunities.

By dinnertime, Adam's agent, Zelda, had been contacted by three different publishers inquiring if Adam would consider writing his family's story. "Zelda said she thinks she can get me a six-figure advance."

"That's great. Not like we need the money, though."

"It's validating to know your work is desired."

"Yes. Of course." She said, but thought: *The advance isn't because of the quality of your writing; it's because of that salacious headline.*

Olivia felt dismissed. Granted, she had let go of the discussion about the article. But it was like he forgot she was impacted by it, that *they* were impacted by it.

The more attention Adam got, the more distance she felt between them. At first, she had thought the distance came from him. Adam spent long hours writing and needed a lot of time alone and a lot of space from her. But their nights were spent together, talking, making love, watching movies, reading books, hanging around. Nothing had changed in that regard, and yet, something felt vastly different. Maybe she needed to figure out who she was in this new life, in their new life.

On a number of occasions, she awoke in the middle of the night from dreams of Justin, tears burning in her eyes. She would think of him longingly for a moment, then would force herself to think about something else, anything else.

She knew she would miss Justin sometimes. She knew she would never love Adam quite the same way as she had loved Justin. Of course, she would dream of him. The thing was, when she woke up from these dreams, she had the vague feeling that she loved who she was when she was with Justin, freer, more spontaneous, at her most honest; he brought something out in her that she felt like she couldn't find without him. When she followed the idea through, it didn't make any sense, though. She was a strong, independent woman; she hadn't been Justin's girlfriend for more than seventeen years. She was who she was with or without him. The dreams kept coming, though, and along with the dreams this nagging, annoying sense that nothing made sense anymore.

Then one morning it occurred to her, and when the thought came, she tried to rid herself of it: Maybe Adam and Justin *were* alike. Maybe her family had been right. Maybe Adam's transformation, now that he was liberated from his past, made him feel less like Justin. What if she had fallen for Adam, because he had been so much like Justin?

They were both reserved, except now Adam was suddenly more open with people. Olivia had always liked Justin's quiet nature; it made her feel special, because he was selective about what he shared with others. Adam had been like that too. But now he was different. He was more extroverted, more talkative. He was more willing to share his personal experiences with the world and not in a metaphorical or hidden manner, like he did in his fiction and Justin did in his poems and lyrics, but rather openly in interviews.

Like Justin, Adam thought deeply about life. Both of them were sensitive, but had an edge. Both were artists. Both looked at her with helpless abandon.

She thought about the first night she had seen Adam's writing area and the piles of notebooks on his desk. Just like Justin's desk. Both had piles of notebooks, pages and pages of their souls poured out inside.

No. *That IS insane,* she told herself as she got out of bed. Besides, her family had said they looked alike. And they didn't look anything alike.

Adam and she were in a bit of a disagreement on their wedding venue, too. Olivia wanted to be married on the ocean where they had released her mom's ashes, a small ceremony with only close family and friends. Adam wanted a big gala at an expensive hotel in Manhattan. Suddenly, he wanted to include all of these people from his parents' life.

She had always envisioned a smaller, more intimate wedding. But it seemed so important to him to reconnect with these people, so she agreed. They were going to look at the various locations and hoped to a have place within the month.

Then Becka messaged her on Facebook on New Year's Day.

> *Becka: Happy New Year Liv! Sorry I have been out of touch. Kids will do that. I loved seeing you. Can we meet for lunch soon? How are you?*
> *Olivia: Hi Becka! Happy New Year! I loved seeing you too. How's Christopher?*
> *Becka: He's great! We took him skiing for the first time during Christmas week.*
> *Olivia: How cute.*
> *Becka: I heard you were getting married. Congratulations!*
> *Olivia: Thank you! Yes, we're very excited.*
> *Becka: It was in Choice Magazine. What happened with that?*

Olivia felt heat course through her.

> *Olivia: It's a long story. Most of that article wasn't true.*
> *Becka: We figured. That magazine is crap. But it was shocking to see you on the cover.*
> *Olivia: What do you mean "we"?*
> *Becka: Oh, haha, me and C.J. and well, Justin and Travis too. They didn't believe the stuff about Adam's brother, either.*
> *Olivia: It's not true.*
> *Becka: We figured.*

Olivia: I'll explain more when we meet for lunch.
Becka: OK. I wanted to show this to you. Not sure if you saw it on my Facebook page. I don't know why I thought you should see it. I guess it reminded me of the old days. I miss those times.
Olivia: What is it?
Becka: Play it. You'll see. Love you, Liv. Lunch very soon.
Olivia: Yes. Very soon. I'll call you next time I'm in Jersey. Xo
Becka: Congrats again.
Olivia: Thank you!

Olivia clicked on the video. It was Justin singing "Wonderwall" on stage with Furious Whiskers. The band's name was on the drums. Scully on electric and doing backup vocals, Parker on base and doing backup vocals, Kylie playing keyboards, someone she never met on drums. God, he looked handsome and dynamic. Justin's band was back together, and they sounded better than ever. *They sound amazing; he sounds amazing.* She wished Becka hadn't sent it. It made her miss him. She watched it again, making the sound louder so she could really hear the affectation in his voice. A small lump sat stubbornly in her throat. Justin had let his hair grow to just above his shoulders and he had facial scruff, both of which made him look exactly like he had seventeen years ago, very sexy. And as he came alive onstage, she saw it in his mannerisms. The way he held his shoulders, his tall, lean stature, the intensity in his expression. Her family was right; there was a resemblance between Justin and Adam. She placed her hand over her mouth. *My God.*

"What is that?" Adam leaned over her shoulder. She was on her laptop in the library, engrossed in the video and hadn't heard him come in.

"Nothing." She jumped, then tried to click it off, inconspicuously, but it didn't close right away.

"Isn't that Justin?"

"Yes." She said softly.

"You said he played with a band when you guys were younger. Didn't know he still did that."

"Oh, yeah, I think he recently got back into it. Becka sent this to me."

"He's got some voice. Surprised he never made it big with that voice."

"I'm not sure that's what Justin wanted, now thinking back. I think he was happy playing with his band and having room for other things in his life. I think he liked balance."

"That's a waste of talent. And probably about fear."

"I don't agree. I don't think everyone wants the same things. And I think Justin saw success as balance, not as money and/or fame. I think it was only about love. Loving what he did." *And loving me,* she thought.

And then it hit her, Justin didn't lack direction. She had always worried that Justin didn't know what he wanted. Truth was, Justin had always known exactly what he wanted. He wanted to be with her, support her in whatever she wanted to do, play his music, write, work as a teacher, or now as a carpenter, and enjoy life, together. Now, he pursued his dream, but without her. "Excuse me." She rushed to the bathroom, tears welling in her eyes.

Adam watched her hurry away, a pensive look in his eyes.

41

Being back at school felt strange; she was back in her normal routine, but nothing felt the way it used to. It felt like someone else teaching those classes, responding to enthusiastic and critical students. It was someone else grading papers. She didn't feel connected to the work or passionate about it. She almost felt apathetic, like there was no meaning in anything she did. She went through the motions, feeling like her feet were stuck in quicksand.

Planning the wedding felt all wrong, too. She didn't say that to Adam. They had visited a few hotels, still had more to see, but none of them felt right to Olivia, too big, too fancy, not warm or intimate the way she had imagined. It was already painful to be getting married without her mother; his desire for this big gala of a wedding was making her feel worse.

She asked about being married in Central Park. Maybe that was a compromise. Adam had said that he worried about an outdoor ceremony. "Weather can be unpredictable, Liv," he had remarked.

"Life is unpredictable." She had said back, trying to sound playful.

He gave her a serious look, then smiled. "The hotel is more secure."

"Sometimes it's fun to be insecure and take a chance, to not worry. An outside wedding would be beautiful. If it rains we can give umbrellas as guest gifts. And people can dress down. I always imagined a wedding with originality and character. Something that says 'this is me — this is us.'"

"We'll make sure that the wedding screams, Olivia and Adam. I promise. Let's just look at a few more hotels." He rubbed the scruff on his chin, then kissed her.

"OK." She said in a defeated voice. "OK."

Adam got a six-figure contract for his memoir. She didn't ask the details of the agreement. Between his new novel being in the final stages of editing, with a pre-release date of May 1st, his concentration on writing his memoir, and all of the new attention he received now that it was public that he was a Siegfried, Adam had become much less attentive. When they spent time together it was wonderful, but his life was big, maybe too big. And she couldn't quite figure out where she fit in.

She wished Becka had never sent that video with Justin. Maybe Olivia would have found out Furious Whiskers was back together anyway, maybe not. Regardless, when she felt really lost, she would watch those videos. There were a bunch of them on the Furious Whiskers' Facebook page, which she discovered one night.

She wasn't really looking.

Or maybe she was.

She watched those videos feeling such warmth toward him, remembering wistfully, how good she felt being close with Justin, and their times together. Whenever she saw Justin's resemblance to Adam, it would send a shiver down her spine. *Adam is a replacement for Justin*, she would think, and her stomach would ball. She would push that idea out of her mind, telling herself that she had a type. Adam and Justin were the same "type." It was that simple.

A few times, she thought of calling Justin, but then she remembered how she felt when she saw those pictures of Petal and him, the actual piercing sensation that shot through her heart like a bullet, when the reality of his life resonated. Besides, she *was* marrying Adam. And Justin had told her never to call him again. Any contact with Justin would potentially mess up her life.

Problem was, her life already felt messed up, and she wasn't sure how to fix it.

January became February became March, like a monotonous blur. She began to wonder if maybe she had made a mistake saying yes to Adam's proposal. Maybe she hadn't really known him well enough or long enough to say "yes." People say you should know someone for all four seasons before moving in with them and/or marrying them because people change just like the seasons do. But then they would have a nice weekend together and she would remember why she had fallen for him in the first place. Her feelings of uncertainty with her life weren't about him. It was something going on with her. Maybe she was commitment phobic. Maybe transitioning from single to married was troubling her. Life transitions were hard. This was an existential crisis of meaning being stirred up by a major life change.

Or maybe not.

Then the second Sunday in March, her phone rang.

She thought he didn't know. And, honestly, he wished he didn't. Olivia had not been the same since her mother's death. At first, Adam thought it had to do with the loss. Of course, she was grieving. He knew all too well what that was like. It was after he proposed that he began to suspect something. Olivia changed. She became preoccupied with meticulous and obsessive organizing of the apartment and trying to be a better homemaker: cleaning, cooking, ordering all kinds of kitchen items, making lists of what she wanted to move around and purchase for their place.

She moved through her days like the Energizer Bunny, never stopping to pause. It was all just, do, do, do, go, go, go. It's not that he didn't appreciate her will and drive to be more domesticated; he did. It was that this wasn't the woman he had proposed to. That woman was strong and independent, had intellectual and un-conventional interests. She was someone who enjoyed sitting and thinking, someone who enjoyed contempla-tion of the big questions, someone with philosophical sensibilities.

Olivia almost seemed manic and not about their en-gagement. She spent more and more time busying her-self with these mundane tasks. It was odd. She was not excited about the wedding, either. They hadn't agreed on a venue. And he started to think it was more than a difference in the vision of what the wedding would be like. Something made her hold back. He wasn't sure what.

Then he saw her watching that video of her ex-fiancé and all the scattered pieces coalesced. Liv had had some sort of relations with him while she was staying in New Jersey, after her mother died. Her distance during that time made sense now. She had been involved with Justin. He saw it in her body language when she got up from watching his video on her laptop; he saw it in her eyes, pain, longing, love. Tears.

He thought of bringing it up with her, but decided to give her some time. She *was* grieving; Justin was from her past; maybe she was going through something. But she became more and more disengaged. Then he heard her on the phone. Of course, he only heard one side of the conversation. But it wasn't even what she said, neces-sarily. It was the tone of her voice. Her body language after she hung up.

He had to say something.

The phone rang, an unfamiliar number, Jersey area code. Olivia debated letting it go to voicemail, but there was always this nagging concern that something had happened to her dad now that he lived alone. So, after a few rings, she accepted the call.

"Hello?"

"Liv. Hi."

Shit. She shouldn't have picked up.

"Hi Petal. What's going on?" She wondered if something happened to Justin. Or maybe Petal called to tell her off in some retaliatory act because she found out Justin had had an affair with Olivia. Olivia felt defensive.

"I'm calling to make amends. I don't know if you know. I'm guessing you do. I'm in rehab."

"Good for you."

"I'm at the point in my recovery where I'm looking back on the people I've hurt and calling to make amends. To take responsibility for poor decisions I made because of my addiction. I know I hurt you. And I am very, very sorry."

Olivia took a heavy breath. Petal put her in a bad situation. She didn't think her drinking led her to sleep with Justin; it was selfishness. But she didn't want to say anything that would negatively impact her recovery. "I don't know what to say. You did hurt me. You think it was because of the alcohol?"

"The alcohol and family issues together made me make decisions that were bad for me and people close to me. You were my closest friend, but I always felt so jealous. I didn't understand it too well back then. But you always got everything you wanted, and I would have given one of my hands to be like you. I never really considered your feelings because I figured that no matter what, you would be OK. That was very wrong and very childish. I will always regret it."

"Thank you for that. It means a lot to me to hear you say that. You sound good."

"I am good. This is very hard for me to say, and I hope it doesn't come out wrong. I– I know you saw Justin after your mother's funeral. I don't think he ever stopped loving you. I complained for years, yelling, drinking, angry that he wouldn't give me what I wanted. But the truth is, he couldn't. His heart belonged to you. It's so painful thinking of the wasted time, the choices I made out of desperation. I hurt you. I hurt him. And I hurt myself. We're separated now. Justin has moved out. When I leave here next week, I will be on my own. And I have made a commitment to myself to start my life over."

Olivia's breath caught. *Justin and Petal are separated. Why hasn't he called me? Well, why would he?* "I'm glad you are making changes. I don't think it's a good idea for you and me to discuss Justin, though."

"Of course. Thank you for talking. Maybe we can catch up sometime."

"Yeah, maybe. Keep up the recovery. You sound great."

"Bye."

"Bye."

Justin, separated, living on his own? Why wouldn't he call? You told him not to. Well, actually, he told you to never contact him ever again. You'd hurt him too much. Something was really gone between them. She turned around to find Adam standing a few feet behind her. Looking at him, she reminded herself that it was totally over with Justin and that she had committed to Adam. Besides, Justin knew she was getting married. *That's why he didn't call.* He knew from that damn magazine article that she was marrying, Adam. *No, that's not why he didn't call. YOU'RE why he didn't call.*

Her mind spun in a messy whirl when Adam said, "Liv, we need to talk." His tone had an uncharacteristic severity. Her stomach flipped.

"What is it?"

"Why don't you tell me."

"There's nothing to tell." She said, defensively.

"I believe there is." He took her hand and led her to the couch. "I know you've been with Justin. I don't know the extent, and you don't need to tell me details. But I think the secrecy is causing distance between us. You can tell me the truth."

Tears welled in her eyes. "I don't know what to say."

"Just tell me the truth, so we can work through it."

She wiped the tears from her cheeks and sighed. "I spent some time with Justin while I was staying at my dad's. He's an old friend."

He gave her a shrewd look. "Friend? Come on, Olivia. Ex-fiancé."

"I– I." She stood up and paced.

Adam watched her go back and forth.

She sat back down and looked at him. "I still love him. I have been so unfair to you. And you deserve better." She took his hands. "You are a wonderful man. And I do love you, but I can't love you the way that I want to because my heart has always belonged to him."

"It's OK, Liv. He was your first love, and you reunited during a vulnerable time in your life. It makes sense that it would ignite old feelings."

"True. But it's not only old feeling. I didn't want to admit it to myself because he hurt me so much, but I have loved Justin my whole life."

"What are you saying? You want to go back to him?"

"No." She took a sharp breath. "I really wanted to make this work between you and me. Me and Justin are over. But it doesn't change how I feel. I'm still in love with him."

He took her hands. "We can work this out, Olivia. "Maybe you need time to heal. From losing your mother, from being with him."

"No. I can't give you what you want and deserve."

"You would rather be alone than be with me?"

"No, I'd rather be alone than trap you in a marriage when I'm in love with another man." Her lips dropped into a frown. "I am so sorry."

They shared a pained look. She tried to pull him in for a hug, but he put his hand out. "No. I need you to leave."

She looked at the ring, her mouth quivering. She took it off and placed it on the living room table.

What was she supposed to do now? She had no apartment to go back to. "I guess, I'll go to my dad's until I can find an apartment. Can I leave my stuff here?"

"That's fine."

She bowed her head. "I'm sorry."

"Me too." He whispered.

She packed a small bag, almost in slow motion. Before she left, she looked at his steadfast expression. She had really hurt him. Handsome, dignified Adam wasn't going to show it, but she had. She wanted to want a life with him, but she didn't. She kissed his cheek, said her goodbyes and left.

As she stepped outside, looking for a taxi to the Port Authority, she admitted what she had been denying for months: Adam was Justin, just a safer, less complicated version.

She wanted Justin. It was harder, messy. There were things she had to get past, things she had to let go of. She ran out on him that night, so hurt by the pictures, so hurt by his choices, she didn't even give herself a chance to think it through. Everything that had felt wrong since her engagement to Adam was because she wanted Justin. Suddenly, she wanted to run to New Jersey and find Justin and tell him that she never wanted to be without him. She had been a complete idiot — afraid, stupid, selfish.

Then she realized that she didn't know where Justin lived or what he was doing. She acted like he was sitting around waiting for her to come back. He had asked her never to call him again. And he hadn't reached out to her despite the fact that he was separated. Maybe it was really done for him.

No.

Yes.

She went back and forth in a painful, internal banter about whether or not she should call him. Once the bus was in New Jersey riding along the Hudson, the impulse to call him overwhelmed her. She had to take a chance. Maybe she could get off the bus and go to him. If she didn't play it safe, maybe, hopefully, she had the chance to see him tonight.

She called. Her heart raced with every ring. *Please, pick up. I miss you. I don't know what I was thinking running out that night, not even giving myself a chance to think about what I was really feeling. Pick up.*

No answer.

"Hey Jus, um. It's Liv. Um. Call me if you have a chance."

42

Things were go fucking fantastic, then Liv called and left a voicemail. He was shocked when he saw her number. Hearing her voice — God her voice, that raspy tone, he missed it, but hearing her voice felt like someone had tossed salt in his wound. He hoped to God that she was all right. That magazine article left a lot open for speculation about Liv's choices and her life.

Justin played the message over a bunch of times. He wanted to call her back and see what she wanted, talk to her. It was a bad idea, though. A future with Liv had slipped through his fingers — again. She was like a ray of light, beautiful, illuminating, strong, and impossible to grasp, at least for him. He would never be the man capable of holding on to Liv. Too many mistakes, mistakes that could never be undone. She had made her choice.

He had been running after Liv his whole life. Now it was time for him to chase dreams unrelated to her.

Damnit, though, it was really fucking hard not to return her call — which is why he had asked her never to call him again; he knew hearing her voice would leave him vulnerable — because deep down he knew Liv was part of the reason his life moved in such a positive direction. She saw the best in him and because of that, he discovered it in himself. Liv was an inspiration even when they weren't together.

Liv would always have a place in his heart, but he wanted to try, now that he separated from Petal, to find love with someone else. He'd never be able to do that if Liv was still in his life. He deleted the message.

Petal got out of rehab a few weeks after Justin had moved into his new apartment. She had never seemed better, less angry, even stable. She was focused on her emotional well-being and her recovery. She saw an outpatient therapist and went to meetings at night.

Justin helped her out financially the first month after she came out. They saw each other a few times for dinner. One afternoon, he went over to fix a loose cabinet in the kitchen and brought Jules so she could see her.

"I met someone. In my meeting. I just– I thought you should know."

"How long has he been clean?"

"You're upset."

"No. I'm concerned."

"He's been in recovery just over six years. He's forty. He's really nice. You've been there for me when no one else was, but I want someone who really loves me." She squared her shoulders. "Someone who loves me like you love Liv." She searched his face for insight into his feelings for Liv, for his reaction to her interest in someone other than him. But his expression revealed nothing.

"You deserve someone who can give you everything you want. You think it's him?"

"So far so good, but I'm not jumping in. I'm supposed to stay unattached for the first year of recovery. We're taking it slow, as Wanda advised."

"That's good."

"And you?"

"Just focusing on my music."

"I want you to be happy too, Jus."

"I am." He smiled.

She leaned in and they hugged.

The music had never been better. Going into spring, between Furious Whiskers and The Ragged Gems, he played out two nights a week, usually Thursday night and Saturday night, occasionally Thursday, Friday and Saturday. When he wasn't out playing, he worked on new stuff with Furious Whiskers. The new lyrics poured out of Justin. He would be in the middle of work or in the grocery store or visiting with his family, and a new rhythm along with phrases would come into his mind. He would rush to write it down.

Furious Whiskers had already recorded a number of new songs, one of which was *Forever and One Day*, a song he had originally written when he was with Liv in college. One morning he woke up with those lines repeating in his mind again. He lay in bed singing the lines to the melody of *Forever and One Day*. It sounded perfect. He got his guitar, rewrote all of the lyrics. Scully loved the new rendition, calling it fucking brilliant. They recorded it right away.

Scully and he sent the new stuff off to agents, exploring the possibility of representation. Justin wanted it, but had some reservations. It would be nice to make enough money to be able to focus exclusively on the music. But he wondered what making it mainstream would do to the quality of the art. He knew a few people who had had their big break. The music they wanted to do changed into a mix between what they wanted and what they had to write and sing, what the agents and producers thought would sell the most.

Justin didn't share his uncertainties with Scully. He decided to go through the steps and see where the efforts took them.

Toward the end of April, a conversation with Sam White opened up a surprising opportunity. While Justin worked on making those cabinets exactly the way Sam had envisioned, Sam hung around the building a lot. They developed a warm rapport, often talking about their respective lives. Sam had gone through an ugly divorce about ten years earlier. At sixty-two years old, he had met a new woman and was getting remarried. Sam had a soft side to him, which made Justin feel comfortable enough to tell Sam more about his life than he shared with most people. He told him the whole reason for his recent separation and soon-to-be divorce. He shared his regrets about Liv, mistakes of his youth, changes he worked on.

"I admire you, son. You've got more sense to you in your late thirties than I had in my late forties, even fifties."

"I don't know about that. I'm just trying really hard not to make mistakes that waste time and hurt people I care about."

Then he began to tell Sam more about his writing. Sam knew he played with a few bands, but he didn't know that Justin was also a songwriter. Sometimes being more reserved really was a disadvantage. When Sam heard this, his eyes lit up. As it turned out, his brother was a big movie producer in Hollywood. Sam thought some of Justin's music might be good for the film he was currently producing.

"Can you get me some of your music tonight? Let me send it over to him. Can't hurt. Right?"

Justin was speechless for a moment. "Yeah, sure, I can do that." He finally blurted. "That's very generous of you."

"If your music is as good as your carpentry, then you may get yourself an easy deal with my brother. All I'm doing is making the contact, which I'm more than glad to do."

"I really appreciate it, Sam."

That night after work, he went for a long run along the river. A warm breeze blew in from the Hudson.

Spring came, and with that it seemed everything flourished, more people were out, traffic was nuts, flowers and greenery exploded everywhere. The trees danced easily in the light spring breeze.

It was a time of growth and new beginnings and now, for Justin, it was a time of great possibility. This new opportunity with Sam's brother excited him. His mind wandered down a path from what their initial meeting might be like to having his music on the original soundtrack for this movie, a love story called *Bring Me Back*.

He stopped running and gazed across the river. It was one of those clear nights when he could see the cars driving through midtown Manhattan. He thought of Liv. She would be squealing with excitement over the possibility with Sam White's brother.

She had been his greatest support and inspiration when they were younger. And truth be told, he had to give her much of the credit for him getting back into it. If he hadn't been trying to better his life, to motivate himself to make better choices in order to be the man he thought she wanted, he never would have found this part of himself that really could accomplish things he set his mind to. She saw who he was deep down before he even saw it himself. If his music would be used in any way for this film, he'd have to shoot her an email or even give her a call and tell her. Thank her.

43

If it weren't for her dad, she might have lost her mind. Temporary insanity. Lost in her life, never so confused, grieving the loss her mother and now — homeless. She gave up her apartment, only now to have to find a new place. Her father insisted that she stay in New Jersey for the rest of the semester and commute into the city. "I'm worried about you, Liv. I've never seen you so stressed. Don't cause yourself more stress by adding another move. Ask Adam if you can keep your stuff there. We'll find you a place and you can move in the summer when you're only teaching one or two classes."

She really didn't want to stay at her dad's and commute, but she didn't have the strength to look for an apartment, never mind go back to Adam's, pack, get movers and move again. So, she stayed at her dad's. Adam said it was fine for her to leave her stuff there for a few months.

She watched Adam's social media to see how his writing was going. It was amazing, in a sort of mind-boggling way, how that awful article seemed to boost Adam from great, but not well-known writer, to famous. Thank goodness the media never bothered her again. That was a godsend.

Justin never called her back. She had always taken for granted that he would be there. Even over those seventeen years when she did her best to forget him, deep down she believed that he would respond if and when she decided she wanted to talk.

She wanted to call him again, but she didn't know how. He had asked her never to call him again; clearly his lack of response showed that he meant that. Nevertheless, a few times she held the phone, wanting to call, and then stopping herself before she dialed.

Being at her dad's made it worse. She wasn't sure where he lived, but it probably wasn't far. And she found herself thinking she saw Justin whenever she was out in the neighborhood. Her heart would vault up, then sink just as quickly when she realized it wasn't him. Some nights she would jog along the river hoping to run into him. She even messaged Becka to tell her that her engagement was off. Wondering if Justin didn't call her back because she was engaged, she hoped Becka's affinity for gossip would lead her to tell Justin that it was called off, and that Liv was staying at her dad's for a while. She kept imagining Justin ringing the bell one night, pulling her into an embrace, telling her that he still loved her. But nothing.

When May rolled in and she still hadn't heard from him, she assumed that he simply didn't want to talk to her. Thinking of the way women were hypnotized by Justin when he played and knowing — because she looked at the band's Facebook page and Twitter account nearly every day — that he played a few times a week, she felt certain that he was dating, or at the very least, having regular sex with fangirls. She felt ill when she thought about it, feverish and nauseous.

Nevertheless, she had to learn to live her life again. So, when springtime was in full bloom and the air was sweet from the flowers, she pushed herself to regain her focus. To begin again. She wanted to find a man she could open her whole heart to.

Match.com depressed her, but Abbee had found a new man on there and insisted that Olivia give it a try. So, she set up a profile and searched for interesting men on the Internet. That was a start.

Abbee came the second week in May so they could go through her mother's things. Abbee asked, "How's the dating going?"

"Not great. I'm still getting used to searching through men's profiles the way I look for new clothes online."

"It is a different experience." Abbee chuckled. "You look tired." Abbee looked at her, sympathetically. "Are you OK?"

"I'm getting better. I am tired, though."

"Talk to me. You're upset about Adam?"

"Not really. I was immediately after it happened. But you were right, marrying him would have been a mistake. It's painful to admit that because I really did enjoy him. I loved him too, just not as much as I think I should have."

"Because of Justin?"

She hated admitting it to Abbee, but she was too tired to lie and deflect her piercing glances. "Yes." She sighed. "But I need to totally move on from the idea of being with Justin, otherwise I'm never going to find what I want."

"What if Justin *is* what you want?" Abbee raised her brow.

Olivia's shoulders dropped. "Yeah. There's that. Except this time, I think Justin is the one who doesn't want me. I called him over two months ago. He never returned the call."

"One call? And you gave up? That's not like you. Whenever you have wanted something, you've gone after it."

"Yes. But this is different." As she said it, she thought: *Is it? And why is it?*

"Liv. It's what mom said. It's pride. Calling Justin again, it risks something of yourself. You don't have control and you have no clue how he'll respond. And you're terrified."

She contemplated what Abbee said, "Maybe. I dunno. He told me never to call him again. And I'm guessing Justin has moved on. Is dating."

She bunched her lips up. "So you don't even try? Liv, if you want him, you are making the worse choice of your life by not at least reaching out one more time."

"You're right." *I just don't know how to do it. It's like I can't even get myself to dial the number.* "I need air."

Olivia went into the backyard. It was Saturday, late afternoon. The May air felt warm and comforting along her skin. She inhaled the sweetness of the early spring flowers.

Then she saw it.

Her mother's rosebush, one red rose in full bloom. She smiled and walked toward the beautiful crimson flower. Bending down to inhale the sweet scent, tears pricked behind her eyes. She imagined her mom outside planting. Then she thought of the last lines of "The Rose," her mother's favorite part of the song. The lines about how the sun helps the seeds of the rose become a blossoming flower in the springtime. Tears rolled down her cheeks, a mix of sadness and nostalgia and joy. Her father had released some of her mother's ashes into her garden. And now this single red rose had bloomed, standing glorious, proud, soft, elegant, a quiet beauty, like her mother. "Dad." She hollered into the house.

Her dad and Abbee came out. The three of them looked at the rose, smiling.

"You think it's her communicating with us?"

"I think so, Liv." Her dad said.

Abbee, with her science mind, said, "Maybe not. But it doesn't matter. Does it? It's all in our interpretation. How we choose to understand it."

"This isn't a science experiment. There are things that are beyond scientific measurement. Love is one of them."

"That's your interpretation. C'mon Liv, you've studied philosophy. You know better than anyone that truth is all about interpretation. We understand things the way we need to. That's why I've always liked science. It attempts to remove interpreter bias to get to the truth."

Olivia didn't respond, because she had tuned Abbee out after that last comment.

"Liv." She heard Abbee's voice.

The rose, the blossoming of love, the line from "The Rose" about never taking a chance on love because of fear, all swarmed through her mind. Then she thought of her mother's words before she died, that Olivia's pride was her downfall, and then Abbee saying upstairs that not taking a chance with Justin could be just about the worst choice she ever made. *Justin.*

Justin, she needed to talk to him. She couldn't call him though. No, she needed to go there.

She walked into the house to search for Justin's address on the Internet.

"Liv." Abbee followed her inside. "What is it? You're pissed. I didn't mean anything by it. It really could be a message from mom. Who knows? Anything's possible."

"I'm not angry. Do you know where Justin moved to?"

"How would I know?"

"C'mon. We have mutual friends. Aren't you Facebook friends with him?"

"Yeah. I never go on that thing though."

"Go on and look. Please. You're right. I need to go and try. Take a risk. Tell him exactly how I feel. And I want to go *now*."

"Jeez. Calm down. Let me look."

Abbee went onto Justin's Facebook page. "Well, there's no private info, like where he's living, which is no surprise considering it's Justin. However, he has tons of posts about his bands' gigs."

"SHIT."

"Not necessarily. His band does have a show tonight."

"Yeah. I saw that yesterday."

"It's in Hoboken. We could go."

"Are you nuts? It's hard enough for me to swallow my pride and take a chance going to him not knowing what he's thinking at all. Never mind showing up and seeing him with all of his band members, the crowd at the bar. I mean, Abbee, he could have a girlfriend. It would be totally humiliating. And hurtful. I don't want to see him with someone else."

"Then call him. Or text."

"Text? Justin? I don't want to text with Justin. I want to talk to him, hear his voice, see him. This is NOT a text conversation."

"Then just call."

"What if he doesn't call back again? I have to talk to him face to face."

"Liv. Calm down." Abbee watched her pace the room. "Why don't we go to his show. He'll be onstage, you can decide when we get there if you want him to see you or not."

She huffed. "I don't know."

"Liv. What are you going to do, pace all night?"

"OK. Fine. But I don't want him to see me unless I decide it. Don't you jump out and make it known that we're there."

"I wouldn't do that."

44

Sam's brother, Michael White, called that morning with the news. "We loved the music you sent over. We'd like to use your song, *Forever and One Day* for one of the scenes. It's perfect. And your voice, you've got great range. If it's OK with you, I'm going to send your demos over to a friend of mine who does voiceover casting. Would you be interested in that?"

"That would be great. Although, to be fair, I think you should know that I wouldn't move out to Hollywood. I'm happy here and I wouldn't leave my band."

"They do voiceovers in New York City, too. Let me send it over and if he's interested, you can work out the details. In the meantime, you should hire an entertainment lawyer to have them look over the contract. I'll be sending it over early next week."

"Sounds perfect."

"I'll be in New York in two weeks. I'll have my assistant call to set up a meeting."

"Excellent. I look forward to it."

"Me too."

Justin hung up, thrilled. He couldn't believe he was being paid for one of his songs and that it was going to be in a movie. The opportunity for the voiceover was also fucking fantastic. He called Scully, his parents and Travis to share the good news. He had a meeting that afternoon with another building owner on River Road, who saw the work he did for Sam and wanted some chairs for a new bar he opened. He was busy. All good stuff, but busier than he had ever been.

He thought of calling Liv as he drove back from his meeting. Man, he really wanted to share the news with her, especially since she had been the inspiration for *Forever and One Day*. Loving her, losing her, knowing she'd always be in his heart, those feelings spurred the lyrics. That song came from the part of him that would always be with her. Their forever and one day.

Such as the mixed bag of life, though, the timing was way off. Kylie had introduced him to her friend, Sabrina, another musician. Justin liked her. They had only gone out twice and he wasn't jumping into anything, but he wanted to remain open to feeling something real. Calling Liv would fuck with his head.

He did miss her, though. More than he wanted to.

As he drove home, he sang *Forever and One Day* while thinking of Liv, tapping his fingers on the steering wheel.

Spanning an inch and crossed with a finger,
Echoes of words in the air that would linger,
Sounds of passion explode under the sheets,
Two bodies whispering where the skin meets.

Hungry fingers waiting, time move so slow,
All the time without you, I wish I didn't know.
Forever and one day to fill in the lines,
A place without pain cause there's no time.

Absence between the whirl of gyration,
And moments of pain replaced by temptation,
The distance remains in the space in between,
And loneliness courses with promises dreamed,

Hungry fingers waiting, time move so slow,
All the time without you, I wish I didn't know.
Forever and one day to fill in the lines,
A place without pain cause there's no time.

There's a journey to find what I wanna believe,
Ripping down walls only you can relieve.
Forever and one day to fill in the lines,
A place without pain cause there's no time.

Forever and one day to fill in the lines,
A place without pain cause there's no time.

45

"Mom would be proud. No matter what happens with Justin tonight, you have grown from the experience."

"I'm not reassured."

"It's Justin. He has loved you as long as you have loved him. I'm sure there's a reasonable reason he never called you back."

"I just hope he's not there with another woman. That would be really hard."

"It would. But no matter what, I know you'll be fine."

She shook off the pent-up tension. "Yeah."

Abbee drove into Hoboken and down Washington Avenue. They were almost to Maroon's. "Liv. Relax. Your foot's tapping like crazy."

"I can't calm down."

"Yeah, no shit. We'll get a shot when we go in."

"Maybe three."

Abbee parked in the same lot Justin and Olivia had parked in the last time she saw him. "Here goes," she said to Abbee as she opened the door. She squared her shoulders and took a deep breath. Olivia's stomach felt like ten butterflies were fluttering about in it as they walked through the sea of people toward the bar.

Justin sang, "I Wanna Be Sedated," by The Ramones. The crowd jammed, bobbed and sang along. Justin wore his white T-shirt with a flannel over it, jeans and black sneakers. He looked so handsome. Olivia kept her head down as they snuck to the back bar through the crowd. Abbee bought them each a beer and a shot of tequila, both of which eased her angst. She was a strong, independent woman, taking a risk. There was no shame in loving someone, even if they no longer loved you back or wanted the same thing.

Abbee bought another shot. They clicked glasses and threw it back.

"It's amazing how tequila makes everything seem less intense." Olivia said.

Abbee laughed. "In this case, it's medicinal."

Olivia gazed over at Justin. People danced in front of the band. And then she noticed two women right in front, swinging their hips back-and-forth. Justin sang, "Semi-Charmed Life," by Third Eye Blind. Olivia watched his long fingers changing chords, his other hand strumming, his voice affecting, his emotions apparent with every movement. He kept returning his gaze toward those two women. And it reminded her of how he always had returned his gaze toward her.

She observed their exchanges, trying to talk herself out of the idea that Justin was involved with one of them. The crowd whistled and screamed when they finished the song. Then she heard the first chords of "Wonderwall." Her stomach flipped. His dark eyes looked intense as he strummed that song and sang. She felt him next to her, his arms, his lips, his breath wispy through her hair

Those two women still stood in front. "I can't do this," she said to Abbee.

"Why not?"

"I think he's with one of those women."

"Where?"

She pointed them out to Abbee.

"No way. They're super young."

"So, Justin's hot. Why couldn't he be with a younger woman?"

"I dunno, Liv. I think you're running again. I think you need to take a fucking chance with Justin. For once, let go of the control."

Olivia nodded. "You're probably right. But I can't do it here. I'll call him."

"No, you won't. He's not with one of those girls. You're making it all up because you are scared."

"Please." Olivia's eyes moistened.

Abbee gave her a steely look. "Fine. But I really think you are making a mistake."

"Let's go now, before the song ends. I bet they're near the end of the set."

They weaved through the thick of the crowd so that Justin wouldn't see them.

Olivia hesitated before she opened the door, but then walked out, tears brimming in her eyes. "What was I thinking coming here?"

"That you love him." Abbee put her arm around Olivia. "What're you gonna do?"

"I dunno." She shook her head. "Let's go for dessert."

Justin spied Liv slipping through the crowd while he was onstage. He followed her with his eyes, trying to be inconspicuous until she was out of sight. Had she wound up there by coincidence? Or had she come to hear him play? As soon as the song ended, he turned to Scully, "I need to step out." Thank God the set was over.

Scully gave him a knowing look. "I'll pack your stuff up. Do your thing, man."

Justin nodded and hurried outside. From a block away, he thought he saw Liv and Abbee walking toward a diner he and Liv used to frequent. He rushed down the block.

What was she doing? If she came to see him, why wouldn't she talk to him? And what was he doing running after her again?

When he opened the front door to the diner, he glanced around and saw Abbee getting up from a table, heading toward the bathroom. Liv's back was to the door, but he saw her thick, red hair from behind. He swallowed. He couldn't let fear stop him from taking another chance.

As his eyes wandered over her wavy, red mane, he realized that love was always worth the risk. He could live with rejection. The only thing that could break him was the regret of not taking another chance with the woman he loved.

He took a deep breath, inhaling all of his courage.

And walked toward her.

He scooted into the booth across from her, his breath catching just looking at her. "Hi." He extended his hand across the table. "I'm Justin."

Liv's breath caught. She hesitated, then smiled knowingly and slipped her hand into his. "Olivia."

NOTE TO READERS

Thank you for reading *Forever and One Day*. I am always grateful to those who take the time to read my work. I hope you enjoyed reading it as much as I enjoyed writing it. As with all of my writing, I am always looking to gain new insight into the human experience. This story offered me the opportunity to explore the power of our choices and their concurrent fragility; the relationship between fear and risk and courage; the strength of enduring love in the face of loss and genuine forgiveness. I am indebted to these amazing characters who filled my life for over a year, allowing me to use their narrative to grow.

I am currently working on another romance novel, all new characters. It takes place on South Beach in Miami and revolves around students in a clinical psychology graduate program. It is another love story with a stunning love triangle. (If you follow my writing, you have probably noticed that my mind loves love triangles). In this book, I'm exploring the interrelations between people: how we come together to learn and grow, how different people draw out different sides of us, how all relationships are journeys within and how we break against each other, for better or worse. It's been quite a passionate journey, very intense, filled with emotion and drama, just the way I like it.

I also have outlines for a few other books, in both the thriller and romance genres. In addition, I have been busy with my health and wellness writing for my freelance work.

For more information about my writing, updates on releases and giveaways, please sign up for my newsletter here: **http://www.jsgunn.com/blog/**

Also, please feel free to contact me through my website if you have any comments or questions. I always enjoy hearing from my readers. And thank you, again, for your interest in my work.

ACKNOWLEDGEMENTS

Thank you to my editor and longtime friend, Carlo DeCarlo, not only for his brilliant edits and expertise, but also for his collaborations on the content and characters in this story. This book was the hardest book I have written so far. I had a vision of a complex multiple-perspective love story involving a betrayal. It was not easy to create a sympathetic character that had betrayed the protagonist. I had fallen in love with Justin's character and, akin to the idealization that happens when we first fall in love, I became blinded to all of the deficits and unsympathetic characteristics in his character in the original drafts.

It's not easy to tell a writer, who is also a friend for nearly thirty years, that there are major problems in a story that the writer loves. But he did just that, because he knew how I imagined the book in my mind and he wanted to help me bring my ideas to fruition. He offered extensive constructive feedback on the draft, and even managed to make me laugh in some of his editorial comments. As I went through the arduous rewrite process, I could see the depth of the characters growing and their motivations gaining complexity and believability.

This book would not have become what I had hoped without his help. Thank you, Carlo, as always, for your generosity, you have helped along every step of the way, and you have encouraged and pushed me to be a better writer. Thank you, thank you, thank you. I could not have done this without your help.

To my husband, Joseph Gunn, for always supporting me and believing in me, and for creating another amazing book cover. Also, thank you for showing me what real love feels like, for being my true romance. To my father, Philip Simon, for always being there and supporting me. I am so grateful, always, for everything. And to my sister, Sharon Simon, who admittedly does not read or watch romance, but helped, nonetheless, with some questions I had about Olivia's inner narrative.

To Heather Ricco, Michael Alonzo, Ross Kenyata Marshall, Lisa Vainieri Marshall, Dawn Dalessio Carambatos, Jeff Ent, Brooke Ent, Gina Jorge Valentin, Paula Sadlon-Pascual, Sherie Piniella and Lanna Lebet for reading drafts, for offering thoughtful feedback, for talking through some plot holes, for listening endlessly while I was writing the book. Your time and generosity are greatly appreciated. As always, thank you so much for your help and support.

ABOUT THE AUTHOR

Jacqueline Simon Gunn is a Manhattan-based clinical psychologist and writer. She has authored two non-fiction books, and co-authored two others. She has published many articles, both scholarly and mainstream, and currently works as a freelance writer. With her academic and clinical experience in psychology, Gunn is now writing psychological fiction. Always in search of truth, fiction writing, like psychology, is a way for her to explore human nature – motivation, emotions, relationships.

In addition to her clinical work and writing, Gunn is an avid runner and reader. She is currently working on multiple writing projects, including her second romance novel.

OTHER BOOKS BY JACQUELINE SIMON GUNN

Non-Fiction

Bare: Psychotherapy Stripped (co-authored with Carlo DeCarlo)

Borderline Personality Disorder: New Perspectives on a Stigmatizing and Overused Diagnosis (co-authored with Brent Potter)

In the Long Run: Reflections from the Road

In the Therapist's Chair

Fiction

Circle of Betrayal (Close Enough to Kill series – Book 1)

Circle of Trust (Close Enough to Kill series – Book 2)

Circle of Truth (Close Enough to Kill series – Book 3)

What He Didn't See (Close Enough to Kill series – Novella)

Noah's Story (Close Enough to Kill series – Novella)